# Praise for

## *INTENT TO HARM*

"There are some things most people take for granted. Small towns are safe. Police officers can handle anything that comes their way. Rape happens to somebody else. In this frighteningly suspenseful crime novel, these assumptions and others are swept away. . . . *Intent to Harm* is a . . . fast-moving police procedural whose nonstop plot twists keep you reading. . . . Washburn forces his characters to face the darkest sort of evil, and to consider how best to overcome it. That he does so in a no-nonsense, conversational style only makes the experience more intense and the novel more powerful."

—Christine Watson, *West Coast Review of Books*

"A chilling but very human portrayal. . . . This police procedural . . . is no ordinary blend of research and office tedium. As the suspense builds and investigators grow increasingly frustrated with their lack of success, so grows the humanity of their concerns, both personal and civic. . . . Washburn holds [the] suspense to [the] end."

—Florence Gilkeson, *The Pilot* (Southern Pines, NC)

"Washburn does the best job since Thomas Harris' *Red Dragon* in setting the reader inside a victim's home. . . . Then Washburn takes it further . . . from her mind into her heart after the crime."

—Paul Foreman, *The Birmingham News* (AL)

*(more)*

**Books by Stan Washburn**

Intent to Harm
Into Thin Air

Published by POCKET BOOKS

# INTO THIN AIR

## STAN WASHBURN

**POCKET BOOKS**

New York   London   Toronto   Sydney   Tokyo   Singapore

This book is for
Andy, Anne, and John

_____

An *Original* Publication of POCKET BOOKS

POCKET BOOKS, a division of Simon & Schuster Inc.
1230 Avenue of the Americas, New York, NY 10020

ISBN: 0-671-56246-0

First Pocket Books printing November 1996

10 9 8 7 6 5 4 3 2 1

POCKET and colophon are registered trademarks of
Simon & Schuster Inc.

Cover art by Brian Bailey

Printed in the U.S.A.

Thanks to Berkeley Police Inspectors Al Bierce and Dan Wolke, Sergeant Frank Reynolds, and psychiatrist Owen Renik, for discussing their work and reviewing mine for errors. Any that remain are mine alone.

Thanks to Margaret Rodriguez, Katie Bails, and my students at the College Preparatory School in Oakland, who gave me their views on issues of loyalty, responsibility, and calamity in teen life.

# 1

After several years of cautious self-denial, Paul Greber resolved that the time had come to steal a child. He was aware of the difficulties. It is easy enough to find a child unattended, but much harder to be sure that an adult will not show up suddenly or that there will be no witnesses. And if there is any sort of commotion, someone might run out to interfere or copy down a license number. You have to have the right situation, the right approach, the right child.

When Paul was out and about, he would sometimes see a child in the street and think, I could take that one right now. If he was not pressed for time, he would hang around to see whether he had sized things up correctly. He would think, I'm approaching; now I'm getting his attention; now I'm talking him into the car; now I'm pulling away from the curb. Sometimes during these imagined abductions the projected victim would move or an adult would appear in a manner that would have disrupted an approach if he had actually been making one. But sometimes not. Sometimes he would reach the point where he would think, Now I'm at the end of the block; I'm turning the corner; I'm away clean—into thin air. On those occasions the blood would rise to his face and his breath would tighten; he would think, *I could have done it that time.* And he would continue to watch and picture what it would be like to possess that particular child—think how exciting it would be if that child were actually in his car right now, driving away for real.

Over the course of time Paul found that he was getting better at these imaginary kidnappings. He did not see openings every day, but often enough. He got more adept at picking promising opportunities. He was quicker to recognize awkward or risky situations. It happened less and less that some circumstance arose that would have forced him to give up an attempt if he had really been making one, and very seldom that anything happened that would have made the attempt hazardous for him.

He began to think, I really could do it.

As the idea grew more solid in his mind, it also grew in urgency. He would see a likely child and think, There, *that* one. I could take that one right now. I could have that one at home in a couple of hours. In his mind he would make his approach and plan what he would say. And when, as happened almost invariably now, he was convinced that he would have gotten away with the child, his succeeding emotion was not one of satisfaction at the ensuing daydream but grievance that the child was not then actually his.

He began to think, Why not? I've had a lot of disappointments—I've got it coming. And one day he said to himself, I will.

Paul worked the 3 to 11 P.M. shift at the Bancroft, California, police department, where he was an aide with miscellaneous duties in the Service Division. He was a civilian employee. He wore a uniform with a simple cloth insignia sewn on the shirt where an officer would wear a badge. He carried handcuffs because his work sometimes involved processing prisoners, but he did not wear a pistol.

Paul had come by his job in an odd way.

In his small hometown in a different state he had volunteered since early adulthood as a coach in various after-school sports. Over a dozen years he had seduced or forced a considerable number of the children entrusted to his care. When this was discovered, the prevailing view among the parents—themselves frightened and ashamed—was to hush the matter up, but Paul—suddenly the object of the most virulent loathing, astounded, badly scared—had to leave town.

Without any connections or obvious place to go, he wandered. Before long he found himself in San Francisco, where he felt himself invisible in a place where he knew no one, and no one knew him.

Paul was a cautious, private man. He cruised the city to see what he could find. He found it dense and teeming, and Paul needed privacy for the sort of life he wanted to lead. He cruised the areas outside the city. On one of these scouting expeditions, moved by the old appetite, he stopped by a park to watch a soccer game of seven- to ten-year-old boys and girls. He loitered by the line of trees along the street, away from the parents and coaches clustered around midfield, and watched hungrily, tracing the line of tight, smooth legs up into billowing shorts, searching for the lines of the underwear, watching tensely for the chance exposure as they darted and tumbled.

It was not the most impressive children, the bold and confident athletes, who interested him. Reflexively his eye sought out the shy, the anxious and tentative, hanging back on the fringes of the action. He knew from experience that these would be grateful for encouragement, for a kind word, a special treat. These would not have the assurance to question or object as one thing led to another, or to tell afterward. Distinguishing the vulnerable was something Paul was good at, and he practiced his skill at it now with a tense pleasure.

Paul had a great asset in his unremarkable appearance. Witnesses would describe him as being in his mid-thirties, average height, a little stocky, slightly balding, ordinary clothes. He looked just like that.

People tended not to notice him when he was present and had trouble remembering him when he was gone.

Still, he had no intention of approaching. He had been badly frightened by his recent experiences, and he shrank from any repetition. Reflexively, he flinched away if any of the adults across the field seemed to be noticing him.

It was in the act of averting his face that his eye fell on the pamphlet discarded by a tree, which would make him an employee of the Bancroft police department. It was a listing of city jobs. Paul's money was dwindling rapidly, and he needed work. Most of the jobs required experience he did not have, but among those he was qualified for was police aide. The pay was more than he was used to, there were positions open, and there did not seem to be any extensive background check. He applied. He was hired.

Paul was not a humorous person, but when he first looked in the mirror and saw himself in uniform it gave him quite a chuckle.

Bancroft was home to a great university, and consequently home to a hundred species of free spirits in whom Paul recognized the sort of cover that a wolf finds in the tangle of the forest. But although Paul saw many possibilities in Bancroft, he decided not to live there. After much questing he found a secluded place on a tributary of the Russian River, a hilly, wooded district between the Pacific and the wine-growing valleys, more than ninety minutes' drive to the north. This distance was not onerous to Paul; the long drive soothed him, each of the many turnings he made on the way signifying to him another layer of seclusion and security. He drove the freeway, then a good county road, then a smaller road, and finally a one-lane track, first paved, then paved in two strips with a grassy strip down the middle, then gravel. At the end of the track there was a padlocked gate; beyond the gate was Paul's cabin.

His landlady occupied the next house, a quarter of a mile back up the track, set off in the woods. She said, "I'm not the social type. You don't visit me, I won't visit you. You need a cup of sugar, you go to town or do without. When I want to inspect, I'll give you plenty of notice. That's my mailbox, down by that tree. You just put every penny of the rent in there on the first of each and every month, and we'll get along fine. You comfortable with that?" Paul was entirely comfortable with that.

He unpacked the collection of videos and photographs that he had taken over the previous years, which constituted his only important personal possessions. He needed to lick his wounds and think about what had gone wrong. He settled carefully into his new life and lived cautiously and clean for many months.

Sergeant Wren was Paul's supervisor in Service Division. His command consisted of a miscellaneous crew of crime-scene technicians, clerk/typists, computer gurus, and Paul, who did a little of each of these jobs and sometimes assisted the jailer upstairs when Patrol was reeling them in faster than usual. When he was not at his desk, people with undemanding jobs of no great urgency would scribble notes and leave them on his spindle.

"Remind me," said Sergeant Wren to one of his technicians. "When Paul gets back I need to speak to him about rearranging the mailboxes in the squad room. We just stick names on whatever box is empty, and pretty soon they're all out of alphabetical order. You can't find anyone unless you know where to look."

"Where is Paul, anyway?" said the technician.

"Oh, he had a few days of vacation time accumulated, and he decided to take it," said Sergeant Wren. "He said he had some personal business."

# 2

Essie Beal liked to get at least some of her weekend homework done on Friday afternoons and took the rest to her baby-sitting job to finish after her charges were in bed. If she could finish it, she would wake up on Saturday morning without a scholastic claim on her time until Monday. Sometimes she got through it and sometimes she did not, but even the attempt marked a level of discipline unknown among the other high school freshmen and made her the object of a certain awe.

Even more interesting to her friends than her academic prowess, and certainly the subject of more discussion among them, was the possibility of Essie's having been singled out by Elliott, the sophomore math whiz. He would have his driver's license in April and had been promised his own car, albeit his mother's used one. Elliott was pushing six feet and looked older than he was.

Essie had only recently turned fourteen. She was plenty bright and funnier than most people, but she barely came up to Elliott's shoulder, had scarcely half a figure so far, and, except for an alertness about her, seemed younger than she was. Everyone agreed that they would make a very amusing couple, and Essie-and-Elliott-coupling jokes, some of them funny, virtually all of them coarse, sprang up like mushrooms.

These speculations were not without foundation. Elliott was observed to speak to Essie quite unnecessarily on at least three separate occasions: once to ask the time (with the office clock clearly visible through the window); once to ask if *smitten* had two *t*s in it, which everyone thought was pretty transparent (and told her to guess next time and not advise him to go look it up); and at *least* once he had chatted with her on the library steps when there was nobody close enough to hear what they were saying.

Erin and Lizby, emerging from the library, witnessed this conversation, halting and brief as it was. They had known Essie since kindergarten and regarded all personal information as common property. So when Elliott had ended a prolonged and silent inspection of his shoes by saying, "Well, seeya," and Essie had said, "Yeah, seeya," and continued to inspect her own, and he had wandered off with an ambiguous expression, they descended on her and demanded to know what he had said, every word. She looked vague and said, "Oh, nothing."

"Oh, *sure,*" said Erin. *"Sure,* Ess. I could see your face while he was talking, and I can tell you, girl, that it was totally not nothing."

"Was so," said Essie distractedly, who really could not tell whether it was nothing or not.

"Don't let her bug you, Ess," said Lizby. "She's just jealous."

"You've got it," said Erin. "Jealous. Ess is going to have her first VD before I've even got to third base. How would *anyone* feel?"

Scandalized, red-eared, Essie cried, "He was just asking how I like *Great Expectations,*" snatching up the volume and displaying it. But Erin knew what to make of that, and she had barely begun on *Elliott's* great expectations before the bell rang and they had to gather their books together and hurry away.

After school Erin and Lizby tried to rope Essie into going off with them to get wired on cappuccinos, but she shook them off and headed home instead.

7

She opened *Great Expectations* on the bus but had trouble keeping her mind on it. She wondered what Elliott's expectations might be. Suppose they *did* go out, and he had his own car—what if he wanted to go park somewhere? Could she handle that? And then there was Shelly to worry about. Shelly had claimed Elliott on the first day of school—not in his hearing, of course, but among the other freshman girls. Essie doubted that Shelly was terribly bright and knew that she was not funny; but she already had all the figure anyone could want, and she was not shy. Essie wondered why Elliott did not seem to prefer Shelly, and knew she was not the only one who wondered. She felt very uncertain, and wished she were not. Essie longed to be bold.

Essie's father was at home when she arrived, as he usually was on Fridays, deep in a book, as he usually was at all times. He was a professor of literature with a predilection for the abstruse. He sat in the living room where his reading chair and his wife's were joined into a single mass by the small table and large shared lamp pressed between them and by the books and papers that silted up on all sides. The room was bright in the late afternoon, but Essie's essential mental image of her parents was how they looked at night, sitting side by side in a pool of light in the middle of the large room, reading carefully, making notes, sometimes taking up the dictionary that lay between their feet, or one of the papers; their ankles sometimes tangling with each other as they crossed or uncrossed their legs, their little unconscious whispers of interest or surprise at what they were reading, the scratch of a pencil, the breath of a page turning or the clump of a book closing: a tiny, atonal, and much-attenuated musical voice that accompanied their life, unheard and unheeded by them, but deeply familiar and bittersweet to their daughter, who had no part in it.

Essie's table and chair were in the corner. She had

her own lamp. At night there would be a light in the hall and perhaps one in the kitchen, and the two little pools of light in the living room, with a zone of half-light and silence between them.

And yet, if she thought about it, while she was not an equal third in the family, she was also not an orphan. Her parents came to whatever play or recital she might be in; they read her stories and essays—really read them—and gave her thoughtful reactions without giving her answers; they went without fail to Back to School day, met all her teachers, knew them by name, and were known to them; they knew her friends and encouraged them to come to the house. The inviolability of the Beals' dinner hour, that family sacrament, was admired by all who knew them, and especially those who had partaken with them. Her mother, at any rate, noticed when she was glum, made sympathetic noises, and did not leave her until she felt better. There was no corner of Essie's life—at least so far—that she could not discuss with her parents, especially her mother, always provided that she was willing to listen as well as to speak.

Still.

Essie's father had a way of registering change in his environment without markedly altering his state of concentration. He did not seem to have heard her come in, despite her struggle with her key in the sticky front door lock, but the sound of her backpack zipper ten feet away elicited an almost imperceptible bob of the head. After some indeterminate interval, his hand sought and found the empty teacup on the table beside him and clamped it. Since he was quite tall and large-boned, but also very thin, these gestures had an automatonlike quality that uninitiated visitors to the house found fascinating or alarming, according to their dispositions. For a time he did not stir further but continued to read with one elbow cocked awkwardly back and the hand embowering the empty cup.

Essie knew that if she waited long enough—as some-times in rebellious moments she would do—he would alter his focus sufficiently to murmur into his book, "Mmm, would . . . ?" And if she still did nothing, he might rise out of his muse enough to blink around the room until he found someone alive in it to whom he could say, "Ah, would you . . . my tea . . . very kind."

A technically minded classmate of Essie's had re-cently been talking about how lurking submarines are able to dispatch communications without rising to the surface, where danger is; she thought of that now.

Her friend Lizby's father was a hearty man with a firm chin who worked in the open air and would sweep into the room and say to any of his family who might be present, "Aw, I want a *hug!*" If Essie were there he would tousle her hair or fake a punch to the chin and say, "It's *really* good to see you, honey," before bustling off to change his clothes. His manner embarrassed Lizby because it was hokey, but her friends said that at least he was trying.

Essie knew that she was unreasonable to make this comparison, but she made it all the same.

Unnoticed, she took the cup out of his hand. She went into the kitchen, made tea, brought it back, and set it beside him, unnoticed. After an interval, per-haps responding to the heat, his hand crabbed cau-tiously out and took hold of it. Long before this happened, however, Essie was at her own table, immersed in her own work.

Once Essie had tried treating her mother as her father treated both of them, pretending to be entirely absorbed. The experiment was unsuccessful. Her mother thought that Essie was angry about some-thing, and was so patient for the rest of the evening, waiting for the revelation of her offense, that Essie grew increasingly ashamed, and hour by hour more puzzled as to how she could extricate herself. She had genuine grievances, but they seemed too large and too intricate to ventilate so suddenly and backhandedly, and the one or two small-scale issues she could think of at the moment were obviously too petty for the fuss that had been made. Resolution came in an unconscious moment, when she had gone to bed and her mother came in, as she invariably did, to say goodnight. Essie sat up suddenly in bed, hugged her, and said, "I'm a teenager, Mom. You'll just have to put up with me." And her mother, visibly relieved, said, "Well, well," and hugged her back so sincerely that Essie added, "I'm *really* sorry," and resolved that after that she would not be so self-indulgent.

This was recent enough that when her mother came in from work on this Friday, Essie jumped up and ran a little self-consciously to the door and kissed her, receiving her sincere, if distracted, smile and cheek peck in a spirit of thankfulness. Her friend Lizby's mom looked Essie in the eye when she held her preparatory to kissing her and always kissed her twice, because, as she said about one time in three, she was so glad that her daughter had brought such a good friend into the house. Lizby's mom also took some care with her appearance, which Esther Beal did only sporadically, when she happened to notice. She was almost as tall as her husband and very small-boned, and also thin. They both usually looked as if they had slept in their clothes. Their friends had learned to smile, but their daughter had not, as yet.

Essie reproached herself for having these thoughts. Lizby just lucked out, she thought. Erin says, At least your parents are around some of the time. Pull yourself together, girl. Get real.

"Now let's see," said her mother, hanging up her coat. "You'll be eating at the Broomes?"

"Yeah," said Essie, who thought that a crisp "Yes" to a parent was servile, however guilty she might be feeling. "I'm making dinner for the munchkins. And Gabriella said it wouldn't be a late evening. Is it okay if I meet Erin and Lizby downtown afterward?"

"So long as you're home by midnight," said Esther in the tone of one who means 11:59 and not 12:01.

"Sure," said Essie. That would not leave them much time, but she did not question midnight. She glanced at her watch—she would be picked up any minute. She hastened to her table to gather her books together.

Paul was a romantic. He longed for an uncomplicated, sunlit life in which he would give and receive a child's happy, simple love. But while Paul was a romantic, he was not a dreamer. He realized that he would have to be realistic about the sort of child he proposed to steal. His preference was for children between six and twelve. If they were above the age of eight or so he preferred boys; if younger, he was impartial—he did not distinctly notice the difference. But he knew that an older child would be hard to steal in the first place and hard to control afterward. He decided that he would limit himself to something at the young end of that range, or even a little younger. He would look around. Opportunity would be a big part of it. Boy, girl, precise age—he'd have to be flexible. There was something attractive about the indefiniteness of it: whoever he got would be the fated one, the one destined for him. There's no fighting these things. And although he did not expressly formulate the thought in his mind, the fact was that when the child reached puberty, Paul's interest would end. A younger child would not only be easier to train but would not develop so soon and have to be replaced by another.

Paul took the long view. In the past he had taken advantage of his opportunities with a brusqueness that cost his victims great emotional as well as physical distress. This was not a problem for Paul because he simply moved on to another child. But if he were going to keep one for several years and realize his dream of willing and reciprocal love, he would have to be patient. Too much haste would not do. Make friends first, and they would naturally become lovers later. Paul was prepared to wait for days, or even weeks, until the child was really ready.

There were not a lot of preparations to make. He put a large duffel bag on the floor of his car on the passenger side and kept the gas tank topped up so that when he made a grab he would not have to stop on the way home. With some boldness of calculation, Paul had decided to begin his search in Bancroft. He knew the town fairly well now, while nobody except his colleagues in the department knew him—both important advantages. And the Hall of Justice being the gossipy place that such places are, he would be able to keep abreast of the police investigation that would follow a disappearance—and that would be helpful as well.

Paul was very excited on the Sunday morning when he set out to cruise the parks. He would have to be careful not to wear himself out. It would be bliss if he could get the first child he saw, but he knew perfectly well that it might be days and days before he came across the right opportunity.

He thought that he would concentrate on the areas around neighborhood parks, where people feel safe and relaxed. Unattended children were clearly best; failing that, he would look for younger children in the charge of older ones or baby-sitters, who might not be completely in control.

He cruised on Sunday without result. The children he saw were too young, or too old, or too mobile, or in inaccessible places; they were clustered in groups rather than by themselves; there were too many watchful adults around. It wasn't going to be easy. The uncertainty was very tiring, staying keyed up: windows of opportunity open and close very fast. He couldn't hesitate: If he saw what he was looking for, he would have to grab and go. The thing could happen literally at any moment.

On Monday he repeated his pattern with similar results.

On Tuesday he had hopes of a young woman with a girl of five or six. The girl seemed quite independent, moving to the edges of the park while the mother or au pair or whatever she was gave the bulk of her attention to lying on the grass and rearranging her skirt and blouse to expose as much of herself as possible to the sun. The park was too open to make the grab right there, but Paul went back and waited in his car. The woman at last became bored, gathered in her charge, and crossed the street. Paul hoped that in her abstraction she would not keep the child close as they walked. But her car was right there; she tucked the child safely inside and drove away.

Paul cruised most of Wednesday without result. But just at dusk he spotted a girl of seven or thereabouts playing by herself on the jungle gym at the corner of an otherwise deserted school yard. It was perfect: there was only a low fence between the school yard and the street, and there was nobody else around. All he had to do was pull in, roll down the window, and ask her to hand him his cane from the passenger side so he could get out. He had practiced this speech many times to get the half-humorous, half-pitiful note just right. She comes over, opens the door, leans in, and there you are.

But Paul was heading in the wrong direction, and

by the time he had driven up to the next corner, made a U-turn, and come back, she had skipped off down the street.

It was bad luck. A disappointment. Another minute and he would have had her.

On Thursday Paul cruised the jungle gym several times, looking for another setup like Wednesday's, but he did not find one. He found unsupervised children, but they were always too old, or too many, or inaccessible.

At a neighborhood park late on Friday afternoon he found a girl—in her early teens by the look of her, small, most likely a sitter—with three energetic children. He parked at a discreet distance and watched them. The youngest, about three, was of no interest to him, but the other two, a boy and a girl, were two or three years older. They were running, climbing, rolling in the sand. He watched them with longing, and when finally the sitter gathered the three together and started off with them down one of the adjacent streets, he followed. One of them might lag behind, he thought.

It was not hard for Paul to follow without being observed; he had every advantage. The sitter was entirely engaged with carrying the youngest child, along with some odd clothing, and keeping the two older ones reined in. She was getting the sort of alternate cooperation and testing that young sitters get from children. She was too busy to notice the nondescript sedan that circled past them once or twice, parked not far behind them as they walked along, and then pulled forward until it was almost up to them before parking again.

Paul followed for three or four blocks before seeing the children run up onto the lawn of a good-size house near the corner of the block. There was a parking space in front of the adjacent house—too close, really, but the sitter seemed entirely absorbed. Paul pulled past the space, and then began to back in, and here he had a piece of bad luck. A car came up behind and, being slightly incommoded by Paul's deliberate maneuvering, honked irritably. The sitter glanced up distractedly and looked right at him before looking away. He did not think she had looked at him to notice—she was responding to the other car's honking. Still, she had looked at him. If she looked again, he decided, he would leave.

But she did not look again. She had set down her burdens by the walk, and for a few minutes all four played a game that seemed to begin as tag and ended with everyone in a noisy pile. Several times they crossed onto the neighbors' lawns, and several times the two older children passed quite close to Paul.

After a few repetitions of this game, the sitter began to calm the children down and gather their odds and ends together. Her arms were full when she led them up the steps.

The middle child, a boy of about five, was lagging.

There were no neighbors around that Paul could see, no one to interfere. But the sitter was slowing as she crossed the porch. She was calling the boy. If she would just go on inside, Paul thought, the kid might linger long enough. No. She had paused in the doorway. She settled her weight on one leg with that "I'm going to stand here all day" expression on her face.

Oh, hell, thought Paul. It was looking so good up to now.

The boy went past the sitter into the house. She turned to follow him, arms still full. With her shoulder she heaved the door closed.

With hungry eyes Paul saw it swing shut, saw it touch the jamb, fail to catch, and swing slowly open again.

There was no one visible in the hallway beyond.

Sometimes things just work out, he thought. It was about time. He had taken many unfair knocks in his life, but today, perhaps, he was going to be treated better.

Tightening all over and breathing faster now, but with what he hoped was an air of unconcern, Paul got out of his car and started up the walk.

Essie was a big girl in comparison with the Broome children, but she was not bossy by nature, and she was fully absorbed in keeping order. She dumped the pile of clothes on the kitchen floor. There would be no dinner, she said in her most firm-sounding voice, until everything was claimed and removed.

The announcement was received with a storm of protest. Essie had seen the father of these three, Trevor, make more or less the same ultimatum, and even though—or perhaps because—he said it with that odd smirk he had, they hastened to obey him. She did not get the same quick result; still, she stuck to her guns, and when they saw she meant it they began to move. She helped Amy find her sweater and Noah collect his socks. Amy was six and a half and had trouble finding things. Noah was three and had an aversion to socks. Jeremy was five and a half and made a point of self-sufficiency.

The universal opinion was that dinner should be soon. Essie began warming things, pouring juice, putting out napkins and silver. Amy wanted to sing songs, and they sang pretty loud, all four, while the meal took shape.

Then Amy wanted a sweater, *not* the sweater that was right there, a *different* sweater, from her room. But she could not get it herself, because the lights were not turned on upstairs, and the house was getting dark. Okay, they would go up and turn on lights together. And, of course, Noah had to have a different sweater, too, since Amy was having one. Jeremy had begun a drawing at the kitchen table; he declared that he was contented with the sweater he had, and he was going to stay where he was.

Amy and Noah and Essie went up the little back stairs by the kitchen. The kids' bedrooms were right above, and it was much the fastest way.

At one point Essie thought she heard Jeremy's voice. She could not hear what he was saying. She shushed Amy and Noah and called, but he did not answer. He's talking to his drawing, she thought.

She called a second time. Amy and Noah burst out again with demands for admiration of their sweater selections, and she could not hear whether Jeremy had answered. He wants to know when dinner is going to be, she thought. She called, "Pretty soon," and said to the little kids, "C'mon, guys, let's go get dinner." They had been upstairs for four or five minutes.

When they got back down to the kitchen again, Jeremy was gone from the table. That was surprising because once he got going on something, he tended to stick to it.

She called him, but there was no answer.

She called again.

He had not followed them upstairs—he shared a room with Noah, and that room and Amy's were the only ones with lights on. He would not be anyplace else—he did not like the dark.

Sometimes he liked to curl up on the living room couch. She jogged quickly through the dining room into the living room with its square, pale windows, but there was nothing to see. Then she ran to the front door, astonished to find it open, wondering even at that moment whether it had been open all the time, out across the porch and down past the front of the house where she could see up and down the block. There were four or five pedestrians visible at a distance; a car was just disappearing down the cross street at the far end of the block. She called. No response. Back around the house, through the side gate, into the backyard. She called. Nothing. She raced back around to the front and up the front stairs. She ran from room to room, calling, throwing open closets, and looking under beds on the off chance that he was hiding. She could not find him.

"Oh, God!" she sobbed, leaping down the stairs two at a time, passing Amy, frightened, in the front hall. "Stay *there!*" she called to Amy as she passed. *"You guys stay inside!"*

Out to the street again. She ran to the near corner.

From the corner she could see two moving cars, one quite close, approaching from the east, and the other moving away northward. There was a bicyclist wearing spandex, and obviously not concealing anything, and three or four pedestrians. Three of the pedestrians were fairly near, but all were walking in different directions. Two of them wore clothes bulky enough to cover a child. The farthest was a nomad pushing a shopping cart covered by some sort of tarp.

She hesitated, anguished, and looked back toward the house. Amy had come out to the sidewalk. Noah would not be far behind.

"Amy!" she screamed, frantically waving her back. "Go inside! *Right now!*" The child hesitated, frightened at the sudden uproar and Essie's wild behavior. The house at the top of the walk was dark. Only the kitchen light was on downstairs, and Amy knew that to get to it she would have to pass again among the black laurels to the dark porch and creep down the unlit hallway past the dining room, full of shadows.

She could hear Noah, somewhere inside, beginning to cry. Essie was the best comfort and protection, hysterical or not. She took a step or two toward the corner.

*"Go inside!"* Essie called.

The pedestrians were getting farther off. The nomad with the shopping cart turned the next corner and was gone from sight. Gasping, almost screaming with fright and vexation, Essie dashed away after the nearest person she could see, a man, pretty big, wearing a big, loose coat. He was half a long block away from her, walking fairly fast. She was still barefoot from playing on the lawn. She could not run very fast.

She called for the man to stop, but he did not, at first. When at last he heard her, he hesitated and looked around; he did not realize that he was the one she meant. He stared at her as she darted up, wild-eyed, tears pouring down her cheeks.

Two yards away she stopped, and they stared at one another. She could not think what to say. She leaped up to him and jerked his coat open. He was too astounded to offer any resistance. He did not have Jeremy.

"Oh, God!" she moaned, and ran a few steps back. She stopped. All the other pedestrians who had been in sight when she first came out were gone.

She heard a car horn, several toots. There was a light blue van stopped back in the intersection, its headlights slightly augmenting the gray twilight. The driver was standing in the street by his open door, waving feebly at Amy, who was attempting to cross, and at Noah, who stood disoriented and crying in the middle of the intersection. Back she ran. As she approached the intersection, a dark sedan came up the cross street too fast, swung impatiently around the van, and jerked to a stop within a yard of striking Noah. She screamed. The van driver snatched up Noah and looked toward her.

"POLICE!" she screamed, as she ran into the

intersection. "POLICE! PLEASE CALL THE PO-
LICE!" She plucked Noah away from the man and
caught Amy by the shirt. "PLEASE!" Her voice was
cracking. "PLEASE CALL THE POLICE! SOME-
BODY HAS KIDNAPPED JEREMY!" She was circling backward around the intersection, clutching the
two terrorized, howling children, wildly scanning up
and down the darkening lines of parked cars and
somber, gloaming elms for some by-now unhoped-for
sight that would put everything right. The van driver
looked vaguely around as if a phone were likely to
materialize close by. Neighbors began parting their
curtains and lifting their blinds, and one or two of the
boldest stepped out onto their porches to discover the
cause of all the fuss.

The sedan was full of teens out for an evening's
cruise. This was excitement, but they had beer in the
car. They could smell cops any minute, and they did
not want to be caught with the beer. The girl and her
kids were blocking the way. The driver threw the car
into reverse and roared backward down the street
until he found a driveway he could turn into. Then
with tires squealing, the sedan roared off again the
way it had come.

These last few moments—the screaming teenager
in the street, the van stopped in the middle of the
intersection, and the abrupt departure of the sedan—
were the observations of the first neighbor who got to
the phone to call the police.

Patrol units could tell by the tightness in her voice
that the dispatcher thought this call was hot.

"For cars in the south campus area, we have a
report of a woman screaming in the street." There
was a brief pause, and then she announced the cross
streets. Toby Parkman was a mile away to the west,
out of his patrol car, writing a parking ticket. He
started running.

Another pause. Dispatch was putting this out in bits as she got it from the reporting party.

"Cars responding to the woman screaming. We have multiple calls now. This is a possible kidnap in progress. Reports of two vehicles involved. Number one is a light blue van, license unknown, still at the scene. Number two is a dark blue or black sedan, no further description, possible multiple occupants, last seen west from there at high speed. More to follow."

Back in his car, Toby flicked on his roof lights and charged off to the east. Almost immediately he encountered a dark sedan with two occupants moving westward at a sedate pace. He turned off his roof lights, hung a U-turn and started back after it, at the same time reaching for his mike. There was time for this car to have covered the distance from the location of occurrence.

"Control ninety-three, I've got a dark sedan westbound, two visible occupants. Any more description of the responsible vehicle, and do we know who the victim is?"

"Cars responding, all we have so far is possible kidnap. Victim unknown. Nothing further on the sedan. Any car close to the scene?"

A woman's voice said, "Sixteen. I'm almost there."

"Okay, sixteen. Try to hook up with the party in the street and advise. Other cars stand by for more."

Toby could not stand by. He had a dark sedan, it had two people in it, he thought they were both men, and the timing was about right.

"Control ninety-three, I'll be making a stop. No assistance required." He gave the vehicle description and plate, the street and the nearest intersection, and put on the red roof lights. He did not ask for backup because the probability was that this was not the car—the streets are full of dark sedans. On the radio he could hear two other cars in quick succession making stops on dark sedans. The whole shift was bogging down far away from the scene.

Both men seemed relaxed enough when he came up to the driver's window.

"Gents," he said, "I stopped you because we had a disturbance near here, and you match the description of one of the involved parties. Can you tell me anything about it?" They looked blank—either genuinely perplexed, or the world's greatest actors.

"Disturbance?" said the passenger. "We were just going out to dinner. We just left his place," indicating the driver. The driver's license gave him an address two blocks away. This was going to check out okay. Toby got the driver out, patted him quickly for weapons, and asked him if he would please open the trunk. He started to do it, with a puzzled expression on his face, when suddenly the feisty spirit of a free land blossomed and he said, "Is this legal? What if I don't want to open this?"

"It's legal," said Toby, speaking quickly. "If you won't, I will. Please don't waste time, sir. If I don't find what I'm looking for, you're free to go."

He opened. There was no kidnap victim.

"Thank you," said Toby, and handed him both licenses. "You're not the one I'm looking for. Sorry to have troubled you."

"Well, ah . . ." he said, but Toby was already running back to his car, moving a little sideways so as not to turn his back completely. He turned off the lights and swung around again toward the east end.

"Control ninety-three, clear my stop."

"Check, ninety-three. Head for the scene and hook up with sixteen. S-five is moving that way, too."

"Sixteen, Control?" There was no response. "One-six, Control." Another pause. "Sixteen, are you there?"

There was a burst of yelling over the air. "Control, are you calling sixteen?" Her voice was almost covered with loud voices and crying in the background. She sounded harassed.

"Sixteen, how are you coming there?"

More wailing. "Control, we've got a missing boy, age five years. Last seen about five minutes prior to time of report. It's definitely a possible kidnap. I've got the baby-sitter here. We're trying to get sorted out. Stand by."

"Check. Ninety-three?"

"Ninety-three."

"Ninety-three, when you get there, make an effort to get us something more about the dark sedan. We'll be stopping half the cars in town if we can't narrow it down."

"Check," said Toby. "I'm there now." He was approaching the intersection. The light van was sitting in the middle of the street with Lindy Webb's black and white just opposite. On the sidewalk Lindy was trying to bring order to a considerable convocation of neighbors, some of whom might have useful information. Toby added his car to the jumble in the intersection and hurried over.

"Take the neighbors," she said when he came up. "I haven't even gotten started with them. The family's house is the big brown shingle there. I'm going to take the sitter and kids in." She nodded at the barefoot teenager huddled with two little kids on the grass. Toby knew her. She was a friend of the girl who usually sat for Toby's two children and had sat for them several times herself. He liked her—organized and polite. He went over. He could not tell whether she was glad to see him in those circumstances or not.

"It's the end of the world," she whispered.

"No," he said, kneeling down beside her. "Keep your wits about you, Essie. We'll try to sort this out."

"Please tell me you're going to find him," she said.

"I don't know," he said in his slightly remote way. "I don't know what's happened."

"Oh, *God*," she whispered.

"I think it *is* going to be a kidnap," said Lindy, coming up behind him. "This is what we've got so far." She handed him a scrawled page from her daybook and turned to Essie. "Come on inside, honey. Keep the little ones close." She got them moving up the lawn.

Most of the onlookers were standing on the corner nearest the house.

"People," Toby said as loud as he could without actually shouting. "People, could I have your attention? Over here?" They gathered in a little tighter, and stopped chatting among themselves.

"People, we have a missing child . . ." he consulted Lindy's notes. ". . . named Jeremy Broome, five years old. He lives in the house right there. He's been missing for the last ten or fifteen minutes. Who knows Jeremy by sight?" A dozen people made slight gestures. "Have you seen him in the last half hour, by himself or with anybody else?"

"He was with the sitter on the lawn a while ago," said a woman.

"Since then?"

No response.

"Has anyone seen an unaccompanied child during the last half hour?" They looked glumly at each other. Nothing.

"Has anyone seen any child at all leaving this area with an adult or with an older kid?"

Nothing.

"Maybe not leaving, maybe just standing around. Any child you may have seen that you couldn't place, whether it looked suspicious or not?"

Silence.

"Before this commotion here in the intersection, did anyone hear anything unusual? Yelling, or crying? No?"

Nothing.

"Any time in the last day or two, have you seen anyone hanging around here? Anyone watching kids? A man, a woman, anyone at all. No?"

They'd stopped referring to each other with each question. They stood in a silent semicircle around him, eyes fixed on his face; with each question they looked thoughtful, then negative. They were trying.

A plain black supervisor's car pulled up, and Sergeant D'Honnencourt got out, looking serious. Toby pointed to the brown house, and D'Honnencourt passed through the neighbors in that direction.

"There was a report of a dark sedan seen leaving this intersection in a hurry," Toby said. "Did anyone see that?" Several hands went up. "Could you come forward, please?" He got out his daybook, and started taking notes.

Paul was confident that his departure had been unobtrusive. He had only been in the house for a moment, and he did not think anyone had seen him leave with the boy. There had been no commotion. It was not until he was just turning the corner, a block away, with the boy huddled on the floor, that the teenager had come running out to the street. He doubted that she had seen him at all, and he was certainly too far away for her to see the license plate on the car. The only way he could get in difficulties now would be to get pulled over for some traffic violation, and that was unlikely because he was driving carefully, just below the speed limit.

A large, shapeless canvas bag lay on the floor in front of the passenger seat. A couple of blocks from the house he had stopped and put the boy into it. That had taken some doing. The boy had made quite a fuss at that, and enough noise to be heard outside the car, even with the windows closed. Paul had had to give the bag a few sharp punches. Now there was no sound, and the only movement was a very slight, fast rise and fall toward the bottom. That was good—that was being well-behaved.

"You'll like it, where we're going," he said to the bag. When there was no reply he said, "It's pretty. We'll have some good times."

They pulled onto the freeway, heading north.

"There's a river there," he said, coaxing a little. "We can go skinny-dipping, just the two of us."

The bag seemed to freeze—even the breathing seemed to stop.

"Well, I guess you're a shy one," he said. Paul liked shy children. He had been shy himself as a child. Better not be sullen, he thought. Paul hated sullen children.

"We'll get along fine," he said.

There was a long drive ahead of them. But Paul was glad to have an interval to get used to the reality of having a real child—not a concept, not a daydream, but a friend—before they had to begin the process of getting to know each other. He had been thinking about this for a long time. They would be happy, he and this child. Paul's own childhood had not been happy.

"It's a black or midnight blue domestic macho-type two-door sedan," said Sergeant D'Honnencourt into the cellular phone, standing at the kitchen counter. He glanced across to the table where the ID tech was photographing Jeremy's drawing and dusting for fingerprints. There would be no place to sit down until she was done.

"Five people saw it. It has an air scoop on the

hood—everyone agreed on that—and fat tires. It's got a dent on the left side just behind the front wheel—two people saw that. And it's probably got gray primer on the whole right rear quarter panel. Two people reported that, but not the same two who saw the dent. The license number begins with a two, and has a K in it."

He was reading from the notes in Toby's daybook and a sheaf of little slips from other sources while Toby stood beside him to help decipher scrawls and reconcile inconsistencies. The most likely description had long since gone out over the air, and now he was reading out the whole range of observations to the press officer at the Hall of Justice, who was preparing a quickie leaflet for distribution to Patrol, neighbors, and the media.

The mother, Gabriella Broome, was not at the number she had left on the refrigerator. She had been there, and then gone on. Efforts were being made to reach her, but the uncomfortable possibility was that she might hear about her son's abduction on TV or radio. News media monitor police transmissions, and the first radio reports had been broadcast already.

Lindy sat near the kitchen phone, ready to answer if the kidnapper should call.

Essie slumped at the dining room table, hollow-eyed, beyond tears. She had been questioned by several officers, hastily at first, while the nature and dimensions of the problem were being assessed and the possibility still existed of a direct pursuit and interception; and then more closely and carefully, each repetition beginning farther back in time and proceeding more minutely to the present. Now she was beginning again with Detective Sergeant Leo Gadek, who would have case responsibility, and an FBI agent. They would have greatly preferred to get her away from all the noise and confusion to some quiet place, but she had turned white at the thought of leaving the other children before their mother returned, so they did not press her. Now the three of them sat at one end of the table with their backs to the kitchen door, papers and a tape recorder before them, systematically working their way through it. Like any witness, Essie would sift through her impressions when presented with a new question, and respond with her best recollection. After that, a similar question would tend to evoke the previous answer rather than a fresh recollection. Unconsciously, she would make the answers to new questions consistent with the older ones. And soon her answers would become her recollections, until a membrane of narration separated her from the actual events. Gadek wanted to make sure he got in the most important questions before this process had gone too far.

Gadek typically was in brisk motion, or about to be, or looking as if he wished he were. He was carefully suppressing this appearance now, his manner attentive and relaxed, his body still, and his voice measured. Toby knew the effort it cost him.

The children were in bed upstairs. Every few minutes Essie had to interrupt her interview to go check on them. Each time she checked Jeremy's bed, too. She wanted to believe that when she came to the bed and ran her hand over the pillow he would suddenly hurl back the covers and be there, safe, and delighted with his naughtiness. She had searched the whole house, every space large enough for a child to hide if he could overcome the hunger for his missed supper and his fear of the dark and of remote places. The police had searched it, too, half a dozen of them, intense-looking officers with flashlights who had sought out spaces she had not suspected, sounded the walls for cavities or disguised closets, and gone around the outside of the house as thoroughly as they had gone through the inside. Still, as she approached the smooth, tightly tucked-in bed, she wished so ardently to find him that she could almost believe that the serious-minded little five-year-old, in a puckish humor, would have concealed himself so carefully as to elude a whole platoon of searchers. Miraculously, he would pick *this* moment, out of these three terrifying hours past, to burst merrily forth and cry, *ta da!* Again and again she looked under the pillow and ran her hand down the bed over the taut blankets, as if they could conceal a boy.

Paul emerged from the car a little stiffly but in good spirits to unlock his gate. Inside, pressing the padlock shut while the car idled among the trees just beyond, he felt a great surge of exhilaration. This was a rebirth, the beginning of a new life, a new self-assertion. Paul was no longer to be content with dreams: Paul was going to live.

He had not tarried along the way. The rush hour was past, but the Friday traffic was still heavy. The freeways were brilliant with headlights, and crossing the long, snaky bridge across the north end of the bay they passed under the bridge lights, blink, blink, blink, mile after mile; and all through this part of the drive Paul delighted in looking down at the bag and thinking that it actually contained a boy, not a dream—this was it, this was really it. Once onto secondary roads, it was very dark. He could see the bag only occasionally, when they passed through major intersections and the lights of the two or three little towns that lay along the route. It was at one of the few stoplights in the largest of these towns—a place where the local cop lurked, bored and hostile, in the hope of writing citations—that the boy had started crying and fussing again and suddenly began to scream out loud. It was dangerous and infuriating. The cop *was* there, on the cross street. Paul did not dare do anything but stare straight ahead and hope he did not hear. But as soon as they reached the outskirts, away from lights and passersby, Paul pulled over and slapped the bag several times, more or less at random. After that, there were only a few tight sobs, and for the last half hour not even those.

Paul had expected a certain emotional upset in the early stages and was prepared to make allowances, but he was not going to put up with self-indulgence. He had known plenty of whimpering kids, and he was not going to put up with it.

From the gate there were another two hundred yards of track through what had once been a field and was now reverting to forest. The cabin nestled in a loose copse of trees, and miscellaneous bushes had been permitted to grow up close around it so that only the porch and parts of the roof could be distinctly seen from any distance. Just short of the porch he stopped his car, leaving the lights on to guide him to the door.

Inside the cabin Paul felt his way across the first room. There were lights, but he did not intend to use them. He wanted candlelight. He came to the mantelpiece and placed his hand on the box of matches. The first match flared, revealing a cozy room gone to seed—a bed and chair, comfortably ratty. Opposite the chair a new television and tape player, and a stack of tape cassettes with handwritten labels. A considerable stone fireplace. At each end of the mantelpiece stood candles in tall holders and votive lights in cups, all of which he now proceeded to light.

A mass of photographs and illustrations crowded among these candles like Christmas cards, and a further vast array rose above that, taped densely over the stone as high as the arm could reach. Most of the pictures were small and hard to make out at first, but they were all of children, of both sexes and various ages. Some were posed singly, some in groups. Some of the photographs were snapshots that Paul had taken or traded from friends; some were from books or magazines. Some were in color, others in black and white. Naked children from specialist magazines, figures from underwear ads. Little girls hanging upside down from jungle gyms, skirts over their faces. Naked children displaying themselves. Masturbation. Sexual acts.

The pictures were cut or torn close to the figures to get rid of backgrounds and incidentals. Adults figured in some of them for particular purposes; their faces were invariably torn off, large headless bodies anonymous among the small ones. The pictures fitted intricately together, smaller pressed in among the larger, hundreds of figures overlapping, teeming over the rounded irregular chimney stones so that in the flickering light the whole surface seemed to writhe. Paul never tired of his pictures.

By the time the candles were all lit the room was quite bright and already getting hot, which was how Paul liked it. But tonight he could not linger. He hurried back outside to the car.

He had devoted a lot of thought to these next days.

He opened the passenger-side door and lifted the sack out onto the wet, rutted ground. The boy was stiff as a board.

"Time to wake up," Paul said with an easy kindness, but the boy did not respond.

"Aw, c'mon now," he said. He gave the foot of the bag a good-natured shake, but there was no response. He opened the head of the bag fully and yanked the foot of it several times to get it clear. The boy lay in a tight ball in the dirt, arms and legs pulled up under him, his mouth drawn into a tight line. His face was bright with sweat, his hair wild, his clothes clinging to his body. Only his eyes moved, following Paul.

He's shy, Paul thought.

Essie searched the house again when the investigators had finished with her, and then hovered in the kitchen, anxious for news. Whenever the front door opened she jerked up in terror, although the mother was not expected home so early. She would come around the corner and see police cars in the street, the ID tech's van in the driveway, anxious clusters of neighbors standing around, her house lit up from end to end.

"Tell you what, Essie," said Lindy. "You go on upstairs and stay with the kids. I'll come up and tell you when we need you. We're going to explain things when she comes."

Essie's look of gratitude and relief induced a guilty start in Toby. It had never occurred to him that she would think that the announcement was going to be her responsibility, but plainly she had. They could have spared her that pain, if no other, hours before. When she stood up she seemed still like a child herself, with that thoroughly polite manner that even a lively teen will adopt around adults. But she did not immediately leave.

"Go ahead," said Lindy. "I'll come and tell you the minute we hear anything, I promise."

When the footsteps had receded up the stairs Lindy murmured, "Let's try to keep her out of sight until matters are clear to the mother. No point things getting any more hysterical than they have to be."

"At least four occupants, all male, late teens, early twenties," said Sergeant D'Honnencourt, juggling phone and papers. "Dark clothes. The driver may have dark hair, but nobody was certain. And of course, this car is the best description we've got, but we haven't actually established that it's connected . . . No, nobody even thinks they saw the actual grab. Whoever it was must have come right into the house. You'll see when you get here—it's a long hall straight to the kitchen where the boy was. The responsible must have come way inside, or else he got the victim to come to the door."

There was a flurry of sound toward the front of the house. A woman's voice, wild, crying, "What do you *mean,* one of them's missing? Who? One of my *children? Tell me!"*

"Here it comes," said Lindy.

"The mother's here," said D'Honnencourt into the phone. "I'll get back to you." He tossed Toby his daybook and turned to the doorway.

Shocked with adrenaline, shaking with anxiety and frustration, the mother heard the bare details from D'Honnencourt while she jinked back and forth around the kitchen, too pumped to stand still, too riveted to obey her instinct to dart out into the street to begin searching immediately. There were several cops in the house, and when they would appear in the doorway she would spin to face them as if each would be the one who would appear with Jeremy in his arms and end this hideous impossibility.

A slight sound from the back hall jerked her around in that direction and brought her face-to-face with the tottering Essie, white-faced, come to face the music.

For a moment the mother froze; Essie had been the last thing on her mind. There was just time for Toby to wonder whether her reaction was going to be sympathetic or reproachful. Then she said, "Where is he?"

All her feelings had suddenly found a focus. Essie put a hand to the doorway to steady herself.

*"Oh, Essie—where were you?"* She was starting to move in. Lindy put a hand on her arm, but she shook it off, advancing. D'Honnencourt stepped quickly in front of her.

"No," he said, and tossed his head from Toby to Essie. "Take her home."

"WHERE IS HE?"

"I know everything there is to know," D'Honnencourt was saying as Toby threw an arm over Essie's shoulders and swept her out the back door.

"WHAT HAS SHE DONE WITH . . ." The door closed sharply, but she was still audible outside.

"Oh my *God!*" said Essie as they walked quickly down the driveway and ducked through the loose circle of onlookers. "Oh my *God,*" she said, over and over again.

**6**

So far as Toby could tell, the whole thing was just very bad luck, and that was what he told Essie on the way home. It was not the moment to split hairs—he told her these things just happen. She listened hungrily, but she shook her head. The closer they got to her house, the smaller and tighter became her gestures of negation. It was as if she were in the process of freezing, right there in his patrol car.

He went in with her to explain the situation to her parents. The department's own investigators, the FBI, heaven knows who else would want to talk to her during the next day or two.

Essie let them in, struggling as her key stuck in the lock. Her parents were visible from the door in their chairs in their pool of light. Old sweaters and stay-at-home clothes. Essie's mother looked up at the sound of the door. She started at the sight of the uniform, and her husband's head jerked up abruptly.

"I'm sorry to disturb you," Toby said, standing in the living room doorway, Essie in front and a bit to the side. "We have some real trouble."

They stirred, fumbled. They recognized Toby, but they had never seen him in his uniform, and it confused them. Essie's father started to stand up, dropped his pen and bookmark, groped for them, abandoned them. Her mother almost knocked over the glass beside her. It was almost completely dark away from their chairs, and Essie turned on the light in the entryway. Toby launched into it, Essie flinching visibly at each detail, trying not to. Both her parents were up now and coming across the room.

A moment before, they had been absorbed in their books. After a few moments they made him stop and repeat the basic information: Jeremy missing— presumed kidnapped—search in progress. They were both standing close to him now, the two of them touching. Essie a little apart.

He was explaining and thinking, Hey, fercrissake, put your arm around her. It was the obvious thing to do, but they did not do it, and she did not seem to expect it. As if people in this household did their thinking and their hugging one at a time.

It flustered him. He knew them as people know the parents of their children's baby-sitters, from standing in the living room chatting while the kid dashes around looking for her shoes and her math notes. Norman, he knew, was a professor of something or other. Esther had a Ph.D. and did some sort of research work. Toby always had the feeling talking with both of them that they were thinking about something else. But reasonable people.

On this occasion Toby had the professor's entire attention, but he was clearly running on several tracks at once. "You have . . ." he said at one point. "You have eliminated—criminal investigation, of course, is not my field—but you have *eliminated* other innocent explanations for his absence? Or not? Or you don't know?" Toby explained why they thought what they thought. The professor's eyes were fixed on some point on the wall opposite. His wife's eyes were fixed on Toby's face.

"And our daughter . . ." the professor said, glancing over at her, as if he had said, Next slide, please,

and was checking to make sure it was the right one
". . . she was not—ah, where she should have been? Is
that what I hear you saying?"

Toby went over it again: Essie upstairs with the
other two; the possibly open door.

"It's one of the things we're not sure about," he
said. "Whether the kidnapper came into the kitchen
or Jeremy went to the door. Or whether he was lured
or forced."

The professor looked bewildered, and his wife
looked as bewildered as he did. She mirrored his
expressions as he spoke, standing very close. They
looked waiflike and inward in the face of this event,
sure only of each other.

"I can only conclude . . ." he said, without concluding. They both looked at Essie, not with accusation
but for confirmation.

Perhaps this was a formal moment amongst the
Beals in crisis. No evasions. Essie's eyes flickered past
her mother's. She nodded and then looked at the
floor.

Toby temporized. He could not say, Well, I can see
that you're making this a whole lot more complicated
than it needs to be—let me straighten you out, so he
tried to be indirect, hoping just to talk long enough
that they would start to pick up on his point of view.
He had only a spotty command of the facts, but he
chatted them up. He laid all the stress he reasonably
could on the element of misfortune, the inescapable
hazards of existence. They were not buying it, he
could see. Too tough-minded to be worked on so
indirectly. They were not responding.

"My opinion," he said a little abruptly, "which I've
told Essie, is that what happened is bad luck. We're all
vulnerable from time to time, and she's been caught
out." Their gaze rose off Essie and settled back on
him. Considering his audience, he stretched the point
and said, "I don't think any blame attaches to her."

The professor turned toward him a little more

frontally, shoulders curving gently under the faded sweater, facing the crisp midnight blue, black leather, pistol, baton. Esther's eyes were on Toby's face. Their expressions changed together now, as they had this whole time, without conscious reference to each other, expressing sorrow and regret.

"Thank you for your opinion," the professor said gently, stressing "opinion" just perceptibly. "The fact is that our daughter was in a position of trust. If, as it appears, this catastrophe stems from her negligence"—he took a deep breath as if steeling himself to the pain of pronouncing it—"she is at fault. And because we agreed that she was ready to be trusted with these responsibilities and encouraged her to baby-sit, we are also at fault. Blame *does* attach to her, as you put it. And to us."

Toby had known some unhappiness in his life, and a great deal of it in his work. He knew how it will feed upon itself like fire, gorging on the most improbable fuels, devouring everything that seemed safe and comfortable. Still, he had not expected that here, and he was astonished to discover this whole new horizon of unjust and gratuitous misery spreading out before him.

But he had said whatever he knew and could invent. He had made no impression; he had no more business; there was nothing to do but go.

From the top step he caught a glimpse of Essie standing right where she had been, her eyes fixed on the opposite wall, the tendons of her wrists standing as her hands gripped each other. Plucky. The door closed behind him.

God*damn*.

He stepped back up and clamped down on the bell.

The door opened again. The professor with his quizzing look. His wife just beyond. Essie not turning her head.

"Uh, look," he said. He knew what he wanted to

say, but he could not say that. He tried to think of something else, something helpful. "Look, uh, she's really been through the wringer tonight. It's a terrible thing for her, too. Maybe if you don't discuss it with her tonight, that would be best. I . . ."

They waited, looking at him without speaking. Not rude, but simply not engaging. They had heard his views.

"Well, she's been through it. Really."

A pause.

"Thank you, Toby," said the professor. "Or is it Officer Parkman, since you are in uniform?"

"Oh . . ." He shrugged. Another pause. "Well . . ."

There was nothing to do but turn away. The door closed again.

*Goddamn!*

The house was not crawling with detectives, Toby was surprised to find when he returned. Lindy had moved her watch on the phone to the living room. The telephone company was supposed to have a trap and trace lock on the line by this time, and if the kidnapper made the mistake of calling from his home, they might be able to wrap the whole thing up practically before it began. It happens sometimes.

Sergeant Gadek was in the kitchen conferring with D'Honnencourt. The children's mother was perched at the kitchen table, nursing a cigarette with one hand while an ID technician took fingerprints off the other. She sprang halfway to her feet when Toby appeared in the doorway, saw he was empty-handed, and dropped back into her chair. The prints were smeared. The ID technician clucked sympathetically and reached for a new card.

"Ah, Toby," said Gadek. He had been Toby's training sergeant at one time and had used him before for special tasks in Detective Division. "Listen, this is going to be my case. I want you to organize the neighborhood check. Let's see, it's almost nine-thirty. We better get shaking on that before the neighbors go to bed. I'll have Control send all the uniforms who can be spared, and you brief 'em and get 'em working. A two-block radius would be great, but we won't get that far. Do the best you can. Do the door-to-door first, then have a couple of cars start cruising a four-block radius looking for some vehicles the sitter remembers seeing. Most likely they're from right around here, and if we can establish that they were doing something innocent, we can forget about 'em. Here's the best list we have of people and vehicles that might be involved. Get that back to me ASAP—it's the only copy. Questions?" His lips were already forming the first *g* in "get going."

"No," said Toby. Neighborhood checks are bread-and-butter stuff.

"Get going," he said, and as Toby hustled down the hall, he heard him phoning in for the necessary hands.

Six cars appeared almost at once and double-parked in front. Toby read out Gadek's list while everyone industriously copied the information into their notebooks.

Essie Beal had seen three moving cars. The one disappearing around the corner seemed the most likely prospect, considering the timing, but she could say only that it was "light" and "not too big." Another car had come down the cross street and passed her pretty close, a blue sports car driven by a woman. The third car she described only as "old" and "maybe white." These were not great descriptions, but they might jog someone's memory.

Then there was the dark sedan. If there was a kid in the neighborhood with a car like that, and who drove like that, people would know about it. Every patrol car on the street was on the lookout for that dark sedan. Word had been passed to neighboring jurisdictions and to the Highway Patrol. Dark sedans with air scoops and fat tires were going to be having a hectic time of it.

Then there was that guy—if it was a guy—Essie could not be sure about the gender—with the shopping cart. He might be known. Nomads will sometimes make regular circuits looking for aluminum cans or deposit bottles. For days to come, nobody was going to be able to move a shopping cart without getting rousted.

Toby divided up the work, assigning a block and a direction to each checker. They would start at the near end of each block and work outward until they were told to stop. At a little before ten they fanned out into the neighborhood and began knocking on doors. He went back inside to return Gadek's list. The children's father, he gathered from what the mother was saying, was away from home. Gadek was listening carefully, taking notes, his face neutral to a degree that suggested to Toby that he was thinking hard about what he was hearing.

Back to the street.

Their bit of luck came almost immediately. One of the checkers found a blue sports car parked just around the block from the victim's house. He determined that the registered owner was a woman who lived two doors away. He got on the radio, raised D'Honnencourt, was passed on to Gadek, and described what he had. Despite all the possibilities, the probability was low that the sports car would turn out to be involved. Gadek told the checker to go ahead and make contact but be alert. So he rang the bell, and spoke to the owner. She matched Essie's description, such as it was. She said that she had driven around the block at about the time in question on her way to the grocery store. She got the shopping bag off the top of the refrigerator and found the receipt inside. The receipt showed the date and time. The officer carefully verified her ID and long-standing residence at that address—in all of which process he found her entirely forthcoming and cooperative—thanked her, and departed. This little coup meant that one element in the investigation had been pinned down and could probably be put aside.

At some addresses the checkers were told positively that nobody knew anything. At other addresses the people they spoke to knew nothing, but other residents who were absent might have information and would have to be recontacted. At quite a few addresses no contact was made at all, and these would have to be checked periodically until a resident could be found. The elimination of the blue sports car was the sole item of profit derived from the neighborhood check.

# 7

Toby went in search of Leo Gadek when he came in to the Hall of Justice at the completion of the neighborhood check. He found him in the classroom, the only large space in the building that could be taken over in a hurry and, therefore, designated as the command center for whatever emergency might arise. In the first hectic hours the detectives from all the various specialty details reported here to Gadek, who started them on the numerous tasks, large and small, with which a kidnapping investigation is begun. Now, the immediate rush out of the way, Gadek was beginning to cut them loose so that they could get a few hours' sleep before the work settled into the twenty-four-hour pattern it would follow until the victim was recovered or the leads dried up. He was perched at a table near the door, combing briskly through piles of raw field reports.

"Ah, Toby," said Gadek when he caught sight of him. "We're going to need uniforms tomorrow. Why don't you volunteer." It was one of Gadek's nonquestions. He added, "I understand you know Essie Beal."

"Yes, she baby-sits for us sometimes," said Toby.

"Do you know the Broomes, by any chance? Gabriella and Trevor, but especially Trevor?"

"No. Are we worried about him?"

"He supposedly went out of town," said Gadek. "He runs a little educational foundation—y'know, gives out money to schools and that sort of thing—and he's supposed to be at this retreat center over the weekend—coming back Sunday. Left no phone number—said they're not supposed to be getting calls because they're retreating about education. I got the number and called the place. Turns out they're closed until the end of the year for renovations. So Trevor is not where he said he'd be. Gabriella looked unhappy when I told her this, but not surprised. I asked her if there was something she wasn't telling me, and she said no, no, she really thought he was at the retreat. I called the secretary of the foundation—*she* thought he was at the retreat. I explained to her that if she was covering for him, there might be big trouble—she *still* thought he was at the retreat. I don't like that, not knowing where the dad is when the kid gets abducted."

"Any reason why he would kidnap his own kid?" said Toby.

"It happens all the time," said Gadek. "For a dozen different reasons. Who knows? But something's going on with Gabriella, that's for sure. And Essie Beal looked uncomfortable when his name came up. When I pushed her a bit she said he's always getting his hands on her in a small way—helping her into her coat, that sort of thing. He's beginning to sound like quite a slime."

"Sounds to me like a little extramarital action," said Toby. "You don't think of slimes kidnapping people. That's a long way from copping feels off baby-sitters."

Gadek put his notebook in his pocket and got up. "I don't know, one way or the other," he said. "But I want to know where he was tonight while his kid was getting pinched. Broome's secretary said he has a cot at his office, and it's conceivable that he's camping out there. Before I hit the hay I want to drop by for a peek."

Toby trotted straight upstairs when he got home. He wanted to check on Adam and Joss and watch them sleeping peacefully in their messy beds. They looked younger than eight and ten. He sat beside Adam for several minutes. He watched him breathe. Adam's cat, Robert Peel, lay pooled atop the chest of drawers opposite, eyes open, watchful. Toby scooped him up and put him in the hollow behind Adam's knees, which was where he often liked to sleep, but he rose immediately with a mordant look and sauntered out of the room.

Then Toby went into Joss's room and sat on *her* bed and watched *her* breathe. Her cat, John Marshall—a female, but John Marshall nevertheless—occupied most of the pillow in a very chummy way. That seemed satisfactory.

What he wanted to do was plump up their pillows and pull the covers right up to their chins so that they would look cozy and protected. But he knew that if he did that they would get too hot and have bad dreams. The best thing was just to leave them alone.

Across the landing, Sara had fallen asleep with the lights on, her briefcase open and papers spread over the bed. He gathered her work together and put it on the floor. He noticed the name of the case and remembered her talking about it: a take-no-prisoners divorce, with the children clawed, battered, and used, in the middle. He turned off most of the lights. He unholstered his pistol and began to unload it with the lush metallic slithering and clacking noises that automatic pistols make.

Violent crime was beyond the personal experience of Essie's parents, but they knew about negligence and failure of trust, and they believed in calling things by their right names. Their daughter's baby-sitting loomed large in their own lives. They made a point of staying home when she was sitting so that she could reach them for any advice or assistance she might need. They knew the Broomes slightly, and once the three Broome children had spent a weekend at the Beals', all in a tumble of pillows and sleeping bags on the floor around Essie's bed. Jeremy was no anonymous individual to them: he had played a game of checkers with Norman Beal, setting up the game and reminding him when it was his turn. He had been the greatest help to Esther—so she assured him—in peeling carrots. He had helped set the table for dinner—had *asked* to help.

They felt a responsibility for action. A kidnapping—the motivation for such an act, the nature of the person who could be capable of it—stumped them. But Jeremy must be somewhere. They felt it their duty to get to the bottom of it.

Essie was their only source of information, and the moment they were alone with her they began to question her, not in a blaming way but for information. They began with the moment Essie had been picked up that evening, and worked their way slowly forward to the moment she was returned to their door in a patrol car, examining everything minutely. They operated in light of their own experience; they assumed that something had been overlooked. If only it could be recalled, they fully expected, Essie would jump up and say, Oh! I forgot about that! and Jeremy would be found sleeping peacefully in a cupboard, or with some old and trusted neighbor, whom, it would turn out, he had gone to visit, and who had lost track of the time. They did not enunciate their fear that she had somehow been remiss. They did not need to enunciate it; their opinion was evident to her—it was half her own—and it lay on her heart like fire.

They could see that she was deeply stricken; they were stricken themselves. How could anyone not be, looking straightforwardly at the facts? They did not try to comfort her or each other; comfort is something that you earn. When the mystery was solved, then they could all be comfortable.

Essie had grown up in that house and expected no other reaction from them. She respected it: the truth is the truth and should not be flinched from. But inconsistently, as she recognized, she also yearned to be rallied around and supported. She desperately wanted to be held and convinced against her own judgment that all would soon be well. Instead, she was deeply alarmed to observe that her parents were nearly as distraught as she was. Their Olympian detachment was shattered. They floundered in helplessness and dismay, and in an anguished conviction of their own responsibility which added to Essie's pain without in any way sharing or diminishing her burdens.

They stayed up far, far into the night, examining her every step. The professor's attention span was prodigious. She bore her torture patiently until, with fatigue and excitement and the sudden, pulsing eruptions of shame and the realization of loss, she became simply incapable of putting ideas and words together. Her father, finally noticing, reluctantly told her to go to bed. Essie did not hear him; in her mind she was in Amy's bedroom, hearing Jeremy's voice below. *Was* he speaking to the kidnapper at that moment? *Had* he said something she should have heard? What if she had rushed down, right at that moment? Would that have changed anything? In her fatigue she could form the images in her mind but not hold or combine them; they flocked tumultuously around her like so many filthy, wrathful birds bent on some meaningless revenge.

Esther crept into Essie's room to say good night. She found her daughter wide-eyed and huddled in the dark. She sat down on the edge of the bed. Tentatively she laid a hand on Essie's shoulder, and as if she had touched some spring, Essie lurched up and clapped her arms around her, sobbing in great heaving gasps, clinging. "Well, well, well," said Esther wearily, enfolding her child. She could not in good conscience say, Don't take on so, because she thought Essie *should* take on. She could not say, It'll be all right, when she had no reason to hope that it would. She said, "Well, well," again; she held Essie and rocked her gently in her arms. She sat with her a long time, sharing her grief.

At the Hall of Justice a night clerk was entering the latest kidnapping update into the statewide computer net. For the last several hours, in dozens of agencies near and far, dispatchers had been broadcasting the updates to units in the field. Cruising officers in their dark cars had been scribbling down the essential information and glancing reflexively around them. A few had remembered their local bad characters and drifted past their known haunts, on the off chance. Lonely sheriff's deputies cruising the backwoods counties had settled into unobtrusive spots overlooking the most promising roads, carefully scanning the sparse traffic for the dark-colored sedan with air scoop and fat tires, which reason assured them would not be within two hundred miles.

Paul awoke unsettled after a restless night. The arrival
the previous evening had been unsatisfactory. The
boy would not say a word, would not even move from
the ground where he had landed when Paul shucked
him out of the bag, until Paul had given him a couple
of slaps across the bottom. Then he moved. Paul
could perfectly well have picked him up and carried
him, but Paul had not himself been coddled as a child,
and he did not think that it was good for children to
be coddled.

Nor had the boy been interested in his new home.
Once inside the cabin he crept to the nearest wall and
stood pressed against it, only his eyes moving. Beautiful as they were, the candles seemed only to frighten
him.

"Now listen," said Paul kindly. He reached into the
kitchen, swung one of the two chairs into the main
room, and placed it so that he could sit backward on
it, facing the boy. Paul thought, He's shy. Don't rush
things. He said, "This is where you are going to live
from now on, here with me." The eyes widened.
"Your mother doesn't want you anymore. She said
you'd been bad. You've been giving her too much
grief. So she gave you to me, and she and the other
kids have moved away."

Paul had given this explanation some thought. He
thought it was very smooth—a kid has to love somebody, and if his mom does not love him, then he will
find somebody else. In his earlier life Paul had always

been careful to pick children who felt unloved, often with good reason. In those days, of course, he had plenty of opportunity to confirm his hunches before making his move; he had picked this child not because he was psychologically ripe for adoption but because he was available. Paul had no way of knowing about his emotional makeup. But detaching him from his family seemed like a sound beginning in any case.

"She said, 'You just take him. He'll like you.'"

At first the only visible reaction was that the boy's eyes seemed to grow deeper, but bit by bit he began to tremble and then shake, a howl rising behind his tight-closed lips, his knees giving way until he huddled, seemingly boneless, along the floor by the wall. After a while the howls turned to rapid little sobs, his eyes fixed on something far away.

Paul watched with interest. He had found the credulity of the young to be virtually boundless and had often taken advantage of it in the past. The boy believed what he had been told, Paul could see that. It's a little rough now, he thought, but it'll save a lot of time in the long run.

The boy did seem to be taking it very hard.

Paul had hoped to show the boy the pictures over the mantel—introduce the idea, in case he didn't know about these things already—get him interested. Who knows how far they might get? Paul was prepared to be patient, but if the boy was hot—no, he was just getting more and more worked up. He wept until Paul began to wonder if there was going to be any end to it.

His first time ought to be a good one, he thought. Give him a while. A little patience now would pay big dividends later on.

The boy fell asleep at last, right where he lay, from sheer exhaustion.

He can't be all that upset, Paul thought. He's having his cry and his sleep. He'll feel better in the morning.

But it was a difficult night for Paul. The boy kept

waking up shrieking, and he would take no comfort from Paul, who gave up trying and tried not to let his own sleep be completely ruined.

The boy was sleeping again—only the tiniest visible rise and fall of his chest to show that he was still alive—when Paul awoke in the morning.

Paul loitered in bed for some time, his eyes shifting uneasily back and forth between the huddled figure by the wall and the clutter of pictures over the mantelpiece. The first ten hours, at any rate, had been very trying. His dream and the reality hovered side by side in his mind, equally insubstantial. Once or twice he heaved himself over in frustration to face the other way, but each time he rolled back the boy was still there, just as he had been. Paul tried to turn his mind into optimistic channels, but his thoughts wandered.

Paul had grievances, and they tended to well up in moments of abstraction.

Paul's fantasies had always involved idyllic interludes in which little boys and girls loved him and discovered their true sexual natures and were eager and grateful. He had tried in various ways to make it work out like that in real life, but it never had.

So many teams he had coached, season by season. Team sports—sports that involve changing clothes break down sissy inhibitions about undressing around other people. Of course, Paul changed with the boys. He knew how to play their desire for acceptance against their modesty so that they resolved the tension by affecting a brazen unreserve, which Paul encouraged as a becoming and manly confidence. Paul put on a frank, confiding manner on these private occasions. He made them feel in the know.

He took them on trips in groups of two or three— rivers, lakes. These were all boys, of course. Parents' blessings, of course—busy, no time themselves— grateful. Hiking. Canoes. Skinny-dipping. Campfires in secluded places. It was all very smooth. One thing led to another. There was no moment of decision, no sudden shift of subject that would jar a kid into saying, Hey, wait a minute—I don't understand—I'm scared.

Kids talk among themselves, up to a point. All the kids knew that things happened on those trips, but nobody told an adult. Human nature ran Paul's way. Nobody goes blabbing about what puzzles and shames them—children least of all.

Then one day a conversation was overheard, explanations demanded, things blurted out. The head coach was called.

The head coach thought back, saw the pattern. Horrified, he recognized what had been happening. He fired Paul immediately and denied everything, hotly, indignantly, to everyone. Rumors flying everywhere. A meeting called at someone's house.

Half the parents denied the possibility, the other half wished they could.

Someone said, it means testifying in court. It'll go on for years.

They were all thinking, Does this mean my boy is queer? Is my daughter still a virgin if he only . . . ? How will we live? Police and lawyers and reporters? What about the other children? The whole school will know. The whole town will know. The whole family will hear, aunts and uncles, grandparents, saying . . . ?

Angry speeches. We can't paper over it, he'll go on doing it. It's water over the dam, begin the healing now. There was no agreement.

Nobody acted. The authorities were never told. But they all turned on Paul. They didn't want to hear about their own shortcomings or their children's eagerness. They wanted only to find someone to blame, and they picked Paul.

He pondered the sleeping boy. He wondered what that kid had had in mind, yelling the way he had in the car. Probably wanted to signal a cop and get Paul into trouble. Well, it was no surprise; it had certainly happened before. Paul had been a good friend to so many kids during his coaching days, but so many of them had turned on him once the word got out. Kids will fink on you if you so much as turn your head.

He slipped into a fretful reverie. The world never turns out to be as good as you think it ought to be—that was Paul's experience.

Early Saturday afternoon found Toby stepping smartly up the stairs, but Gadek passed him, taking them two at a time, a sheaf of papers in each hand. Toby was early—it was ridiculous for him to run simply because Gadek was running—but he ran anyway, with a hand on his long baton to keep from tripping himself up, and caught the classroom door before it could swing shut.

Most of the people working the case were elsewhere, but there was some action here. A detective was assessing the likely profit in culling a Department of Motor Vehicles printout listing the 26,847 locally registered makes and models which might correspond to the dark sedan. "I don't think this is going to be worth the trouble," he said. "What we really know about it—color, fat tires, and hood scoop—none of that is included on DMV records 'cause those things come and go. We could cut it down by running the names of all the registered owners and then looking for youngish males, but we'd still have thousands. We can't run around trying to eyeball thousands of different cars."

A small party of detectives was in the midst of backgrounding the Broomes and Essie Beal.

Walt Kramer, Toby's college roommate, old friend, and fellow patrol officer, appeared in the door. Characteristically, his shirttail had managed to work loose enough to hang out over his gunbelt in the time it took to climb the two stories from the locker room. Walt had owned a bookstore after college; its failure had brought him to police work as a temporary safe haven. Toby had joined for the same reason after being laid off by a small publishing house. They became engaged with the work and stayed, somewhat to the dismay of their wives, who were both professionals and who—especially Walt's wife, Melanie—dreamed of neckties and gentility for their husbands.

"Well, this is cheerful," said Walt, observing the bustle. "I was stuck in the other end of town last night when this thing went down, and I never did get in on any of the action."

"I don't know that I'd call what we're likely to be doing today action," said Toby.

"Ah, Parkman, Kramer," said Gadek, spotting them and waving briskly from his desk. They hastened over. "Two tasks for you, to start. From now till six o'clock, I want you to see if you can find any prior sightings of suspicious characters hanging around kids. Working out from the victim's house, visit all the places where you get concentrations of young children—school yards, parks, shopping areas. Leave the little kids alone, but leaflet all the parents you can find, and older kids—baby-sitting age. Ask 'em if they're around much and whether they've seen anyone hanging around recently. We don't know whether our responsible knew about Jeremy and went after him specifically, or whether he was just cruising for a lucky grab. If he's been cruising, somebody may have noticed him. That clear?"

"Yes," they said.

"Then, starting at six, we want an area sift at the house. People have routines, and a lot of people who were driving or walking through at the time of the grab last night will be doing the same tonight. It won't be just the same, because this is Saturday, but there'll be a lot of the same people. Stop every car and every pedestrian that passes through the intersections at each end of the block. Give 'em a leaflet and ask 'em if they went through the area between six and seven-thirty last night. If they did, find out what they observed. Do it till eight-thirty. I've been promised some help for you on that. They'll meet you there at six.

"We're monitoring Channel Two up here, so you can hit me on the air. Let me know ASAP if you get anything promising—don't wait until the end of the detail. We're updating all the time. Questions? No? Pick up a box of leaflets from the press office on your way out. Oh, and by the way, Toby. Charlie Footer went to see Essie Beal this morning to see what more she could remember after a night's sleep. He didn't think she'd had one. The parents"—he ran his eye over a sheet of notes on the table beside him—"ah, Norman and Esther Beal—you know them?"

"Just from saying 'hello' at the door when I go by to pick Essie up to baby-sit. And from my discussion with them when I dropped her off last night."

"Footer characterized them as terribly upset and blaming Essie."

"That was my impression last night, too."

"Essie couldn't talk in front of them, and they couldn't stop asking questions and making suggestions. Finally, Footer had to ask them to leave the room."

"That's certainly how it was last night," said Toby. "That poor kid is really in for it."

Toby and Walt spent a hectic afternoon in the

watery autumn sun, hurrying around with their leaflets from one playground to the next, querying parents while the children played, trying to be relaxed
enough to encourage confidence while still covering a
lot of ground. They were well received. The kidnapping had been on the news and in the papers and
much discussed around the sandboxes, and people
who would not give a cop the time of day in most
circumstances made a real effort when they saw the
leaflet. Mothers would think hard about where they
had been with their children recently, and who
they might have noticed hanging around. While
they talked they would keep looking back at their
children, and when the cops moved on, they would
get up and move to another bench to be closer.

They got no fewer than three descriptions, all more
or less the same: male, roughly 5′ 10″, stocky, between
thirty and forty years old, clean shaven, thinning hair,
flannel shirt or light jacket, light pants, work shoes.
They phoned these in to Gadek one by one as they
received them. This man had been noticed nearby or
observing from the edge of the park. What all three
informants remembered was that he would watch the
children unless he saw someone looking at him, then
he would look away and watch something else, but a
minute later he would be watching the children again.
They didn't call the police because—they tried to
remember why they hadn't: he hadn't seemed threatening at the time; he hadn't seemed sneaky so much
as bashful about eye contact. Otherwise they surely
would have done something about it, they said unhappily.

From six to eight-thirty, Toby and Walt and several
other officers stopped every vehicle and pedestrian
passing through the intersections at each end of the
Broomes' block. They identified who had been by
during those hours on Friday, and these people were
questioned more closely about anything they might

have observed. Most of the people they talked to were well disposed, but nobody had any useful information to add.

There had been little or no sleep for any of the Beals on Friday night, and their Saturday began in the gray hours. They moped and wandered to and fro all day. Sometimes they stumbled into new rounds of interrogation. Questions and doubts rose over them like scalding tides that receded to leave them raw and new-blistered. Esther called Gabriella with all the right motives and had a broken conversation of regrets, false starts, cross purposes, and reproaches, suddenly cut off, which stunned her.

There seemed to be no way to proceed with life, even on the most ordinary level. Without actually considering or choosing, they hewed futilely to their normal weekend duties and routine, except that any ordinary duty seemed too trivial for consideration. There were no little chats about mutual concerns. None of those, Oh, would you mind, or While you're up, or Oh, thanks. All day Norman picked up his books and put them down again, drifting. He had run out of information and had no access to more. Detectives came and spent some time with Essie but declined to discuss the case in detail with him. His bewilderment and his frustration mounted together. Esther stayed near him to strengthen and to receive strength. Essie floated numbly in isolation and despair.

Word of the kidnapping spread quickly among Essie's friends, and several of them appeared at the Beals' door. The first of these was Heather, an older girl, a junior, Walt Kramer's stepdaughter, who had heard the night before when Walt came home at the end of his shift. Heather's friendship with Essie was of long standing, and she had always been reckoned a semi-resident in the Beals' home, but now Esther stopped her short. Essie could not have visitors,

Heather was informed; she had better go on home. Heather instantly assumed some further catastrophe. Had Essie been hurt? No. Couldn't she help? No. Could she see her just for a minute to tell she was thinking about her?

No.

Bewildered, Heather drifted away.

Erin and Lizby appeared; they were sent away. From time to time the phone rang. Essie knew better than to answer it. Each time the caller was told firmly, "I'm sorry, but Essie can't come to the phone now." There was no offer to take messages.

Toward the middle of the afternoon, stifling, Essie asked if she could go out for a while. Her parents looked up at her.

"Go out?" said the professor. For the last eighteen hours he had merely been presented with information, but this called for a decision.

The picture in his mind of "going out" was the café downtown where Essie's circle often met, a noisy, frenetic place crusted with rock band posters and antiestablishment graffiti. Loud and obnoxious music and much whooping and greeting of friends across the room. The antithesis of his own state of mind, which he felt was also properly hers. How was this to be cleared up if they stopped thinking about it, if they just went back to their ordinary lives as if nothing had happened? It made him angry just to think about it.

She was standing near their chairs. They gazed at her, minds humming away, getting madder. The professor began to get up.

"No," said her mother firmly, to head him off. "No, I don't think going out is the right thing to do."

"No," said her father, with heat.

"I think you should consider yourself grounded," said her mother.

"Yes, grounded," said her father, astonished to find the bizarre expression on his tongue, relieved to have a specific course of action proposed. They had never "grounded" Essie before or thought of "grounding" her. But it was a decision, it was something to do. His anguish overflowed, and he cried, "I think you ought to take this situation *seriously*."

He was not watching her face, or he would have taken it back and held her and begged her pardon. But he was looking into infinite space, and Esther was looking at him, her hand on his arm; neither of them saw Essie's expression.

That was that. Essie wept in her room, instead.

She stood for a long time by a window. She observed the perfection of the gentle autumn at a great distance, as if it were a recollection.

# 10

When Heather returned home in defeat from the Beals', she hastened to her mother to describe this very strange event. It never crossed her mind that Melanie, whom she had abused on Friday night as bourgeois, small-minded, and power-mad (the subject under discussion being Heather's curfew), would be in any way reluctant to listen, sympathize, and advise on Saturday morning; and to the extent that Melanie may in fact still have been nursing her wounds, Heather was much too full of her immediate concern to notice. She described her interview on the doorstep. And Melanie was aghast at what she heard.

Melanie had known Esther Beal for years in the way that parents know other parents, putting on bake sales and chaperoning dances—not personally, but in a practical way. She had always gotten on well with Esther, who always promised to do more than her share, and she always did what she promised. Essie was the same way. Melanie could see where she got it.

"They must still be very excited and upset," Melanie said. "Give them a little time to get themselves together. I'll call Esther tomorrow. I certainly think you ought to see Essie."

Accordingly, on Sunday morning she called, thinking to be helpful—two mothers with a good deal of history together. Esther cut her right off, not rudely but not wasting any time. Esther's view was that Essie had a trust, and something had gone terribly wrong. That was the long and the short of it. The whole family was stewing, and she thought they *ought* to be stewing. Melanie was taken considerably aback. The best she could do was get Esther to agree to let Essie and Heather talk on the phone for ten minutes.

She called Sara Parkman, an old friend, to vent.

"Ten minutes!" she told Sara, who made sympathetic noises.

"And then the *worst,*" said Melanie, sounding perplexed and frustrated, "the *worst,* as Heather found out when they had their ten-minute talk, is that Essie is half convinced herself. She wonders if maybe she *is* to blame. I don't know, I suppose it's partly her fault in the sense that one could always have been more careful. But she takes the whole thing on her own shoulders."

"Toby told them it was a bad break," said Sara, chewing her lip. "It wasn't her fault."

"No," said Melanie. "That's what Walt said, too. They've been told, it's been explained to them. It's what you'd think parents would *want* to believe about their child, in any case. You'd think that if they were going to make a miscalculation one way or the other, it would be on her side."

"You'd think so," Sara said with some heat, because she liked and respected Essie. "I can't believe they're going around in circles and not helping and protecting their daughter. I can't believe they don't simply put first things first."

Melanie said, "Oh, it just makes you want to put your arms around her and tell her that *somebody* loves her."

They both thought so; and when they hung up, they both examined their consciences, and finding evidence of recent imperfections, they both resolved to be less selfish, more patient, and more supportive toward their loved ones in future.

It did not occur to Jeremy to doubt that his mother had stopped loving him, or that she had given him away. It did not occur to him that she did not know this man and this cabin, or the pattern of his new life. He knew that he did bad things. He got out of bed sometimes when he was supposed to be asleep. He was saucy sometimes. He lost things. When he was two and a half he threw a little toy car at baby Noah and made a tiny cut on his forehead where a drop of blood had gradually formed, perfect, scarlet, mesmerizing in its ripeness.

Not long ago, playing with the telephone, he had found himself connected to a bartender in Sri Lanka, and they had chatted for some time before he was discovered. His mother was irritated. That night at bedtime when his father came upstairs, he said that there would be no bedtime story and, instead, lectured him about the telephone bill.

Later, Jeremy was just dozing off when he heard contentious voices in the kitchen. They were arguing about him. He pressed into the covers, trying to shut them out. He could not distinguish most of the words, but he could hear the rhythm of his father's speech, like marching feet, and his mother's, like the sea roiling among rocks. The angry words and hard looks were all on his account. If only he could be better, he knew, everything would be easy and loving between them; only he never seemed able to be better.

He awoke some time after that to find his mother holding him. She did not mention Sri Lanka, or anger. She kissed him and told him that she loved him and would *always* love him.

He had inferred from this that his mother would love him despite his badness. And yet, just a day or two later, he had pressed too hard and broken Amy's orange crayon, her favorite color. His mother had given him a cross look and said, *"Honestly,* Jeremy, what am I going to *do* with you?"

Now he knew what she had done. She would not have told Paul that she did not love him anymore unless it were true; she was so serious about things like that. She did not joke about loving and not loving.

She must have changed her mind.

Jeremy knew the despair of one who realizes too late that he has acted wrongly, and that the wrong is irrecoverable. He knew that crayons cannot be fixed once they are broken. His mother did not want him anymore.

The place by the wall was his place now. There was nothing to distinguish it—no corner or piece of furniture—but it was the place he had first stood when he came into that habitation, and it remained the most familiar place. He stayed there every moment he could, pressed against the floor, neither moving nor speaking. He slept there again on Saturday night. Paul wanted him to come sleep on the bed, but he would not. Paul lost his temper and shouted and stamped; Jeremy curled tighter and covered his face with his arm. Finally, Paul gave up and left him there.

Paul was baffled by the boy's collapse. He struggled with his anger, but inwardly he thought he had a right to it. He had known a lot of kids, and he had never seen one so wrapped up in himself. The boy would not talk at all; he would scarcely eat a thing, although Paul had been careful to lay in a supply of the sure favorites. He would not even pick up the controller for the video game, and when Paul played a videotape that he had taken on a canoe trip—a *funny* tape, largely consisting of skinny-dipping scenes with several kids vying to strike the grossest pose for the camera—the boy shut his eyes and would not open them again until he heard by the sounds that the VCR and the television had been turned off. He absolutely refused to look at the pictures over the mantel. He lay curled by the wall, unmoving, unless he was positively commanded to leave it, and unless the commands were reinforced with threats or slaps.

It was frustrating, Paul thought. He would have been delighted to have been paid so much attention when he was that age. This weekend was to have got them off on the right foot—clearly, very important— and instead, the boy was being impossible, and Paul's minimal efforts to keep order were only creating panic and negative impressions that would have to be overcome in the future.

On Monday he would have to go back to work, and he would have much less time to spend. It was very frustrating.

Well, it's only been two days, he thought. Don't give up on things too easily. Show a little character. You just have to find the right approach.

But he could scarcely believe that his years of dreaming and weeks of preparation had come down to the possession of this speechless, huddled creature. He had been under considerable stress for several days while he was looking for children he might take. He had been shaking with excitement—literally shaking—when he went to get the boy out of the car. And then to get no response at all . . . well, who wouldn't be upset? And stymied. How do you make friends with a kid like that? He would not talk, he would not play—there was nothing to get a grip on. It was only asleep that he made noise, and only in a nightmare that Paul had heard him speak: on the second night he convulsed suddenly into a sitting position, eyes wide open, and screamed, *"I sorry!"*

Paul thought it was creepy, having this kid who slept with his eyes open and talked to the air but not to him. Maybe he had taken a kid with a screw loose—Christ, he'd never considered that.

On Sunday Paul needed to make an expedition into town. He did not do this lightly. He locked the boy carefully into the closet off the kitchen, closing bolts he had installed both at top and bottom. He made sure that all of the windows were locked, and carefully locked the front and back doors. He locked the gate across the track once he was past.

Paul regarded the passage of this track in ritual terms. Coming in was the emotional equivalent of a warm bath, relaxing and reassuring, but going out was the reverse, a process of arming himself against a hostile and suspicious world. It had always made him uneasy to think that when he was away someone might find some excuse to go into his cabin, where his pictures were in plain view. Now he had the further uneasiness of leaving the boy, who might try to escape or somehow make enough noise to attract attention. Or start a fire. Paul had no idea how he might start a fire, but it was an alarming possibility. The cabin was not so retired that nobody would notice, and the fire department would be called. Even if the pictures were completely destroyed, there would still be a body. There is almost always something left. How would he explain that? All he could do was hope it did not happen.

He was still revolving these unsettling possibilities when he arrived at the market. On the bulletin board outside he saw for the first time one of the first flyers with the boy's picture.

## HAVE YOU SEEN THIS CHILD?

Yes, he thought.

Jeremy Broome. So that's his name. Paul had not thought to ask the boy what his name was; he was not much interested. Paul did not think of him as a name; he thought of him as an image in his mind: the boy. And since he did not plan to speak of him to anyone, this served him perfectly well.

He read the description and the little narrative with interest, especially the part about the dark sedan.

He thought, They won't find him—but the thought sounded boastful to him even as he formed it, and he reached up to the nearest piece of wood and softly knocked three times.

Paul hastened to complete his marketing and return. His side road turned off from the winding two-lane, unmarked and almost invisible amidst a substantial grove of redwoods, and from this moment he breathed more easily. For the first mile the road meandered along the side of a ridge, with forest overarching on the uphill side, and on the other a steep, shrubby embankment with narrow, meandering grassy fields and a small wooded river at the bottom. Sometimes there was a horse or two, or a half acre of vineyard laid out by some enthusiast. The pavement was patched and potholed, and here and there, especially during the rains, little dirt slides sent fingers of yellow soil out across the tarmac. Occasional side roads branched off, each with a few houses lost in the trees; after each side road, the main artery suffered a further diminution of width and surface, sometimes brushing through foliage on either side until the pavement ended and gravel continued, rougher and ever more irregular, encroached on at the edges and down the middle by advancing swaths of grass and weed, until gravel gave way to dirt—at this season, to mud—and finally all pretense of public maintenance ended at Paul's gate.

Jeremy was faintly audible even from outside the house, weeping, and patting on the closet door.

I guess he doesn't like the dark, thought Paul. I didn't, either, when I was his age. But he's got to learn that he can't make so much noise. I've got to do something about that.

In the locker room on Sunday afternoon Toby and Walt saw Charlie Footer.

"Trevor the Slime has come home to his nest," said Footer. He sat and jittered one foot, as he always did, and talked while Toby changed into uniform. "Gadek and I were in the kitchen running a list of names past Gabriella. She heard his key in the door and went out into the hall to meet him. We could hear him start right in about what a good retreat it had been and how fascinating everybody was, all this horsepucky. Can you believe this guy? I mean, you don't have to look very hard at Gabriella to see that something ain't right—she hasn't slept since Thursday night, she's been scared to death—she isn't trying to hide it, and she's his wife, right? Not paying close attention. Just chattering away." Footer's hands were resting on the bench on either side of him, and all ten fingers drummed away at the wood. "Well, she manages to cut into this stream of malarkey long enough to tell him that their kid's been kidnapped, which I wish hadn't happened in the hall because we really wanted to watch his face, see what he looks like when he's told. But she brings him into the kitchen about twenty seconds later, and he's clearly disbelieving—doesn't get it at all. There's no doubt in my mind that he didn't know before, and Gadek felt the same. So he takes about five minutes to be disbelieving and have the whole thing explained to him again, and then he gets furious. And at who? Guess. G'wan, guess."

"At Gabriella," said Toby. Footer gave him an approving look.

"Good for you, Parkman. Right. Gabriella. Had a few nasty things to say about the baby-sitter, too, but mostly he was mad at Gabriella. Why didn't she let 'im know, why didn't she call, blah, blah, blah. It's like, if one of the kids had just been run over or lost a leg or something he couldn't do anything about, well *then* of course she shouldn't bother 'im, but a kidnapping—he wants to be on the scene. He wants to be in charge. And can you believe it, she's taking this shit? Just standing there looking deserted. She knows perfectly well the retreat never happened, and whatever he's been up to it hasn't been retreating, but she's just letting him pour all this crap on her. Probably a Buddhist or something."

"But you digress," said Walt.

"No," said Footer, "I don't. But in any case, we didn't interrupt 'im—let 'im go on, to hear what he'd say. Our mistake. Because then he turns on us and wants to know who is in charge of the investigation, the *top man*. I said—I couldn't help myself—I, of all people, said, The top *person* is Sergeant Gadek. Don't think he noticed. He says, he demands to meet immediately—*immediately*—with 'this Sergeant Gadek,' blah, blah, blah. Well, you know Gadek. He listens to this horsepucky for a while and then he cuts right into the middle of a sentence and says, 'Mr. Broome, I'm Sergeant Gadek. Where have you been since Friday morning?' And the slime actually says—I mean, not smart—at a retreat. He gives us the whole retreat story. So Gadek tells him that lying to the police isn't going to get him his son back, but it may land him in jail. He says, 'What are you talking about?' and Gadek says, 'Let's go downtown and you can talk as much as you like, or even more—probably more.'

"And then something *funny* happens. Gabriella, who has been standing there taking this all in, suddenly says, 'And when you're done talking downtown, go find yourself another place to live.'

"Dead silence. The two of 'em just staring at each other. Then she says, 'I don't have the strength for you now, in the middle of all this. I'll pack a bag. You'll find it on the porch. Don't even think about coming into this house again.'

"It was beautiful, Parkman. There's so much injustice in the world, and it's a real pleasure to see a little of it tidied up. He didn't say a word. He just gave her this *wounded* look—like, How could you stab me in the back this way?—and then he walked out, as if taking himself off was the worst thing he could think of to do to her. But she seemed calm enough.

"Anyway, he's upstairs now, talking with Gadek. I'm going home because I was last in bed Friday night, I think, and I'm kinda flat."

"Yes," said Toby, "that's what I thought when I saw you. Charlie looks flat, I thought."

"But I'll bet you I'm not missing anything," said Footer. "The slime ain't our man. He's all kinds of crap, but he ain't crazy, and he'd have to be *really* crazy to behave the way he's behaving if he thought he had anything to hide. To hide from us, at any rate."

"Well, I'm glad to hear it," said Walt. "You don't like to think of fathers kidnapping their own children. You'd rather think it was some kook off the street."

"Of course if it *had* been Trevor," said Toby, "the kid's chances of being alive right now would be a lot better."

"That's the other way to look at it," said Walt.

On Sunday evening the dark sedan was spotted, run to earth in a hazardous high-speed chase that Toby and everyone else enjoyed immensely, and eliminated from any connection with the kidnapping.

The chase was the subject of discussion in the squad room at the end of the shift.

"The sedan is a bust," said someone who had brought the driver in and helped with the paperwork.

"They were just kids out cruising the night of the Broome thing. When they saw a black and white taking an interest in them tonight, they figured they'd gotten blamed, and that's why they ran. Now they're in the soup for real."

"But no connection," said Toby.

"Nah. Just coincidence. There'll be plenty of prodding to make sure, but it won't pan out."

# 11

On Monday morning Essie left her house for the first time since she had returned there with Toby on Friday night. Her going to school had in itself been the subject of prolonged discussion, with her mother considering that the activity would do her good, and her father arguing that it would be an unbearable diversion of attention from the central problem. In his fatigue and confusion he could not abandon the idea that one more effort of concentration, one more convulsive exertion of the mind, would somehow produce a resolution and a restoration of peace and comfort. Esther labored under no such illusion, but she was uneasy at the idea of sloughing the tragedy off and resuming their normal routine simply because Monday had come. Without consciously framing the thought, she extended the normal scale of domestic expectation into this new and entirely novel situation. If Essie had carelessly broken a plate, her mother would have expected her to apologize and clean it up and be ostentatiously careful for the rest of the day.

Only instead of a plate, it was Jeremy. The difference was scale: If one should be sorry a certain amount for breaking a plate, how sorry should she be for losing a child? A mother's sympathy could soften this reckoning a certain amount—a great deal—but there still remained a terrible sum which she felt must in conscience be acknowledged. She pictured Essie at school, smiling and laughing among her friends, and shook her head.

But in the end they decided that Essie would go, if only because there seemed to be no probable end to it if they kept her home.

She was glad to go. Arriving was harder. Everyone knew, of course. Some of the students and teachers she passed before class gave her a sympathetic nod, or spoke briefly to her; others looked away, embarrassed, or self-consciously reenacted their customary greeting as if nothing had happened at all.

Her group was there on the library steps. Erin and Lizby ran down to her as soon as she appeared and threw their arms around her.

"We tried to come," said Lizby. "We tried to call."

"We're on your side," said Erin. "It was totally not your fault."

The others approached more circumspectly, but they all tried in their various ways to be reassuring. Latasha and Moll and Addie, afraid of saying the wrong thing, said uncertainly that it could happen to anyone. Robert, who was self-absorbed, said that she would feel better soon and began to tell about his own unhappy experience at summer camp before Rhea told him to shut up.

Essie had scarcely slept for three nights. She had scarcely eaten. Physical and emotional exhaustion had flattened her defenses, but her perceptions were keen. She was glad to be hugged, she was grateful that they had tried to call, but Erin had no way of knowing that it was not her fault. There was no comfort in unthinking support. In the more tentative consolations of her other friends she heard the implied accusation which, she reasoned to herself, was really the only honest position for uninformed people to take. Yet there was solace in the end of her isolation; she was surrounded two deep, arms draped around and reaching in, voices pressing in; her eyes filled.

Elliott appeared at the fringe of the group and murmured something inaudible.

She threw up her hands abruptly and heaved her shoulders, shaking off the teeming arms.

*"Get your hands OFF me!"* she cried. *"Leave me ALONE!"*

They froze for a moment, uncomprehending.

*"You don't know anything about it!"* she shouted. The circle stirred, loosened. Expressions were stunned, perplexed. Suddenly she was turning this way and that, looking for a way out. The clearest route was toward Elliott; she spun back the other way and cannoned straight into Lizby who backed a step and said, *"Ess! Just tell us what you want.* That's what we'll do. Promise."

They were a foot apart.

*"Just don't tell me it wasn't my fault, okay?"* Essie hissed, the tears streaming down her face. She rounded on Erin, shaking with rage. *"Just don't talk a lot of shit, okay? Just don't talk about things you don't know anything about."*

Early Monday afternoon Paul put the boy in the closet again and got the first word the boy had spoken to him. As he opened the door and guided the boy in he tried to break away, and as Paul seized him more firmly and pushed him in, he cried *"No!"* several times in a high, scared voice. Paul had to give him several sharp swats on the behind.

Paul knew that he would not be home from work until well after midnight, so he also put in a peanut butter sandwich and two screw-top bottles of soda and a jar to use as a toilet. Then he closed the door and carefully set the bolts at top and bottom. The boy was crying and thumping on the door, but Paul did not think he could keep it up for long. It'll get hot in there if he keeps that up, he thought.

He arrived at work to find the Hall of Justice all aflutter, FBI agents trotting through, reporters hanging out—the whole three-ring circus that unfolds its tents and settles in for a juicy crime. He knew in ten minutes from the buzz that they had nothing, and a few perfectly natural questions to Sergeant Wren confirmed it. Not that Sergeant Wren was in on the investigation, but as he said himself, winking, "Those Detective Division boys are through here fifty times a day, and you only have to watch their expressions. A barometer couldn't be more accurate. Even Gadek is looking worried." He shook his head. "I'll tell you, Greber, it doesn't look good for that kid. Whoever grabbed him has really lucked out."

Paul shook his head sadly and said what was appropriate. Old Mother Superior could call it luck if he liked.

Paul was fascinated to think of the police searching diligently for a child who was presently in his kitchen closet. He was fascinated that they would be thinking about this for a long time. He was thrilled to think that they knew him perfectly well and saw him every day, but it would not occur to them to put those two pieces together.

They keep those cases open for years and years. He would hear occasionally about some gross old detective, red-nosed and obese, still chewing over a crime decades cold. That was a funny term they use, a cold case. The boy's case would be a cold case, he thought. A cold case for a cold boy. The play on words pleased him. He wondered what relation it bore to the actual future. Fate. You never know what's going to happen.

\* \* \*

On Monday afternoon Toby headed upstairs to the classroom. Gadek was not calling for support from Patrol.

"We're getting calls from all over the country," he said, "and mostly the FBI is dealing with them. Local leads we're handling, but we blitzed all the good stuff, and now there isn't a lot that needs more than a quick look."

"It's over?" said Toby. "Just like that?"

"No, it's not over. But what we've got is a quick elimination of the obvious suspects, and nothing new coming in. I assume at this point that it was a stranger grab, but whatever it was, it was very, very clean. We'll keep chewing on what we've got and hope for a break from someplace unexpected."

"I don't suppose there's anything I can do?" said Toby. "If it's a budgetary matter, I could take some vacation time. I guess I've gotten involved with this one. I keep thinking, just throw a little more weight on and something'll give."

"Thanks," said Gadek. "But it isn't budgetary. We're doing everything we can with what there is. If there's something for you, I'll let you know."


Essie was still grounded, and so immediately after school she returned home. Both her parents were there, huddled together in their chair nest, not reading, scarcely talking. Her eyes met theirs as she stood in the open doorway, trying to get her key out of the lock. She thought, I could just back out again and close the door. I could be a long way off.

But the key came loose; she went inside and closed the door behind her.

She had been thinking. She wanted a formal conference with her parents to discuss the whole thing and get them to say what they were planning to do with her, so she could know. Not knowing what to expect was killing her. Was she grounded forever?

What . . . ? But they were not ready to discuss it—it all depended—they did not know. She crept to her room and closed the door, but soon her mother appeared to say that hiding wasn't going to cure anything: the door was to remain open.

It was perfectly dark in the closet, and it was hot. The air became stale almost at once and grew steadily worse. Jeremy scarcely noticed. He could smell the peanut butter, but he was not hungry. His thirst was terrible. His eyes had been shut when Paul put the bottles into the closet. He had not seen them, and he did not know that they were there. He was not strong enough to open them, in any case. Paul had put the jar next to him, so he knew about that, but Paul had not told him what it was for, and it never occurred to him to put it to the intended use. After some hours he could not help wetting himself. He had not wet himself for a long time. He trembled with the old, newly remembered shame and a vivid, newly discovered apprehension. He curled more tightly, unmoving, in the corner where he had been put. He was awake most of the time, eyes open, staring into the dark—a teeming place of visions, frights, and the consciousness of an infinite regret, unworthiness, and loss.

On Tuesday Erin and Lizby watched the noontime crowd shifting and jostling.

"Essie's off talking to Heather again," said Erin. "I don't know what Heather's got to say that's so important."

"Her mom and dad aren't any help," said Lizby. The sunny library steps were crowded with little groups, and they were speaking in low voices so as not to be overheard. "Heather's helping her deal with it."

"So?" said Erin. *"We* help her deal with it."

"Heather's older," said Lizby.

"So?" said Erin. "So *she* can help so much? By the time you're a junior you've been kidnapped a bunch of times so you know all about it?"

*"Oh,"* said Lizby.

Someone nearby was saying, "I'll tell you *one* thing—nobody's getting *me* to baby-sit again for a *long* time. Hell, no! My mom's all like, Your college money, your college money, and I'm like, *Forget* it, Mom."

*"I've* talked to her about it, *too,"* said Erin. *"I've* talked to her about it 'till I'm turning *purple.* Half the time she wants me to hug her 'till I get cramps, and the other half of the time she screams at me. *I'm* so bored with it I'm beginning to wish it hadn't even happened."

"Don't joke about it," said Lizby. "I baby-sat for the Broomes a bunch of times. Amy's a little brat, but Jeremy was *so* cute."

*"Was?"* said Erin reflexively, and then looked awkward.

For a moment neither of them spoke. Lizby shivered suddenly. "She needs *lots* of help, y'know," she said. "It *wasn't* her fault. She wants so bad to make it right, and there's nothing she can do. She keeps looking around, as if he was going to be right here somewhere, and she could grab him up and that would be the end of it."

"Well, you don't need to tell me that," said Erin. "I know it wasn't her fault." She waved voguishly to a friend across the courtyard. She glanced around to be sure she would not be overheard, and then she said, "But it wouldn't have happened to you, would it?"

"Oh, c'mon," said Lizby, uncomfortably.

"You wouldn't have let it happen," said Erin.

*"Oh . . ."* said Lizby.

"Well, you wouldn't," said Erin. "And it wouldn't have happened to me, either."

"Oh . . ." said Lizby.

"Would it?"

"Oh, c'mon."

*"Would* it?"

"No," said Lizby after a pause.

"I would have closed that door," said Erin.

"So would I," said Lizby.

"I would *never* have left that door open."

"No."

"It was *really* stupid," said Erin.

"But maybe we've . . . well, we've never done *that,* but maybe *we've* done dumb things. Maybe without even knowing. And just gotten away with it."

*"That* dumb?"

"Well . . ."

*"That* dumb? Leaving the door open?"

"But it's still not very *fair,"* said Lizby. "Essie's the only one getting blamed and it's not *just* her fault." She was whispering, but her voice was quick and urgent. "There was the *kidnapper,* too. I mean that's significant *too,* isn't it, that there was a kidnapper? 'Cause there usually *isn't* a kidnapper, no matter *what* you leave open, right? 'Cause . . . well, *shit."* She nestled her head in her arms and rocked her face back and forth against her sleeve to dry her eyes without being obvious about it.

"No," said Erin. "It's not very fair. But it is a *little."* She shivered in her turn. "And you think so, too. That it's a *little* fair. Even if it sucks. Right?"

"Yeah," said Lizby bleakly. "Yeah, so don't say it anymore."

"I think it's important to be honest," said Erin. And then she burst into a dazzling smile and said, "Hey, *Elliott!* Don't be like, *shy* or anything. It's just us bitches havin' a bitchfest. Stick around. You can talk to us till someone better shows up. *God,* we'd be *so* grateful."

# 12

On Wednesday morning Erin said, "How's it going at home?"

Essie shook her head in a tight downward curl, a gesture newly habitual. "Nothing's changed," she whispered.

"That's tough," said Erin. "You're not used to it. My folks get like that a lot—throw these big tantrums, turn blue in the face. I just hunker down till they get tired of it."

Essie shook her head again. She knew better. Her parents were not throwing a tantrum. They were bewildered, lost, clinging to each other. It had always been the pair of them as a unit, and then Essie. It was not something they had thought to conceal or she to resent. They had always seemed to her a unit, a single two-headed parent, bedrock for her life to be built on, strong and reassuring. But now they were revealed as two individuals needing all their strength for themselves, and none left for her. Unblinkered, knowing that this was how they were, she could see no possibility of change. And she was woven inextricably into their bewilderment, their frustration. She could not come into the room without agitating them; the most trivial interchange with her father would touch off writhing, futile interrogations. Family dinnertime, that holy of holies, shuddered past in tortured, seething silences burst through with agonized eruptions. That was not going to change, either.

On Tuesday she had called Charlie Footer, who had

interviewed her the day after the kidnapping, and asked him directly how long he thought it would take to find Jeremy. He told her that he was not going to mislead her; there was simply no way of knowing. She asked him if Jeremy would ever be found; he said he was not going to lie to her there, either; he did not know. He said some reassuring things as well, but she scarcely heard them.

When something had to be done, Esther Beal was given to saying, "Well, it's the best sort of day for it," by which she meant, mingling optimism and resignation, that right now is as good as opportunity gets. Usually she was talking about doing dishes or the laundry, but it was a maxim that the household was inclined to apply to human affairs in general. Essie pondered these questions late into Tuesday night.

On Wednesday morning Essie spent her free period and study hall composing farewell notes. She wrote several long, discursive ones which she crumpled up and threw away. The one she settled on simply said,

Dear Mom & Dad,
I'm sorry.
Love, Essie

This seemed to her to meet the requirements of the occasion. Her parents could apply her apology to whichever of her failings vexed them most, without its being watered down by application to a too-long list. And in attempting to explain her feelings, she had found that her sorrows were far too numerous and intricate for the discussion of specifics.

Essie's parents had resumed their own normal work schedules, and Essie found the house empty, as she expected, when she got home. She put on what she supposed was a sensible running-away outfit: jeans, a simple button-up blouse, a favorite sweater with a pattern of reindeer, and a pink windbreaker. In a small gym duffel with a shoulder strap she packed a sweatshirt, some changes of underwear, a few indispensable toiletries, and *Great Expectations*. Essie's time horizon was almost at her feet: Present desperation was moving her, but beyond a few hours, she did not consider how long running away might be. She had some baby-sitting money on hand—forty-two dollars and some change. Thus provided, she slipped out the door and headed for the bus stop.

For the most part, Essie recognized that her motives in running away were selfish ones. She could not bear to answer a million more useless questions. She could not bear the stricken looks. She could not bear to be the focus of such emotion, such agony, without the power to say or do anything that would undo any part of the evil or atone for whatever her own error might have been. But she was also conscious that wherever Jeremy might be, he was not safely at home, as she was, and that by going out into the world, she was more likely to come across him than if she were to remain huddled in her room. And if she did not have it in her power to find him, she could at least destroy her own comfort and share exile with him. It was not much, she recognized, but it was something she could do.

San Francisco was half an hour away by commuter express, and the very bus she wanted was pulling into the stop as she scampered down to the corner. She had feared that the driver would recognize at once that she was running away and order her off or take her into custody, but instead he watched incuriously as she deposited her fare and immediately pulled back out into the traffic, leaving her to wallow down the aisle and plop into a seat as best she could.

The driver was later able to recall that he had picked up a teenager at one of the stops in that neighborhood. She had been carrying a bag. He could not remember where she got off.

The neighborhood that the bus passed through was Essie's own, familiar from childhood; seen through a fugitive's eyes, the rows of houses seemed inexpressibly remote in the hazy light of late afternoon. She was frightened and unhappy. She was entirely unsure. Her mother would be home from work in a few minutes; the bus had not advanced more than a few stops before she knew that it was too late to get off, pick up a returning bus, and get home in time to conceal her sortie. Her mother would know perfectly well what to make of the duffel and the forty-two dollars, what defiance she had conceived—had almost carried off. Essie played out in her mind various scenarios of return under those circumstances, abandoning each before the end and starting again while the bus carried her along unregarded streets, the freeway, and finally the bridge, deeper and deeper into the irremediable toils of her rebellion.

Toby spent his whole day off on Wednesday repairing gutters and down spouts. By the time dinner approached, he had no interest in transferring his labors to the kitchen. He called Sara at her office. He said, "Look, why don't you meet the kids and me at that Chinese restaurant. Then a movie, if we can find one that doesn't consist of wall-to-wall disembowelments and mindless sex. We'll eat popcorn and drink fattening carbonated beverages. No expense will be spared."

"Let's do," she said.

"Whadda ya say, guys?" he said to Adam and Joss, who were standing right beside him, ears pressed to the outside of the receiver.

*"Yeah!"* they said, which made it unanimous.

It was still light and Essie was still engrossed in fantasies of forgiveness and reconciliation when her bus arrived at the commuter terminal in San Francisco. The bus stopped, and the passengers got out while another group waited to get on. She tagged along into the large waiting room and through it to the street beyond where there were other, local buses, a street-car line, and a rank of taxis. Here she stopped. All around was downtown: tall office buildings, some with windows still lit, some dark, all part of lives and routines. These people had places to go. Someone bumped into her, grunted something ambiguous, and moved on. She moved over to the wall, out of the way, clutching her duffel, and watched in growing bewilderment as the succession of vehicles drew into the lanes along the front of the building, emptied, filled, and passed on into the street again, bound . . . where?

What now?

Where to? She had arrived at the end, the utter limit, of her plan and her imagination.

She had no idea at all where or how runaway fourteen-year-olds find places to stay, or sustain themselves, or pass their time. She knew very few parts of the city. She knew a few stores in the downtown where she sometimes went shopping with her mother; there were one or two residential districts where she had been taken to visit family friends, but these would not do her any good, even if she could find them.

She wondered if she should just walk out into a strange city and trust to luck.

There was a line of phone booths.

There were news racks. One of the papers had a story about the kidnapping; the part of the story that showed above the fold said that there was no progress. She did not want to read further.

A maintenance man noticed her looking at the news racks. He thought she had nice legs. When she moved a bit, he decided she was too thin to be worth watching—he liked a girl to have a little meat on her. But later, when he was asked, he remembered seeing her.

On the other side of the building, where she had got off, buses were filling every minute or two, and returning, ultimately, to her stop, a block from her house.

No.

She thought, What am I going to do?

She went back into the waiting room. She did not want to sit down, she wanted to go and be settled someplace. But she could not see any obvious first step. She sat down. The schedule of arrivals and departures was opposite. She recognized the destination of the next departing bus, a town where her family had rented a vacation house two years before. She remembered a friendly, tree-lined square and a balmy summer evening. It was an inviting recollection and an immediate objective. Aimlessness was frightening. Without hesitation, she paid fourteen dollars for a one-way ticket.

The clerk remembered her afterward because she was so polite and seemed so young—the reindeer sweater and the pink windbreaker.

It was not until her new bus had pulled out into the evening traffic that it occurred to Essie that she was not going to have any more specific plan for her new destination than she had had for San Francisco; that the evening would not be balmy in early November; and that her cash now amounted to twenty-eight dollars. Her sense of well-being evaporated. She thought, *Now* what?

The question remained unanswered when she stood with her duffel over her shoulder on the edge of the square, which was much as she had remembered it, except that the lamplit trees were golden now, and the wind was cold.

She had scarcely eaten all day, and she was seriously hungry. Several of the eating places around the square were open. A café with kitsch statuary and a moose head in the window seemed less intimidating than the others, and she went in.

There was no other customer. She ordered the

cheapest sandwich listed on the blackboard—avocado and bean sprouts for $3.25, which seemed like an awful lot—and tried to admire the old neon signs on the walls and the stuffed ferret by the cash register as the woman behind the counter sliced and spread. She seemed weary, and Essie conceived a bold scheme. She gave the woman a five-dollar bill for her sandwich, and as she put out her hand for the change, she tried to sound as old and relaxed as possible and said, "I'm looking for a job. Need any help?"

The woman's face clouded. She glanced around the empty tables.

"Sure doesn't look like it, does it?" she said. Her eye fell on the cup by the cash register which contained loose change and a little sign saying "Support counter intelligence."

Clearly, she expected a tip. Essie had already put her change in her pocket. She wasn't sure how much a tip at a café counter ought to be. She thrust her hand down into her pocket and produced a quarter, which she dropped in the cup. She was sorry to see it go. She was dismayed when the woman rolled her eyes and turned away. She fled back to the sidewalk.

The wind was at least as cold as it had been ten minutes before. The café was toasty and cheerful and she was certainly entitled to eat her sandwich inside, but she could not face the woman. She crossed the street to the square and found a bench by a large bush. It was muddy underfoot there, and still cold, but a little out of the wind. She unwrapped one end of the sandwich, and took a bite.

Then suddenly she bent down and placed the sandwich on the ground, like an offering. Methodically she stamped it into the muck, thinking, There's no way to make it right. I don't know *what* I'm supposed to do. God, I really don't.

# 13

One of Sergeant Wren's clerks said, "I've just been talking to the receptionist in DD. She says they've got something going on the Broome thing. A neighbor who got missed by the neighborhood check is sure that he saw a man sitting in a car almost in front of the Broomes' house on the evening of the kidnapping. He wasn't close enough himself to give much of a description, but he's sure that the baby-sitter was outside with the kids while this guy was there. She probably saw him right up close and just didn't think about it. But if the neighbor's right—if she got a look at him—then she might be able to ID him. So of course they rushed right out to talk to the baby-sitter, and they found she's gone—missing. They think she's run away. *Big* commotion. The FBI is getting on it. They really want to find her."

"How much chance is there that the baby-sitter will be able to ID the man in the car?" said Paul, trying not to sound alarmed. He remembered the glance the sitter had given him in front of the house. It was a fleeting glance, and she had other things on her mind. He did not *think* she could remember.

"Who knows?" said the clerk. "But she was close, the neighbor says. If she looked that way at all, she must have seen him."

"Who'd believe a baby-sitter, anyway, eh?" said Paul with half a laugh. "*Kids.* Kids'll say anything to get themselves out of trouble."

"Perhaps it depends on the kid, don't you think?" said the clerk, staring rudely at Paul. He expected to be a sworn officer in the near future, and he was modeling his behavior on the aggressive young patrolmen he admired. "The receptionist says that Gadek says that Parkman thinks that the baby-sitter's pretty smart. Anyway, if she IDs, then they can corroborate in other ways. There's usually *something,* if you know what to look for. They just need somewhere to start."

That was perfectly true, Paul knew. There were his pictures and tapes—if they got into the cabin they couldn't miss them. The boy was in the goddamn kitchen closet—still whining and beating on the door, for all he knew. If once they got inside his door, he was dead.

Paul did not *think* the baby-sitter had been paying attention that one time she looked at him. In fact, he was sure—but then, how can you be completely sure? And maybe that wasn't the only time—maybe she looked at him while he was looking somewhere else, watching the children—who knows? She wouldn't have had to stare—just glance over. He might have missed it. She might be able to recall it, if she were reminded.

Perhaps she *could* ID him.

Most runaways are found, he knew. Or at any rate, findable—if the authorities know where to look. If there were a big effort they might find her, and then—well, it did not bear thinking about.

They'll get you if they can. He knew that perfectly well. He didn't have any friends here, he could see that—this jumped-up little fool snapping at him, and Mother Superior just sitting there. He remembered what it had been like in his old town when those parents got done working themselves up: the convulsive anger, the reckless unfairness, *all* directed at him. Too busy to pay attention to their children, but not too busy to turn on him.

He had done their parenting for them. He had never asked for thanks.

Which was a good thing, because far from thanking him, they had turned on him.

And it would be the same thing here, again. That baby-sitter wouldn't hesitate to strike at him. Nobody was going to look after Paul except Paul. He could see that perfectly well.

The answering machine was emitting a long succession of blinks when the Parkmans got home from the movie shortly before nine. Sara pressed the message button while Toby took off his jacket. There was a prolonged whirring while the tape rewound, and then the first voice, tight and worried.

"Mr. Parkman, this is Esther Beal, Essie's mother. Could you call me, please?"

Click.

"Mr. Parkman, this is Esther Beal again. It's about six-thirty. Please call me right away."

Click.

"Toby, Leo. It's . . . ah . . . six-fifty. Call me at my office ASAP."

Click.

"Sara, Toby, it's Melanie. Esther Beal has been calling here, trying to get ahold of Heather. Essie isn't where she's supposed to be. She left a note just saying, I'm sorry. Esther's scared to death—she's afraid it might be a suicide note. I called school and had Heather dragged out of Chorus, but she doesn't know anything. I don't know if there's anything you can do, but I thought you ought to know."

Click.

There were two of the little chirrups the machine makes when someone has called but left no message.

Click.

"Esther Beal. It's almost seven-thirty."

Click.

"It's Melanie. Call when you get the chance."

Click.

Another chirrup.

Click.

"It's Melanie. Let's see, it's eight-twenty. Esther called again. Still no word. I'm going to pick Heather up now. I'll call you later."

Click.

Adam and Joss had started off for bed, but now they were frozen on the stairs. Joss said, "Essie . . ."

"Sssssh," Sara and Toby said together.

The tape stopped, and the light resumed blinking. Sara went and sat with the kids on the stairs. Toby called Gadek.

"Ah," said Gadek, "thanks for getting back. Look, it appears that Essie Beal is missing. Know anything?"

"No," said Toby. "I just got home. I found a lot of messages on the machine from her mother."

"Anything helpful?"

"No. She left a note?"

"She left a note simply saying, I'm sorry. Her parents fear the worst. They're going ape—remorse and the whole bit."

"Well, god*damn,"* said Toby. He slapped his hand down on the table. "That's great. God*damn,* that's just timely. I'm really . . ."

"Toby, Toby, Toby," said Gadek, chuckling. "Don't break down on me."

"Sorry," said Toby after a moment. "I'm with you."

"Good. Footer had the same reaction, by the way. But listen. The note is not a prime example of declarative prose. It works equally well as a runaway announcement. Look, I know she sits for your kids. D'you think she might have given them any idea where she might go if she decided to do something like this?"

Toby looked up the staircase. Joss and Adam were

sitting on either side of Sara, just below the landing, looking solemn and worried.

"No," he said. "I'll ask 'em, of course, but I don't think there'll be anything. They haven't seen her since the kidnapping, and before that she's the last kid you'd think would even fantasize about running away."

"Well, ask 'em. And while we're on the subject of asking people, the Beals are sure that Walt's step-daughter—ah, Heather—would know all about this if it's a runaway. I'll be talking to her tonight. What's your take on how close she is with Essie?"

"Close," said Toby. "Melanie says they've done a lot of talking over the last few days, but how confidential, I don't know."

"Do you think she'll tell, if she knows anything?"

"I don't know, Leo," he said. Toby and Sara had known Heather for years, they had entrusted her with their children, but Toby could see that this was very partial knowledge. "My sense of her is that she's very straight, and she's not stupid. But this is way out of her experience with life and my experience with her. I don't know what she'll do."

"Okay," Gadek said, with that little exhalation people make when they're checking off an item on a pad. "Then we're dealing with your basic unpredictable kid acting on her gut. Let's see. We're working her friends. We're trying to track down bus drivers from the routes past her house and school. We're looking at the prime hitchhiking spots. Her parents are pretty sure she didn't have any close friends who drive—does that sound right?"

"I don't know of any."

"Anything useful I seem to be missing?"

"I don't think so. Well, wait a minute—her school counselor might know if there'd been problems she hadn't talked to anyone else about."

"Ah, good thought." Scribbling noises. "Schooool coun . . . selor. Well, it's just the worst timing. We

want to see her. We think she might be able to ID the
Broome responsible. Footer was just picking up his
keys to go get her when her mother called. Call me
back if you get anything from your brood. This is a
complication we didn't need."

"Right," said Toby, and Gadek hung up.

They all sat together on the stairs and tried to think
of things that would be helpful, if for no other reason
than it gave Adam and Joss something positive to do.
Twenty minutes later Gadek called again.

"Quick update. It's going to be a runaway. A
neighbor saw her get on a bus carrying a bag right
after school. That bus goes downtown and then to San
Francisco, so by this time she could have transferred
and be anywhere at all. I assume she's either on the
road or tucked away somewhere by now. The FBI is
starting to work on it tonight. Nothing from your
kids?"

"Nothing. But thanks for calling back, Leo."

"Sure thing," he said, and hung up.

"Guys," said Toby, "she's okay. At least for now."

# 14

Essie had never gone altogether without eating. She
had never faced a night without a safe and comfortable bed. She had occasionally dealt with informal
toilet facilities on camping trips, but she had never
faced the indignity of such necessities in an urban
area. Luckily, the town was small. She struck out at
random from the square, and in twenty minutes she

found herself looking at a little finger of trees beside a small stream bisecting a vast vineyard. It looked dirty and uncomfortable, but it was cover, and there during the course of a bleak and weary night she had her first experience of getting by without a roof, a tent, a sleeping bag, a campfire, a copious dinner, and friendly companions.

In the last sleepless hours before dawn she leaned against the downwind side of a tree, stared at the lights of the town, and thought, I'm freezing, hungry, and miserable, I'm freezing, hungry and miserable, I'm freezing, hungry, and miserable, over and over until she began to giggle. She was sustained in her misery by the conviction that she deserved it, and she was able to find some amusement in that paradox. She giggled until she wept, and giggled and wept again, until sleep overcame her in spite of everything.

She dreamed vividly that Jeremy was near her, somewhere among the trees, calling her name. She woke abruptly. She scrambled up and wobbled back and forth in the undergrowth until, moment by moment, she had to realize that it was a dream. She came fully awake at the margin of the trees, staring in bitterest disappointment across the endless rows of gnarled gray grapevines into the first pale rays of the sun. Oh, God, she thought. I'm just where I was.

"The FBI worked the buses last night," Gadek said to Toby. "They found the driver of the bus she took to the city, they found two people at the terminal who remembered her, and the driver who took her north. It's a small town. The family spent a vacation there, but they don't know any local people, and they can't think of any other connection.

"Somebody must have seen her when she got off the bus last night. We've contacted the local department, and the FBI has had two people there since last night. They were going to start working eating places and food stores first thing this morning, and they'll go through the stores around the downtown as they open. There aren't that many. We ought to have our answer one way or another, pretty soon. Anyway, I want you to go on up there this morning. You're up on what we've got here. You may be able to help with the search, and if she's found, you'll bring her back."

It was a comforting image for Toby—Essie tucked safely into his car, none the worse for wear, on the road home. He associated the young with soon-stanched tears and runny noses. Unconsciously, he felt in his jacket pocket to see if he had clean tissues so he would be ready to deal with her needs.

"We've really got no special tips on this one," said Gadek. "Runaways are vulnerable at the best of times, and she's got problems. She may be just fine, holed up someplace safe, or she could be in real trouble by now. Use your judgment. Keep in touch."

Essie had fallen asleep again, warmed by the sun, and slept on into the morning. Hunger woke her. At home the moment of waking is the prelude to a prolonged ritual of ablution, dressing, and breakfast. At the edge of the vineyard she had only to grab her duffel and stand up.

*Now* what?

For a few minutes she stared helplessly across the fields to distant hills. When you have nothing, where do you start? How do you get ahold of something? How do you live? What do you do?

Hunger decided her. She dusted herself off, ran a comb through her hair, and started back toward the town to try again.

A decrepit-looking car stood on the shoulder of the road where it crossed the stream. The passenger-side door gaped open, and beside it a distracted-looking woman was helping a child of four or five to be sick. A three-year-old stood a few feet away. Car, mother, and children seemed of a piece, not old but worn and faded, as if each of them, animate and inanimate alike, had known more use than maintenance. The woman held the heaving older child, but her eyes were on the younger, who was edging off.

"Dylan, you stay here," said the woman, without conviction. Dylan, knowing a good game when he saw one, was moving along the shoulder of the roadway. The older child, seized with a fresh series of heaves, groaned and gasped.

"Dylan!"

Dylan was beginning to run, angling up toward the roadway. Traffic was sparse but fast. Essie trotted out of the bushes, scooped him up, and carried him squirming back to his mother.

*"Thank* you," she said, attention still greatly divided. The older child straightened up. "Well, you just about done?" She produced a tissue with a clean corner and dabbed ineffectually at the pale lips. "I guess the Lord had a bad day when he made a child's insides," she said, shaking her head. She retrieved Dylan from Essie and ran her eye over the surrounding fields. "Where did *you* come from? You live on one of the farms?"

"Uh, yeah," said Essie.

"Well, you've still got a ways to go, wherever you're going. Like a lift?"

"That'd be great," said Essie, who was feeling her empty stomach and her sleepless night. You sit down in cars, and that seemed like an attractive idea.

"We're headed for San Francisco," said the mother.

Essie hesitated. There was nothing here. Memories of summers past were not going to feed her. San Francisco was a big city. That was where she should have gone in the first place.

"I am, too," she said. She fully expected to be asked why she was not in school at this hour in the middle of the week, but the woman's interest, such as it was, seemed entirely taken up with her own affairs. She simply said, "Well, hop in," and began plucking up miscellaneous objects from the front seat and dropping them behind, where Essie was surprised to notice two more children, asleep.

"It'd be nice to have someone to talk to," she said. "The radio doesn't work, and I could sure use some help with the kids."

"Sure," said Essie.

"Well, that's great. My name's Nora, by the way."

"I'm Essie."

The passenger door creaked savagely as she pulled it, and closed with a disconcertingly tentative sound. She tried again with the same result. The lock stem was stiff but without apparent connection to any mechanism within.

The engine cranked slowly for an anxious time, but at length it caught and permitted itself to be coaxed into a sort of life.

"Kids can be a handful, there's no doubt about it," said Nora, fumbling for the parking brake as if it were seldom to be found in the same place twice. "I don't know why the Lord had to arrange kids coming so close together, but then what do I know, anyway." She inclined her head a little toward Essie and in a cheerful, conspiratorial way, but without in the least lowering her voice, added, "I turn up my cunt for a lot of busy men."

Essie glanced reflexively into the backseat, and found the eyes of the two wakeful children fixed on her face, passive, watchful. The car was moving— there was no graceful retreat now. Nora looked over again, narrowed her eyes a little and said, "Got a boyfriend?"

"No," said Essie quickly. In fact, if Shelly were not in the picture, Essie might have dared to think of Elliott as a boyfriend; but she did not want to be asked if she turned up her cunt for Elliott.

"When the time comes, maybe you wouldn't mind

chipping in a little for gas," said the busy mother, craning over her shoulder at the traffic.

"No, sure," said Essie, reflexively anxious that she would not be able to do the civil, expected thing, wondering what that would come to. In her mind's eye she was putting her own mother in the passenger seat and wondering what the conversation would be like.

"That'd be swell." Nora stared at the greasy instrument panel long enough to find the gas gauge. "Looks like the time's going to come pretty soon. Gas costs an arm and a leg these days, it surely does."

"Yeah," said Essie.

"I'll tell you one thing you *don't* have to worry about with this car, and that's traveling at unsafe speeds. Not with this car."

Toby checked in with the local police department. The two FBI agents were out beating the bushes, along with most of the on-duty officers.

"She bought a sandwich at a café on the square last night," said the watch commander. "That's the last anyone's seen of her. Three buses went out this morning, but she wasn't on any of them. She might have hitchhiked out during the night, but there isn't much traffic through here and we had two cars cruising, mostly on the main road, and they didn't see anything. So chances are she's still here somewhere. We're knocking on doors, working outward from the square. Some of the houses in that area will have a room they rent in the summer. You ever come here in the summer?"

"No, but I hear it's very nice," said Toby politely.

"It *is* great," said the watch commander. "Tour the vineyards. Water sports in the river—rent a canoe."

"Do you go out in canoes?" said Toby.

"You bet," said the watch commander. "Builds up the shoulder girdle like you wouldn't believe. Very elegant, river sports—tans, bathing suits—and my

Lord, *such* bathing suits. I read somewhere that in Florida the cops are supposed to arrest chicks in thongs, but around here, I'm glad to say, our duties don't extend beyond admiration.

"Anyway, your fugitive may be tucked away in one of those rooms right now, and if she is, we'll find her. That would wrap it up quick."

"Her parents didn't think she'd have much money," said Toby. "I doubt she could afford a room."

The whole group was huddled on the library stairs at lunchtime, shifting, anxious.

"How could she just go off like that?" said Rhea. "Not even a word or where she's going or *anything*? What about *us*? What are *we* supposed to do?"

"Well, what are you getting mad at *her* for?" said Latasha.

"Yeah, if we're such good friends, how come we totally didn't know?" said Moll, and Lizby and Addie nodded and said, Yeah.

"Did Heather know?" said Robert.

"No," said Erin. "Heather's just as wiped out as everybody else. Ess didn't tell *anyone*."

"Well, *I* think everyone is just totally on the wrong track," said Addie. "*I* think something's going on. Look. How likely is it, I mean some crazy just hypes in off the street and grabs him? How often does that happen? *Not* very often. *I* think it's someone who knows the family, knows the house. She *thought* she closed the door, only everybody's like, Well, it couldn't have been closed, or how would the kidnapper have gotten in? But maybe she *did* close it. Maybe the kidnapper had a key and walked right in. How come Jeremy didn't make a fuss that Ess could hear? She was right upstairs. Who would Jeremy just quietly walk out of the house with? *Someone he knew.*"

"Why?" said Elliott.

"Well, how do *I* know why? All *I* know is that what

we know doesn't make any sense. Maybe his parents gave someone the key, and they're blaming Ess to distract attention from what really happened."

"They are such *total* jerks," said Rhea. "I don't care what anyone says. It just wasn't her fault at all."

"That's way true," said Moll.

"Except they wouldn't kidnap their own kid," said Lizby.

"Look," said Addie. "If Castro and the CIA can assassinate Kennedy, and the Supreme Court knows all about it, and everyone's like, Well, how's the weather?— Y'know what I mean?"

*"Totally,"* said Moll.

*"Wow,"* said Robert.

"No," said Elliott. "That doesn't make any sense."

*"Anyway,"* said Lizby, "what about Ess? What's she going to do? She doesn't have any money. How's she supposed to live?"

Paul was determined to be friends with the boy, and each morning he tried something new. Before he left for work early on Monday afternoon he had taken the boy for a walk along the river, which lay two hundred yards down the hillside from the cabin. It was an engaging landscape, with scruffy little meadows reverting to forest, and here and there substantial groves of old timber. Paul had always been very good at introducing the young to nature. He knew the names of trees and plants, he could identify common birds, he knew where to find animal tracks, and how to spot the places where they might see fish. His skills were wasted. The boy looked when things were pointed out to him—out of fear, but without the slightest engagement, so far as Paul could tell.

On Tuesday Paul brought out his heavy ammunition: a video game that a middle-aged couple at a garage sale had assured him had kept *their* youngsters entertained for years. He had envisioned it as a special reward, but after three discouraging days in which the boy had not loosened up at all, he thought it might be better employed to shock him out of his shell.

Just get him relating a little, Paul thought, and everything else will follow.

But the boy only held the controller in a nerveless hand and stared limply at the screen. It was utterly infuriating.

And there were concerns quite apart from questions of fellowship and amusement. Paul wondered if he was going to have to rethink his security arrangements. The kitchen closet was certainly large enough to hold the boy, and the door was strong enough, but Paul had to wonder if it was a good place to leave him for long periods. He was half dead by the time Paul got home on Monday night and let him out. It should not have been a surprise, Paul realized—he had been in there for almost twelve hours and had not eaten or drunk anything. Paul put one of the sodas into the boy's hand and told him to drink it. He struggled with the top. Paul thought he was pretending he could not open it so that Paul would have to wait on him. Paul slapped him and got a real effort out of him, but it seemed that he could not, in fact, open the soda by himself.

On Tuesday Paul started the bottletops himself and showed the boy; but despite that, he literally had to stuff him in, howling and struggling.

On Wednesday morning Paul's irritation overcame him and he sulked. He told the boy that he wasn't going to knock himself out for someone who wasn't even making an effort. But despite his anger he could see that the closet was not going to work, simply because it terrified the boy. Paul was torn between his determination not to let himself be jerked around and his desire to ingratiate himself. Fuming, he nailed a piece of wire mesh over the bathroom window and installed bolts on the outside of the door. That afternoon he locked Jeremy in there instead of in the closet. The boy wasn't any good to him dead, after all, he thought.

And if the closet would not work for housing, it clearly gave Paul an effective tool for discipline. The boy could have a choice: shape up, start talking, and get cheerful—or back into the closet. Day *and* night, until you decide to be cooperative.

*That* might work. Every kid has his formula, Paul knew, and sooner or later he would find what it was for this one. They just needed to break through this first stage. They would be friends yet, Paul was sure of it. It was a thrilling thought. Paul had never really had a friend.

Then on Wednesday afternoon these hopeful auguries were dashed by the alarming news about the baby-sitter. Paul was shaken. He hated to leave work at the end of his shift, for fear that something important might develop in his absence. When finally he went home, he felt anxious and irritable. He unlocked the bathroom, woke the boy up, and gave him a snack. But he found himself unsettled at the thought that the boy would be loose in the house, unwatched while Paul slept, and he locked him back up in the bathroom for the night.

On Thursday morning he found himself dreading going in to work. He told the boy to play by himself, and spent hours in pacing up and down. He wanted to know what was going on, but the prospect of what might await him when he first walked in, before he could know the status of things, appalled him. They might be waiting for him. He pictured coming around the corner into Service Division to find Gadek sitting mockingly at Paul's desk with his henchmen lounging around him—every eye fixed on him, and a vengeful, taunting grin on every face.

In the end he went anyway. Nothing happened.

He kept on the move around the building all through his shift, keen to pick up whatever gossip there might be. He had little thought to give to the boy, but when he did think of him it was more food for unease. By the time Paul got home at the end of Thursday's shift, the boy would have been in the bathroom for most of Wednesday, all Wednesday night, and most of Thursday; the way Paul felt just then, he was going to want to keep him there Thursday night, as well. Paul wondered how the boy would react to it. Probably not well.

It was an unfair bind: if the boy was loose, Paul would be uneasy; if he was locked up he would resent it, and blame Paul. Either way, it was Paul who would suffer in the end. The realization of it angered him: where is the justice in a situation in which one person is invariably blamed?

Toward the end of Thursday afternoon, Toby phoned Gadek.

"We know she was on the square last night," he said, "but that's the last we know. Between the locals and the FBI and me, we've hit every business in the downtown, every eating place to the city limits, every gas station, every motel, and every house known to rent rooms. Zip all around. There are a couple of intersections that are common hitchhiking spots. They're both near late-night gas stations and restaurants. Nobody's seen anyone who looks at all like her. The people in Juvenile here did some checking at the high school. Zip. If she has friends here, they're not talking."

"We've been through her friends here, too," said Gadek. "Nobody admits to knowing that she has contacts in that area."

"So what do you make of all this?" said Toby.

"Well, the fact that we don't know about contacts in that area doesn't mean she hasn't got any," he said. "She may be all set, or she may have moved on without anyone happening to see her. She could be a long way off by this time."

"Where does that leave us?"

"The press officer did a news conference this morning, saying that we're looking for her, that she has potentially vital information, and asking her to call. Her parents did an appeal, too. Footer says they're half dead with worry, and they look it. Anyway, those pieces have been all over the radio news already, and they'll be on the tube tonight and the papers tomorrow, at least locally. She's supposed to be a responsible kid—all that may bring her in. Or it may not. Or she may simply be out of touch and not hear any of it.

"The FBI is going to keep on casting around up there for another day or two, and the locals will keep their eyes open, but it doesn't look as if we're going to get quick results from gumshoe work. You may as well come on back."

"Is anything else moving on this thing?" said Toby.

"Nope," he said. "Nothing at all. Finding Essie Beal is still our best shot. I'm sorry she slipped through. We really want that kidnapper."

"That too," said Toby.

Erin had her own phone in her room, but Lizby had to sneak into her parents' bedroom and whisper, keeping an ear cocked at the stairs. They were supposed to be doing their homework.

"She's never even *joked* about running away," murmured Lizby. "She never talks about going places. She wouldn't go to a relative. I don't think she knows anyplace to go."

"Well, *c'mon,* girl," said Erin. "She got on a bus. A bus goes someplace, and when you get off, there you are. Problem solved."

"Yeah, yeah, yeah," said Lizby. "But *then* what? If she knew someone who'd take her in, that's one thing. But if you just get on the bus and ride, what *happens* when you get off? What's she supposed to do? Like for money?"

"Well, baby-sit or something," said Erin.

"Oh, *c'mon,* dummer," said Lizby. "You don't just walk into some strange place and go up to some total stranger and say, Lemme baby-sit."

"Well, how do *I* know what she's going to do?" said Erin. "Be a busboy. Do yard work. Scalp tickets—God, you see people doing that all the time. They make bundles. Ess is smart. She'll think of something."

"Did you see her parents on the news?" said Lizby. "Their faces? I thought her dad was going to start crying right there."

"Well, isn't that just like parents?" said Erin. "I mean, isn't it? My mom and dad are just the same way. So busy all the time it's like you're *invisible,* and when you go and really *need* to talk to them it's like, Oh, God, sweetie, we're going to the symphony tonight and we don't have time *now,* sweetie. That's *just* what they're like. If Ess's parents are so goddamn concerned, why weren't they there for her when she needed them?"

# 15

The trip north had taken Essie a little less than two hours on the bus. The drive south took almost nine. Nora disliked freeways, and so they traveled secondary roads. She was far from being an alert navigator, and so they were often lost. There had been a flat tire, and stops for provisions, and several other stops for no special reason other than that Nora found consistent effort fatiguing and liked to do something else from time to time. She liked to sit under a tree and stare into the distance and chat. Since she tended to choose accessible trees close to the road, Essie spent much of this time restraining the children from running out into the traffic, a game they enjoyed greatly once they discovered that Essie would chase them earnestly into the road as often as they ran there. Nora laughed as heartily as they did until watching the game bored her, and then she slapped whomever was near and made them all go sit in the car.

Nora dropped her off in front of the bus terminal in San Francisco where she had arrived the previous afternoon. The back window seemed full of mournful eyes all fixed on her as the old car steamed off. Contributions toward gas, fixing the flat, and purchasing groceries to be shared by all left Essie with four dollars and change in her pocket.

I'm right where I was, she thought, and I still don't know what I'm going to do.

She went into the waiting room to use the women's room but she did not like the look of the people clustered around the door, and shied off. She slumped down for a moment in an out-of-the-way corner. She tried to remember where she had been shopping in downtown San Francisco with her mother; the place was thick with glittering department stores, and they all had glittering bathrooms. She tried to think if there were any nearby, but she discovered on examination that her sense of downtown geography was almost nil. Her mother had always known where to go, and she had simply tagged along. She felt utterly helpless, and the more she felt helpless the more she felt miserable.

A young man detached himself from the wall near the door and perched next to her on the edge of the bench in a way that was both respectful and intimate, a way he had spent a good deal of time practicing.

"Hi," he said. He was clean, earnest looking. His

clothes were casual. He had poetic brown eyes and long lashes. He did not look tough or even particularly strong.

"Hi," said Essie.

"Look," he said, meeting her eyes gently, "maybe I've got you sized up wrong. I hope I have. But you look to me like you don't have any place to go."

Essie gulped.

"Well, look, I'm a counselor for Mother Hubbard's. We're a shelter for young people who need to get out from under for a while. I've got a card here. Somewhere . . ." He felt in his shirt pocket—made a face—tried the inside pocket of his jacket—both outside pockets. "Well. I guess . . ." He looked bewildered in a sweet, engaging way, not angry at all. "Well, at the top it says Mother Hubbard's and the address and phone, and then down at the bottom it says Kit Jamison, counselor. It's a nice card. You'd like it if you saw one." He made a wry face and chuckled ruefully.

Essie laughed, too. He was funny. She liked him.

"Well, look, uh . . ."

"Essie," she said. She had planned to use a false name, but she had not thought of one. And she wanted to be honest with Kit.

"Essie," he repeated, thoughtfully, as if it were already a special name to him. He looked down at the floor and then back at her. "Well, look, Essie, I'm right, am I? You're taking a little . . . a little vacation?" He laughed again, very sympathetically. He said "vacation" as if it were perfectly normal, no big deal. Everyone needs to get away.

"Yes," she said, looking down and then meeting his eyes. He nodded. He was cool, but he took things seriously.

"Well, look, Essie, it's getting late. Nighttime's not a good time to be out by yourself in the city—there are a lot of heavy folks." He gave a discreet shrug in the direction of a hulking pair of filthy derelicts who were just finishing a large bottle of something wrapped in a brown paper bag.

"The cops don't really keep an eye on this place," said Kit. "Not enough to make it safe. And I guess you don't really want to talk to the cops anyway."

"No," she said. He was realistic. He knew how the world could be.

"Well," he said, cheering up, "let me tell you about Mother Hubbard's, Essie. We're a shelter for young people, like I said, girls and guys. We take twenty when we're full, but we have three beds open. It's not fancy—it's four to a room—all the same sex, I'm afraid . . ." He made a droll face of apology and laughed, and she laughed with him.

"I'll live," she said, reassured.

"We've got a common room where there are some old broken-down couches you don't have to worry about putting your feet on, and a TV, and games. Kids can stay as long as they like. It's a pretty cool bunch—pretty much like you. We won't call your parents, but we have counselors—me and Jane— she's cool. You'll like her. We'll help you figure out what to do about your home situation or school or whatever, and then when you're ready we'll help you do whatever you think the right thing is. Sound fair?"

"Yeah," she said.

"It's kind of like a slumber party that just goes on nonstop," he said. Without Essie's quite noticing, he had taken her duffel and they had gotten up and started out the door together. They were heading away from the downtown.

"Now, there are chores. We're casual but it's not a pigsty. You have to make your bed—well, sort of— pull it together, anyway. Jane's not very uptight about things like that. Everyone helps keep the place picked up and takes a turn setting table—we all eat together at one long table—and doing dishes. Some kids like to help Mrs. O'Brian out with the cooking 'cause she's the kind of person you want to be around. Do you like spaghetti?"

"Yeah, I love spaghetti," said Essie.

"Oh, well, you'll love the way Mrs. O'Brian cooks it, but maybe you can show her how you like it, too—she loves to learn from young people."

"Sure," said Essie. "Sure. I'd love to help."

"Dinner's pretty soon," he said, glancing at his watch. "We'd better not dawdle. Everyone'll be glad to see a new face."

A whole bunch of nice kids, some cool, reassuring adults, and all glad to see her. She'd be funny. She'd laugh at her troubles and they'd all laugh with her, sitting together at the long table.

Maybe they could convince her that it wasn't really her fault.

They chatted busily while they walked briskly along, down streets and through alleys. Essie was preoccupied with the images of Mother Hubbard's, and with the glances she took at Kit. When their eyes met she smiled—she couldn't help it. She'd felt so lost twenty minutes ago.

She was too preoccupied to notice the names of any of the streets, and after ten minutes' walking she would not have been able to say where she was.

They turned into the top of a narrow alley that sloped noticeably downhill, a sweep of facades of two and three stories, of every shape and material and every age. Some were the backs of large buildings fronting on the main streets on either side, and others were the fronts of small buildings that opened only on the alley. One of the first places they passed was entirely overgrown with trumpet vine, and an older brick building farther down was rich with ivy. Some of the second-story windows and metal fire escapes carried bright pots and window boxes. Trees arched out from midblock courtyards and met in the middle.

Many of the doors were painted in bright colors and blazoned the company name in gold letters. To Essie's small-town eye it was all arty and bohemian.

One or two of the businesses were still open; they passed a printing shop where a weary man was still cleaning up, a design studio where three vexed-looking individuals could be seen glaring at something on a drawing board, and the kitchen doors of two restaurants. When a car passed they had to step into a doorway: there was barely room for a car to pass the line of vehicles parked close along the buildings on one side of the way below the closely spaced No Parking At Any Time signs.

They were several doors down the block when Kit began digging in the pockets of his tight jeans for his keys. The door where he stopped was unlike most of its neighbors in that it was filthy, and the paint was old and peeling. The building itself seemed too small to house the sort of residential spaces that Kit had described. On the ground level there was a roll-up vehicle entrance of normal size, and next to that a door; above were three windows. There was no name on the door, which opened directly to the foot of a long, narrow, and dreary-looking staircase illuminated at the top by a bare bulb in the ceiling.

"We don't get very much money from the city, Essie," said Kit, laughing, as they went up, "and we've got better things to spend it on than carpets." His voice grew serious. "I don't understand the attitude. Young people are the future of the world, and the fat cats downtown don't want to shell out for a few gallons of paint. I guess I'm naive. But maybe your generation will do better."

The stairs gave onto a short hallway with three or four doors locked with padlocks, the hasps screwed haphazardly to the faces of the doors. It was very quiet.

"Doesn't seem to be anyone around," said Kit

cheerfully, unfastening the padlock on one of the doors. "The common room and the kitchen are over on the other side. We'll go over in a few minutes. This is my office. C'mon in."

A small room with a shaded window, a table with miscellaneous detritus, an obtrusively new-looking TV set on the floor, some clothes on hangers hung on a nail, a few crusty-looking containers of food, a paper bag of garbage, and in the corner, on the floor, a mattress with an uncased pillow and a couple of disheveled blankets.

"Why don't you relax for a few minutes," said Kit over his shoulder, nodding at the mattress. "Then we'll go find everyone."

His voice sounded a little tighter than it had before, and his body seemed tighter. He seemed less casual as he slung the strap of Essie's duffel over the back of the chair. The mattress was brown-stained and filthy. The pillow was filthy. The blankets were torn and filthy. She did not want to lie on it. She did not want to go into that corner.

Kit had followed her eyes.

"I bet your parents don't let you drink," he said abruptly, producing a bottle from the bottom drawer of the desk. In size and shape it resembled the bottle she had seen the two derelicts drinking from at the terminal.

She was still near the door. Her parents did *not* let her drink, to speak of. She did not want to drink now. She wondered where the other people—"the other side"—were; that hallway did not lead anywhere.

"You'll like this," he said, unscrewing the cap.

"I need to . . . I need to use the bathroom," she said.

"Sure," said Kit. "No prob. Next door over. Here . . . here, make yourself at home." He took her windbreaker by the collar and helped her out of it. He was very smooth. She suddenly realized that she did not want to take it off, but she did not want to be rude, and then it was gone. He slung it into the corner by the mattress.

"Look, Essie," he said. "Y'know, there are some kids in this program . . . they're all nice kids, but some of 'em are a little, like, casual, y'know, with personal property. Maybe you'd better let me lock your money up in my desk. That way you won't have to worry about it." He held out his hand. She hesitated. "Sorry," he said. "It's the rule."

She fished her four dollar bills out of her pocket and put them in his hand. His face fell just for a moment.

"C'mon," he said cheerfully, putting the money in his pocket and producing his keyring. "I'll unlock the bathroom." He was in the doorway. He was chewing his lip.

"I need my bag," she said, turning toward the table, but he put a hand on her neck in a friendly way and propelled her past him out the door.

*"C'mon,"* he laughed. "You don't need to touch up your lipstick." His hand lingered for a moment on her neck, the fingers passing down to the collarbone, the thumb along her spine. When she was past he did not lift it off, but drew it away, his fingertips gliding around deep under the collar of her blouse, tracing her shoulder and the base of her neck so that she was very conscious of her skin. She had never been touched in that way before, but she knew what had happened.

The bathroom was close kin to the mattress. Old, paint-chipped door with a rusty little wire hook and a big, bright keyhole. She slipped the hook into place as quietly as she could. She wiped the seat with toilet paper, which made some difference. The bowl was appalling. She looked again at the door. There was no light now beyond the keyhole. She could not hear Kit. She could not hear anything at all except the sounds of the city at a great distance through the tiny window, partially open, above the toilet. She unzipped her jeans.

She did not want to pull them down.

The keyhole.

Holding her waistband closed she leaned down toward the keyhole. Footsteps just outside, and now she could see light.

"C'mon." It was Kit's voice from across the hall. "Does it take all day to pee?"

She screwed up a piece of toilet paper and stuck it in the hole. Pulled down her jeans, hovered over the seat. She did not flush.

She lowered the seat and lid, climbed up on the toilet and looked out. The window opened onto a flat gravel roof. On the other side of that the twin top rails of a fire escape.

She pushed on the sash. It went up easily enough. Standing on the toilet tank the sill was just above her waist. She began to pull herself through. It was a very small window. Her shoulders stuck. When she pressed with her feet the tank lid rocked and made a clanking sound. She thought, He'll hear, he'll pop that little hook and come bombing in and grab my legs. He'll pull me back in. She could still feel his fingers on her neck. She could almost feel his hands, one around each ankle, yanking.

There was nothing to pull on the roof outside, she could not bend her arms far enough to get purchase on the outside of the sill, and there was nothing firm that she could reach to push with her feet.

"C'mon," Kit called. His voice sounded as if he were standing just outside the door. The lid clanked. Oh, God, he'll hear, oh, God, he'll know what it means. She jerked her shoulders around a little, tearing her sweater, but she had thrown her shoulders through. She squirmed out onto the roof, into the November wind, cold enough to notice even at such a moment. Behind her, inside, she heard the door rattle. *"Essie!"* She darted across the gravel and plummeted down the ladder to a landing where a counterbalanced stair floated horizontally at the level of the second story. She stepped out onto it; ponderously and with a prodigious squeaking, it dipped toward the roadway and she clattered on down, regardless of the racket. In a moment she was in the alley, next door to the building she had entered with Kit.

"Essie! Hey, Essie!" He was on the staircase inside. She could hear his footsteps coming fast. In a moment he would burst out the doorway into the alley, and they would be twenty feet apart.

Up and down the alley were blank walls and locked doors. The printer was closed; the design studio was dark. There was not time to get out of sight in either direction. Directly opposite was an open door, and she darted into it.

A back room, hot. Boxes. Big cans. Right beside her the doors of an enormous freezer. Sounds of water running, dishes clashing. A restaurant. The storeroom of a restaurant.

Kit was in the street right outside.

"Essie! Hey! Essie! It's cool! C'mon back!" The softness was gone altogether from his voice, and she heard a resonance of his mattress, a willful, crusted filthiness.

Running feet, and then he was gone.

She was in a small room with the kitchen straight ahead down a short passage. Anyone coming back here couldn't miss seeing her—couldn't miss stepping on her.

Against the wall, a ladder and a dumbwaiter to a storage loft. She slipped up the ladder. There were a few bags of rice and boxes of this and that. Not a lot of stuff—it was an inconvenient place to store things, even with the dumbwaiter. There was plenty of room for Essie.

The loft had been built in close to the false ceiling, where it ended. From the loft Essie could see between ceiling and roof all the way to the front of the building, except for a cluster of vents and chimneys from the kitchen. Sheets of plywood had been laid across the rafters here for access to these vents, and a jumble of large boxes had been put down along the plywood as if it were a big shelf. She climbed in through a cobwebbed gap and dropped down on the other side, invisible, warm, and, as she felt, safe again.

# 16

A piece of duct had at some point been removed from the ceiling and the hole covered with a piece of wire screen. From that vantage point Essie could see the entire kitchen. Immediately below her hiding place was the pot washer, an Asian man of middle age. The waiters deposited trays of dirty dishes on the steel counter beside him. These he rinsed and deposited in the dishwasher by his side. The two chefs would occasionally thrust cooking pots and pans onto the counter, calling out, "Hot, Jim," as they did it. He swept them into the sink with his bare hands, pursued and cleaned them, dried and returned them to their hooks and racks above and below the big wooden work table in the middle of the room, immediately returning to deal with the dishes that had appeared meanwhile. It went on and on, everyone working very hard.

Essie believed in working hard. She thought she was conscientious, with lapses. But it had not been enough.

She fell asleep pondering great themes.

It was the lights changing and the sounds in the almost silent kitchen below that woke her.

"Well, I don't know what you're *kvetching* about," said a man's voice. "It's just one of the best nights we've ever *had*. Look at the register tape. And the bar, my *God!*"

"Oh, it was okay, Nicky," said another man's voice, tired, discouraged. "God, I thought, God, just this once let Harry not overcook the lamb. Was it overcooked? Eh? Was it?"

"No, Charles, it was not. We don't all like our lamb still bleating. And the squab was magnificent. And with all the wine we sold tonight, do you think anyone was in any condition to notice either way? I mean, baby, *c'mon.*"

The lights in the kitchen went out. The voices receded toward the front of the building.

"Now, *c'mon,*" Nicky was saying. "Let's go *home*, for God's sake. You'll make us tea. You'll feel better. I promise." Essie could not hear what they said after that, but soon she heard the sound of keys in locks and, except for the hum of the big freezer, the place was silent.

For a little while she lay quite still, listening. It was scary, at fourteen, to be alone in a strange place, especially a strange place where she was not supposed to be. But soon her hunger brought her cautiously down the ladder. She found a light switch just where one would likely be, by the back door, which illuminated the storeroom and cast an indirect glow into the kitchen. The door, she saw, the door that lay most immediately between her and Kit, was secured with a heavy wooden beam laid into large steel brackets.

Essie could not form any very accurate conception of what would happen to her if someone were to find her here. She could imagine what her mother would say, but beyond that . . . ? Someone looking in the window could see that there was a light on in the kitchen, but she knew that many businesses left lights on, so that was not necessarily dangerous unless the owners came back for some reason. The clock over the wall phone said 12:48. Their coming back did not seem very likely.

With considerable trepidation she examined the kitchen, the pantry, and the dining room beyond. There was a lot of wood and black and glass and murals that she guessed were of the Mediterranean coast. At the front the maître d's desk, and the cashier's desk by the window fronting on a narrow, tree-lined park, were now quiet. At the desk she found a stack of menus emblazoned with the name of the place: Le Coq d'Or. She opened one and ran her eye over the offerings. Most of it consisted of things she had never had—at least, not as described—but it all sounded wonderful. She was very hungry. Nora's notions of meals were rudimentary, and the dinner that Kit had promised had never materialized. Still, she was in a restaurant—there must be something. She went back to the kitchen and opened the refrigerator.

Among other things she found a plate with a full entrée serving of lamb.

Essie had never stolen. Not as a prank, not out of adolescent rebellion, not for any reason. She did not see any alternative now. First you talk to strangers and then you steal. She put the plate on the worktable and found a knife and fork. A spasm of conscience drove her back out to the maître d's desk for another look at the menu. The lamb seemed terribly expensive. Back in the kitchen she inspected the refrigerator again, but everything else she found required preparation.

She threw up her hands. She turned again to the plate she had put out and ate every bite. Even cold, it was astonishingly good; she had never eaten good lamb prepared by someone who knew what he was doing.

Last night, she remembered, she had slept in a field. Today had begun with Nora and continued with Kit. It was ending in trespassing and theft.

Having eaten, she carefully washed and dried her plate and found the pantry where it belonged.

The restrooms were in the passage between dining room and kitchen. She used the ladies'.

Back in the kitchen, she wondered if anyone could tell that she had been there. She thought, I should clean. At first she meant merely that she should expunge any traces of her presence, but the thought broadened almost instantly; it was a way to pay for what she had taken. There was a janitor's closet with a deep sink below the loft; she found supplies and set to work. The ladies' room was already respectable; when she was done it was positively clean. She cleaned the men's room. Then she cleaned the pantry, taking down dishes and glasses and wiping the shelves. Someone standing at the front window might have caught a glimpse of her from time to time, way at the back, passing to and fro, head down, moving fast.

While she worked she whispered incessantly to herself, monologues, conversations, trying to reason out what had become of her, and what she ought to do. She had gone from one great failure, in not safeguarding Jeremy, to another, in her failure to abide by the consequences. Flight had been one misery after another. She felt as if she were tumbling, and her instinct, since change seemed to be only for the worse, was to arrest it, to make herself stable. The kitchen was a big, square room with a solid utilitarian presence, and above it was the odd nest she had discovered. The alley door with its reassuring beam enclosed her; on the other side lurked Kit, and beyond him, homeward, stretched concentric circles of alienation, uncertainty, and reproach. In the familiar, unassailable act of cleaning she felt comfortable and useful as she had not done since these calamities befell. The theft of a plate of food cost her conscience a sore pang, but it was something she could put a value on, a value that could be requited with scrubbing and polishing. It was one wrong she could put right. Essie had a great need to put things right.

She wore out near two in the morning. She replaced everything exactly as she had found it, turned out the light, and retreated again to her hideaway.

The crawl space stretched away toward the front of the building. It was too dark to see, but Essie could feel the expanse of it once she had squeezed through the boxes. It was secluded but not cozy. And it was cold. The heat was off and the kitchen had been out of operation for hours.

She simply could not lie out among the rafters and shiver herself to sleep. Down the ladder she crept, turned on the lights again, and looked about. There were some old newspapers, and two rice sacks. She took the two sacks and a pile of the newspapers and bore them up the ladder. Several of the boxes in places less accessible from the front were dust-covered and obviously not in great demand. These she arranged so that they formed a bed-size enclosure on the plywood. She laid the sacks and most of the newspapers inside. The result was a nest with at least the illusion of privacy and comfort. Then down the ladder again to turn out the light, back up and through the gap in the boxes, which she closed behind her. She stuffed more newspapers into her sweater, back and front, and layered the rest over her as thickly as she could manage. It was uncomfortable and not really warm enough, but she was exhausted, and soon she was asleep.

While Paul was wearily unlocking the gate he debated within himself whether it might not be counterproductive to confine the boy in the bathroom for a second night. The boy, after all, was not interested in Paul's peace of mind. Paul considered explaining his difficulties and the reasons for doing what he was doing, but he rejected the idea. Other people aren't interested in you, they are interested in *themselves*. That was Paul's experience. The boy would simply resent being locked up, however good the reason, and his resentment would then have to be undone before their relationship could make progress. Things had not gone well in the first days, and giving the boy another grievance, whether real or imagined, would inevitably protract this awkward period. So Paul resolved that in the interests of their long-term friendship he would simply swallow his anxiety, let the boy loose in the cabin, and hope for the best.

And of course it was the middle of the night. Paul would just put him to bed in his own bed, and they would sleep together. That would be nice.

The boy was asleep when Paul unlocked the bathroom door, but he struggled up and, without a word or a sign, staggering a little from sleepiness, trotted straight past Paul, and curled up in his place by the wall.

"You'll be cold there on the bare floor, you know," Paul said, carefully keeping his voice gentle and reasonable. "You'll be nice and warm and cozy if you sleep in the bed with me."

The boy did not look at him but curled tighter on the floor.

"I'm not going to give you a blanket," Paul said, but the boy did not respond.

*"Just try it!"* yelled Paul, suddenly furious. Suddenly he was at the end of his patience. He was being generous, he was taking risks to make the boy's life more pleasant, and what he got for it was to be treated as if he were invisible in his own living room. *"God-damn it, what the fuck's the matter with you?"* He

stamped across the room and snatched the boy up by the waist. *"I've fuckin' had it with you."* He dropped him roughly on the bed. Instantly, not looking up, the boy uncurled, slipped off the bed, and darted around Paul and back to his place where he dropped to the floor and curled up again.

"Well, *shit!*" yelled Paul. He stamped. "Well, *shit!* I've *had* it with you. This is *not my fault.* This is *your* fault. I have *tried* and *tried* to figure out what you want, and you are not playing ball at *all.* You are just *sulking* and being *spoiled,* and I have *just fuckin' had* it. You're going back to the closet till you learn some manners." He grabbed one arm. The boy's eyes were wide now, and he shrank back and shook off Paul's hand. "You have got some *serious thinking* to do, my friend," Paul said, grabbing again, "and you can do it better where you won't be distracted." He yanked him along the floor. The boy was struggling and shrieking so frantically now that it was all Paul could do to hold him with one hand while he opened the closet door with the other. When he started to close the door the boy thrust an arm out, grasping for purchase along the wall, trying to widen the gap. Paul opened the door again and rapped it shut across the arm, and when the arm jerked back, he slammed the door completely closed. He heard a muffled, *"Noooooooooo,"* and instantly there was scrabbling and thumping against the inside.

"If you're good, I'll let you out," Paul said loudly to the door. There was triumph in his voice. He had this little brat's number.

The boy was beating on the door. "I be *good!*" he called. "I *promise!*"

"You think about it for tonight," said Paul. "Tomorrow we'll see."

*"I prommmmmmmise!"*

"You think about it," said Paul, turning away.

**116**

# 17

Ringing phones woke Essie. There were phones in the kitchen, the pantry, the tiny office cubby adjacent to the pantry, and the maître d's desk in front. They all had different-sounding rings. They all rang together three times, and then an answering machine clicked on. She recognized the words Le Coq d'Or, but could not make out the rest, a scratchy whispering somewhere beyond the passage.

The big front windows faced the morning sun, still fairly low, and the restaurant was bright with a pinkish glare, even back into the kitchen.

Essie had no idea when the working day at a restaurant began. She pulled the newspapers out of her sweater and slipped quickly down the ladder. She used the ladies' room, giving everything a last lick with the sponge when she was done, and came back to the kitchen. She was hungry. She ate some bread that seemed to be surplus and drank milk from the refrigerator. She felt that she should compensate the establishment for this latest inroad, but she doubted that there would be time to do more cleaning. She had given her four dollars to Kit, but she still had the eighty-seven cents in change, and she was putting this on a corner of the counter when she heard a key in the front door and darted back up to the loft.

A man and a woman appeared. They were in the middle of some animated conversation, which they continued as they prepared for work, merely raising their voices when they were in different places. Essie recognized the language, but she could not follow what they said. They filled buckets at the slop sink under the ladder, chattering away at a great rate, and returned to the kitchen. The man carried his bucket into the corner by the stove and began taking up the big rubber mats that covered the floor. Essie saw him notice the little pile of change on the counter. The woman propped open the restroom doors and went into the men's. There was a surprised exclamation, and she emerged, voluble. The man put down his mop and went in to see. There was some discussion and some laughing before he emerged and returned to his mop. The woman moved into the ladies', and a moment later popped out again. The man had scarcely picked up his mop when he put it down and followed his companion into the ladies'.

Essie watched these discoveries with growing alarm. She had never considered what would happen when the staff arrived in the morning to find that several parts of the establishment had been mysteriously cleaned during the night. She had not cleaned the whole place, of course, but she had cleaned a lot here and there, and these people would keep finding the places. Surely they would tell whoever was in charge, and then—well, what?

It was clear that the discovery of the restrooms had changed the focus of the couple's conversation. They continued to discuss it while the man carried the mats to the alley door, unbarred it, and leaned them up against the wall outside to hose off. They chatted as he went in and out, she clearly trying to decide who had done the cleaning, he whimsical. They were both in the kitchen when a knock sounded on the alley door and a voice called, "Hey, anybody home?"

It was Kit's voice, friendly and disarming.

Essie jammed herself flat into her nest of newspapers as if his sight could penetrate the loft and the boxes that concealed her. She could not see the doorway from where she lay, but she could see the couple turning toward it. She pictured Kit darting into the middle of the kitchen and suddenly looking up to the hole and seeing her. She braced herself to drop back out of sight.

"Hey, okay if I use the phone? Just a local call."

"Está cerrado," said the man, not moving.

"Just wantta use the phone. Hey, man, won't be a minute."

"Cerrado," said the man, very definitely.

"Yeah, I know you're cerrado. Tel-ee-fone. Just use the tel-ee-fone. Right there on the wall. Okay?"

"Cerrado," said the woman. "No hay teléfono aquí."

"Sure there's a telephone. Look. See, on the wall? It's okay. I know the boss real well. We're buddies."

"Cerrado," said the man, making brisk crisscross gestures with both hands. "Cerrado."

"Cerrado," said the woman.

"Assholes." It was almost inaudible. And then, apparently, he was gone. Essie listened for his foot on the ladder. But the cleaners were turning back to their work. He must be gone.

The chef appeared, a heavy, deliberate man, and shortly afterward his assistant, slight and nervous, given to grinning suddenly when spoken to. They put on coffee and then fell to compiling lists, moving around the kitchen peering into jars, running their eyes over the contents of shelves, and making a careful survey of the refrigerator. Essie wondered if they would notice the missing lamb plate, but they did not appear to.

The cleaners made an attempt to interest them in the restrooms but failed.

"Busy," said the chef, miming rapid motion with his fingertips, and declining to inspect the ladies' room. "Muy busy." Soon the assistant departed with the lists. The chef poured himself coffee and settled at the counter on a tall stool to study a scrapbook of recipes that lay open before him. The vacuum cleaner whined in the dining room.

"Good *morning!*" cried a voice from the alley door.

"Mornin', Nicky," said the chef, looking up from his reading.

"Oh, I just *love* owning a restaurant," said Nicky, sweeping into Essie's line of vision. He was trim and movie-star handsome. "You get to work all day and all night and pay everybody in the world a *fortune* to sit around on their *cute* buns and drink coffee. Oh, *God,* I just *love* it."

"Fuck you, Nicky," said the chef amiably, turning a page.

"Promises, promises," said Nicky. He disappeared into the office. The cleaners followed him, and after a long, inaudible negotiation, all three reappeared and went into the ladies' room. Moments later they were out again.

*"Yes,"* said Nicky, *"yes,* it's just *lovely.* Oh, you do *such good work.* I put in a little note to your boss last month when I paid the bill. Thank you *so* much." He began to turn back to the office, but the cleaners burst out into further explanations in which gestures toward the restrooms were mixed with gestures of negation toward themselves. Nicky listened with a small, polite smile.

"Something is not right?" he said at last. "Something is broken?" He went back into the ladies' room. Essie could hear water running in the sink. The toilet flushed. Nicky emerged.

"It all seems *just fine,"* he said. "You do *such* good work. Thank you so much. And now I really *have* to get down to brass tacks." He swept off to the office. Defeated, the cleaners replaced their equipment under the ladder and departed in intense colloquy.

"Morning, Harry," said a new voice, a young man with a ponytail and bodybuilder shoulders.

"Nathan," said the chef, without looking up.

"I don't like my new schedule," said Nathan.

"Well, don't talk to me," said Harry. "Talk to Charles. You know that."

"Well, is Charles here?"

"Nope. Nicky is here."

"Well, is Charles coming in?"

"Beats me."

Nathan noticed the little pile of change on the end of the counter. He said, "This yours?" Harry glanced over and shook his head. "Must be mine," said Nathan, and swept it into his pocket.

There was a moment's silence while the freezer hummed. Then Nathan said, "Y'know, Harry, you and I are the only two straight guys in this place. Don't you think we ought to stick together?" He massaged one palm with the other and grimaced conspiratorially.

Harry cast him a look of settled dislike.

"No," he said, after a moment. "No, I don't. If we're the only two straight guys in this place I would think that sticking together would be the last thing we'd want to do. And speaking of doing things, Nicky's in the office and he's probably got a list."

"I bet he does. He . . ."

"Don't start in again telling me about Nicky," said Harry. "I know about Nicky. He knows how to run a restaurant. He puts a paycheck in my hand every Saturday without fail, and he doesn't waste my time. You could learn a few things from Nicky."

Nathan made a disdainful mug, drew his shoulders back, and puffed out his chest, rocking back on the balls of his feet. Then he turned abruptly and stalked off down the passage.

Essie lay by her opening all morning, sometimes staring at the ceiling, sometimes watching while the staff prepared lunch. She was hungry and she knew she wasn't going to get anything, so she tried to distract herself by watching what the chefs did and pretending that they were not doing it to food. It was hard to see because she was several feet above them and they tended to lean over their work. So far as she could observe, they did the same things that are done in domestic kitchens, but they did them in larger quantities, more deftly, and much faster. She watched the assistant, whom Harry addressed as Al, mincing garlic with a knife of alarming size and producing almost magically a succession first of neat slices, then strips, and finally tiny cubes. He did several, and by the time he had moved on to something else, Essie thought that she could do it pretty well if she ever had the chance.

But she was not successful at pretending that it was not food. She was quite hungry. And sooner or later she would need to visit the ladies' again.

Gadek's interest in Essie was that she might be able to put him onto Jeremy Broome's kidnapper, but Bill Franklin was the Juvenile Bureau officer who held Essie's case as a runaway.

"It's too bad Gadek didn't snap her up right away," he mused to Toby. "I've got reinterviews lined up with some of her friends—y'know, remind 'em how important it is, and hope if they know anything they'll spill it now they've had time to think about it—but I'm not hopeful. There's no romantic interest that anyone's telling about, no fantasies about running off to join the circus, nothing to suggest a direction."

"So what can you do?" said Toby.

"Very little, really, beyond what's been done. The press conference would have been good, but it got crowded out by other stories that day. Most of the stations I checked didn't even show her picture. Of course it's old news now, barring some sensational development. We put out the usual teletype. I'll work on her friends. If we can get any idea where she is, we'll go after her. If she doesn't turn up in the next few days, I'll get a copy of her dental charts, just in case."

"Jesus."

"Yeah, well, better safe than sorry. It isn't so alarming to the family if you get the dental charts as a matter of routine. Otherwise, you may have to go and say, Golly, we've found a stiff that might be your daughter or it might not, and we'd like to check it out. *That's* hard on 'em."

"I can see that."

"But let's not go completely ape about this. Some kids stay out for a night or two, get scared, and come right back home. She might still fall into that category. Some get arrested—get hungry and order a hamburger they can't pay for, that sort of thing. Those we get back fast. Some hook up with one of these runaway shelters where they give them counseling and help them reconnect with their families. There are a lot of ways kids come back safe and sound."

He stirred a little and his swivel chair creaked.

"Of course, then there are the other ones. A lot of 'em start turning tricks. They can stay out a long time then 'cause they're making money. And there's a lot of dope, especially for the ones who are selling sex. It helps 'em get through what the customers want 'em to do. The street's hard on 'em, what with one thing and another. They can be in pretty bad shape when they come back, if they come back at all."

**18**

More waiters appeared in the kitchen of Le Coq d'Or. Jim, the dishwasher, arrived with an air of fortitude that fascinated and worried Essie.

The dining room began to fill. The work went

rapidly, even Harry's deliberate movements quickened, and Al fairly flew, his grin coming and going automatically like a blinking sign. They cooked and prepared, arranged the plates, and set them out for the waiters who darted in and out. From time to time a diner would appear in the corridor to use the restrooms just opposite and pause in the kitchen doorway to watch. For an hour they all worked at a great pace, and then more slowly. The waiters slowed to a walk, and there were whole minutes when the chefs could stand still or even sit on one of the high stools. One by one, the waiters passed through the kitchen on their way out for the afternoon. Jim went out. Harry went out. Al puttered back and forth between storeroom and kitchen and dining room.

All this Essie watched in increasing despair from above. There seemed no way to escape without being seen—and if she escaped, where would she go without a penny in her pocket and no more than the clothes she was wearing? On the other hand, she did not see how she could stay where she was until the restaurant closed for the night. And even if she could, what about tomorrow?

Harry returned, hanging his jacket and hat by the back door with the comfortable air of one who has come back to his own fireside. Al went out.

The clock on the kitchen wall showed a little after three. If she were in school, it would be the end of the school day. She would be hurrying down the hall to her locker and then to Chorus or Drama, calculating how much free time she would be able to squeeze out between the end of after-school activities and the beginning of homework.

And this train of thought suggested an expedient.

Essie slid out from behind her rampart of boxes onto the loft. She dusted herself off as well as she could, teased her hair into some sort of order with her fingers (her comb had been in her duffel), and ghosted silently down the ladder. From the storeroom she stepped sideways into the kitchen doorway so that she would seem to have come from the alley, and stopped. Harry looked up.

"Hi," she said in her most engaging way.

He raised an interrogative eyebrow.

"Hi," she said again, and then, rather quickly as if reciting something she had memorized, "My name is Jo March." She half expected him to snort and say, No it isn't, but he did not, and she pressed on. "I'm in Ms. Dorsey's class, y'know, at Bray? And we have an assignment to observe work and then write a paper about what we've seen? And I'd like to observe a restaurant . . . well, *this* restaurant—would that be okay? I'll just stay in a corner and be quiet as a mouse and not get in anybody's way."

Harry had heard many pitches, but this was a new one. He hesitated.

"Most work they'll let you see is outside," she said. She ran her finger into the rent that Kit's window had made in her sweater, and added in what she hoped was a convincingly brave but hopeful tone, "It's warm here."

Harry looked at the hole and glanced out through the dining room toward the big window. It was a chill and dreary afternoon.

"That's the warmest thing you've got?" he asked.

"Yeah," said Essie truthfully.

Harry looked up. He looked down. Harry minded his own business and expected others to do the same. He had never had a child of his own. He was a solitary man. When in doubt, his instinct was to say No. When he looked back, Essie's gaze was fixed on the remains of his lunch. He felt a pang.

"Okay," he said, surprising himself. "Just don't get in the way."

Essie gave him an earnest nod and said nothing.

For a moment he sat and she stood.

"Here," he said, getting up and bringing one of the tall stools to the end of the big table. "Sit here."

She nodded humbly, and sat down. Moments later he had forgotten her. When Al returned there was a brief explanation, and then they both forgot her. They conferred about the preparation of dinner, timing, and quantities, and then set to work. They did not talk much. Essie sat quietly and observed. She was hoping to worm her way into the establishment—a restaurant kitchen seemed like the sort of place where people would be noshing all the time, for example, and what would be more natural, since she was there, than to cut her in? And chat? And then, who knows? But although Harry looked like a very hearty feeder, and Al as if he could use all the feeding he could get, nothing, so far as Essie could see, went into their mouths except the tiniest bits for the most stringently professional reasons.

But then Harry set out several heads of garlic, laid out a knife next to them, and sighed, and Essie's heart jumped. Usually she found the voice of Fortune obscured in riddles, but sometimes it rings out like a bell.

"Can I help?" she said.

Harry looked up, surprised. "What do you know how to do," he said, not asking.

"I can mince garlic," she said.

Harry glanced down at the garlic, and up at her. He broke out a clove and laid it on the table. He nudged the knife so that it lay next to the clove.

"Don't cut yourself," he said, and turned to another task.

Essie hopped off the stool and walked quickly around the table. She peeled the clove rather awkwardly, and then began the process of slicing she had observed from above. It was harder than it looked; her slices were not even, and the little cubes, when she was done, were wildly irregular, but she knew the steps. She looked up bravely. Harry did not seem to be paying attention. She cleared her throat. He glanced at the board.

126

"Hmm," he said. "D'you cut yourself?"

"No," she said.

"Okay, young lady," he said. "You wash your hands at the sink. You know what a sink is?"

A *joke,* thought Essie. He's making a *joke.* She got it. She nodded judiciously and said, "Yes. We have one at home. I've seen Mom use it." She expected him to smile, but he did not. She could not tell whether he was amused or not.

"Okay," he said. "When you've washed your hands, you can mince all these, if you like. Take your time and do it neat. And don't cut yourself." Then he said something unrelated to Al, whose attention was entirely taken up in something he was doing to several chickens.

Okay, she thought. He didn't go on about what a great job I did, but it must have been good enough. She set to work. Soon the three of them were laboring silently around the table while the freezer hummed.

She was in the middle of peeling when Nicky hurried into the kitchen.

"Hell-*o,*" he said. "What have we *here?*"

"That's Jo, my new assistant," said Harry.

"Jo . . . ?"

"March," said Essie resolutely, and explained about Ms. Dorsey at Bray.

"Oh *God,*" said Nicky. "Ms. *Dorsey.* I can just *imagine. 'Ms. Dorsey'* sounds like a *total* bitch. *Is* she a total bitch? Still, I think education is a wonderful thing. I wish *I'd* had some." Then with a raised eyebrow and a glance at Harry he added, "So you're going to be observing here this afternoon?" Harry shrugged a tiny shrug. *"Wonderful,"* said Nicky, and hurried out the alley door.

The garlic was minced, the later batches not discreditably. She waited for a moment to be noticed and then said, "All done."

Harry glanced over, nodded, and continued what he was doing. He glanced at the clock and said, "Al, those greens are going to need to get wilted pretty quick."

"Ah, right," said Al, putting down the chicken he was working on and turning to the sink, grinning hugely.

"Wilting something I could do?" said Essie.

"No," said Harry. He was mixing ingredients in a bowl. He reached for a spatula from a large jar of implements behind her, and she had to jump out of the way. This was not working in the manner it was supposed to. Harry noticed her expression. He sighed and glanced around the table.

"Would you know a potato if you saw one?" he asked.

"I think so," said Essie, eyes down, and paid careful attention to the hurried demonstration that followed.

The afternoon waned. One task became another. The waiters reappeared a little before five. Emile was almost as gorgeous as Nicky, Essie thought, and without Nicky's tense edge, much warmer, always smiling. He had a French accent to die for. Arthur was dour. They seemed to be great pals. The third waiter was the bodybuilder, Nathan, who said nothing but who disconcerted Essie by standing near her and staring openly at her behind. When he left the room she put her thumbs in her pockets and baggied her jeans as much as she could, although not as much as she wanted.

Jim, the dishwasher, returned. He nodded to Harry and Al and then began gathering and cleaning the accumulations of the afternoon.

At five Harry looked over at Essie and said, "You'd better go on home now." She looked disconcerted and said, "Oh, but I'm learning so much. Do I have to go?" He considered and said, "No, I guess you can stay for a while. See if you can give Al a hand."

At seven Emile said, "Doesn't she 'ave a 'ome to go to? Jo, won't your mother be worried?"

"No," said Essie. She had anticipated this question.

"She doesn't worry about me much." But she looked thankfully at Emile, and he gave her a dazzling smile, which charmed her.

"You are a mystery girl," he said in a stage whisper. "A mystery girl with a secret," and smiled again. Then he darted off.

*God,* thought Essie. If Emile had been safely distant, she would have thought, *Hunk, hunk, hunk!* But since he was right there, she was not so bold, and she thought, *God,* again.

It was very busy.

At eight Al said, "Can you handle those?" nodding at some dirty saucepans that needed to be handed across to the dishwasher. She threw a dish towel over the bunched handles as she had seen him do and took them all at once, calling out "Hot, Jim," as she put them down, and feeling like a pro.

At eight-thirty Nicky said, "Jo, dear, you really *must* go home now. I mean, there are *laws* about this sort of thing." And then he said, "Have you had anything to eat?"

"Uh, no," said Essie bravely.

*"Oh!"* cried Nicky. "Harry, my *God.* What are you *thinking* of? You are un*fit* to be a mother. Food for Jo this *instant.* What would you like, my dear?"

Essie hesitated. She knew that when you eat out on somebody else's nickel you never order the most expensive thing. She knew how much the lamb was, but she had not noticed whether it was more or less than other possibilities.

"How about the lamb," said Nicky, divining her difficulty. "Do you like lamb?"

"Yes," said Essie. "I love it."

"It's a little *pink,* my dear, as you must have noticed," said Nicky. "Do you mind it pink? When I was your age I *hated* pink meat."

"No, I like it," said Essie.

"Lamb it shall be," said Nicky. "So *sophisticated,*

my *God.*" He swept a plate together with his own hand, added a glass of milk and perched her at a corner of the worktable to eat it. He was passing through the kitchen as she finished and said, "I hope you enjoyed that. We *so* liked having you here. I'm sure you were a great help. And do come show us your paper when it's done."

"Oh, but can't I come again tomorrow?" said Essie quickly. "It's supposed to be a big paper. I was hoping . . ."

Nicky was rushed. They were all rushed. He glanced at Harry, who shrugged.

"We'd *love* it," said Nicky, and hastened off.

From the doorway Essie said, "Thank you, Harry. Thank you, Al." They glanced up, and Al smiled distractedly. Then there was no one looking. Just before she reached the alley door she edged sideways into the storeroom and flew up the ladder. Safe, warm, fed. And she could do it again tomorrow. That was a future, the first she'd had since leaving home.

She woke at some point later in the evening. From the sounds, the kitchen was less rushed but still serving. Someone was in the loft just on the other side of the line of boxes, almost within arm's reach, loading things onto the dumbwaiter. There was no place to go where she would be any more hidden than she was. She stopped breathing. She heard whoever it was go down the ladder, and then the dumbwaiter descended.

She fell asleep again.

She woke later in darkness and silence. She was cold.

She missed home. She missed her friends and school. She missed everything.

On an impulse she pulled herself out of her nest of newspapers and felt her way between the boxes and down the ladder to the kitchen. The clock said one forty-five.

She stood for some minutes looking at the wall phone in the kitchen. She wanted to call home, just to say that she was okay. What do you say? Mom, it's me, I'm okay—and hang up? She took up the receiver and dialed, but before the connection was made she snapped down the hook. A moment later she was curled up on the cold concrete by the wall below the phone, sobbing uncontrollably. *Jeremy, Jeremy, Jeremy.* Why *can't* something be undone, if you wish for it hard enough, if you'd do *anything?* She couldn't understand it. It just seemed *wrong.*

# 19

Essie could not get by very well with one pair of underwear and one pair of socks. She needed more than one shirt and one pair of pants. She wanted a book: she could not spend eighteen hours a day concealed in a space less than five feet high with nothing to do but observe the kitchen below. But in order to do anything else, Essie realized, she needed to regularize her position and accumulate some funds. So during her second day in the loft, while she watched the preparation of lunch to pick up what professional skills she might, she also ruminated on ways and means.

That evening after she had been fed, she watched carefully for a relatively quiet moment when Nicky was in the kitchen and said, "Nicky?"

"Yes, Jo? I bet you want dessert. You know, last night we never gave you dessert. We're low on the truffle cake, so I can't offer you that, as a man of business, but I can recommend the crème brûlée. Would you like a crème brûlée?"

"I'd love a crème brûlée," said Essie, whatever a crème brûlée might be. She liked dessert on general principle, but beyond that she could see that Nicky considered that he was being generous, and she had observed that people are more likely to do you a big favor if they have done you a small one first.

He placed the dish before her, and she tasted appreciatively. He explained to her how to distinguish between a humdrum crème brûlée and a crème brûlée of distinction, and pointed out in some detail how the present specimen fell into the latter category—the quality of the heavy cream, the unbroken surface, the timing of the finish so that the caramel had hardened properly but had not begun to lose its crispness. She praised it and then quickly, before he could rush off again she said, "Nicky? I know you've been very nice to me, letting me do research and learn so much. I don't want to be a pest."

"*Jo,* dear, you're not a *pest*. What an *idea.*" He sounded just a little distracted.

"But I was wondering if I could come here after school and work. I mean every day." He looked surprised, and she hastened on. "You don't have to pay me a lot. Whatever you want. I don't . . . I mean, I don't have . . ." She lost her way for a moment. "I like it here," she said. She wasn't pretending, and it showed.

Suddenly she seemed to have his entire attention. He looked at her a long moment. He said, "Jo, we need to talk."

Essie tried to look innocent, but her ears were turning red, and she could feel it. He noticed it, too, she could see. So she did not try any goo-goo eyes on him, she just waited.

"I don't *know* about you, my dear," he said. Perhaps he hoped this would jog some revelation out of her, and waited, but she was silent. He said, "Do you even *have* a mom? Is there *anyone* who looks after you?"

"Oh, yes," said Essie. At that moment, in one sense and another, both of those propositions were true.

"Because when someone your age is hanging out at this time of night, and hungry, and shows up wearing the same clothes two days in a row, I worry if I should call the police or something."

"Please don't," she said very quietly, looking at the floor.

"Jo," he said carefully, "listen to me. Look up, please. You can't tell me *anything* about growing up tough. Honey, I know *all* about it, *all* about it. Now there's no question you've got a lot on the ball, so it can't be *all* bad. I don't want to play *games* with you, my dear, and you mustn't play games with me. Are you getting by okay?"

"Yes," she said.

"You have a place to stay?"

"Yes," she said, and almost laughed.

"Nobody is taking advantage? Beating you? Whatever?"

She shook her head.

"If anybody was, would you tell me?"

She hesitated and then she said, "Maybe."

Nicky studied her, but there was nothing to see that he had not seen already. Neither laws nor bones were being broken, so far as he could tell; sometimes you only make things worse when you meddle. The kid seemed to have her reasons. He said, "Jo, I've worked very hard for this restaurant. I can't afford any trouble."

Essie shook her head. No trouble.

He opened his mouth and then closed it. He lifted his hands and then dropped them against his thighs.

"I hope I'm doing the right thing," he said.

"Thank you, Nicky."

* * *

"We've lost her," said Gadek. "Either she's moved on without anyone seeing her, or she's holed up in a really serious way."

"Or something could have happened to her," said Toby.

"Yes," he said. "Or something's happened to her. In any case, she was the best thing we had going on the Broome thing, and now we're stuck again."

On the third day Nicky gave Essie fifty dollars. "Go do a little shopping," he said.

The fourth day was Monday, and the restaurant was closed. Essie had gathered from the talk in the kitchen that nobody was planning to come in, but when she got up she moved about warily, alert for the sound of a key in the front door.

She needed to get out to buy clothes. Simply getting out was a vexing problem. She had no key for the front door, so the only possibility was to come and go by the alley. The alley door had an interior deadbolt and then the wooden beam. She undid the lock and removed the beam, and with cardboard made a wedge that should hold the door closed while she was gone.

Kit's door was just opposite. There was no rear window in the restaurant, so the only way to find out if the coast was clear was to open the door and look. The wedge was ready. Carefully, she eased the door until she had a narrow view across the alley. Kit's door was closed, and he was not visible in the window above. She opened a little farther and peered out. There were cars parked up and down under the tow-away signs. There were one or two people going to and fro, but none of them was Kit. He might come out his door at any moment, or he might appear at either end of the alley, but he was not there now. Quickly she stepped out, placed the wedge, and closed the door. It felt firm enough so long as nobody pushed against it. Reflexively avoiding the route that she had followed with Kit, she sprinted for the lower end of the block, glancing back just before she turned the corner to be sure she was not followed. This isn't going to work forever, she thought.

Jeremy's face stopped her, surreally elevated a head's height above her own, smiling carefully out from a utility pole at her and at the blank wall opposite.

Above the face large letters said,

## HAVE YOU SEEN THIS CHILD?

She read the flyer through several times, although there was little in it that she did not know. The picture looked so lifeless, unblinking, although the sun shone directly on it.

She said to herself, He's dead.

It was the first time she had permitted herself to frame that thought. She thought of Gabriella's face on the night of the kidnapping, almost heard her crying, *Oh, Essie. Where were you . . .*

She ran.

The next pole up the street had another flyer, and so did the one after that.

They were all over the district. Essie quickly taught herself to look past them, but it occurred to her for the first time that her life would always be shaded by his loss—that there would never be a happy return for either of them.

It was a mercy in such a mood to have a task, even if the task was shopping. Decay and gentrification still contended for the district. Some of the businesses she passed were entirely too chichi and upscale for her means, but here and there she found pockets of commerce that would not despise her. She discovered a thrift store where she expanded the visible parts of her wardrobe and doubled the invisible parts so she could have one to wear and one to wash. She stumbled on a used bookstore where she bought another copy of *Great Expectations* and a space fantasy. Her last dollar and change bought a bag of the cheapest possible cookies. Returning, she passed an office that was being recarpeted, and rescued two bed-size remnants from the Dumpster outside. With considerable precaution she crept back into the alley from the lower end. She moved cautiously, pausing here and there behind parked cars until she was close to the door, and then darting the last few yards, arms full of treasures.

She lined her nest with the carpet pieces, extracted a handful of cookies, and then, reclining luxuriously, opened *Great Expectations*. After a page or two she closed it, picked up the space fantasy, and was for some hours lost to the world.

Toby got to the Hall of Justice in enough time to go by the classroom before roll call. Gadek was looking harassed.

"It's the crazy stuff that wears me down," he said. "The pointless stuff. A couple of days ago we were approached by a psychic."

"Oh, Jesus," said Toby.

"Yes," said Gadek. "Not convincing. A lot of mumbo jumbo about visualizing where Jeremy is, but nothing specific that would actually guide you in going out and finding him. And she wanted cash down. We said thanks but no thanks. Sometimes you pay informants, and sometimes you listen to batty ideas, but you don't pay to listen to batty ideas."

"Good for you," said Toby.

"Well, so off she goes to Gabriella Broome, tells her that Jeremy is alive, that she knows where he is, and that the cops don't care."

"Where is the dunking stool now that we really need it?" said Toby.

"Well," said Gadek, "think of a mother's heart. It's

ten days since the kidnapping, the cops aren't making any progress, the one possible witness has dropped out of sight, and now here's someone telling you that your kid is okay and she'll tell you where to find him. All it takes is a little cash. Well, quite a lot of cash. Up front."

"Which she paid, I bet."

"Which she was going to pay this morning, except that Trevor got on his high horse and decided that *we* should pay it instead of them."

"I thought she threw Trevor out."

"She did, but he's still the father, and he wants to be consulted. He called me this morning and harangued me about it. The upshot was that I talked them out of it. I told them that we simply wouldn't spend an hour investigating airy-fairy stuff. If someone has information, great. Smoke and vibrations, no."

"And?"

"Well, Trevor agreed with me—he thought it was all baloney anyway. That's one reason he wanted us to pay, I guess. If we wouldn't, fine. He figured he'd shifted the blame just in case anything *were* to come of it.

"Gabriella, on the other hand, is absolutely frantic. She's thinking, pay the psychic, get the tip, go out and get Jeremy—just like that. She's thinking she could have her boy home tonight. You can imagine the state she's in.

"It's a human problem. It just isn't in human nature to say, Well, this is an eighty percent chance so I'll get eighty percent excited, and this other is only a five percent chance so I'll only get five percent excited. Gabriella cares a hundred percent. She gets a hundred percent excited about an eighty percent chance, or five, or zip. If a shadow is the best thing she's got going, she'll be a hundred percent excited about a shadow. The trouble is that remote possibilities usually don't pan out, and she's a hundred percent disappointed every time. But that doesn't make her any the less committed to chasing the next shadow. Her kid's missing, and she can't just say, Well, I've taken enough knocks over this and now I'm going to protect myself. She's thinking, What if I relax and the important thing gets by me, just because I wasn't paying attention? So she stays jacked up. And it's rough, going up and down, up and down. It takes a real toll."

One of Sergeant Wren's clerks said, "I was just over in DD. The Broome task force is running out of leads to work on. They're going to start cutting people loose."

"Well, that's only sensible," said Sergeant Wren. "That's only putting a little reality back into the situation. The media gets onto a case, and suddenly you'd think it was the only case going on in the world."

"I hear you," said somebody else. "I feel sorry for that little kid, but there're folks hurtin' all over town who can't get a detective to give 'em the time of day."

Paul thought, I wonder why she feels sorry for *him?* I'm the one who has to put up with him and his moods. I don't see why the rules shouldn't apply to him as well as to me.

Still, he thought, it was good news. He had been under real pressure over the last few days, worrying that he might be blamed again. He had not altogether realized until that moment how keenly he had felt it.

He had been fighting on two fronts at once: the boy being ridiculous—well, that was over, anyway—it wasn't all sweetness and light yet, but no more rebellion, thanks to the closet. And then threatened from the outside. He had held himself together—but suddenly, now that the danger was past, he felt the menace, the injustice that had been hanging over him.

He felt it like a series of shocks. His face flushed and his fists knotted as the recognition jolted him.

Paul knew that he had been ill used. He knew it very well. This baby-sitter was only the latest example. They'll fink on you, he knew. They'll make you the goat. They didn't even attempt to put an innocent face on it. Glad to have money spent on them, glad to have a good time, to be initiated, and then suddenly it's "He made me do it." Loyalty meant nothing to them.

But he had never made anyone do anything they didn't want to do. They all wanted it until they got caught. Then they remembered their supposed shame and said anything to please the authorities, to get out of trouble themselves.

You never knew where you were with these kids. They all hated their parents. They didn't need much encouragement to talk about all the ways their parents jacked them around, piling up examples, topping each other, but they all went whining back to their parents in the end. Where did that capacity for double-talk and betrayal come from? Who fed them this poison? And the lies they told about him . . . Paul swayed in his chair. Sergeant Wren pontificated in the background, unheard.

*Who fed them this poison?* In his old town, one of the first boys he had befriended—Steven, that was his name—Steven had been so grateful when he was ten, but when he was seventeen he began coming back. He began hanging around, sitting on his bike across the street, riding off when Paul came out, but pretty soon he'd be there again. He tried to break into Paul's house—literally attempted a burglary. Paul came home unexpectedly and caught him at it. *He'd been after the pictures that Paul had taken of him.* That was his game. He was going to get those back, and then, when *he* was nicely out of it, when *his* name would not be in the papers, when *he* would not be exposed, he was going to go to the police. Going to rat on Paul. And who was Steven? Nothing: simply nothing at all. A hippie father long gone, and his hippie mother stoned all the time. A runt: a whipped, skinny, lonely, loveless, longing, cringing runt. Do *anything* to please, *anything* for a kind word. No pride. Anything at all. Then along comes Paul and pays some attention—along comes Paul and treats him like a somebody, talks to him, listens to him and encourages him, spends money on him, teaches him about life— and how does he repay? He's going to go to the police. And it's not as if Steven was the only one ready to betray him. When the coach found out, they *all* betrayed him. They *all* did. Not *one* of them stood by him. Not *one*.

Sergeant Wren was watching him.

He pulled himself up. His knew his face was red, and he could feel sweat on his forehead. His hands were clamped on the arms of his chair, and guiltily he relaxed them.

"I don't feel so well," he said, too loud.

"Well, you don't look well," said Sergeant Wren, sounding suspicious to Paul.

"I . . . I have to go home."

"Well, I would," said Sergeant Wren. "I would if I felt the way you look."

"I'm going to take a few days off," said Paul, suddenly deciding and hauling himself to his feet. "I'm going to take a little sick leave. I'm going to try to get caught up with myself." He was reaching for his jacket.

"I certainly would," said Sergeant Wren.

The restaurant was open on Tuesday. Essie appeared in the doorway punctually at a quarter past three.

"Here," said Harry, putting a list in her hand. "You're good at walking, I bet. We need some things from Park's Market. The address is at the top—go up the alley and turn left. It's the best place around here for produce on short notice, and we go there a lot. Tell 'em I sent you, and if they don't give you the best they've got, I'm going to send you right back again. Now skedaddle. No, you don't run errands through the dining room—use the alley."

A moment later she was scooting out the door. Kit was not in sight, but it was blind luck. Twenty minutes later, more carefully, she had to return the same way. Blind luck again. Essie wondered how long it was going to last. She wondered what Kit would do if they met in the alley or if he found out where she spent her time.

There was a steam table at one end of the kitchen with deep steel containers where the items that could be finished ahead of time were kept, and where each plate was prepared before being sent out to the diners. Harry stationed Essie here, and showed her how to arrange the vegetables on the plate—"No more, no less, and just like this"—and checked each plate before it could go. He did the meats and sauces himself. It was hectic work, but she was adroit for a beginner.

The cream of asparagus soup had to have a sprinkle of bright green tips arranged in the middle. "You try," said Al, not noticing Harry's shake of the head. Essie tried; her sprinkle had an undeniable springy energy. Al grinned delightedly and said, "That's pretty good. Good, huh?" he added to Harry, who looked disapproving but could not deny that it looked good.

So Essie took on the soup as well as the vegetables.

"You do eet so beautiful," said Emile, without stopping—he said it as if it were four words, bee *you* tee full—"The lady at table four says eet eez too nice to eat." Starting out into the passage he smiled his tremendous smile and added over his shoulder, "I tell 'er, you'll be missing the best part."

Nicky rushed past on an errand to replenish the ready stocks of wine. *"Like* the clothes," he said, running his eye over her.

Nathan did not like the clothes. "Too baggy," he said. He paused for a moment, staring grossly at her behind, which seemed to her suddenly protuberant and completely naked. He tilted his head this way and that as if in profound critical assessment. *"Don't,"* she said. She was right in the middle of a job—there was nothing she could do about it. Harry glanced over with a sour look at Nathan but said nothing. Nathan laughed as he picked up plates. But when Nicky came back into the kitchen and gave him a sharp look, he went off quickly into the passage.

"Nicky . . ." said Essie as he zipped past, but he was gone; did not want to stop, it seemed to her. He knew what she was going to say, and he did not want to hear about it.

Essie had been asleep for some time when she woke. The only sound was Nicky's voice below her in the silent kitchen.

". . . but I worry about her anyway. Nathan was giving her a hard time this evening. She wanted to *kvetch* about it, but I wouldn't hang around to hear it. I worry that she's not mature enough to take care of herself."

Essie did not need to look down. Nicky was standing at the kitchen phone on the wall by the passageway. She lay silently, listening.

"Yes, Nathan is *certainly* a prick, *and* a prima donna—my *God,* you don't have to tell *me*—but he moves more appetizers and desserts than anyone else, and sells better wine. Let's not forget we're trying to run a business here . . . It won't do *any* good if we speak to him. He *knows* I'm not going to fire him. If *I* can put up with him, *she'd* better be able to . . . Well, Charles, we *don't* know, do we? We know there's no Bray school or Ms. Dorsey. There's no March listed at any address around here, but maybe they don't have a telephone . . . I agree. But if we turn her away, *then* where would she wind up? When I was her age, I had *no* place to go, and it was *hell,* my dear, simply hell. And it's not as if she's really in the way . . . Well, look, I'll be home in ten minutes. We can think it through."

She heard him hang up the phone. A moment later the kitchen lights went out, then the passage, then the dining room. The ceiling space, illuminated from below by gaps and holes all along its length, at last was dark. She heard the front door close and the locks click.

She did not know what to make of it—she had thought she was doing well. She stirred restlessly in her nest of papers and carpet scraps, miserable in the low dark space, oppressed by the loom of the outer roof, invisible just above her.

# 20

Harry dispatched Essie to the market again. The alley door was visible from most of the kitchen; she simply could not be cautious about going out. She darted, hoping for the best, and got safely away. Darkness was falling as she returned, and she was on the street scant yards from the top of the alley when Kit emerged in front of her. She sidestepped into the closest doorway, and didn't think he had seen her.

He was entirely absorbed in talking to a girl of Essie's age or a little older. She was wearing a short skirt in the cold wind. She looked scared as well as cold, trying not to show either. He was driving her. The self-deprecating bend in his body, the gentle looseness, was gone. He hung over her like a gibbet.

Then, with a parting injunction, he sidled back into the alley, and the girl, with some hesitation and several backward glances, moved forward to the curb. She began to scan the stream of traffic, making eye contact with the drivers as they passed. Leaning a little out of her doorway, Essie could see Kit standing in the shelter of a telephone pole that stood close beside the brick wall just inside the alley, watching the girl, watching the street. Once he called out something to her, and she began to peer more actively at the traffic.

She was a pretty girl, and in her fright she looked younger than she was. It was less than a minute later that a car, an expensive sedan, pulled over to the curb beside her. The passenger window glided down. The girl glanced back at Kit, fear all over her. He cocked his head abruptly toward the sedan. She bent down to the window.

The driver, the girl, Kit, and Essie were all too intent to see the patrol car that ghosted up behind the sedan. The door opened and a large, very spruce-looking cop emerged. Kit, focused on his project, noticed too late and called out. The girl started up from the window and the driver jolted upright. His hand shot to the gearshift lever.

"Hold it," bellowed the cop, rapping forcefully for attention on the sedan's trunk lid with his metal flashlight, leaving a visible dent. The driver's hand fell to his lap and they all froze, the driver, the girl, Kit, and Essie unseen in her doorway, waiting for the next step.

The cop looked the girl up and down, and then shouted to Kit in the alley, "Found some new kiddie talent, you asshole? You stay right where you are."

Essie could see the driver's eyes widen and the girl

looking gray. She could not see Kit without showing herself, and she was not about to show herself.

The cop walked slowly along the street side of the sedan. He had unhooked his key chain from his belt, and he dragged a key along the side from the taillight to the driver's door, making a loud scratching noise and scoring the paint to the metal. When he reached the front, he knocked sardonically on the window with his metal flashlight. Knock. Knock. Knock.

"Could I trouble you for a moment of your *valuable* time?" he bellowed in a voice that carried for half a block. The window glided down. In a voice only slightly moderated he said, "Your driver's license, *sir,* if you please, if you would be so kind."

The driver hastened to produce it, and in a leisurely fashion the spruce cop produced his daybook and a pen and began to transcribe the information. While he wrote, he talked.

"I'll try not to hold you up, *sir.* I know you must want to get back to your cozy suburban home and your wife, even if she doesn't understand your needs. I'm not going to arrest you, *sir,* because, as you know, I probably can't prove that you've solicited a juvenile for an act of prostitution. If I could, I'd send you to prison to get butt-fucked by every syphilitic, clapped-up hard-timer in the system. Shits like you really disgust me. But instead, I'm just going to tell you to get your fucking ass off my beat. Is that fair?" The driver opened his mouth and closed it again, goggle-eyed. The cop flicked the door-mounted mirror with his flashlight, popping it off its mounting so that it hung quivering by a wire. "Is that *fair?*" he said again.

"Uh, yes," gabbled the driver. And when that response seemed inadequate, he added, "Uh, yes. Yes, it's fair. Uh, officer."

"*Good,*" said the cop, staring down, eye to eye. "Then it never has to get into the papers that you have a taste for underage whores. I was hoping you'd think that was fair. Well, *sir*, I won't keep you from the warmth of your family circle." He flicked the license through the window and stepped back. As the sedan pulled hastily past he dragged his key down the side again from front to rear.

Now there was nothing between him and the girl, who goggled at him from the curb, horror-struck.

"Be my guest," he said, and cocked his head at the patrol car. He watched her get in on the passenger side and close the door, and then his gaze settled on Kit.

He strode across the sidewalk, the heavy aluminum three-cell flashlight describing brisk little arcs beside his leg. He glanced around as he stepped into the alley, and Essie drew back into her doorway. There was the first syllable of a plea from Kit, a welter of thumps, shoes scraping, fabric dragging across brick. Essie saw the girl in the car, watching, jerk back in her seat. A moment later the cop reappeared, got in, and drove away with his capture.

Kit was collapsed in the little space between the telephone pole and the brick wall where he had been standing. His eyes clenched shut. His hand cupped over his bloody mouth, each breath a falsetto shrilling. He was trying to control his heaving chest, trying to hold himself perfectly still. Essie clung to the wall opposite, moving as silently as she could, staring, fascinated beyond judgment. When she was a few yards past, she broke into a run. From just outside the storeroom door she could see him, still in the same position.

If Kit had been a wounded dog, Essie would have spoken to somebody or made phone calls to some authority. But Kit was infinitely remote from her, from all community. It did not occur to her that the spruce cop might have performed a rogue act; what she had seen must be the way things are done in the places kids go to when they run away.

And it was by no means clear to her who was in the right. If the spruce cop was wild and violent, Kit was a predator; Essie knew what to think about Kit. And Essie could see that she was safer now than she had been ten minutes before. The scared girl was safer. What about that?

Later in the evening she wondered if Kit was still lying between pole and wall where he had been, but Emile was doing a very droll imitation of the couple at table seven while she finished ladling out four bowls of an opulent lobster bisque, and she didn't hold the thought.

# 21

Sara said, "I was walking down the street today, and I saw a man sitting in his car at a stop sign. A nice, prosperous-looking man. There was no cross traffic, but he was just sitting. It was as if he had pulled up at the stop sign and then forgotten where he was.

"He was talking furiously to himself, mouth wide open, big gestures with both hands, big discussion. He just sat there, obviously talking to someone situated somewhere right in the middle of the engine. He wasn't holding anybody up—there was no particular reason why he *shouldn't* sit there at the stop sign and talk—except that people usually don't. He just wasn't aware of where he was.

"Maybe I need a vacation. When you're pregnant, the streets are full of pregnant women. When you have a little kid, all you see are strollers. What I notice these days is people looking frazzled and talking to themselves. People standing by the side of the road watching their radiators boil over. I see those things all the time."

Toby said, "I wonder why you mentioned that the man was prosperous?"

She said, "Never mind." And then, "Heather will be here in half an hour. I think you should take me to a movie."

Heather appeared punctually with her homework and her clarinet, which she flourished and said, "I've written this really neat new piece, 'Ice Arbor Number One.' I've been listening to John Cage. Do you like John Cage?"

"I don't think so," said Toby vaguely.

"I guess he doesn't write for everyone," said Heather. "He's just *totally* awesome. I'm dedicating 'Ice Arbor' to him. I'm going to play it for Adam and Joss. It's atonal and arrhythmic. It's about sex. Mom hates it. I play it all the time around the house."

"I wonder if the kids will . . ."

"Oh, sure. They're eight and ten, y'know," she said, as if the ages of Toby's children had probably escaped his attention. "Don't be an old fogy. They'll really get into it."

In the car he said, "Am I getting stuffy, or is Heather getting saucy?"

"Well, I'll have to think about you," said Sara, "but Heather is definitely getting saucy. I guess she's doing it a little late. I got into it when I was about fourteen. Oh, I hate to think about it. Bitchy, fault-finding, and superior are what I was. I don't know how my mother survived. I don't know how *I'm* going to survive when Joss gets around to it."

"Maybe Joss won't get around to it," said Toby.

"What goes around comes around," said Sara glumly.

\* \* \*

The next morning at breakfast Toby asked the kids whether Heather had played her new composition for them.

"Yeah!" they said.

"And how did you like it?"

*"Awesome,"* said Adam.

*"Totally,"* said Joss.

"And the subject?" he said. "Heather said . . ."

"Oh, you mean about love," said Joss.

*"Love,"* said Adam, throwing his arms around Joss and making smooching noises.

"I dunno," said Joss, evading him. "Heather said that's what it was about, but . . ."

"It was kind of . . ." said Adam.

"But you could *really* tell how good it was," said Joss. "Maybe Heather just needs to work on it a little more, but we really liked it."

"Totally," said Adam. "Don't be an old fogy."

"Heather, this is Toby."

"Oh. Hi." A little hesitant.

"Heather, did you tell Adam and Joss that I'm an old fogy?" There was an audible intake of air at the other end of the line, which he took for confirmation.

"Listen, Heather," he said. "You have no right to call me names. I don't expect you to like or agree with all my attitudes, but I expect you to support me with my children."

"You're right," she said quickly. She sounded genuinely contrite, suddenly younger. "I shouldn't have said it, and I won't do anything like that again. I'm really sorry."

Oblique acknowledgment was all he had expected to get out of her. His lungs were still full of air.

"I'm sorry," she said again.

There was an awkward pause. He was still in full charge. He did not know how to stop.

"Well, I . . ."

149

Another pause.

"Well, look," he said, feeling lame and sounding lame as well. "Okay, let's call it quits."

"Thank you," she said, her voice small. And then, "Am I still working for you?"

"Well, Heather, of course . . ."

"Thank you," she said. "It won't happen again."

When he hung up, he turned to Sara and said, "Would you explain Heather to me?" She laughed and laughed.

Joss said, "Dad, if Adam or I ran away, would you want us back?"

Toby's mouth was full. Sara said, "Of course we would, cupcake. But I hope you're not thinking about running away."

"No," said Joss. "But how do you know you would?"

"Because we love you, honey."

"But wouldn't you be mad?"

"Yes, I suppose, and a lot of other things. But we love you, even if you make us mad."

"As you may have noticed," said Toby, but Joss ignored this. She said, "Dad was talking about a woman he took to the hospital because she was sick, and her parents didn't want her back because she was a heroin addict and stole their things to buy heroin."

"That was different," said Toby. "There was a lot of history there. She was a grown woman."

"Did they love her?"

Toby said, "That was a very complicated situation."

"But what if *Essie* has a lot of problems?" said Joss. "You and Dad were talking in the living room last night. You said a lot of runaways get into trouble and start doing dope. What if *Essie* starts stealing things? What if it gets to be a very complicated situation?"

"Essie's still a kid," said Toby.

"But before, when I asked you if she was going to be okay, you said you hoped so because she's pretty grown up, and you hoped she could take care of herself."

"It sounds like a complicated situation," said Adam. "Can she still come home, even if it's a complicated situation?"

"Y'know, guys," said Sara, putting on her lawyerly voice, "let's not talk hypotheticals. I don't know about the whole world. I can't tell what's going to happen. I hope Essie's all right. If I knew where she was, I'd jump in the car this minute and go get her. And if her parents didn't want her back, I'd bring her here to live with us. You two aren't running away, but if you do, you can *always* come back, however complicated it is."

"The woman in the hospital," said Joss. "Did *her* parents tell her *she* could always come back?"

"Come here," said Sara. "I want a squeeze. I don't know what that woman's parents said. I don't know what's going to happen."


The first time Essie sat for the Broomes, she had finished reading Jeremy his bedtime story, reaching for the light, when he said, "Do you love me?"

She gave him a funny look and said, "Like, I'm just the baby-sitter."

He looked so disappointed, she said quickly, "Just kiiidddding! Of course I love you."

Now there was doubt written all over him, but very seriously he said, "I love you, too."

Huddling in her nest, she thought, How could I possibly have said that to him? He was *so* shot down. How could I possibly have treated a little kid that way?

# 22

Essie could scarcely connect the pieces of her life. In unconscious moments she thought of herself as rooted in a thousand ways. Family and friends, school and after-school, her room, her possessions—all seemed at her elbow, just outside her vision. If she thought about them directly, however, they seemed immeasurably distant. Essie was vulnerable to a painful pulse of guilt if the school bell caught her not yet at her desk, binder open at the proper place, and the appropriate writing instrument at the ready. Erin would cut a class occasionally and leave Essie almost frantic with anxiety on her account; when Erin suggested once that Essie cut, too, her knees had sagged under her at the very idea.

And now she was cutting not a class or two but her whole life—classes, chorus rehearsals, family dinnertime, yard chores, homework, the dishes—every variety of order, connection, obedience, and discipline known to her. She had cast off authority and also protection. Nobody had any effective responsibility for her; she could not assume anything.

She knew that the ceiling of Le Coq d'Or could not last forever, but she was not going to abandon this haven as lightly as she had launched herself from home. As matters stood, she was housed, clothed, and fed on decent terms. Change would likely be for the worse. Errands for Harry, only two or three blocks' walk, had taken her to parts of downtown where kids her own age hustled dope and sold themselves on street corners. She was neither customer nor predator, all but invisible to them, but they fascinated her. Looking at them was like seeing her own reflection in store windows, a dark likeness.

In one sense, normal existence seemed merely interrupted, as if she had been out sick. Home and friends were half an hour away. The nightmare days between the kidnapping and her flight faded into a dreamlike distance almost immediately, and her long-established sense of home as a place of slightly pressured contentment and security returned to her. She thought of herself as having been happy. She missed her home.

But now petty sin had become the pattern of her life, however unwillingly. She was profoundly uncomfortable with lying, stealing, sneaking, truancy, and irresponsible behavior of all varieties. She had always been reliable about schoolwork, and the thought that she was falling behind nagged at her. Idleness bored her and offended her sense of thrift.

She found a certain satisfaction in her life—it was hard, but she had run away to join Jeremy in hardship. And one day, perhaps—some indeterminate day, not today, not tomorrow—she might see a headline: BOY FOUND. Perhaps that would resolve matters. Since seeing his picture on the telephone pole she had thought of him as dead, but humility insulated her from complete despair; she mistrusted her judgment on that point, as she did on so many others.

And in the meantime the elements of her life hovered, never altogether abandoned, never quite resolved. Waking and sleeping, she dreamed of things within reach that, nevertheless, her hand could not manage to touch. She became accustomed to trains of thought that did not have ends but merely abeyances.

The practical aspects of her life were pressing and constant. In the morning she had to be up early enough to use the ladies' room, bathe herself, and do essential washing in the big janitor's sink under the loft, scrounge something that would not be missed for breakfast, expunge all traces of her presence, and then either get back into hiding or be far enough away from the restaurant so that she would not cross paths with the staff as they arrived. She had discovered that there were always two or three spare keys to the front door hanging on a nail by Nicky's desk. She would borrow one and let herself out the front door so that the alley door would not be found unbarred.

Essie had not seen Kit since his encounter with the spruce cop, but she treated the alley as a hostile place to be entered cautiously and as seldom as possible. Even beyond the alley, the street was worrisome. She was far from clear about truancy issues, but she knew that her situation was irregular. She made it a point to go out as little as possible during school hours. When she did go out she always headed directly for the most crowded streets. Nicky tipped her odd amounts at irregular intervals, and when she was in funds, she would sometimes sneak out around noon for an hour, buying fast food, doing necessary shopping, and returning while the staff was still absorbed with the lunchtime rush. As she approached from either end of the alley she could usually see Nicky's green convertible parked by the storeroom door. If it was not there, it meant that he was likely to show up at any moment, and the passage of the alley accordingly became tenser.

On Mondays the restaurant was closed. Nicky and Charles made a point of staying away on that day, regardless of what needed to be done. Essie could sleep late and come and go as she liked without having to worry about being seen.

The front of Le Coq d'Or opened on a prospect entirely more spacious than the rear. Here a park, perhaps a hundred feet across and engirdled by a narrow one-way street, ran most of the length of the block. A ring of mature trees surrounded it, with grass and a large climbing structure in the middle. The buildings that surrounded it, where they were visible through the trees, were of that happy, unpretentious, small industrial sort that still survive in pockets in San Francisco, with two- and three-story fronts of brick and concrete and great steel-framed windows, some tall and square, and some with fan lights. These disgorged on sunny days all the rich human variety of the city to patronize the several restaurants, of which Le Coq d'Or was the most upscale, or to brown-bag it on the grass amidst coworkers, scampering dogs, and bouncing children. There was a laundromat; while her clothes were washing, Essie would go across the street and sit on a bench near the sandbox. Reflexively, she ran her eye over the children in case Jeremy might be among them. Then, with a dedication that would have astonished and alarmed the parents if they had been aware of it, she set herself to watch—for what, she did not exactly know. But she thought she might see something if she just looked hard enough.

Usually she brought a book to read, or at any rate, to hold, which made it easier to avoid conversation. It was an effort for her in that friendly place, but she stayed solitary. She did not want one of these people paying attention to her, wondering where they had seen her before.

And she had things to chew on. *Was* the door left open? If it was, how had the kidnapper known? If it was not, how had he gotten in? How had he known it would be safe? She could not make up her mind about it.

Once a terrible idea occurred to her: whether it was possible that Jeremy had never left the house. Whether he might have crept into—what?—some closet, some place under the house or in the attic—and passed out or been overcome by fumes from the heater or something, or just gotten stuck, and just never come out or been found. Might be there still, wedged in some tight place.

Nobody had actually seen him leave, after all. Nobody had actually seen any kidnapper.

He might have been there all the time they were running around looking—everywhere except the right place. She remembered those cops who had been searching, looking competent and very active.

Was it possible that there had been, in fact, no kidnapping? She could not rule it out. She pictured the Broome house, the nooks and crannies that she knew, the places she had never been into. How sure could the police be that they had looked in every possible place?

He would not still be alive, of course. She thought of them searching again and finding him—she pictured some cramped space where joists and rafters form a tight angle behind the chimney—and knowing that he had been there dying, right above their heads, while they pursued other possibilities. *God!*

And yet it would be closure of a sort. At least everyone would know. Not knowing was the worst.

She bought a postcard, which she was careful to handle only by the edges, and a stamp. Late that night she used the typewriter in Nicky's office to write,

Jeremy Broome still in house?

She addressed it to the police department. The telegraphic style made her feel anonymous. She had no specific suggestions to make, so there was no point in enumerating possibilities. Maybe someone would think again and come up with something.

She brought back odds and ends encountered in her travels and furnished her nest with them. She tied together her enclosure of boxes to make it more substantial, and decorated it with pages torn from magazines and wrapping paper scraps and bits of ribbon she found in a bag. One of the boxes was empty; she used it for a closet. She rescued an old-fashioned alarm clock, inoperable, with bells and a brass ring on the top, and hung it by a string from a rafter overhead, slightly askew, its four stout conical legs poking bravely into space. She named it The Mom Clock because it hung over her and reminded her of things. Idling sometimes in her nest, she would watch chance drafts nudge it slightly, fretfully, this way and that. She assigned fanciful significance to its movements, sometimes commands, sometimes auguries. If it turns to the left, she would think, I must eat two cookies very slowly. If it turns to the right, it means that tomorrow Nicky will not be worried-looking.

She bought a small flashlight that she could keep beside her to turn on and hold when she woke from nightmare.

On days when the fictional Bray would not be in session, she arrived in the kitchen in time to work on lunch and stayed as far into the evening as she was permitted. Nicky laid down eight hours as her maximum, but Harry was inclined to let her stretch it. Work reassured her. So long as she was busy and useful, she felt she was not entirely reprobate.

On weekdays, if she did not go out, she lay quietly in her nest and read or watched the kitchen, busy below her, or pondered the riddles of The Mom Clock.

*Great Expectations* was finished. Ms. Dieter would assign a paper at this point: when you finish a ponderous book, you write an earnest essay. Writing one appealed to Essie as a comfortable and accessible piece of her old routine. She bought a scholastic-looking spiral notebook and a pen and curled in her nest to write while the noontime rush clattered heedlessly away below her. What would Ms. Dieter assign? "Compare and contrast . . ." what?

If she were at home and forgot an assignment, she would call up one of her friends.

Wow.

She pictured a phone. She had their numbers in her fingertips, an abstract pattern of darting little jabs.

Why not?

*Wow!*

For a moment she was so carried away with it that she forgot where she was, and when her eyes suddenly registered the forest of kitchen vents in the shadowy 'tween-space she jerked physically, as when she would fall in dreams. The wave of homesickness that followed struck her like a blow.

But why not?

The next day, Monday, Essie had plenty of time to think about things. Why *not* call? Erin would not tell. Lizby would not. She thought that Elliott would not, if she dared to call him in the first place. Erin even had her own phone.

No one would know.

Why not?

She knew that some calls can be traced and others cannot, but she did not know any details. All that she knew about calling from undisclosed locations she had learned from movies.

She could not risk calling from the restaurant—not for herself, not for Nicky. She had promised him that there would be no trouble—that was fair. But a public phone seemed safe enough.

Do it.

She skipped down to the phone booth at the gas station around the corner. She had four quarters in her pocket. She inserted one and dialed Erin's number. An automaton's voice demanded another quarter and, when she had complied, thanked her. The phone rang less than once before being snatched up.

Erin's voice: "C'est moi."

"Hey," said Essie, which was what she said to announce herself on the phone.

*"Ess! Ess, is that you?"*

"Yeah. C'est moi, too," said Essie.

*"Oh, GOD! God God God God GOD!"* said Erin. "Where *ARE* you? Are you *back?"*

"No, uh, no, I'm not back, I . . ."

"Where *are* you? *Oh God God God!* Where *are* you?"

She was prepared for this.

"I'm *somewhere,"* she said, in a mock creepy voice. "Somewhere *mysterious."*

"Somewhere mysterious like *where?"* said Erin. "Like omigod *where?"*

"Can't say, dummer. You don't want to know. In case they torture you or something."

"Well, *God,* Ess," said Erin. "That's kinda weird. Like I don't think they torture the friends of runaways very often." But there was a hesitation in her voice; all she knew about the juvenile justice system was that it is a murky business.

"They haven't found Jeremy?" said Essie abruptly.

"No," said Erin, a little surprised that Essie was asking—all the local channels had followed the story as long as it lasted. "Like, they wouldn't be keeping it a secret."

"No," said Essie. And quickly, to head off any more questions she said, "Now *tell.* What's been happening? Tell all."

Erin was supposed to be doing her homework; the conversation was conducted at her end in an urgent whisper threatening at frequent intervals to burst into full-throated shrieks, and at Essie's in tones ranging from normal to a shout when the haphazard din of passing traffic threatened to drown her out. Erin had scarcely begun telling all before the automaton demanded her last fifty cents. She was in the middle of a minute description of how Shelly was taking advantage of Essie's absence to throw herself at Elliott when the automaton spoke again.

"That's it," said Essie bravely. "Gotta go."

"Reverse the charges," said Erin.

That made sense.

They were on the phone for some time. Erin was doing what she could to keep Essie's memory green with Elliott, but it was a desperate situation. "I can't hold Shelly off forever," she said. "How long are you going to be wherever you are, Ess, instead of here?"

"Till they find Jeremy," she said.

"God," said Erin. It did not occur to her that Essie had not seen the press conferences and news coverage following her disappearance, and with the curiously selective delicacy of friendship, she refrained from mentioning it.

But there was a great deal of other news. Whenever Rhea's mom and dad are fighting really bad, her dad takes Rhea out and buys her clothes, and she showed up at school in this megacool new outfit, and Lizby took one look and said, God, I'm sorry, and Rhea broke down crying right there on the library steps. And Addie won some totally important poetry contest—big announcement in assembly—so everyone read it, only no one can understand it. If you ask Addie what it means she's all like, Don't ask *me,* I only wrote it. Ms. Dieter says that's fair, but I think it's totally pompous. Latasha cheated on a chemistry test and almost got caught and thought her heart had stopped and swore never to do it again, but of course she will 'cause chemistry is not her subject. Her parents say she has to be the best, so they'll totally kill her if she doesn't get an A, but of course they'll also totally kill her if she gets caught cheating, so don't switch channels 'cause there's gonna be a show either way. And Ms. Dieter and Mr. Coley are a thing— *everyone* thinks so, and she goes around smiling all the time. And Moll is anorexic again and trying to hide it, which is pathetic.

There was a lot of news, and they talked for a long time. Essie promised to call again the following night, if she could, and Erin promised that Lizby would be there.

Wow! thought Essie when she hung up.

As a child she had been enthralled by an old engraving of a foundering ship, the rescue line arcing out from the shore toward a little cluster of mariners awash on the canting deck reaching desperately out to it. It was unclear from the engraving whether they would succeed in catching it or not. Tantalized, she had pondered the fate of those poor souls, trying to decide if the story ended happily. Now I know, she thought.

She skipped a step. She could not go back and be cooped up in the restaurant. She had to move. She sprinted half a block, walked, ran again, walked, ran, once or twice skipping a few steps in sheer high spirits. It was not until she had let off steam and returned safely to her nest again that it occurred to her that she never asked Erin about the paper assignment for *Great Expectations*.

That night Essie thought of home, not as a vague gray longing but as a bright beam. Anything might be possible, even if she could not yet see how.

Gadek said, "We've cut most of our own people loose from the Broome thing, and the FBI has been cut back for some time. They're with us if there's anything to do. They got a call from Cleveland yesterday—some guy who was going to miss his favorite true crime program the night the segment on Jeremy played, so he taped it and just got around to watching it. Said he'd been visiting relatives in Kansas, and they were telling him about some weirdo who just moved in down the road from them and has a little kid. He was sure the kid was Jeremy. The timing seemed about right. The local FBI office is checking it out, but I'm not holding my breath."

"And apart from that . . . ?" said Toby.

"Zip. Well, a smattering—a couple of calls from theorists. An anonymous postcard wanting us to search the house again. But substantially zip."

"Well, where would new leads be coming from? He's probably been dead since day one or two, don't you think?"

"Yeah," said Gadek. "Yeah. That's what I think. But it isn't what I know, and we're still treating it as a life-or-death matter. I can't have people just sitting around waiting for something to turn up, but if anything does, we'll be onto it big time."

# 23

Paul and Jeremy stood on the riverbank below the cabin. Paul was throwing sticks upstream, and Jeremy was trying to hit them with stones as they floated past. Paul leaned over in a kindly way and said, "Okay, I'm going to throw this one a little farther out. You ready for that?" Jeremy nodded a very small nod.

"Feet a little farther apart," said Paul, stick in hand, giving the boy's stance a last check. Some days before, his first attempts at this had been feeble, partly from lack of enthusiasm, but also from utter ignorance of technique. Paul demonstrated, observed the boy's form, critiqued. This was Paul's strength. Now Jeremy was noticeably improved, knew it, and was proud of it.

He adjusted his feet and glanced up at Paul. He got an encouraging smile and a professional-sounding, "That's right. Now, don't take your eyes off it after it hits the water."

Paul threw the stick, and they watched it sweep back along the quick, turbulent surface. The boy threw and raised a splash only inches short.

*"Hey!"* cried Paul. *"Hey!* You almost *had* that sucker! *Outstanding!"*

The boy cracked the faintest glimmer of a smile, not the first that morning. Paul saw it and knew what it meant. It meant that he was coming around, adjusting. It meant that he could not cling to his old life forever.

"But you gotta put more *meat* into it. You can't do it with just your arm. Here's another, and this time I want to see you *lean into* it."

He threw the sticks and cheered or groaned good-naturedly each time. They had been there for a while, but Paul was content to stay as long as the boy's arm held up. Those smiles were virtually the first cracks in the kid's armor. There would be more to come. Then suddenly it would be as if they had been friends always, and the past had never been.

Paul felt at peace for the first time he could remember. He considered in retrospect that he had overestimated the danger that the baby-sitter had represented to him. Most probably she had never noticed him and would not have been able to identify him. In any case, she was not to be found, and with luck, would never be found. The task force had given up trying to find her. Whatever the danger had been, it was past. He was home free, and home was looking up.

*"Hey!"* he cheered. *"You hit that sucker! Outstanding!"*

His whole mistake, if in fact he had made one, was to persevere after the sitter had looked at him. That was a simple error, easy to avoid another time, when another time came, as sooner or later it would. Of course he had been concerned during the time the investigation was hot, but who would not be? The stakes were very high, even if the risk was very small.

And now the boy was beginning to come around.

He certainly was not yet the carefree and uninhibited friend, who was to have been the point of all this fuss, but he would be, given enough time and patience.

In the first days Paul had begun to suspect that he had picked a boy who was simply a joyless personality. He never smiled. He spoke very little and almost entirely in disconnected words or phrases, like a very young child. If he wanted more milk, he would not ask for it; he would nudge his empty glass a little and look in the direction of the refrigerator. This incensed Paul. Clearly he was supposed to say, Oh, would you like some more milk? and then go get it, and serve it like some sort of butler. So Paul chose not to notice any wordless clue that would customarily be expressed as a polite request, and Jeremy did without.

He cringed when Paul approached him, however kindly, which was aggravating in the last degree. He would not hug or express affection in any way. He would not say "please" or "thank you" until Paul instituted a policy of slapping him whenever he forgot these or similar courtesies. Paul felt that it was demeaning to have to enforce the forms of a respect that should be freely rendered to him as an adult, a caregiver, and a friend.

He wet his pants—pushing six years old and still wetting his pants.

It had been very discouraging, but Paul had persevered. He brought little presents, he brought special treats, he was gentle and cajoling. The boy was unresponsive, but he could not hold out indefinitely. Paul had many advantages. He put an end to sullenness and noncooperation with the closet; he enforced respect with quick, sharp punishment. And he was getting results.

"We're out of sticks," Paul said.

"More, please?" said the boy hopefully. He looked shyly at Paul.

"Okay," said Paul indulgently. "Let's go look up

there, under those trees. We've already gotten all the good ones around here."

The boy did not run to the trees—he was still very self-conscious, and careful not to let go—but he walked pretty fast.

It was not that the struggle for his affections was won yet, by any means. Paul realized that. The usual pattern was that if Paul planned some fun sort of time for the two of them, the boy had unspoken conditions or reservations so that there was always some fiasco and it always looked like Paul's fault. Each time Paul swore to himself that he was not going to be provoked, and each time he wound up in the wrong. It made him simply furious, and every time he lost his temper, he knew perfectly well, he set them back again, and that only made him madder.

The boy moved around through the trees, selecting appropriate sticks and bringing them to Paul to carry.

"Maybe this is enough," said Paul.

"More, please," said the boy.

"Well, a few more," said Paul, chuckling. "We have to fix lunch, y'know, and then I have to go to work."

"Work," said the boy, sadly. "Work" meant being locked up in the bathroom.

Paul heard the note in his voice and thought, He doesn't want me to go. He's getting to like me.

Of course, the boy still had plenty of odd ways. If Paul was home, he often lay huddled in his place by the wall for hours together, sometimes playing silently with a toy, sometimes just moping. At night, when he thought Paul was asleep, he would creep out of bed and return there. He was half a night creature, sleeping during the day while Paul was gone, and frequently awake at night. He would take a toy into the bathroom, close the door, turn on the light, and play there—urgent murmuring narrative fantasies, never rising above a whisper. When he did sleep, so far as Paul could tell, he dreamed constantly, jerking and trembling, mumbling and sometimes screaming. Once Paul threw a shoe at him, which panicked him and only made it worse.

And yet, and yet, Paul kept reminding himself, there *had* been progress. There *had* been progress. Control was firmly established. When Paul told him to do something, he jumped to do it. And getting rid of the sulky behavior meant that they could have pleasant times like this one.

"This is it," said Paul, throwing a last stick. "Now we have to get lunch ready."

"More, please?" said the boy.

"What did I just say?" said Paul, suddenly annoyed. He'd been letting the kid have his way all morning, and now everything was an argument. "Eh? Answer me. What did I just say?"

"Lunch," said the boy, looking at the ground, instantly submissive.

"How many times do I have to say things?" demanded Paul. "Eh? I told you that was it, and that had better be the end of it."

"I'm good," whispered the boy. There was a stone in his hand. He dropped it into the trampled grass as unobtrusively as he could.

"Well, sometimes you are and sometimes you aren't," said Paul. "Sometimes you're good, and sometimes you're a royal pain in the ass. I really put myself out for you, and what I expect in return is a little consideration and not a lot of back talk. Get it?"

The boy nodded several times, not looking up.

"Think you can remember? Or do I need to remind you?"

The boy shook his head, holding the rest of himself as still as possible, as if he were invisible. Paul stood over him for a few moments in silence. Then without a word he turned and started back up the hillside toward the cabin. The boy hastened along right behind.

Paul had not realized how much patience would be

required and how much restraint. He had thought that they would be lovers before this. It was very hard to have the boy right there, right next to him, and not do anything about it. He managed it by visualizing their happiness together, not this week, or even next, but soon enough. So Paul was hopeful. Guardedly optimistic. But he had to be alert every minute.

They ate lunch in silence, Paul still paradingly silent and offended, the boy never looking up. He went quickly to the bathroom when Paul called him, and suffered himself to be locked in without a word.

On the way to work Paul wondered if he had been too quick to take offense. They had been having a very pleasant time up until then, and the mood had certainly been spoiled. But he reflected that once you let a kid start making an issue out of just every little thing, that was the end of all peace. It was order and respect that had made the morning possible. No. He had been right. End of subject.

But there were other concerns. As he considered the matter, Paul realized that in planning to keep the boy in his cabin he had not really considered all the security ramifications. Keeping the boy from escaping was taken care of: Paul had nailed wire mesh over all the windows; he installed strong bolts high on the doors and purposely set the sockets askew so that the bolts were not only inaccessible but also required considerable strength to draw. When he had to leave the house, he locked the boy in the bathroom and then locked the front and back doors with keyed dead bolts from the outside. He inspected all these arrangements regularly for signs of tampering and never found any.

But the other big security issue had escaped him: what would happen if suspicion were suddenly to fall upon him, as it conceivably might. The wire mesh and locks he could explain away, but there were clothes—not many, but they were obviously not Paul's. There was an increasing accumulation of toys and games.

And there was the boy himself. What would he do about the boy? He might have very little notice.

After much cogitation on his long drive home that night, he got a flashlight and visited the derelict shed that stood a few yards beyond the kitchen door. The structure was wood frame and corrugated iron sheathing, now largely rusted, and it was all overgrown with blackberry vines. Part of the dirt floor inside was covered with duckboards. He decided that he could lift a section of the flooring and dig a hole underneath. He could leave everything ready just like that. Then if danger threatened, he could simply bury the boy and everything connected to him in the hole, and drop the duckboards back into place. It would look perfectly natural and undisturbed. That ought to do the trick.

Paul's father had been fond of saying, "Never put off until tomorrow what you can do today." The precept sat strangely on the lips of a man who never did anything if it could be put off or avoided altogether. The indolence of Paul's mother precluded even the offering of good advice. But Paul in the earnest stage of childhood had seen competence as an unoccupied niche where he might find distinction, and had bustled about being as helpful as he could. Sometimes this provoked his parents to good-natured ribbing about his efficiency and sometimes to bitter reproaches for trying to be better than his kin. But whether smiling or swearing, they ingrained in him— among many other, less positive concepts—that he was one who sees what is necessary and acts on what he sees.

So the very next morning Paul bustled about the kitchen and began the preparation of a breakfast of unprecedented magnificence. He made the boy come and sit at the kitchen table and butter the toast. Paul believed that the sharing of tasks contributes to a sense of commitment and common purpose, and the toast was merely the beginning of what he intended to be a jolly bonding day. They were going to have breakfast together, and then they were going to go dig the grave in the shed: pick-and-shovel work, like two men. Get sweaty and use bad language and laugh a lot. It would do them both good.

He fried bacon and scrambled reckless quantities of eggs. He poured glasses of orange juice to the very brim, and milk for Jeremy, and coffee for himself. He sang hymns remembered from his days in choir—his face clouding only slightly as he recalled the face of the choirmaster, his first serious adult friend. He repeated the first verse of one hymn several times so that Jeremy could learn it, and then insisted that they sing it together, his booming voice and Jeremy's faint one, until he turned back to the stove and Jeremy's died off altogether. It was a noble spread when at last Paul sat down, rubbed his hands eagerly together, and urged the boy to eat hearty.

The boy's heart sank. He disliked scrambled eggs if they were not very thoroughly cooked, which these were not, and even if they had been his special favorite, he could never have eaten so many as Paul had heaped up on his plate. The butter had been hard and the toast soft, so that he had squashed and mangled the pieces he had buttered. He trembled at what Paul would say when he noticed. He could not possibly eat the two slices in front of him, in any case, and there was more on the table. The bacon was irregularly cooked so that great white gobbits of disgusting undercooked fat obtruded everywhere. He wanted the juice and milk, but the glasses were filled so full that he could never hope to lift them without spilling—a day or two before, Paul had slapped him for spilling. And he recognized plainly in Paul's present manner that artful, squeezed bonhomie which could turn to hurt in a breath, and fury in two breaths.

But he had to do something. Greatly fearing, he took up a slice of toast and bit gingerly into a corner of it. He tried not to meet Paul's eyes.

Paul had not taken his first bite before he could see how his gesture was going to be received. The boy was going to show him that any overtures he might make were overtures thrown away. Paul had made this breakfast? Then Paul could eat it himself or he could scrape it into the garbage, but he was not going to get any thanks or even simple acceptance. Paul's mother had once dropped on his plate a fried egg that was obviously bad—his father refused it, and either Paul or his mother would have to eat it. They made him eat it. Now he was tempted to pile it all on the boy's plate—both their breakfasts, the extra toast, the bacon now congealing in the pan—and make him eat every last bite of it, standing behind his chair and pinching him if he hesitated, as Paul had been—and say, "Thank you, God," after every bite, as he had been made to say. His face began to fill; he was tensing to rise and do it.

Then he remembered his plan for the morning, and with an effort he drew back from the emotional brink. Breakfast was only a part of the day, he told himself—keep things in proportion. You're the grown-up here. Yesterday they had a good time. They could do it again today.

And to show that the boy was not going to be able to make him angry about the breakfast, he folded a piece of toast in two, crammed a large bite into his mouth, added a loud dollop of coffee, and before he had finished chewing it, said jovially, "Listen, buddy, we have got a *job* to do today." He smiled and winked conspiratorially.

"Job?" said the boy.

"A *big* job," said Paul, pressing a slice of bacon into his maw. "Too big a job for me to do by myself. *Much* too big. That's why I need *you* to help me. I figure the two of us can just about get it done today before I have to go to work."

"Work," said the boy. His mouth was dry from the toast, and he was wondering if he dared try to pick up the juice.

"We've got some *excavating* to do. Do you know what *excavating* is?"

The boy shook his head.

"Well, you're about to find out," said Paul. "Every man has to know how to do things. You want to be a man, don't you?"

The boy had been asked that question before and knew that only one answer was acceptable. He nodded gingerly and made a slight sibilant exhalation that might pass for "yes," but in any case was clearly not "no."

"Good," said Paul. "And now, if you're finished with breakfast"—his frustration welled up into his voice at the word, but he controlled it—"we can get going."

He led the way out to the shed and explained about excavation. They lifted a section of the duckboards, and Paul marked out the hole by dragging the end of his pickax through the clay. He explained how one person picks and the other shovels. He took a few strokes with the pick and then stood back and encouraged the boy to go to work with a gardener's trowel. After the boy had gotten out a lump or two, Paul praised him and told him to rest, and then set to work seriously with the pick. They traded tools, and the boy made a few entirely ineffectual attempts while Paul cheered him and interrupted several times to correct his grip and show him how to get the most power out of his swing. Then Paul took his big shovel and cleared what had been loosened; and so they proceeded.

But while Paul was jolly and encouraging, the boy was flat and dutiful. Paul's fantasy was that the boy would get into the spirit of the thing—swinging that pick for all he was worth, laughing and joking about the work and how muddy they were getting, the way Paul was doing. Paul did not expect him to contribute to the progress of the actual work in any great degree, but he did expect him to loosen up and show a little spirit. This was supposed to be quality time.

But the boy was simply being sullen, not taking any sort of interest in the project, and staring out the doorway at the meadow beyond instead of cheering and encouraging Paul as Paul cheered and encouraged him. All through the digging Paul kept up a happy banter, but he was growing more and more offended. He knew how important it is to be patient with children, but it is also important not to reinforce negative behavior. It was hard to judge how to handle a situation like this one.

At length the pit seemed sufficiently large and deep. To make sure, Paul had Jeremy get down into it to dig out the last loose bits in the bottom while he watched. Yes. It was not a very big hole, but it was big enough, and when it was filled in, the duckboards would conceal any telltale irregularities in the surface.

They cleaned the mud off the tools and put them away, and Paul led the way back to the cabin. Before they started he had put two cans of soda in the refrigerator—he had planned this all out—and they were going to sit on the back steps and drink them and laugh and talk about how much work they had accomplished together. But the boy had not broken a smile the whole time, and he was not smiling now. Paul told him to sit on the step while he got the sodas—he had planned each step of this—but the kitchen was still littered with the remains of the calamitous breakfast, the boy's plate practically untouched, and when he came back out, the boy was so whipped looking, so miserable, that Paul finally had to admit to himself that they had not had any sort of bonding experience at all. He thrust the boy's soda into his hand and flopped down on the step beside him, scowling.

He had been knocking himself out all morning for nothing, that was clear. He had been making a fool of himself. Or rather—to be perfectly frank about what had been going on—the boy had been making a fool of him. The boy was taking, taking, taking, and giving nothing back—nothing at all. And Paul would be just *crazy* to put up with it. When a kid does the right thing, you show him that you've noticed and you approve. When he does the wrong thing, you punish him. Or what you wind up with is a sullen, spoiled kid. Paul put down his soda so suddenly that foam burst over the top. He pointed to the boy's.

"Put it down," he said. His brow lowered, his mouth was working. The boy looked up and flinched. "I said *put it down!*" Paul shouted. "Did you *hear* me? *When are you going to put that goddamn can down?*"

The boy did not know what to do. He was terrified of spilling. He put the can down as carefully as he could, holding it with both hands, but what Paul wanted was speed—instant obedience—and not care.

"Stand up," he hissed. He unbuckled his belt and began to pull it free. The boy's eyes widened, but he stood, shifting uneasily from foot to foot, his hands shaking. He did not know what was happening. He was watching Paul's face. A dark stain spread rapidly down the inside of one leg of his pants.

"You're getting a couple of the best," said Paul. "Turn around."

When the boy did not turn instantly Paul clamped one big hand over his shoulder and yanked him around.

*"Sullen little shit,"* Paul shouted, yanking the boy's pants and underpants down to his ankles and forcing him hard over. "Don't you move! Don't you dare move a muscle!"

He stepped back, utterly intent on hurting, suffused

with an exultant sense of his strength, of his power to see that justice was done, as it had never been before in his life. Paul had choked down many grievances, many insults. Not this time. Not any more. He swept the belt out and then swung. It was far less than the full force of his arm, but the belt whizzed in the air and snapped loudly across the bare skin. The boy shrieked from the soul and jerked forward; hobbled by his pants he stumbled and fell over on his face, covering the pink track with his hands as he struggled on the ground, amazement, utter incomprehension, on his face.

*"I told you not to move,"* Paul shouted. *"That one doesn't count. They don't count if you move. You still have two to go. You get back over here right now, and don't be such a sissy."*

Toby ran into Franklin from Juvenile.

"On my way to court," said Franklin, waving a thick sheaf of papers. "This thirty-five-year-old guy is screwing his twenty-five-year-old girlfriend's twelve-year-old daughter. The girlfriend finds out, and what does she do? She starts thumping on her daughter for cutting her out with the boyfriend. One of our people almost ran over them fighting in the middle of the street, which is how it came to our attention. Daughter was winning, too. Big girl."

"Sounds great," said Toby.

"It's great for you," said Franklin. "You don't have to spend hours talking to these specimens. It wears me out. Then I go home and find my wife has rented *Silence of the Lambs.*"

Later, as he drove to work, Paul thought, I guess I kind of lost my temper this morning. He'd try the patience of a saint, but digging that hole was a chore, and kids don't like chores. I have to try to do better than that.

And he wondered if the pit would really be an effective way to conceal the boy, if it came to that. He could sprinkle a lot of pepper around—he thought that would defeat dogs if the searchers used dogs. But the boy's scent would be all over the cabin, to say nothing of fingerprints—how would he deal with that? Paul's job did not involve training in the investigation of crime scenes. He had picked up quite a lot of information here and there, but he was aware that his knowledge was patchy. There were probably very obvious points that had not happened to come under his observation. That was worrisome. He could not very well strike up a conversation with a detective and solicit a lecture on investigations—even if he knew a detective who was on easy terms with him, which he did not. There were training manuals—perhaps he could get his hands on one.

But the whole question made him anxious. He felt as if things hung over him.

It doesn't make me any easier to live with, he thought. It makes me short-fused. That's probably what happened this morning.

Essie found the kitchen full of beauty. She had once noticed in an art museum to which her mother had taken her a small painting in a lush, buttery style showing a kitchen knife with an austere, triangular gray blade lying between the halves of a newly sliced tomato. The viewpoint was a child's, close and low, familiar to Essie. The objects filled the canvas, as if, despite being physically small and common, they were emotionally enormous and important. Essie was still in the completely-on or completely-off stage of childhood and happened, for no explicable reason, to be completely on at that moment. She really looked at this painting.

So it was without surprise, but with a sudden pleasure of recognition, that early in her apprenticeship at Le Coq d'Or Essie noticed one of Harry's knives lying on the cutting board next to three lemons. This prosaic little group she framed tight in her mind's eye, as the painter of *Tomato and Knife* had done, and transformed them into something monumental, symbolic of life's richness. Farther along the table a bunch of bright parsley and a row of boned chicken breasts were reflected, with surreal distortion, in a stainless-steel mixing bowl. Beautiful things, wonderful conjunctions created by the chance operations of the kitchen, coming and going all the time.

Wow, she thought.

She was still in the early stages of these discoveries one afternoon when Emile appeared, heading out to the alley for a smoke. In a sudden moment of confidence Essie stopped him and showed him the way the big pepper grinder cast a shadow of fantastic shape tinted bright red by the light reflected from a box next to it. "It's so pretty," she said. He looked and agreed that it was. She showed him the stove opposite, the gas burning with a pure blue flame against the intense black deep inside the burner ring. He laughed with a quick, unfeigned joy.

"It 'as been there all the time, and I never saw eet," he said in his wonderful French accent, looking straight in her eyes and laughing again. "You are a *funny* kid." Their faces were very close. He dipped forward and kissed her on the mouth, lingering for a moment, working her lips gently with his own. Then he straightened up and said again, "You are *funny,* Jo," winked, and went out for his cigarette.

*Wow!* thought Essie. Her knees wobbled. She had never been kissed half so smoothly or half so well. *Wow!*

Moments later he was back in the doorway, calling her delightedly to the alley door, and pointed out how two power poles were at some distance from each other, but how their shadows lay together—and here he dropped his voice into a mock-confidential, mock-lubricious tone and murmured, *"Like lovers."* He laughed, and when she tittered nervously, he laughed again and said, "You *are* funny."

Essie was delighted and flattered and a little scared.

Later she watched while Harry boned a leg of lamb. Her mind kept slipping off. To discipline her attention she concentrated on how beautiful it was to see, the knife silvery against the deep red muscle and the pallid bone. But her mind kept slipping, just the same. Emile had so much style, and she loved the way he talked. He was sweet and didn't patronize. He must be attracted to her, at least a little. She had never thought that she could be attractive to anyone like that, an older man. It was altogether exciting, and once or twice she blushed suddenly, spontaneously, at a new turn in her train of thought.

At the end of the afternoon she did not hear Nathan come into the kitchen.

"Well," he said, "aren't you busy." He pretended that he had to squeeze between Essie and the wall, and as he passed he dipped down and dragged his crotch lingeringly across her behind.

"Hey, stop it!" she said.

Harry looked up from his knife. "Leave her alone," he said.

Nathan wheeled on him, angry and tight. "Don't give me orders," he said.

"Leave her alone," said Harry. He turned back to his task.

*"I can look at her ass any time I want to,"* Nathan said loudly.

Nobody answered him. Harry julienned. Al sautéed. Jim scoured. Essie diced. Stove hissed and freezer hummed.

"Any time I want to," repeated Nathan. But then he left the kitchen.

Essie's lips formed the words, Thank you, Harry, but for shame she could not pronounce them. She felt tiny and toylike, and she did not like it. At the first opportunity she retreated to the ladies' room. It was a refuge in that all-male establishment, and in the late afternoon, when there were no diners, she could retire for a few minutes to be alone. There was a full-length mirror on the wall opposite the door. She peered at herself unhappily. Le Coq d'Or catered to a stylish clientele. Emile and Nicky and Charles, Arthur—Nathan, too, to be fair—they all looked great and moved well, full of confidence. She felt newly, urgently dissatisfied with herself.

There had been a woman diner the evening before who had stood in the doorway for a few minutes, watching the kitchen. She wore a tiny black minidress and very long bare legs and very short bleached hair, but thick dark eyebrows and purple lipstick. She watched them slaving away with the chin-up, all-devouring air of one who does what she likes and never takes shit from anyone. She seemed interested in what Essie was doing, which made Essie feel important and professional. A moment later she wiggled her nose and disappeared into the ladies' room.

It was a bold look and a bold front, and Essie was impressed. It had never occurred to her that she could be like that, but now suddenly it seemed highly desirable to try. Perhaps if she got the look, the manner would follow. She knew that the dress was out of the question, and the hair, and she wasn't sure about the eyebrows. She wondered if she could pull off purple lipstick. She stared unhappily into the mirror. She thought, Probably not.

She could discuss it on the phone with Erin and Lizby—that was a consolation.

She wondered if she had the raw materials of glamour. The thought of her reindeer sweater made her flinch. It was all right for a pillow in her nest, but she would never, ever wear it again. She pictured herself standing beside Emile, her arm through his, and knew the picture was ridiculous. She wanted to weep. She thought, I wish I wasn't so *mousy* all the time. I wish I could be a little bold.

She thought of the young woman as "the bold girl," and pondered her example a great deal.

Erin had promised a lot when she promised that Lizby would be on hand to receive Essie's next call. The night in question, after all, was a Tuesday, and they would both have homework.

Erin's parents were not a problem; they were in the midst of agonizing over the question of a nursing home for Erin's grandmother and had little thought for anything else. Erin offered a plausible explanation having to do with Lizby coming over so that they could quiz each other on Japanese vocab. Her parents looked thoughtful—which was what they always thought necessary when called upon for judgments— and then said doubtfully, Very well, just this once— which was what they usually said.

Lizby had a more difficult problem. Her parents had no current crises to distract them. They believed in regularity of habit as desirable in itself, and since Lizby was their third child, they had a veteran ear for improbable explanations. A further obstacle was that Lizby disliked lying to her parents, whom she respected. After pondering various approaches, she decided to tell at least part of the truth—that she and

Erin had things to talk about; she promised to get her homework done—they did, in fact, have some Japanese vocab—and besides, she had been good for just weeks and weeks. This was accepted, and after dinner her father drove her to Erin's.

Now Erin and Lizby huddled on Erin's bed, heads together, each with an ear to the receiver between them while Essie enthused as much as she dared about Emile. When that subject exhausted the few known facts and reached the realm of pure speculation, Erin searched her notes for the paper assignment for *Great Expectations.*

"Okay," said Erin, "it's, uh, compare and contrast . . . uh, loyalty and ambition as Pip and Joe understand it. Two to three pages."

"Oh, wow," said Essie.

"I don't know why you're doing this to yourself," said Erin.

"It makes me feel connected," said Essie simply.

"Well, look, Ess," said Erin, "like, there are better ways of feeling connected."

"You can't just stay out there," Lizby said. "You could tell us where you were if you weren't worried about it."

"No," said Essie. "'Cause if anyone finds out you've been talking to me, all you have to say is you don't know where I am, and it'll be the truth."

"I think you ought to trust us, Ess," said Erin, a little stiffly. "I mean, it's not as if someone's going to say, Tell, and we'll be all like, Sure, or something. Anyway, you ought to be somewhere safe."

"I'm safe," said Essie. "And anyway, there isn't anyplace else."

"That is simply not *so,*" said Erin. "That is simply *way* untrue. We were talking about it today. There are the hills up behind Addie's house. You could have a tent up there, and we could bring you food and stuff."

"Or Carol's cousin lives in a dorm," said Lizby.

"It's a megatiny room, but people stay there all the time. You could stay with her."

"I don't think so," said Essie.

"Well, how about staying with Rhea?" said Erin. "It's a humongous house, and her parents pay, like, *no* attention to anything anyway. They're never home, and when they *are* home, they're completely drunk. They never have family dinner or watch TV together or *anything.* Rhea could tell them someone is coming for the weekend, and then you could just stay and stay and stay, and they'd never notice how long it'd been."

"Guess again," said Essie, who had spent the night at Rhea's several times and thought it was the loneliest place she knew. "Look, guys, what's the big deal? What's wrong with how things are?"

"I wish you could hear your voice," said Lizby. "What about Heather? Maybe she could think of something. Have you called her?"

"It's not fair to call Heather," said Essie. "Her stepdad's a cop. It puts her wrong, whatever she does."

"Anyway, *you* don't think things are right," said Erin. "You know you totally don't. And we don't, either. Like who is this old lech who kissed you, anyway?"

"He's not an old lech," said Essie. "He's twenty-six. I heard him say something about it to . . . to someone else."

"He really kissed you right there?" said Lizby. "God, Ess, be careful. Your mom'd wet her pants if she knew."

That was perfectly true. Essie had thought of it before, and it weighed with her.

"He's twice your age. You could *really* mess up," said Erin.

"There's nothing to be careful about," said Essie, glum again. She was not glamorous enough for Emile. "Nothing's happened."

"What's *happened* isn't what you have to be careful about," said Lizby. "It's what's *happening*."

"Nothing's happening," said Essie, who thought that nothing probably was. "And anyway, he is *not* twice my age. He's twenty-six, not twenty-eight."

# 25

When Essie came down the ladder on Wednesday prior to making her usual midafternoon entrance, she saw that the vehicle door in Kit's building was up—something she had never seen before. A van with the name of a commercial cleaning company was parked just inside, and several men were hard at work on the large empty space beyond. A trash Dumpster filled the narrow setback by the staircase door, which was wedged open. A relaxed-looking woman with a long iron gray ponytail, a workshirt, and jeans, supervised the work. A Mom sort of woman, to Essie's eye.

"Hi," said the woman when she noticed Essie across the alley. There was nothing shy or coy about the greeting.

"Hi," said Essie politely.

"You one of my new neighbors?" said the woman.

"I work here," said Essie.

"Well, I'm going to be working here," said the woman. "Downstairs. I'll be living upstairs."

A workman appeared at the door with an armload of debris. He heaved this into the Dumpster and disappeared upstairs again.

"The previous tenant wasn't a neatness freak," said the woman. "It's a real mess up there."

"Kit's *gone?*" said Essie. She felt a huge *whoosh!* She felt lighter by tons, a great dancing-off from her shoulders.

"Friend of yours? The landlord just said the guy had been stiffing him on the rent. Also that he was a pimp. He came last week with eviction papers—more exercised about the rent than the pimping, it seemed to me—and found he'd already moved on. I've been looking for a live-in studio space, so here I am."

*"God!"* said Essie. It was good news—really good news. The alley, virtually her only way in and out, was suddenly converted from a gauntlet to the cheerful lane it had seemed when she first laid eyes on it. Unthinking, she beamed and skipped a step.

"I guess you're not going to miss Kit," said the woman.

"Nope! Not much," said Essie, beaming.

The workman appeared again with another armload in which Essie noticed several of her own things.

"Wait!" she said. The workman stood looking at her, load raised above the Dumpster; the woman looked.

"Uh, some of those . . ." Essie did not want to acknowledge any sort of connection with Kit. "Uh, some of those things look like they might fit me," she said, and then added truthfully, "I don't have a lot of money."

"Okay," said the woman. "Let's look." The workman dumped the pile on the ground and went back upstairs. Essie came across the alley and picked out her sweatshirt and her gym duffel. There was some of her underwear, too, but she could not very well claim what was supposed to be unidentified underwear in front of this woman. There was a pair of expensive jeans, two designer T-shirts, and a silk blouse— perhaps they had belonged to the scared girl. There was a sailor's dark blue peacoat, heavy and new and almost small enough. Essie picked them out.

"Well, that's good stuff," said the woman. "Good

thing for you I'm too big to wear those things. *Much too big*," she said, and laughed without evident amusement. Then she nodded at the doorway opposite and said, "What is that, a restaurant?"

"Yeah," said Essie. "Le Coq d'Or. It's really good. You'll like it."

"Sounds pricey. Your dad runs it or something?"

"Uh, no," said Essie. "I have a job there. After school."

"But you live around here?"

"Yeah," said Essie.

"Well, I'll be moved in in a day or two. Come visit me. We'll have a cup of tea and you can tell me all about the restaurant business. You won't have any competition from me. I figure God would never have given us the microwave if she hadn't meant us to get a lot of use out of it." She laughed again. Then she held out her hand and said, "I'm Charlotte, by the way."

"I'm Essie," said Essie, taking Charlotte's hand and then suddenly turning red.

"Glad to meet you, Essie," said Charlotte, a little surprised, because she had noticed. "That's a nice name. Is that like Esther?"

"Uh, yeah," said Essie, and thought, Omi*god!* How could I have done that?

"But everyone calls me Jo. I don't really like 'Essie' very much." She was flustered, and it showed. It was a moment before Charlotte said, "Well, okay, Jo."

I *think* that'll be okay, Essie thought later. God, I *hate* telling lies—it's so hard to remember. The bold girl wouldn't have made a mistake like that—she'd always be *so* together.

But it was wonderful to know that Kit was gone. And much as she loved her friends and the telephone, she thought that someone live—someone older, to drink tea with—a Mom sort of person—would be very nice. Perhaps Essie could talk to her about Emile.

\* \* \*

The lobby of the Bancroft Hall of Justice is large and unadorned. Walls and ceiling of smooth plaster, floor of linoleum. Everything echoes. Twin staircases lead from the ground floor level, vulnerable to gunfire from the street, up to the front counter on the second floor. Bulletproof glass divides the counter into outer and inner halves and rises to the ceiling, with little burrows such as boys make under school yard fences to pass small objects back and forth. Visible through the glass is an alcove with two desks and two filing cabinets, and beyond that a partition and a sliver of Service Division. Small metal speaking grilles are provided at a height convenient for abnormally tall people, but they are ineffective; whatever their stature, and however painful or private their business, everyone must speak loudly to be heard on the other side.

Just opposite the counter is a line of chairs where citizens wait while the person they need to speak to is paged through the building or summoned in from the street. The entertainment here is to read the lists of bail bondsmen, notices for service organizations, posters for hotlines, guides to associated city services, and the placard with jail visiting hours and rules, and to listen to the shouted troubles of other people.

"Weird place," said Erin, full-voiced, at the top of the stairs.

*"Shhh,"* said Lizby, appalled at the echo. Some of the people waiting glanced up, and a dirty, tired-looking man ran his eye frankly and systematically over their bodies from neck to knee, first Lizby's, then Erin's.

The counter has a button in the middle with a sign taped to the glass next to it saying, For Service Ring ONCE. Erin mashed the button firmly, and a raucous buzzer sounded somewhere beyond the partition.

No one came.

"The service here is terrible," said Erin quite soon,

bouncing the button again several times. The buzzer stuttered, and her voice echoed around the bare lobby.

Lizby hissed, "Keep your voice down."

"It's a free country, isn't it?" said Erin as loud as before. The people on the chairs looked up, then away. The tired-looking man laughed out loud and goggled openly at her chest. She tried glaring at him. "It's a free country," he said, and goggled again.

Sergeant Wren appeared abruptly. Looking back and forth between Erin and Lizby, he wrapped the sign by the button with his knuckle and said, "It says, ring once."

"It says, for service," said Erin. "My dad pays all kinds of taxes. Anyway, we have a question."

"I wouldn't pay taxes to this goddamn country," said the tired-looking man, "but I was here first. And I'm entitled to some service, too." He jerked his chin at Erin. "Even if I haven't got big tits."

"I've explained to you, my friend," said Sergeant Wren, his voice cloudy behind the heavy glass, "that the officer you want to see is . . ."

"I don't *want* to see him. I *gotta* see him. Maybe if I had big tits I *would* see him."

". . . is out on another case. He knows you're here, and he'll be in as soon as he can. And if you can't wait *quietly,*" said Sergeant Wren, raising his voice, because the man was opening his mouth again, "if you can't wait without annoying other people, then you'll have to leave. And that's the last I want to hear from you. The *last,*" he said, raising his hand firmly and holding it until the man sank back in his chair.

"And now, young ladies." Having secured his flank, he turned again to face the new assault. His fingers tapped impatiently on the countertop, his chin jutted slightly, his eyebrows arched. Lizby dropped her eyes, but Erin stared directly back. After a moment her own eyebrows arched, and she said, "Never mind."

"You have some police problem?" said Sergeant Wren, his voice seeming to come from a great distance.

"No," said Erin. "We thought we did, but we don't. C'mon, Liz."

One of Sergeant Wren's elevated eyebrows flickered. He turned abruptly and disappeared behind the partition. The tired-looking man laughed and leaned forward to watch their legs as they headed for the stairs. "Love the free country!" he shouted after them, and his guffaw rang around the lobby for some time after they were gone.

"Well, that was really great," Erin said outside. "That really cleared the situation up for *me*. Got any more great suggestions like asking the cops what to do? Let's hear 'em. We'll try 'em out. The night is still young."

"I just wanted to know what would happen if they found out where she was," said Lizby.

"And now you know," said Erin.

Heather arrived punctually for the Parkmans' evening out, and on this evening her manner was as it had formerly been, warm and cheerful and a little shy. She hugged Sara and smiled happily at Toby. He was misled by this chance moment in her pendulum passage to adulthood. He had opened the door to leave when on an impulse he closed it again and said, "Look, Heather, I hope you won't be offended if I ask you this—I know you've been asked before. Do you know anything that might help us find Essie? Has Walt explained why we're worried about her?"

It was a mistake, he saw instantly; she frosted, face and figure, like a cold glass in a breath of warm air.

"He's told me that Essie might be able to identify Jeremy Broome's kidnapper," she said in a voice redolent of unshakable good breeding, looking him directly in the eye. "He's talked to me about drugs and AIDS and homelessness and sexual degradation." She tossed her head. "I know why you're worried. I worry about her, too, all the time."

*"Heather,"* called Adam from upstairs.

"Just a minute, you guys," she called back. "I'm talking to your dad." From the tone of her voice, she might have been saying, I'm cutting out your dad's liver. She turned back to Toby and said, "Essie never told me what she had in mind. She hasn't called me. I haven't had any contact with her. I have no secrets at all about this." After the slightest hesitation, she added, "And if I had, I would keep them."

"Ah," said Toby. "Well, sorry. But I had to ask."

"Of course," she said. "I understand."

"Well," said Sara brightly. "If that's it, perhaps we should get going."

In the car she said, "It must be very difficult for her, getting grilled every time she turns around." Toby said nothing.

Erin and Lizby huddled cross-legged side by side on Erin's bed, the telephone in front of them, the receiver pressed between their ears. They had been waiting for Essie's call. When it came, it was hard to hear because there was a diesel truck idling right beside the phone booth, but they had important business and they began at once.

"Look, Ess," said Erin, "we need to talk. Can you hear okay?"

"Yeah, I can hear." Her voice floated on a thick plasma of engine noise.

"You sound like you're on Mars or someplace," said Erin. "Anyway, listen. We had a bitchfest yesterday—only it wasn't really a bitchfest because Robert and Elliott were there—we didn't think you'd mind. And listen. We think this whole thing is just *way* stupid. Right, Lizby?"

"Right," said Lizby.

"And it isn't just us. Addie thinks so, too, and Latasha and Moll and Rhea. God, even Shelly. Well, Shelly said there was no rush."

"Stretching like a cat," said Lizby.

"*Right* in front of Elliott," said Erin. "And didn't his eyes bug out. But everyone just *totally* thinks you're being unfair, making us all worry about you all the time. And we've talked about it, and we have a list of demands. Listen, can you hear me? There's so much noise."

"I can hear you," said Essie, sounding very far away.

A mechanical voice demanded more money, and Erin impatiently reversed the charges. "And tell that truck driver to go park his truck somewhere else," she said. "Anyway, we're your friends. You owe us *something*. Right?"

"Right," said Lizby, but noise was all they could hear at the other end.

"Okay, listen," said Erin. She smoothed a much-crumpled piece of blue-lined binder paper. "We know you're around here somewhere. We want to know where you are so we know you're okay and we don't have to worry about you all the time—like we worry about this twenty-six-year-old boyfriend of yours who sounds like *really* bad news to me."

"He's not a boyfriend," said Essie.

"No?" said Erin. "You're *sure?* Anyway, that's number one, we get to know where you are. And we want to be able to come see you, like on weekends and things, and bring you money and make sure you've got clothes and take you out to eat. That's number two. And number three—and we want you to *listen* to this, just *listen,* okay?—we want to go talk to your parents and try to work something out. 'Cause there's *gotta* be *some* way, there's just *gotta.* That's number three. And we won't tell *anyone.* But you have to trust us, 'cause we're your friends. Right, Ess?"

For a long moment there was no sound but the truck.

Lizby said, "Ess, your mom and dad were on TV the day after you ran away. They sounded *so* wrecked." She paused, but there was no answer at the other end. She said, "They really, really, really messed up, but they want you back in the worst way."

A passing bus drowning even the truck.

"Ess?" said Erin.

The distant voice said, "Is there anything new about Jeremy?"

Erin and Lizby looked at each other.

"Oh, *c'mon,* Ess," said Erin, but Lizby twisted the receiver around and said, "No, Ess. Nothing new."

Just the sound of their breathing and the throb of the truck. Then Erin twisted the receiver back and said, "Ess, you have to think things through, girl. Maybe it isn't going to change, y'know? Maybe there isn't going to be any news about Jeremy. Maybe this is a permanent situation. God, get real. You can't just . . ."

They could just hear her say, "I have to go," and she hung up.

"Well, shit," said Erin, snapping down the receiver.

"God," said Lizby, slumping back against the wall. "God, she sounded so far away."

On their way home, Sara suggested the desirability of some slight expression of regret to Heather. Toby did not consider that any such expression was required, but he was careful to be friendly when he paid her. She paused in the doorway as she left, and without quite looking him in the eye said, "I'm sorry if I was rude," with only the slightest emphasis on the "if."

Half an hour later Melanie called to ask if Heather had left yet. "I'm sure it's okay," she said to Sara. "She probably stopped in to visit someone on her way home. She doesn't have to be in for another twenty minutes."

"You sound worried," said Sara.

"I worry about Heather all the time these days," said Melanie. "I don't know that anything is going on, but all that means is that I don't know whether it is or not. If I could be sure that being unpleasant to me was the worst thing she was doing, I could be philosophical and wait it out. That's what *my* mother did—I blush to think about it. But of course I *don't* know.

"And then she's up and down all the time. If she were just consistently abusive I could brace for it, but she isn't. She'll be sweet and responsible for days at a time. It's like having a sister in the house, someone really close. It's quite wonderful. I fall into it, and then, boom! something heartless. That's the worst—never knowing what to expect. Anyway, I get anxious, and now that she's driving, it's worse than ever.

"I don't stay up until her curfew—I'm too tired—but I've got so I wake up spontaneously about ten minutes before she's supposed to come in. I lie in bed listening for the car. She stays out until the last possible moment. I don't know how she does it. Maybe she parks up the street and waits.

"Anyway, a few days ago we had one of those pointless set-tos, and she huffed out. I was uneasy all evening. I was going to stay up until she got home so we could talk about it, but I fell asleep, reading in bed.

"But a few minutes before the hour, sure enough, I

woke up. I lay there listening. I felt so anxious. Then all of a sudden, right out loud I said, 'Lord, protect her.' Then I thought, Where did *that* come from? I'm not religious. It just popped out.

"But the funny thing was, I felt better. And a minute later I heard her car coming down the street. I listened to her pull in and the engine die. The hand brake. The car door opening and closing. I listened to her come trotting up the driveway and her key in the door. I listened to her moving around in the kitchen and then her footsteps on the stairs. There was nothing hasty or abrupt, the way she moves when she's upset. I thought, She's all right.

"Well, religious or not, fair is fair. I said, 'Thank you' out loud. She was just outside my door, and she heard me say it. She thought I was speaking to her, being sarcastic. She said, 'I was home *on time.* I was *downstairs.*' She said it in a very bitchy way.

"I let it go. Maybe I'll explain it to her in a year or two, if it still seems important then."

# 27

Paul often listened to the radio on his long commutes, and on several occasions he had heard discussions of child-rearing. He had not paid much attention to them at the time, but increasingly he brooded on the subject. It was becoming clear to him that having a single child on a long-term basis was quite different than coaching a team a few times a week or taking a small group for a weekend—that all sorts of novel and unanticipated problems arose over time that would have to be surmounted if his dream were to be realized.

Paul had to admit to himself that he was stymied. He did not know how to break through the boy's emotional passivity—or canny, intractable hostility, whichever it was. He had to admit that he was, in the phrase of one of the experts he had heard, "deficient in parenting skills." That belting, for example, had probably been a mistake. It had certainly relieved Paul's feelings, but it had reduced the boy to shrieking panic. If Paul had actually insisted that each belt did not count if the boy jumped or yelped, why, they'd still be there by the back steps, belting and howling. When Paul came home that night, the boy was so scared he soiled his pants. Paul had been feeling some contrition about the morning, and so he controlled himself—when *Paul* did that as a boy, his mother rubbed the pants in his face—but of course he was angry, and the boy was white and literally shaking.

Now, here was precisely the sort of parenting dilemma that bewildered Paul. He had come home in a forgiving mood, with a little fantasy about how the next couple of hours might pass: there was a particular video they could watch, which he hoped would loosen up the boy a bit. That would have pleased Paul very much. It was not a certainty that the boy would enjoy it—he seemed to be frightened by that video when last Paul played it; but since he was also no doubt contrite for having angered Paul, and since Paul would regard cheerful cooperation as a very great amelioration of the boy's offense, was not the generous thing to offer him the opportunity of atonement rather than having everybody going to bed mad? Paul found that a very hard call to make at the time, and no clearer when he thought about it afterward.

What does someone with *superior* parenting skills do with a morose child? In his coaching days Paul had been around plenty of parents, but he had never been much interested in noticing what they did. Paul's interest lay in the children of parents who were distracted or absent; an active, effective parent meant nothing but trouble, and Paul had as little to do with them as he could. He had to admit that it was a fault of his character that he did not pay attention to things unless he had an immediate, practical need for the information.

On the other hand, once he knew he needed to know something, he was energetic enough about finding out. And having recognized that he needed guidance, he determined to act without delay. He would leave the cabin a couple of hours early, go to Bancroft, and hang around a park until it was time to go to work. Some of these mothers were obviously very skillful in getting what they wanted out of their children. He would be a diligent student, and observe how they did it.

And on the way, he would go by a bookstore and see what they had in the way of self-help works on the subject.

He felt a surge of that new energy that comes with a new resolve. Every problem has its solution—you only have to find it. Instead of having lunch together, as usual, Jeremy was locked in the bathroom with two sandwiches—one for lunch, and the other for dinner—and Paul was on the road, all before eleven.

Not long after noon he was seated on a bench in a small neighborhood park. In his lap lay a copy of *The Perfect Parent,* which had caught his eye by its cover photo of a smiling man gently pitching a ball to an eager, worshipful boy of about Jeremy's age. There was no one else in the park, but he knew the pattern at these places: Some little group of mothers will arrive all at once, by prearrangement, so that they can chat while their children play. One minute a park is empty, and the next there are a dozen kids. He unwrapped his sandwich, poured out a cup of coffee, and carefully, so as not to get greasy fingermarks on the pages, Paul Greber turned to the first chapter of *The Perfect Parent*.

# 28

When Essie left work around eight she saw through the open back door that her new neighbor was visible in one of the upstairs windows, and instead of ducking sideways to the ladder, she went on across the alley and knocked. The window opened.

"Who?" called Charlotte from above.

"It's Jo from the restaurant," said Essie, stepping back into the alley where she could be seen, anxious not to stand for long where anyone who came to the back door of the restaurant could not miss seeing her.

"Sec," called Charlotte, and disappeared. A moment later she was back with a key on an enormous metal ring, which she threw down. "Be sure the door catches behind you," she called.

She was waiting at the top of the stairs.

"It's nice to see you," said Charlotte. "I don't seem to be working tonight."

The warren of dingy little rooms Essie remembered was clean and white, still smelling strongly of fresh paint, with paintings and drawings leaning and hung and pinned up everywhere.

"So many paintings and things," said Essie, who was accustomed to slightly gray reproductions of the Old Masters, one per wall.

"It's what I do," said Charlotte.

"You're an artist?" said Essie, who had never known an artist, but had a distinct mental image of intense, disheveled, jowly men with a propensity to depression and drink.

"Me being an artist is a subject of dispute," said Charlotte, "but I did all this stuff."

"Wow," said Essie.

"I might as well enjoy 'em," said Charlotte. "I'm sure not selling 'em. They say hot painters live in bare rooms," she added sadly. She showed Essie into a room that had been padlocked under Kit's administration and was now sparsely furnished as a living room. A television in the corner was tuned to the news. The anchor was concluding one story about a lurid domestic dispute and beginning another about a predatory attack on a helpless widow when Charlotte turned off the sound, leaving the head mouthing harmlessly.

"Surprising how little difference it makes whether you have the sound on or off," she said, nodding at the screen, which showed an uninformative shot of an emergency room and the back of somebody's bandaged head before returning to the anchor. "But it's company." She waved to a chair. "Ever been up here?"

"No," said Essie.

"Landlord said that besides being a pimp, this guy Kit was a weirdo. I guess he must have been. This room was where he kept his dirty magazines. Had a zillion of 'em. A lot of stuff about underage girls. Stone shit. 'Put 'em in the Dumpster,' I told the cleaners. But I think they took 'em home."

Charlotte was drinking wine. She put out another glass and poured.

"Uh, no . . ." began Essie, but Charlotte did not hear. She held out the glass.

"Thanks," said Essie, taking it, wondering how her mother would handle this.

"Sure. But hey, *you're* an underage girl. Kit would have liked you. Got a boyfriend?"

"No," said Essie reflexively. But when Charlotte smiled, she said, "Well, kind of." Emile would not say so, but Charlotte was asking her, not him.

"'Kind of'?" said Charlotte with a droll groan. "'Kind of' doesn't cut it. You oughta have 'Definitely!' You oughta have 'You bet!' Everybody oughta have a boyfriend. Hell, *I* oughta have a boyfriend. I had a husband till a couple of months ago. Much good *that* did me. Well, anyway . . ." she held out her glass ". . . cheers."

Essie said, "Cheers," a little awkwardly, took a sip, and looked dubious. Charlotte said, "Not a heavy drinker, I guess."

"Not too much," said Essie.

"Well, hey, you don't have to . . . what else have I got? There must be . . ."

"No, no, that's okay," said Essie, taking the plunge. Wine wasn't so bad. She was drinking wine with an artist. That was kind of neat—Erin and Lizby would be impressed. She didn't have to drink the whole thing. Or who knows? Maybe she'd get the hang of it.

The silent television flashed images of sleek cars and seminude women.

"My ex could never figure out why I cared about painting," said Charlotte. "He thought painting for a lady meant diddling around with watercolors on weekends. He didn't want me to be serious about it, let alone good at it. He wasn't very interested in my having anything he hadn't given me. He tried to get me to take an interest in cooking lessons instead. Can you believe that?"

"Yeah," said Essie, and then, "I mean, no."

"Crazy," said Charlotte. She gazed glumly around her. "He'd be delighted to see all this stuff piling up, the son of a bitch. My dealer's an old friend of a friend of his. I'm beginning to wonder if that's my problem."

Charlotte enjoyed talking, and she had been by herself more than usual. Essie was content to listen, sitting in a chair in a normal room with an adult, sipping wine. It made her feel a little fixed, a little less at the mercy of the elements. She felt relaxed as she had not been in weeks, and the more she became aware of it, the more she enjoyed being there, listening and laughing at the funny parts, until Charlotte stopped in the middle of something and said, *"Hey!* I've just remembered who you are."

For a moment they gazed at each other, Charlotte delighted, Essie dumbstruck.

"The angel of silence has passed over us," said Charlotte, and chuckled amiably enough. Then she said, "Jo—Essie—whatever. *You* are the missing baby-sitter."

Essie stirred suddenly in her chair, and Charlotte said, "Aw, relax. You must have figured *somebody* in San Francisco would catch the news. I guess I'm the one."

"Oh, God," Essie murmured. She had been completely out of touch herself. "It was on the news?"

"You bet. Weeks ago. News conference, the whole bit—your parents, I guess—a tall stick-up-the-ass couple with glasses and—what would you say—noses? Those were your parents?"

"Oh, God," said Essie. These could only be her parents. "What did they say?"

"Well, I don't know exactly," said Charlotte, scratching her chin. "I had the sound off. But they showed the boy's picture, and I knew who he was, and they showed your picture. I'd heard about it. Two and two, y'know. I guess they wanted you to come back."

"Oh, God."

"I've been scratching my head over it since the other day, trying to remember where I'd seen your face."

"Oh, God."

"Well, don't hit the panic button," said Charlotte.

"I'm not going to do anything about it. I believe in leaving people alone. You look like you can make your own decisions."

Essie gulped. She would not have made such a claim on her own behalf, but she did not want to be sent home. She looked at the floor and held her tongue. Charlotte was saying something about parents not owning kids, and beginning to expatiate on the institution of the family. Essie tried to listen, but she was not equal to a sociological discussion. She had been frightened. She pictured herself being brought home, walked up to the door between two policemen. Their steely fingers would go all the way around her arms so that their fingers and thumbs met on the other side. She pictured her mother opening the door, looking distracted at first, then seeing who it was who trembled there.

"I told my husband right at the get-go—no kids," Charlotte was saying. "I don't have the training for it. I'd only bungle it, like *my* parents. I figure history can go repeat itself somewhere else—it's not as if the world isn't up to the eyeballs in people already. Well, that was fine with him. He'd had a kid with his first wife. Said it spoiled her figure, they couldn't have sex for months, she leaked milk at night and made the sheets smell sour—he wanted her to go sleep in the spare room because of the smell, and they had a big fight about it. And that was just the beginning."

Essie shifted uneasily. She had two young cousins, and some details—quite a different selection of details—of their entrance into the world and the attendant consequences to their parents had been imparted to her, but in a more joyful and reverent spirit.

"So anyway, look, I figure it's none of my business. You seem to be keeping body and soul together. You want to be Jo, well, Jo you will be. I won't pry. I've got my own troubles."

"Okay," said Essie.

"But all I can say is, those guys in your restaurant must keep their noses to the grindstone if they haven't heard about you."

"I guess they do," said Essie.

Then Charlotte surprised Essie and said, "Do you *want* to go home?"

Essie longed for her home-before-all-this-happened, but that was not what "home" meant to her anymore. Now "home" meant where-everything-is-painful. She said, "No," meaning, I don't see how it would be possible to go home, and Charlotte said, "Okay," meaning, It's your call.

Then Charlotte began to describe some of the instances of intrafamilial heartbreak and bitterness that had come within her experience. Essie's mind drifted. A tall, stick-up-the-ass couple with glasses and noses. Who else could it be? She wondered what they had said.

Charlotte was refilling Essie's glass, but she scarcely noticed. She sipped politely and nodded at the hesitations in Charlotte's voice. She wondered what people at home were thinking of her. She studied Charlotte's face, trying to make her out. Of all the people in the world who might know who she was, this was the one who had made the connection. Essie thought that in principle, at any rate, it was a relief that there was somebody she could be open with. There was great relief in sharing secrets with the right person. She shared many secrets with Erin and Lizby, and when the door was closed, they would bitch them over in luxurious unreserve, a tumbling flood of words rattling and overlapping and hugging and giggling or weeping, as occasion suggested.

On the silent television a small man, camera-badgered in heartless closeup, lashed by the video lights, wept frantically in some bleak and featureless corridor. Charlotte was describing the peccadilloes of a certain aunt.

She lost the thread.

Charlotte was shaking her gently by the shoulder.

"Hey," she said. "Hey. Time to wake up. Time to go to bed."

"Oh, wow," said Essie, only half present. She struggled to her feet.

"I talked you out," said Charlotte, laughing, as they descended the stairs. "Sure you can get home okay?" This struck Essie as immoderately funny, and she burst into giggles.

"Shurrr," she said, in teen dialect. "No prob," and giggled again.

"Well, g'night," said Charlotte.

"G'night," said Essie.

The door closed, and Charlotte's footfalls could be heard on the stairs.

Essie took a step into the alley, which swayed slightly. She stopped.

*"Omigod!"* she said out loud. "I'm *tipsy."*

Essie had never been tipsy and rarely seen anyone who was. Her mother, whom Essie had never seen affected by drink, reproved words such as *tipsy* as mere evasions of the word *drunk,* but Essie could see now that there was a worthwhile distinction between those two conditions. She would have to explain that to her mother—if the opportunity ever . . . oh, dear.

The restaurant door was ten feet away. It seemed like a long distance, but she set herself to reach it. Then she discovered her mistake. Nicky's green convertible still sat close along the rear wall of the restaurant by the alley door, but the door itself was closed and, as she discovered by pressing on it, barred on the other side. The restaurant was closed for the night, and she was locked out.

The wind gusted down the alley. She was cold. And getting colder. Oh, dear.

With some difficulty she made her way back to Charlotte's door and knocked. After a minute she knocked again. The window opened, and Charlotte leaned out.

"Who?"

"It's me, Ess—er, Jo," said Essie. Looking up at such a steep angle made it difficult to stand, she discovered.

"Go home, for heaven's sake," said Charlotte. "It's late."

"I'm locked out," said Essie.

"Locked out of what? You just this minute left. You haven't been anywhere to get locked out of."

"No, I mean . . ."

"Go home, for crissakes," said Charlotte. The window closed again, and a moment later the lights in the front room went out. The alley was slightly darker as a result.

Quaint irregularity of alley lighting. Noises of traffic in the streets at either end. Nicky's car heavily beaded with dew.

A scraping sound behind the door of the restaurant—the bar being lifted. It opened, revealing Nicky, car keys in hand, and Harry standing behind him. Essie pressed back into Charlotte's doorway, out of the light. Leaning against walls, she found, she could still manage pretty well.

*"Thank* you, Harry," Nicky was saying as he came out, unlocking his car. "I *couldn't* have done it without you. Charles has *no* idea. I'll meet you around front." The door closed, and immediately opened again.

"The cake," said Harry, deadpan. Nicky threw up his arms.

"Oh *Jesus!"* he said. "Wouldn't *that* be wonderful, *all* this trouble and then forget the damn cake."

"And the present," said Harry.

"Oh *Jesus!"* said Nicky. He hurried back inside.

Essie tottered determinedly across the narrow alleyway, aiming for the door. Saw their backs in the passageway beyond the kitchen, just turning into the office. Through the door, laboriously up the ladder, between the boxes, into her nest while Harry and Nicky hastened back and forth below, still making jokes about what would have happened if they had arrived without the cake and the present. Lights snapped off. Locks clicked toward the front. Faintly on the other side of the blank wall the sound of Nicky's car.

Drifting into sleep she thought, I'm an underage girl. Kit would have loved me. She dreamed that she was huddled on Kit's stained mattress, listening for his key in the padlock—his foul toilet bowl must be cleaned, though no scrubbing would clean it, all night long, tossing and shifting in her nest. Once or twice she cried out sharply in her sleep, but no one was there to hear her.

When Paul got back to the cabin and unlocked the bathroom door, Jeremy awoke and stumbled past to his own place. This reflex always annoyed Paul. But he was in charge, as the first chapter of *The Perfect Parent* had assured him. The boy could not threaten him. He said, "I've been reading a book. A book that's going to make a big difference to you and me." Jeremy looked up at him, sleepy and confused. "What do you think about that?" said Paul. There was a note in his voice: it was quite clear between them now that when he spoke, he expected a reply.

"A book?" said Jeremy.

"Yes," said Paul. "A book."

"A book," said Jeremy. His room at home had been littered with books. His newest one had been about an artist who is too poor to buy paint, and how his mean uncle, charmed by the artist's children, helps them. Paul never read him books. He lay unnaturally still, hoping to be unnoticed, trying not to break any of the rules. "I'm good," he said almost inaudibly, scarcely moving his lips, hoping that would help.

# 29

Thanksgiving Day dawned bleakly upon Essie. It was a day that always began briskly at the Beals', with breakfast and the papers gotten through and then cleared away so that the kitchen would be unencumbered; it continued with all three of them in bustle and business all day long, cooking, cleaning, polishing, and setting out, gradually augmented with early-arriving relations bearing specialties and pitching in; the great gathering, and the dinner at three tables strung end to end from the dining room into the living room; a cataclysm of cleanup involving many inefficient hands bringing things to the wrong places and clogging every necessary passage; and finally, a prolonged evening of visiting, with the youngest members slumbering in corners and on piles of coats in Essie's room, and the adults saying how nice it was to see one another, but surely there must be some more efficient way to go about it. The family festivals of the Beals had always been a trial to Essie and to all her abstracted, quirky clan; but they stretched back in her mind to the beginning of consciousness, like the sun and the rain, not incidents in life but life itself. Family members who were absent, however voluntarily, were spoken of with a certain wonder, as if they had sailed off the edge of the world.

Essie wondered what they would be saying about her. One of her older cousins had missed both Thanksgiving and Christmas one year, and the adults had discussed the matter in earnest whispers, falling silent and frankly shushing each other when the children came near. Perhaps it was like that.

Le Coq d'Or was closed for lunch, but it served a special Thanksgiving dinner, traditional American dishes Frenchified and far, far better than ever Essie had experienced them among her family, where despite the magnitude of the occasion no cook was expected to interrupt a good conversation for the sake of the string beans. She thought it pitiful and depressing that people would come to eat such a meal in a restaurant, surrounded by strangers, however well it was prepared; but after lying in her nest all morning and following in her mind the preparations at home, hour by hour—her father polishing the silver his grandmother had received on her wedding in 1922, her mother attempting, never with complete success, to repeat a much-acclaimed stuffing she had served in 1979, the arrival of the cousin who brought the pumpkin pies—Essie was weepy with homesickness, and heartily glad to be spending that evening, of all evenings, working near Harry and Al, her hands busy and her mind occupied.

Emile would certainly smile at her. Perhaps he would kiss her again.

But when she appeared in the kitchen, tying on her apron and running an eye over the preparations, Nicky drew her aside, saying, "Jo, dear, we have to talk." He had on his serious look.

"It's Thanksgiving, Jo," he said. She had no answer; she glanced miserably at him and then stared miserably at the floor. Nicky regarded her with concern, but he had things on his mind.

"You've been here every day for three weeks, my dear," he said. "You stay late. I thought . . . well, I don't know *what* I thought. But I'm sure . . . ."

"Nicky, don't ask," she said. She did not want to know what he was sure of. He closed his mouth and waited. She had to say more without having any more to say. She said, "Just don't. Please. *Please.*" She drew the back of her hand across her face.

"My life is such a mess, you know that. You . . . My life just totally sucks. Except here." She glanced around the kitchen, warm and purposeful. She knew what was outside. She wore her apron like armor. She thought, He can't make me leave while I'm wearing it and I won't take it off.

"My life is *so* screwed up," she said, louder. She could not explain, could not stop explaining. Her face was turning red, her eyes filling. Harry looked up from the stove. Al stared, grinning, nervous. Jim looked up from the sink. She faced them, turned away, faced them again. She was almost a head shorter than any of them, and it made her feel puny and insignificant.

"I don't know what to *do,*" she cried. "I have . . ." She stamped, but it was feeble. She plucked at the apron to cover her face, but the flap was too short to reach up; she jerked at it, but the strings would not come free from around her waist. There was no wall to turn to out in the middle of the room, hemmed in against the table. In frustration she yanked savagely at the apron, the knot merely hardening, the whole kitchen staring, dumbstruck.

*"Don't look at me!"* she cried, defeated by the apron, sagging back against the big table, feet apart, shaking all over. Face in her hands, trying to hold in her sobs. It was so sudden.

For another moment everyone stared and Essie struggled. It was a response out of nowhere. It made no sense. For that reason Nicky found it apposite and was much affected.

"I tell you *what,*" he said to Essie in a different voice, at the same time making shooing gestures to the onlookers. "I tell you *what.* What if I withdraw the question? How would that be? I won't ask." The circle was breaking up, tasks were resuming. He put his hands on her shoulders, ducking down to her. "Would that be better? Al, bring me a truffle cake. And two forks. And a glass of champagne. We'll have them together," he said. "I won't pry, and we'll go on as we have. Would that be better?"

She heard the plate put down on the table beside her, and the click of silver. This was not the moment to indulge herself. She wiped her eyes and lifted her head. Nicky's hands were still on her shoulders, his face close to hers, intent. Another complication for him. Another thing he didn't need. But she thought, he can handle it and I can't.

She thought that if she tightened her throat she would be able to speak without either squealing or sobbing.

"That would be much better, thank you, Nicky," she said, her voice breaking only a little at the end.

"Good," he said. "You know how much we like having you here." They ate the truffle cake in silence, but she met his eyes several times, and he smiled reassuringly at her. They passed the glass of champagne back and forth, their hands touching.

When they had worked their way down to the last bite and the last sip, and Essie had had the bite and Nicky had had the sip, he turned her around, picked loose the knots on her apron, drew it over her head, folded it over his arm, and said, "Now I want you to go home."

He gave her a small hug. He propelled her gently toward the door.

She did not resist. He was not prying, but perhaps he still had lines drawn. Perhaps he thought that the fact of the holiday would produce a happy family for her to enjoy it with. Perhaps it was simply that her spending the evening in the kitchen undercut their tacit fiction.

She drifted back into the alley.

She had a book, but she was disinclined to hole up in her nest for hours before it was time to sleep. It would be fun to see a movie, but she could not afford a movie, and she would worry about getting locked out again.

She wondered if Emile would ever take her to a movie. She doubted it. She could not believe that she loomed large in his life. He was always friendly when he noticed her, but he did not seem to notice her very much.

But what if he *did* take her? And what if he insisted on coming home with her, to make sure she got in safely? She wondered how she would handle that.

What if he *did* kiss her again?

What if he wanted to take her to *his* place? Can you say, Okay *kind of*? Okay *so long as*? Would the bold girl say that? What if you say it and he doesn't hear it?

What would her mother say if she found out about *that*?

God, she wanted to talk to someone. Erin and Lizby were out of town. Elliott wouldn't have any privacy at that hour, and anyway, she could not very well discuss Emile with Elliott.

There were lights on downstairs at Charlotte's.

Essie thought of Charlotte's conversation, her iron hair, and her easy manner. Charlotte wasn't exactly like a mother, but she was sort of like an aunt.

She knocked, only then wondering whether Charlotte might be having some sort of family celebration and would not find a visitor convenient.

The door opened abruptly and Charlotte appeared, dressed as Essie had first seen her in an old shirt and jeans. She blinked a little and said, "Oh, hi. Hey, listen, I'm working." She looked again at Essie's face, stopped, and finally said, "Look, c'mon in," and showed her into the open ground-floor space. Two or three large tables on wheels, several large canvases around the walls, one as tall as Charlotte on an easel, bright lights on tripods. In a dim corner a small television flickered away, the sound turned low.

"Working," said Charlotte, her eyes slipping away to the canvas on the easel. Then, as if recollecting something she had observed at the door, she looked again at Essie and said, "You okay?" She put a hand on Essie's shoulder.

"Oh, yeah," said Essie. "Sure." She thought for a moment that Charlotte was about to hug her. Suddenly she wanted so much for that to happen. Suddenly she wanted to cry, not by herself in her nest but with someone. She wanted Charlotte to hug her and sit her down and get the whole story out of her and figure out what to do and how to put everything right again. She desperately wanted a grown-up— a friendly, protective grown-up she could trust. Charlotte was friendly enough, grown-up enough. Charlotte would do if she were in the mood. Essie could feel it welling up, these weeks of discipline and pretense, pressure and remorse. She would fold herself into Charlotte's arms and let the many burdens of her heart burst out. She looked up.

Charlotte's hand was still on her shoulder, but her eyes were back to the canvas on the easel.

Essie caught herself, like suppressing a hiccup.

"Hey, look," Charlotte said, noticing Essie again, "let's have some tea. That'd be nice. Sit." She waved to a pair of big overstuffed armchairs in stained canvas slipcovers that stood near the television. She switched on an electric kettle sitting on the floor and brought down a pair of mugs and a saucer of tea bags from a shelf.

"Yeah," said Essie, with a great effort. "Thanksgiving tea."

"Thanksgiving? Hey, yeah, I guess it is," said Charlotte. "D'ja have a turkey, all that?"

"Oh, yeah," said Essie.

"Shoulda brought me some," Charlotte said. "The

water'll just be a minute." Her attention was elsewhere. She put tea bags in the cups and produced
spoons, but instead of putting them down, she stood
and stared at her work, her head tipping a little
forward and then a little back. Essie perched on one of
the chairs and watched guardedly. She wanted to
confide, but she could go on without it; the worst was
not to know whether she might confide or not, whether she might expect comfort or not.

Charlotte had meandered back to the canvas, still
holding the spoons. She picked up a brush.

"Just let me . . ." she said, her voice trailing off.
The canvas consisted largely of tumbled areas of
creamy ochers and off-whites, like a pan of half-
cooked omelets. She drew two short curving lines of a
cold and brilliant blue along the margins of a transi-
tional area, and then scrubbed one of them partially
into the wet surface. Now one of the blue lines seemed
to curl up out of the ocher like cold smoke while the
other seemed to be a sharp glimpse of sky. She backed
off a few steps and stopped.

"Wow," she said, very quietly, obviously to herself
alone. "Goddamn." She had forgotten that Essie was
there.

The kettle began to hiss, then to sing. Charlotte
advanced to the canvas again, softened the harder of
the blue lines by scraping along the edge with one of
the teaspoons, and dragged a brush of pure bright
ocher alongside. Again she backed away.

"Mmm-*mmm*," she whispered. "God*damn.*"

Essie was recovered. You're okay, she said to herself.

She went over to the kettle and made two cups of
tea. One of them she put on the table where Charlotte
stood when she backed up. The other she took back to
her chair in the semidarkness by the television
and snuggled in. She watched Charlotte moving in
and out of the bright light by the easel. She gig-

gled and thought, This is just like home, being ignored and making tea. She thought, Am I happy or sad, right this minute? She could not decide. Would I rather laugh or cry? Cry, definitely. But she did not.

Several more blue lines had appeared, curling in and out of the ocher.

"God*damn,*" Charlotte whispered to herself. She advanced, laid down a stroke or two, and then retreated, back and forth, again and again.

Essie watched her paint. Her mind drifted. She shied away from the thought of Jeremy, but she thought of home. The cleanup would be done by now. They'd all be in the living room, drinking decaf and catching up on things, her father as intent on the family news as he would usually be on his books. "Ah?" he would be saying. "She has musical talent, you think? What, precisely, leads you to think so? And isn't that wonderful? Will she sing Bach, do you think?"

The television anchor, his nearly inaudible voice pumped and urgent, was attempting to titillate any possible listeners with the suggestive circumstances surrounding the employment of somebody's son-in-law in the Municipal Railway, but Essie did not notice.

Sergeant Wren had suggested to Paul that as a single man he might consider working Thanksgiving so that a particular clerk/typist, a single mother, could spend the day with her children. Paul had made it clear that he did not wish to give up his holiday, and although Sergeant Wren did not mention the matter to anyone, the conference had been observed and its subject and outcome guessed, with the result that Paul found himself coldly treated by everyone at work.

On Thanksgiving morning Paul took the boy for a walk by the river. It had been a mere stream when the boy first arrived almost a month before, meandering quietly between steep, wooded banks and broad, sunny beaches of sand and pebble. Now it was rising with the winter rains, no broader than Jeremy could throw a stone but deep and fast and noisy, throwing up impressive wakes where it was impeded by rocks or snags. As they did whenever they came to the river, Paul threw pieces of driftwood upstream, and then he and the boy pelted them as they swept past. The boy's throw was improving. A lot of it was a few lessons, and some of it was more exercise, a better appetite, and a better attitude. He was beginning to get something behind his arm. He hit one of the pieces fair and square. Paul cheered, and the boy shot him an anxious smile.

"You're getting to be a champ," said Paul. "Didn't your dad ever show you how to do this stuff?" The boy looked a little solemn and shook his head.

They stayed there for half an hour, Paul lofting in the target pieces and responding conventionally to each throw. When it was time to go back to the cabin, he reached down on an impulse and took the boy's hand. The boy sobered, but he did not immediately pull it away as he had always done before. He gave Paul an anxious, almost pleading look, which puzzled him.

You never know what they're thinking, Paul thought. It doesn't matter. He's getting to like me.

*The Perfect Parent* made a great point of not feeling you have to understand each and every one of your child's moods, because you will not succeed. Paul was greatly reassured by this advice.

He felt the happy buzz of success. Things were finally working his way. The previous day—before he had any idea that this morning would go so well—he had decided to go ahead with the big home-cooked Thanksgiving blowout, and done all the shopping. Now it seemed perfect—after that happy, easy morning, they could work on the dinner together. Not the whole time—the boy could go off and play his video game or something—but enough to make it *their* dinner. It would be a special celebration. It was all going to be easy from now on. And after dinner they could watch one of Paul's special tapes—one they had not seen before. Perhaps—just perhaps, he cautioned himself, but perhaps, nevertheless—this would be the day things worked out for them.

It would be their first perfect day together.

But when in the early afternoon Paul laid out the turkey and all the other necessaries, a brave show on the little kitchen table, and called the boy in to see, and reminded him what day it was, he saw that it was not his fondest hopes but his worst fears that were to be realized. The boy did not at first make the connection between this pile of groceries and the handsome table at home, with its centerpiece of Indian corn and its crowded miscellany of chairs from all over the house, the gleaming plates and the silvery forest of glasses; but when he did, he burst out crying and screaming as he had not done since his first arrival. He was remembering his mother's face, concentrated but smiling, hurrying in and out between kitchen and dining room, surveying all and making little adjustments. She had little snacks of nuts and fruit for the children to hold them until dinnertime. He remembered how she would feed him tidbits with her fingers and tell him which of his cousins would be coming for the feast and what a good time they were all going to have. It was as vivid to him as if she had been kneeling beside him on the floor of the cabin kitchen. He could see her silver earrings with the little black stones, her gray eyes, the smell of her hair. His shrieks came harshly, as if he would strip the linings from his lungs.

When he cried himself out it was only to sink into a state of the most desolate melancholy.

Paul knew in the first flicker of the boy's expression

what was to become of his dream of their first perfect day. For a brief time he felt himself tottering on an appalling brink. Images of the wildest violence arose in his mind, but they were immediately supplanted by a despair that seemed to drain the strength from his arms and legs and left vengeful violence or any other action equally beyond his power.

Still, he felt he had to do something, or explode, or melt; he could think of nothing better than to proceed as he had planned. Grimly, the boy still weeping frantically, he set himself to prepare their feast. Grimly, he roasted and chopped and mashed while the autumn overcast set in to hide the sun, and the somber gray light dwindled and finally disappeared outside the foggy kitchen window. Grimly, he set it forth as he had planned to do, with all the formality and pomp his meager panoply of pots and bowls would stretch to. Grimly, he summoned the boy to the table and sat him up straight in his place opposite. He carved and served, passed and poured. Silently, struggling bite by bite, he ate, while the boy stared blankly at the table and wept or gasped with trying not to weep.

At one point Paul realized that his hands were fumbling under his napkin for the buckle of his belt, quite without conscious volition. He had been visualizing giving the boy *ten* strokes—ten *real* strokes, with some meat behind them—and if he made the least movement, or any sound at all—so much as an audible breath—before they reached the full ten, he would start the count all over again.

But he did not actually get up from his chair. He was as paralyzed by his loneliness and his disappointment as Jeremy was with homesickness. When he had eaten only half of what was on his plate, he slapped down his fork, and with a cry and a sweep of his arm, scattered bird and plates and everything in a tumbling ruin across the floor. It was his last spasm of energy.

He laid his head down on his arms on the table and covered his face. He rocked slightly, slowly back and forth in his chair, abandoned to his misery, unconscious of Jeremy opposite, entirely silent now, eyes huge, motionless, waiting.

Essie's tea was drunk, and Charlotte's was cold. At one point Charlotte registered her again for a moment and said, "God, I'm terrible. Be with you in a minute. Just . . . I've got this one . . ."

The restaurant kitchen began to slow down around ten, Essie knew, and it would be hard to get in unnoticed if she stayed much longer. She turned off the kettle and crept silently out the door, closing it carefully behind her and pulling it until it latched firmly.

Once in the open she could not face her nest. The kitchen seemed busy enough. She slipped quickly out of the alley and then drifted, feeling the hard wind.

In the corner of a parking lot, a phone booth.

A fresh wave of homesickness engulfed her. She stood outside the booth for a few minutes, watching the streetlights. Then she went inside. She deposited two quarters and heard the dial tone. A timorous fingertip pressed in the number. The passing traffic was noisy, but at the other end she heard two rings, and then her mother's voice. She said, "Mom, it's me. I'm okay," and pressed down the hook. For a few moments she stood gazing at the phone in front of her, still holding the receiver, in her mind's ear hearing again the familiar voice, trying to decide what it was, exactly, that she had done.

# 30

"She called home last night," said Gadek on Friday morning. "We've traced the call—sometimes we can recover the source of an incoming call from a different area code. It was from San Francisco—a public phone, which is too bad. It's nice that it's close, but I was hoping it'd be a residence. All this means is that she was at a public phone sixteen hours ago. Anyway, I want to go eyeball the phone and see who's around. Somebody might have seen her. There might be some sort of vehicle description. She may be living in the area. Somebody might know her or know where we can find her."

"Look, if you need another body . . ." said Toby.

"Good," he said. "I'll speak to your sergeant. Plain clothes at two. We should be ready to go by then. I want Essie Beal here in this office. I want her to make the ID if she can without further loss of time. I want to find Jeremy Broome, or what's left of him, and I want that kidnapper under lock and key before he snatches another kid."

Two-thirty found Gadek and Toby hastening to the city.

"We might have her in an hour," said Toby.

"Yes, and we might not," said Gadek cheerfully. "Christmas doesn't happen every day."

The phone was located in the corner parking lot of a defunct convenience store. There was only one nearby building with windows overlooking the phone, and that was tenanted by a sweatshop whose workers were plainly too busy to be noticing who was using the booth across the street, even if they were working late on Thanksgiving, which they might well have been doing.

"Well," said Gadek. "Let's do the immediate neighborhood and see what we can see."

They saw a beehive district of light industry, warehousing, and garment manufacturing. Delivery trucks great and small came and went, double and triple-parked on the wide, one-way streets. Workers maneuvered clattering, tiny-wheeled racks of clothing along the traffic lanes, and bicycle messengers in bizarre haircuts shot through the traffic in defiance of all law and regulation. There were lots of alleys, and here and there vacant lots that serve the same function for someone on foot. It was a very porous district, and a user of the phone could come with equal convenience from almost anywhere.

"Too bad," said Gadek. "Still, let's take a chance. I brought a couple of pictures. You take that side of the street, I'll take this. A block up, a block down, a block down the cross street, and poke into the courts and alleys. Talk to whoever you can find, show 'em the picture, and see if someone's seen her."

"Right," said Toby.

"And when I say 'whoever,' I mean use some discretion. We can't assume that anyone who knows her will want to help us. Some people would warn Jack the Ripper if they saw a cop coming. If your gut tells you not to trust someone, follow your gut."

"Right."

"Good. I'll meet you back here in an hour, and we'll see how we're doing."

Toby began with an import/export business right across the street that fronted on an alley. The front office did not have a direct view of the phone, but they were right there, and people might have seen her on their way in or out. He showed Essie's picture to the office people, and the manager took him upstairs to see the warehousemen, but nobody remembered seeing her. A little farther into the alley he found a body shop where cars and tools looked as if they hadn't been touched in months, and whatever the citizens inside were doing, it did not seem to be work. His gut said that they would not recognize pictures of their sisters if a cop was showing them, so he saved his time. He cruised up and down, speaking to people on the street and dropping into offices, but he had nothing to report when he got back to the car.

"Too bad," said Gadek. "Once I did one of those little walk-arounds, and the second guy I laid the picture on said, why yes, the guy I was looking for was in the bathroom but he'd be right out. That was fun, but it doesn't happen every time."

Late afternoon found them returning to the station.

"It's not much," said Gadek. "It's one phone call. She might have been just passing through town. It could mean she's getting lonely or needs help. But whatever it means, it's a change. She may call again. In case she does, I think it's worth keeping an eye on that phone for a few days, starting tonight. I take it you're up for that?"

"You bet."

"You'll need someone to work with."

"How about Walt Kramer?"

"Good. I'll see if I can borrow him, too."

Toby said, "I suppose there's another possibility. If she anticipated that she might be connected to the phone she used, she might have been careful *not* to call from her own area. She might have come across town to put us off the scent."

"Yes," said Gadek. "People do that sometimes. But she's fourteen, for crissake. She's led a quiet life. How sly can she be? Let's keep it simple and assume that she picked that phone for convenience."

Toby ran into Walt Kramer in the squad room. He had heard the news already.

"I'm off to the city to sit on Essie's phone," said Toby.

"Sounds pretty dull," said Walt.

"No doubt, but we're not making any progress staying home. Oh, by the way, Gadek wants to see you."

"Concerning?" said Walt, his face falling. He hated surveillances.

"Guess, old buddy. Guess."

"Ah. Well, love to," said Walt. Toby had once reproached him for being too action oriented. "Love to. Love to."

"Good," said Toby. "I'll see you later."

Toby's first decision when he got back to the city was how to work the area.

She might be living right around there, and visible from time to time, even if she was not using that phone booth. So one possibility was to work the area in a roving fashion in his car, hoping to spot her on the street. But simply surviving in that traffic left him no attention for anything else.

He could walk around, which is a far better way to see things, but he had no idea where she might be, and if they were near each other on the street, she would have a perfectly good chance of seeing him before he saw her. If she were inside one of these buildings, and anywhere near a window when he wandered by, the advantage would be entirely hers. If he could find a parking place with a view, he could just sit in his car and be far less conspicuous.

He had trouble finding a parking space of any sort, let alone one with a nice view—which, for his purposes, meant one that was near the intersection with the phone booth where he could watch at least two streets, and one with a view not continually blocked by passing traffic. If he took a spot near an intersection, his view would be blocked by traffic backed up waiting for the light at the corner. Finally he settled on a space half a block away, at the bottom of one of the alleys that run all through that part of town. He could see the approach to Essie's phone. He could not see the phone itself, but if he saw her go in he could just go right on over, and she would not be able to see him coming. It seemed like a promising enough spot. He was settled into it by about five-thirty.

Gadek called on the cellular phone a little before six.

"Walt'll be there pretty soon," he said. "I've told him to hook up with you, and the two of you work out how you want to approach this. The phone company has put a trap on the Beals' phone. If Essie calls, they'll have the location of her phone instantly, which would be especially nice if she isn't calling from the phone you're watching. Dispatch is supposed to call both us and the San Francisco PD and tell us where to find her. If she stays on the phone for more than a minute or two, she should still be talking when we arrive. SFPD has briefed their patrol people, so everyone ought to know what's going on. But they may well not have a unit to send right away, so you're the primary response."

A few minutes later Walt arrived.

"Well, this looks great," he said, squinting down the street. "Rush hour and traffic and all. You can see for yards and yards."

"It'll clear out," said Toby.

They decided to split up after dinner and work independently. Toby settled into his car, trying to look aimless and bored, and Walt drove slowly away to start cruising. In an hour he would come back and they would switch, with Walt sitting and Toby mobile. Splitting up doubled their chances of spotting her, and one of them ought to be enough to gather her in unless she ran, which they doubted she would do, or unless she had a pugnacious friend.

* * *

"Sure seems like a lot of running around in DD this evening," said Paul.

"Oh, that's the Broome thing again," said Sergeant Wren a little crossly. He was still struggling with his irritation about Paul's insistence on taking Thanksgiving. "The missing baby-sitter phoned her mother, and they've traced the call."

Paul felt the floor shift under him.

"They know where to find her, eh?" he said. He had to ask.

"Not yet," said Sergeant Wren, turning back to his work.

Paul sagged in his chair, clapping onto the desk to steady himself. *The whole thing was in the air again— she was right out there, right there close.* It could all come tumbling in at any moment.

Sergeant Wren was not in a communicative mood, and Paul did not dare to ask more questions. But there were slips on his spindle, errands, odd jobs around the building, and he gathered them up and set out to see what he could pick up. He spent as much time as he could hanging around Detective Division, where he heard much to reassure him. They did *not* know where to look. They were hanging around a public telephone from which she had made a single call, hoping that she would come back to it. Well, it wasn't much, he thought.

And yet—why had she called at all? Could there be some change of heart? Kids are all over the place, no one knew that better than he; up one minute and down the next. She could get homesick or something, change her mind, and bop right on back. And if she did, she would be anxious to shift the blame. She would have some story prepared. Kids lie very smoothly, Paul knew. Paul knew all about that. They'd told all sorts of lies about him when it suited them.

She'll try to put the blame on me, he thought. I'd

better check the hole, make sure it's big enough. He remembered the previous night and thought, Hell, maybe it's time to go ahead and *use* the hole. Then he thought, No, no, don't lose it. We're making progress. I can always put him in the hole later, if things don't work out.

Al almost caught her coming down the ladder from the loft. If she had been two seconds later, he *would* have caught her. She thought, I'm not going to get away with this forever.

When Walt returned from his first hour of cruising, he got in Toby's car and they had a map conference. He showed Toby a couple of convenience stores that would be after-hours draws, and he had found a two-block strip not far away where there seemed to be a good deal of action in soft goods.

"It's pretty busy," he said. "You cruise through and look, then come back in fifteen minutes and see different kids. Worth checking out often. If she's working there, she won't be visible for long at a stretch."

So Toby spent an hour winding through alleys, peering into convenience stores and laundromats, rolling slowly up and down the strip that Walt had found. It wasn't all underage trade, but a lot of it was. He saw boys and girls of about Essie's age whose souls, from a certain perspective, a certain distance, were probably as valuable as hers. They stood on the curb scanning the traffic, trying for eye contact, straining to satisfy their pimps and their habits. But he did not see her.

"That strip is really uplifting," he said when he came back to switch off.

"Good thing it's illegal," said Walt. "Otherwise it'd be going on right out in the open."

Gadek had told them to shut down their operation

at ten. They went by his office on their way home and left a note on his desk:

Gadek/Parkman & Kramer   11/25   2255hrs
Zip.

# 31

Paul waffled all through the weekend, seething and calming himself. This was a time for lying low. The baby-sitter was a factor of uncertain menace, and her hovering presence unsettled him. If she were brought in, she would undoubtedly attempt to implicate him, and he contemplated in outrage all the things that she might say.

On the other hand, of course, it was more than likely that all this would blow over. They would not find her. In a week or two, all would be well.

Wait and see, he told himself. Just give it a few days.

Essie went across the alley on Saturday morning to visit Charlotte. Charlotte fixed coffee while Essie sat at the little round kitchen table. There were windows on two sides overlooking the alley on one side and the gray downtown on the other. A small television sat on the counter next to them: a sleek hostess artfully degraded an obese woman and her anorexic daughter before a smirking studio audience until Charlotte turned off the sound and the exploitation continued in pantomime.

"Sorry about the other night," Charlotte said, putting out cups. "I guess you wanted a chin-wag. I just couldn't get out of that piece."

"It's okay," Essie said. "I was happy."

"You didn't look happy."

"I wasn't *very* happy. But I don't think I was sad. At least, not right then."

Very soon they were talking about Life. Essie had passionate opinions on this subject, but Charlotte, incontestably, had more hard information.

"No, let me tell you," said Charlotte, "divorce can be rough. No, I *won't* tell you. You don't need to hear about it. But my ex is *not* doing this gracefully. Possessive. And his latest stunt is, I think he's got gumshoes keeping an eye on me."

"Gumshoes?" said Essie.

"Private investigators. Private eyes. Yesterday I went down past the gas station down on the corner, and there was this guy sitting up the block in a car. He was parked where he could see the end of the alley— see me going in and out."

"That's creepy," said Essie. She tried to picture the streets immediately around and the people she would usually see.

"Two hours later, when I came back, he was still there, and there was another guy, a big guy like a bear, sitting in the car with him. I tell you, it *is* creepy. It's not even as if I had some sort of secret life going. I don't know what they're after."

Essie thought, Maybe it's me they're after. Then she thought, The guilty flee where none pursue—I bet they don't send gumshoes after runaways. But she had to admit to herself that she did not really know, one way or the other. And besides, she had been fleeing for weeks, and she felt guilty. She could not see any way that the presence of gumshoes could be good for her.

Toby and Walt worked the phone and its neighborhood again on Saturday. When they came in on Sunday Gadek said, "I'm folding this detail up after today, assuming we don't get some results. She hasn't called again, she hasn't turned up on the street. That call may have been a unique impulse. In any case, we can't tie up two people on the off chance that she may do it again. We're going back on standby. You guys might as well be back in Patrol busting crime."

"Aw, hell," Toby said. "I can't argue with the logic, but once I get started on something like this, I hate to let go. Every minute I'm thinking she'll pop out right in front of me, I'll reel her in, and there we are."

"Well, you've got tonight to do that very thing," said Gadek. "Enjoy."

"Aw, hell," said Toby.

On Sunday afternoon Nathan dragged his hand across Essie's chest as they passed each other in the kitchen doorway, eyes elaborately elsewhere, but no mistake about it.

*"Stop that!"* she said, surprising herself. He ignored her, gathering silver for the dining room. *"Nathan,"* she said, following him, suddenly fed up, "you better *stop* that." His back was turned, broad and expressive; he did not respond to her at all. Then she said, "I'm going to tell Nicky," and started for the door. Instantly Nathan jumped ahead, blocking her.

"If you do, I'll lose my job," he said, strong, accusing.

Lifelong training in deference. She hesitated.

"No you won't," she said uncertainly. She had no idea what would happen. She wanted Nicky to protect her; she had not thought about the consequences for Nathan.

Don't be hasty, her mother was fond of saying, don't be too sure of yourself. What's done can't be undone.

"I'll be out of work," he said reproachfully. "It'll be your fault." His arms were hanging loose, shoulders slumping. He was staring hard at her, his breath a little shallow, his lip almost trembling.

She held him in her hand. Having him fired would be an enormous responsibility.

"Well, then don't do it," she said, turning back to the stove.

"Don't you tell *me* what to do," he said, instantly masterful again, pulling himself up and shaking his wide shoulders loose, massaging one hand with the other.

"Don't do it," she said, not understanding what had happened, feeling tiny. He laughed sarcastically and turned away with elaborate unconcern.

But a moment later Emile swept into the kitchen and hugged her exuberantly.

"'Ow is my mystery sweet'art?" he whooped, jumping back to arm's length and dropping into a slight crouch so that he still held her shoulders but they were eye to eye. "'Ow eez my beeyootiful girl with a secret?"

"I'm fine, Emile," she said, grinning hugely.

"'Fine'!" he cried, as to the universe, shooting his arms aloft. "My mystery sweet'art eez 'fine'! And she 'as pronounced my name, and now I may die!"

"Well, you may as well die," said Harry without irritation, "because if Jo doesn't get those suprêmes finished sometime this afternoon, there won't be any dinner, and you'll be out of a job."

"I am crushed," said Emile, balancing on one foot and shrinking the rest of himself into a ball. "''Arry 'as crushed me." He gave Essie a prodigious stage wink and disappeared into the passage.

"Emile's sure feeling funny this afternoon," said Al.

"Emile's always funny," said Essie, still smiling excessively.

On Monday afternoon somebody in Service Division said, "Gadek's given up. They weren't getting anything, and he doesn't think one call is enough to justify the detail."

"That makes sense," said Sergeant Wren. "Listen, I

hope everyone's noticed that the new weekend rotation schedule started yesterday."

"Well, they never had much," said somebody. "One teenager picks up the phone once—it doesn't make much of a pattern."

"Kids," said Paul, pooh-poohing. "Say anything." *She's gone!* he thought. *Goddamn!* I shouldn't have lost a minute's sleep over it. They'll never find her. I knew they wouldn't.

During the week following Thanksgiving Essie had spent a good deal of time thinking about her call home. The call had been impulsive, but not out of the blue; she was homesick. She was getting by, but only through the most harassing exertion. Except insofar as she might be sharing Jeremy's lack of comfort, she could not see that she was doing him any good.

And sooner or later someone would catch her on the ladder or move one of those boxes in the loft and find her nest. Then what?

By Thursday she had taken her thinking as far as it would go unaided. She decided that she needed to confide—to giggle, if possible. She slipped out after work and went around the corner to her nearest phone. She fumbled with the coins, waited anxiously while Erin's phone rang—several times, surprisingly—the receiver pressed tightly to one ear and her free hand clamped tightly over the other to shut out the noise of a particularly dense cluster of traffic stalled in the street next to her. It was noisy enough that Essie did not hear the different voice when Erin's mother answered. She was several sentences into the conversation before she realized her mistake.

Erin's mother called Esther Beal. Esther Beal called the police. Gadek called Toby and Walt in off their beats to change into plain clothes and dash off to the city in case she called again.

"It's probably too late," he said, "but we'll try. She

may still be around on the street. We don't know what phone she called from yet, but we're going to assume it's the same one or one in the same area. I'll be coming after you as soon as I can shake loose from here. Get going."

The people in Service Division saw Toby and Walt trotting through on the way to the parking lot, and Gadek a few minutes later. But word had already flown around the building: They know where she is. They've gone to pick her up.

Paul heard the rumors and saw them hurrying by from DD, looking hopeful and determined. He had no way of knowing exactly what had happened. They would be bringing her right back here in the next couple of hours. He thought he would go mad.

# 32

"She's been calling Erin every couple of days for weeks," Melanie told Sara, "and Erin never said a word. It turns out that she's been talking to *several* of her friends. I asked Heather if Essie had called *her,* and she assured me that she hadn't, but then she said very plainly that if Essie *had* called her, and if she had promised not to tell, then she wouldn't, whether she regretted her promise or not. I'm not sure where that leaves us. But I'm inclined to believe her. She seemed hurt. Why *not* her, if people were being called? She's always felt very fond and protective of Essie."

"I wish she'd call *us,*" said Joss. "We wouldn't ask any questions."

"Well, maybe just some short ones," said Adam.

"The phone company's traced it back to a different phone than the time before," Gadek told Toby on Friday morning. "Another public phone. Footer went right over last night and spoke to the girl she called, Erin, ah"—Gadek glanced at his notes—"ah, Erin Conlan, and persuaded her to talk. Essie began calling her a couple of weeks before Thanksgiving. They've been reversing the charges, luckily enough, so any numbers she's been using will appear on the Conlans' bill. We should have all that in an hour or two. Erin isn't admitting to knowing where Essie is, and Footer thinks she actually doesn't know. Essie just refers to 'the place I'm staying.' The only name she's dropped is Emile, which doesn't seem to help us.

"Erin gave Footer several other names, all kids in Essie's school. He's over there this morning, pulling kids out of class and interviewing them. Erin is supposed to be Essie's great friend, and what Essie hasn't told her she probably hasn't told anyone, but if she's been calling a lot she must have dropped things here and there—useful things for us to know.

"I've sent another fax to San Francisco PD. I've given 'em her description and photo again and the location of both phone booths and requested that the beat officer keep an eye peeled for her.

"We're going to restart the surveillance as soon as Footer gets back. If she's been calling all those kids, she's been on the phone a lot, and if she's been calling collect, we'll know where every call came from. We were probably just sitting on the wrong place, before. I expect we'll be organized by three. Meet in my office. Tell Kramer."

\* \* \*

The group huddled on the library steps at noon.

"I feel like such a dork," said Erin. "It was my idea to reverse the charges."

"I would've done the same thing," said Latasha. "Who would have known it showed where the call comes from? The only time I've ever *seen* a phone bill is when it's being shaken in my face, and then it's hard to read the fine print."

"I can't believe the cops are doing this to us," said Rhea. "I think it's just *totally* unfair, putting us in this position."

*"Totally,"* said Moll.

"It really isn't something that's being *done* by anyone," said Elliott. "Essie knows something significant, and we're associated with Essie. That makes us significant."

"Well, I think it sucks," said Rhea.

Lizby said, "If she calls me, I'm going to say that the police are trying to find her, and they think that if she comes back, it may help to find Jeremy. I'm going to tell her just what they told me."

Shelly made kissing noises, and Moll said, "God, girl, lie down and get walked on."

"I want them to find Jeremy," said Lizby. "He's just totally precious. When I'd baby-sit he'd always be making some machine with blocks or drawing something. He hated to be interrupted until it was done, and then he'd show it to me and explain what everything was. He was *so* serious. I've fed him and bandaged his cuts and kissed his bumps and read to him and listened while he read to me, even when he couldn't read yet. I've sat in the dark on the foot of his bed for hours when he wakes up screaming and can't go back to sleep. If the cops told me it'd help, I'd go stand on my head on the library steps at high noon. So go stick it, Moll and Shelly. I don't care."

"Well, excuse *us,"* said Moll.

"Well, I care a lot," said Rhea. "And I'm not doing *anything.* The cops aren't using *me.* Cops, parents—

they're all, Do this, do that, write your paper, clean your room, don't bother us. And I'm saying, don't bother *me*. You want to jerk Ess around, go find her and jerk her around yourself. Leave me out of it."

"I don't blame you for being mad at your parents," said Elliott. "I'll agree with anything you say about your parents. But I think this is one of those situations where you have to cooperate."

"I don't believe a word they say, *ever,*" said Rhea.

"That's unreasonable," said Elliott. Reflexively, Shelly made a face and then realized that Elliott had seen it. "Just kiiiidddddding," she said.

"I'm totally not answering the phone till this is *all* over," said Rhea. "I can't tell what's right, so just leave me out of it."

"I'm with Lizby," said Erin. "Finding Jeremy comes first, and all the dorks had better get with the program." She shook her head violently. "I can't believe I really said that, but that's what I'm going to do."

At noon they all gathered in Gadek's office.

Footer recapitulated his interviews with Essie's circle, which had produced very little in the way of information that might help find her directly.

"She's been real careful," said Footer. "Real discreet. She knows she puts her friends in a box by calling, and she's tried to keep it simple for 'em. They discuss schoolwork some and gossip a lot. Not much else. But she makes the initial call, and then when her time is up, they reverse the charges, so all the calls are itemized on the family phone bills. They didn't think of that."

"The phone company faxed 'em over," said Gadek, flourishing a sheaf of printouts. "Most of the calls come back to six public phones in a fairly small area, but not all—she's used a few other phones once or twice. She's probably living right in the middle of those six somewhere. She obviously knows something about phone tracing. I don't know whether that trip north was a dead end for her or designed to throw us off, but she's been right next door for weeks, and perhaps the whole time. She's trying to be elusive."

"She's succeeding," said Footer. "Swift kid."

"Yes," said Gadek. "So far. Except for the phone bills."

Everybody chuckled comfortably.

"The families have agreed to our putting traps on their lines. The phone company gets the location she's calling from instantly, and then it's just a matter of getting the word to us on the street. According to these bills, she spends half an hour or more on a call—it ought to be plenty of time. We've informed San Francisco PD of the new phone locations, and we'll be over there to sit on the phones starting this evening. The billing information also includes the time of the calls, which helps. She rarely calls before eight-thirty, except on Mondays, when she often calls earlier, and she rarely calls later than ten. So tonight we'll plan on being in place by seven-thirty, to be on the safe side."

"What's different about Mondays?" said Footer, but nobody could think of any possibilities that would advance their thinking in any practical way.

"But guys, let me tell you," said Gadek. "We don't have a sure thing, and we don't want to bobble this one. What's going to happen tonight, with any luck, is that she'll walk right up to a phone we're sitting on, and we grab her. Failing that, she calls a trap line and we go find her before she gets off the phone. Dispatch should have the location of her phone within two or three minutes. Dispatch calls us and San Francisco PD, we pounce, and there we are. Either of those works fine.

"There's always a glitch window, however. In this case we've got a lot of human imponderables. We have *not* told the kids involved about the traps—just the parents. But of course the kids know they've been talked to. We didn't ask 'em to keep it a secret, because they probably won't or won't be able to. So the first thing they're going to say to her when she calls is that the cops spoke to everyone today."

"I explained that Essie might have key information in the Broome case," said Footer.

"Did that seem to impress anyone?" said Toby.

Footer looked at the ceiling and shrugged. "Sometimes more and sometimes less," he said. "Sometimes not a bit. Got an attitude, some of 'em."

"Anyway, they'll take up time telling Essie about it, which is good for us," said Gadek. "What we *don't* want is to have them thinking about what's happening while they're talking, because then she rabbits."

"It's the Broome baby-sitter thing again," somebody said, laughing. "Stop and go, stop and go."

Paul did not know what to think. Last night everyone had been saying that they knew where she was and that they were bringing her in. He had lingered after the end of his shift, mesmerized by his approaching doom—and then they had returned empty-handed but calm, as if they had not really been expecting to pick her up at all. Now there were people running in and out, interviewing—had been, all morning long—holding meetings, and clearly another blitz was being mounted.

It was the uncertainty that was so hard on him. If only he had some way to judge.

"You don't look well," said Sergeant Wren.

"No," said Paul. But he did not want to go home, where he could not keep tabs on things. "I'll be all right," he said. "I've got some odds and ends to do. I'll be here and there today."

"That's fine," said Sergeant Wren. But he did not say it as if it was fine. It was occurring to him that Paul had definitely been behaving very oddly for some time now. He was beginning to wonder if he had a problem that would require some sort of action. His inner question was reflected in his expression and tone of voice. Paul noticed this, and it was one more source of disquiet for him.

By midafternoon on Friday Toby was charging off to San Francisco to scout the newly identified phones and prepare for the arrival of the main force in the early evening.

The new phones were all in the area he and Walt had worked previously. The first phone was in a gas station on a corner. The staff looked friendly enough, and he showed them Essie's picture, but they did not think they recognized her.

The second was the phone he and Gadek had looked at before.

The third was midblock at the end of an alley. Up and down the block were the featureless sides of the warehouses that fronted the two streets on either side, and across the street was much the same. Just inside the alley was an open loading door, and he spoke with the three warehousemen working there. They were sympathetic enough. They said that they saw people using the phone from time to time, but they had never seen anyone who looked like the picture, so far as they could remember. They took Toby's card and promised to call.

The fourth phone was in the parking lot of another service station, out by the street, with the door facing the sidewalk. The glass sides had been pasted over almost completely with posters, so that anyone in the garage itself would have only the most fleeting glimpse of anyone approaching or leaving the phone, and none of anyone standing inside. The staff was dull, busy, and unhelpful.

The fifth was another streetside booth overlooked by a whole building's worth of warehouse windows in which nothing but boxes were visible. He found when he inquired that nobody worked in the front of the building—the office was in the rear—and although the boss very obligingly called everyone in the place together to hear what he had to say, nobody had anything to offer.

The last phone was outside a nightspot with boarded-up windows—not derelict, just indulging in the look. Next door was a silver-plating company. By the window in the front office was a sharp-looking man, and he told Toby that he had seen the young woman in the photo use the phone once, a couple of weeks before, in the evening, oh, about eight-thirty or nine, when the firm had been working into the evening, which they didn't usually do. That was the only time. She'd walked up the block, called, talked at least fifteen minutes, very animated, and then gone back the way she'd come. That was back into the middle of the six-phone area, Toby was pleased to see. Perhaps their basic take on her whereabouts had some merit.

Toby phoned in to the office with these very moderate results, and then went to take a spot on the first phone booth, since the phone company records showed that it was the most used of them all.

At seven Gadek appeared, with Walt, Footer, and Lindy Webb. They rendezvoused a few blocks away because the streets were emptying out and a group would be conspicuous.

"We'll sit on the most used phones, one per phone," said Gadek. "She's made about two-thirds of her calls from those five. That gives us a two-out-of-three chance that she walks right into our arms, assuming she calls at all. Toby's been sitting on number one, so keep it." He parceled them out. "And keep your eyes open. Some of these phones are near other things, so if she goes out for something to eat or whatever, we'll have a good chance of seeing her go by even if she isn't planning to make a call."

"Right," they said, and all trundled off to sit.

But nothing happened. No calls were intercepted. None of the watchers spotted her.

**33**

On Saturday morning Charlotte said, "They're still
there." Essie did not have to ask who she meant.

"When I got in last night, the medium-size one was
right where he was before. And there was this man
and woman strolling along with a big yellow dog, and
I'm thinking, It's the middle of the night in December, and I'm supposed to believe that they're out for a
walk? *They're* looking for me, too. Then I thought, I
must be going utterly paranoid—completely crazy.
Dogs have to be walked in December, too, unless
they're *really* well trained. And anyway, my ex isn't
*that* rich. How many gumshoes can there be?"

They went into the kitchen and sat at the table by
the window. The television on the counter grumbled
about the weather. Charlotte turned off the sound and
set about making tea. There was a drawing pinned to
a drawing board, which leaned against the kitchen
doorway. It was the charcoal equivalent of one of her
paintings, a maelstrom of strokes and smudges in the
midst of which a figure could be discerned. She
paused once or twice in her tea making to squint at it.

Essie wondered whether they were not gumshoes
but cops. *God*, she thought, *why?* They can't be after
me. They don't send detectives and police dogs after
runaways. It's some coincidence. That's the only
explanation.

Still, it jogged her.

She could always just give up and go home. She

236

pictured herself standing in the doorway, struggling with her key, and saying, Hi, Mom and Dad, I ran off and scared everyone to death and now here I am back again, and I sure hope you're going to be good sports about it, and by the way, please don't mention the kidnapping any more 'cause I'm tired of hearing about it?

Sure. The image recurred to her of her mother opening the door. The tight-gripping cop hands clamping her arms.

Would she be in trouble with the police, too? She had never known a runaway. She did not know what the authorities did about these things. With Walt or Toby, perhaps—or at least with Walt, whom she knew better—she would not worry so much. But what if it was not somebody like Walt? What if it was somebody like the spruce cop?

"Y'know," Charlotte said, nodding at the drawing, "there's nothing wrong with that. If my dealer can't sell it, what I need is a new dealer."

"Yeah," said Essie loyally. And then on an impulse she said, "Charlotte, have you ever done anything . . ." She was stuck, unable to find an adequate word.

"Yes, I have," said Charlotte, and when Essie looked startled, she laughed and added, "Most people have. But listen, Jo, if you're thinking about the kidnapping, what you did, what you should have done—all that—there's no point asking me. You haven't told me anything about it, and if you had, I *still* wouldn't know what to think."

"Oh, I wasn't . . ." she began, but clearly she was.

"I don't want to lead you on," Charlotte said. "Wisdom isn't my thing. Look, if it would make you feel better to talk, go ahead and talk. I'll listen. But I don't do advice."

"It doesn't matter," said Essie after a moment, disappointed, pulling herself up. She had been full of hope when she heard the question on her own lips,

237

and it was hard to change direction so quickly. She added after a moment, "It's something I'm trying to work out. I'm okay."

"I'm on your side," Charlotte said, "if that helps. I'm sure you did the best you could."

"It doesn't matter," Essie said, fighting down an impulse to scream.

"Well, good," said Charlotte. "We've all got our own troubles."

"I'm okay," Essie said.

Harry said, "I forgot to put *haricots vert* on the list this morning—went right out of my head. Run up to Park's before they close. Get two pounds."

I do *not* want to go on the street, she thought. Cops or gumshoes hanging around—I'm not ready for it.

"Oh, Harry," she said, "can someone else go?"

"Why? What's the matter with you?"

"Uh, I've got cramps. *Bad* cramps."

"Cramps?"

"My period, Harry."

Her ears turned red to say it, but Harry's ears turned red, too, and he sent Jim.

Essie thought, That'll keep me off the street for the next day or two, and that's a day or two to think of something else.

But at 8:45, despite everything, feeling at least half protected by the dark, she slipped out the alley door. She had to talk. Charlotte would not do; Charlotte was important to Essie in many ways—a fixed point, a buddy of an odd but reassuring sort—but she was not a confidante. Essie wanted to tell and hear without reservation. She wanted to talk to a friend.

She could not see anyone watching, gumshoe or cop, but with a wary intuition she avoided all of her regular phones in favor of a new one on a corner that she had often passed on the way to the market but had never used.

She wished she could talk to Heather, who would know what she ought to do. But she had settled in her mind that it was not fair to call Heather. She called Erin, but there was no answer. She called Elliott.

It was Elliott's mother who answered.

"May I please speak to Elliott?" she said. She did not attempt to disguise her voice; she assumed that Elliott was besieged with calls from girls, and that hers would fall upon incurious ears.

"Oh, uh . . . why yes, of course," said Elliott's mother. "May I tell him . . . oh, uh, never mind. Uh, he's just getting out of the shower. I'll go call him."

But there were none of the accustomed sounds of the receiver being put down, footsteps receding, and the distant calling of his name. Instead there was a rubbing, as when a hand is pressed over the mouthpiece, and a muffled conference. "Just a minute," said Elliott's mother after a minute. "He's coming." And then the rubbing sound again, and another considerable pause. The rubbing sound, and then, "Uh, I don't think he heard me, Es . . . uh, just hold on."

Es . . . ?

Elliott's mom knew who was calling, and she was trying to keep her on the line.

Essie slammed down the receiver and ran like mad. She had covered almost a block when she saw a patrol car shoot past her the other way. At the corner she paused and peered back. She saw the car jink sharply at the far end of the block and lurch to a stop beside the phone booth she had just left. The spruce cop popped out and stood within the open door, one leg still inside the car, one arm clapped across the roof, scanning up and down the adjacent streets as far as he could see. Then he dropped quickly back in, pulled briskly into traffic, and zipped off. It was clear what was going on—he knew that she had been on that phone moments before, that she must still be near. He was beginning a sweep of the neighborhood. Essie did not know how he would go about it, but she knew that she did not want to be on the street to find out; she wanted nothing to do with the spruce cop.

Another half block brought her to the bottom of the alley. She pressed madly along between the walls and the few remaining parked cars and small trucks. At the back door she paused to regain her breath and was just stepping through it when she saw the silhouette of a patrol car, its headlights dark, filling the top of the alley. She jumped inside, turning toward the ladder, but Al was right there, filling a canister from a great sack of rice, looking up, surprised to see her. She glanced off, darted past the startled Harry to the only private place, the ladies', swinging the door shut and turning the rattling little knob lock.

It was a refuge of a sort, and she sank down, panting, on the commode.

*What had happened?*

Elliott's mom had been keeping her on the phone, and the police had come right to her. The *energy* of that car, whizzing past like a great stone. And she had a vivid mental picture of the man inside, tight and violent—she remembered the sounds when he beat Kit, could still hear the sound of Kit's keening breath in the moments after.

Somebody had talked to the police. Erin's mom? Could word have gotten around so fast? It was a bitter, naked-feeling moment. And it meant that she was cut off, they must all be hooked in to the cops. No more calls—no more friends.

And she had come running into the kitchen when she was supposed to have gone home—how was she going to explain *that?* But the restaurant was open, the dining room was full of people, and she could not stay in the bathroom all night.

The spruce cop was not in the kitchen when she emerged, but Nicky was, and waiting for her. He looked concerned. He beckoned her over. She came slowly.

Oh, God, she thought.

He laid an avuncular arm around her neck.

Oh, God, she thought, here it comes.

"*Jo,* dear," he said hesitantly.

Oh, God.

"You know, you're a growing girl and we think you *ought* to take plenty of snacks. I mean, good things."

Snacks?

"And Harry says you're very fond of fruit."

Fruit?

"And of course I *approve* of you eating fruit—but my dear, you take a *long time* in the bathroom."

The bathroom?

"Maybe . . . I mean, perhaps . . . oh, dear, this is embarrassing. Perhaps you shouldn't eat *quite* so much fruit, if it . . . you can always have some *bread* . . . do you know what I mean?"

Ah!

*Thank* you, God.

Red-eared, she hugged him around the waist. He was very lean and muscular through the middle, she was surprised to find. She said, "Thanks for taking care of me, Nicky."

Toby was subject on surveillances to the tantalizing fancy that something was happening just outside his range of vision, something he could pick up on if he moved. But he believed in playing these things by the numbers rather than by hunches, and in this case he considered that moving around would be a losing proposition. So he stayed put.

From his spot he could see a considerable expanse of street in four directions and the mouths of two alleys. She had to be on the street sometimes, even if she wasn't calling friends. There are lots of reasons for getting out. People have business, errands. And there is simple human nature: a kid wants to boogie.

A little before nine a city black-and-white appeared, weaving in and out of streets and alleys, doing a search pattern. A few minutes later it was joined by another, both very active. Whatever they had going, Toby admired their energy. When they were gone the street was quiet, as before.

It was toward ten o'clock that Gadek came on the air and called them all in to his spot. He sounded very tight.

"I just got the word on my cellular," he said. "She made a call from a new phone to a trap number. It was more than an hour ago."

"Aw, *shit,"* said Footer.

"Right," said Gadek.

"How come . . . ?" said Walt.

"Because there was a monumental screwup," said Gadek, as close to turning purple as Toby had ever seen him. "Because Dispatch called SFPD but didn't call us. San Francisco said they had a car there in less than a minute, but she'd disappeared."

"Aw, shit," said Footer.

"She cut off the call and ran," said Gadek. "I don't know why. But it means she knows now that her calls are being traced. It means we're burned. I don't know what she'll do about it, but it's a disaster from every point of view. It's just a stone disaster."

# 34

Paul lived in agonizing, hourly expectation that the baby-sitter would be brought in. The interception of the call to Erin Conlan was reported on Thursday night, Gadek's advance guard had charged out within an hour, and the main force on Friday afternoon. For the first forty-eight hours his people were continually jogging back and forth between the Detective Division and the parking lot. Service Division people were in constant contact with their DD counterparts and bore home a tantalizing dribble of rumors and intimations to add to what he could pick up himself. So much going on, but he did not dare show too much interest or ask more questions than the others did.

On Friday he kept the boy locked in the bathroom all night, but even then he found it hard to sleep—any little noise awakened him, and he had trouble falling to sleep again.

Then Saturday night the grab was fumbled and the baby-sitter dropped out of sight. At the end of Paul's shift on Saturday the first of the task force people had just come in, looking grim, clearly unsuccessful. Paul was encouraged. The baby-sitter was smart and alert—the same qualities that made her dangerous if she were found made finding her less likely.

Now he was up and down, alternately hopeful and despairing. He found work difficult and sitting agony. He loitered as much as possible among the corridors of files, where he was not under everyone's eye but where he could still catch most of what people were saying. He seized on every errand and little job that took him away from his desk for a few minutes.

Half the time he reassured himself with the reflection that even if the baby-sitter were found, she might not have seen him, or if she had, might not be able to describe him or even recognize him if they came face to face. He had seen that a hundred times—someone gets her purse snatched or something, Patrol grabs the guy two blocks away, and the victim has no idea whether that's the one or not. So they bring her in, she says she didn't see anyone, and that's it; the whole thing just blows over. Jeremy Broome becomes one of those cases destined to sit open but unsolved, cluttering file drawers and minds for dreary and unprofitable decades until someone in the next century sits down and calculates that nobody connected to it could possibly still be alive.

The other half of the time it seemed to Paul a certainty that she had seen him, or that she would pick him out as the scapegoat whether she had seen him or not. A kid will say anything to get herself out of trouble. They pick her up and bring her in—they wouldn't call ahead—she'd be in the building before anyone knew she'd been found. The quickest way from the parking lot to DD is right through Service Division. They'd bring her past his desk. She'd spot him and start pointing and screaming. It could happen at any moment. Each time someone came around the corner, Paul's heart jumped—it would be her—there he was at his desk in plain sight.

People came around that corner all the time. It was the water torture: drip, drip, drip.

He considered going home sick for a day or two until there was some resolution, but if he was at home, he would have no idea what was happening. Bad as it was to be in the middle of all the rumors, he could not bear the thought of being cut off.

He did not see what he could do. Get rid of evidence? He had his pictures, his tapes. How could he get rid of them? So much of his life had been taken from him already. What sort of life is it if you have to give up everything that matters to you in the name of security? What's fair about that? Why should he have to cut his own throat just because some hysterical girl . . . he hadn't done anything.

And then there was the boy. The boy was certainly easier to deal with than the pictures because he was replaceable, and they were not. The boy could be put in the hole. But it would mean starting all over again, and they were making real progress. The boy was getting to like him, he could see that. A little more time, and all would be well. It would be agonizing to have to throw it all away when they were so close.

His mind shied away from these things.

Paul looked up at the innocuous-seeming ceiling above his desk. The jail was right upstairs, directly over Service Division. He could see the painted lines on the floor, the jailer's office with the thick wired windows, the little barred cells, the glaring lights. They'd drag him up there in handcuffs. They'd all gather around while he was searched, leering and mocking. *Okay, buddy, strip.* Oh, they'd love to watch that. *Okay, buddy, face the wall. Bend over and spread your buttocks with your hands.*

He'd have to do it. They'd make him do it. The pumped-up wisecracks, the harsh shouts of laughter rang through the mind's ear. Paul's body tightened and his face was pink.

None of them like me, Paul thought. Not one of them. Certainly not Mother Superior. They'd be happy to put the blame on Paul instead of the baby-sitter. Only too glad to get rid of Paul. People always were.

Why did this whole thing have to keep threatening? Why couldn't everyone just do what they had been doing before? All he had ever asked was to be left alone.

"What's gotten into Paul?" said someone during one of his absences. "I mean, he's always been angry inside, but he absolutely goes around muttering all the time."

"Oh, well," said Sergeant Wren mildly. He discouraged personal discussion of people in his command, whatever his own reservations might be.

"No, that's right," said someone else. "He's *snappin'* all the time. Can't ask him for a paper clip—he comes back at you like it's out*rageous*. Wears me out, dealin' with it."

"Well, perhaps I should speak to him," said Sergeant Wren, resolving inwardly that he *would* speak to him.

"It's gotten worse lately, it really has," said someone.

"'Course, *other* times he's chucklin' and bouncin' around," said someone else. "That don't make much sense, either."

"These things can be very complicated," said Sergeant Wren. "I don't know. I'll think about the best way to approach it."

Footer was in the office when Toby and Walt came in on Sunday afternoon.

"Gadek's been in the city since early this morning," he said. "He figured maybe we'd been missing something, concentrating on the evening hours. We know she goes out then, but we don't know she doesn't go out other times."

"Sounds sensible," said Walt.

"Yeah," said Footer, "except it doesn't seem to have panned out. Gadek can be pretty dry sometimes, but I think if he'd gotten her, he would've called in. I guess there's still something for you guys to do."

"Should we hook up with him when we get over there, or is he coming back?" said Toby.

"He should still be there. Raise him on Channel Three. You can hear all about his uneventful day before enjoying your quiet evening."

When they got to the city and found Gadek, he had been up and down and in and out all day long and gotten a pretty good sense of the weekend pulse of the area. But no Essie to show for it.

"She's too smart to call now," he said. "The interesting question is what she *will* do. She may just have broken off that one piece of her pattern. And if she has, it's anyone's guess whether she develops a new one that gives us any sort of handle."

"So how long do you propose hanging out here?" Toby asked.

"We'll do it for a bit," said Gadek. "She may think that she's safe so long as she isn't calling and wander out where we can run into her. But if we don't catch her moving on the street, then we'll just have to think again."

"And?"

"Ask me in a week. We could just start knocking on doors. Or we could put it all on the back burner until she shows again."

"Maybe she just pulled up stakes after we missed her last night," said Walt. "Could be anywhere now."

"I hope not," said Gadek. "In any case, it's just you two tonight. The others have got urgent cases going, and I've got things to do in the office. I seriously doubt she's going to do any calling tonight."

"I just spoke to someone in DD," said one of the clerks to Sergeant Wren. "It was a complete botch last night." Paul pricked up his ears. The clerk explained what had happened and that the task force was burned.

"Well, that's terrible," said Paul. "I heard it didn't go well."

"'Not well' doesn't begin to describe it," said the clerk.

"So they still don't know where she is?"

"That's what they're so worried about," said the clerk. "Now that she knows how close they are, all she has to do is disappear again."

"Well, that's terrible," said Paul.

"She's smart," said the clerk. "They may never find her."

"That's terrible," said Paul.

The Sunday brunch service was easing in the early afternoon. Essie stood at the big table, mixing batter in a large bowl and furiously chewing the fact that her calls had been discovered and traced and that her contacts with her friends were at an end, when Nathan squeezed past her, dipping down to drag his crotch across her behind. Without thinking, she spun around and launched the bowl at him. It was a heavy bowl and a slow movement; it missed Nathan and burst noisily against the wall. Nathan reeled back, furious, the veins in his neck standing, eyes small, lower jaw working.

"What in Christ . . ." said Harry, turning from the stove.

Nicky, just emerging from the office, saw the whole thing.

"Stop that *this instant!*" he shouted. Advancing on Nathan he hissed, "You get out."

"You're crazy," Nathan said, indignant, incredulous. "She threw it at me. *She threw it at me!*"

"I saw what you did."

"We were just playing," said Nathan, suddenly affable. "She's got it, she likes to show it off."

"*Crap,*" said Harry.

"*Likes* it?" said Nicky, turning to Essie. "My *God,*" he cried, turning back to Nathan, "I don't care whether she likes it or not. She's a *child,* simply a child."

"Ha, ha," said Nathan jovially, trying to turn him.

"Ha, ha, *nothing!*" he shouted at Nathan. "Ha, ha your*self.* You are *fired.* I won't have a *per*vert working in my restaurant."

"*Pervert?*" bellowed Nathan. "*You fucking faggot, you . . .*"

"You don't insult me," said Nicky with invincible simplicity, snatching out his wallet. "I *am* a fucking faggot. That's exactly what I am. But I don't go around taking advantage of children. Here." He threw several bills on the table. "That's your severance. Now get, or I'm calling the police."

Harry had come up beside Nicky. Al's hand was on the telephone, the grin frozen on his face. Jim stood immobile on the other side of the room, gripping a heavy crêpe pan. And almost immediately, despite his ferocious appearance and enormous shoulders, Nathan was rushing out the alley door.

*"Prick,"* Nicky called after him, red-faced. And then rounding suddenly on Essie he said, "Now for you, Jo. I want you to know that I've just had to fire the *best* waiter I've *ever* had working for me. I suppose it's my fault for leaving you in a situation you couldn't handle." Essie had just been opening her mouth to say, Thank you, Nicky. "What Nathan did was inexcusable, but I *can't* believe you couldn't have avoided this if you'd tried, I *really* can't. Now I have to look for a *replacement,* and Charles is going to have to cover until I find one. I'm trying to run a business here. I *didn't* need this. I didn't need this at *all."* And then he was gone, too, stalking off to the office.

There was a silent moment in the kitchen, and then Arthur whistled. Al giggled and said, "Well, I think he's pissed." Harry snorted and turned back to his work. Jim turned away, stony-faced.

"Well, well, *well,* w'at a leetle *Amazon* our Jo eez," cried Emile. "You won't catch me putting my 'ands on 'er, not anymore."

"Oh, it's safe enough now," said Harry over his shoulder. "We're not going to let her have any more of those heavy bowls. Christ, if she'd hit him with the thing, he'd've been dead. 'Course, maybe the bowl wouldn't have broken if she'd hit him. That's what I regret. That was a pretty good bowl."

"What was I . . ." said Essie, in bewilderment.

"But how can you blame Nathan?" said Arthur in some glee. "How could he resist our Jo? She has such lovely thighs. If she were a boy, I couldn't control myself." And then he added, "You're *not* a boy? In disguise?" which Emile thought was killing funny.

"Sure," said Essie, trying to be a sport, disconcerted, on the brink of tears. "I'm a boy. You bet." *I wish they'd stop making stupid jokes,* she thought. *I wish they'd stop talking about sex all the time. I didn't want this to happen. I don't want to be responsible for Nathan getting fired. I wish somebody'd speak to me in a normal voice without all the goddamn joking. I wish somebody'd tell me I did the right thing.*

"Well," Harry said, "when you've gathered all the wool you're going to need for right now, perhaps you'd better get that mess cleaned up, and start another batch. Was that the last of the heavy cream?"

"Yes," she said, still reeling.

"Well, then someone'll need to go up to Park's. Preferably you, since they seem to be short-handed in the dining room all of a sudden. Unless your plumbing's still acting up," he added.

*What's going on?* she thought. *My God, what's changed?*

But Al said, "I'll go." And as he was leaving he stopped by her and, lowering his voice and grinning awkwardly, said, "That was kinda rough."

"Yeah," said Essie.

"Well, don't feel bad," he said.

Essie nodded, head down, and he departed. But she was not comforted. She *did* feel bad. Don't feel bad? Why not? It was advice that made no sense after what had happened.

But then Emile appeared beside her and said, "I 'ave come to apologize. I should not 'ave laughed at you." She did not raise her head. He crouched down so that he was looking up at her. "Weel you forgive me? Or must I shoot myself?"

She trembled between pride and loneliness. She shook her head.

"You must say, 'I forgive,'" Emile said. "And you must smile a leetle. Or I weel never sleep."

She glanced at him. His expression was sincere and

terribly funny at the same time. She was afraid she was going to giggle. She whispered, "I forgive."

He did not burst into a laugh, as she expected, or make one of his theatrical gestures, but he smiled happily, leaned up, and again kissed her. She thought she was going to faint. She looked him full in the face with an expression he saw, so that abruptly he straightened up and in a different, slightly concerned tone, as if he had just noticed the effect he had on her, he said, "Jo, there eez no confusion? We are friends, but you know that Art'ur and I are a—'ow you say— a number?"

She looked up sharply, and then, more slowly, down again. Yes, of course she knew, more or less.

Again she whispered, "I forgive."

Which was not completely true, but she thought she ought to say it; and he laughed out loud, relieved, and hugged her, which was a great recompense.

Sunday night had the advantage that apart from the surveillance operation, there was very little moving at all except around the little park and its restaurants. It was easy to sort out that traffic because it was stylish and concentrated on that block. The rest was easy to keep an eye on because it was so intermittent. Anybody moving caught the eye. But Essie did not call and she did not show, and when Toby and Walt conferred on the radio around ten-thirty they agreed to pack it in. They checked in at Gadek's office before going home. There were no messages on the answering machine to review for hot new tips and no notes for them from Gadek. They wrote,

Gadek/Kramer & Parkman    12/4    2315
zip

on a slip of paper and left it on his desk.

Paul saw them going down the corridor to DD, and

a few minutes later coming back, heading home. He only had to look at their faces to see that they hadn't brought home the bacon. His own shift was over. He wandered casually down the quiet hallway, carrying a file folder for an excuse. His work took him all over the building, distributing things or picking things up. No one would question his presence. A common key, which he legitimately carried, opened most offices in DD. He let himself into Gadek's office and examined the desk. He read the note:

>  Gadek/Kramer & Parkman   12/4   2315
>            zip

Too bad, he thought.

The little red message light on the machine shone steadily. No messages. It glowed like a tiny beacon of safety in the night. Nothing going on. No tips, no leads. Zip.

Too bad, he thought.

# 35

Essie opened her eyes on Monday morning and said, "I can't stay here." Nicky's voice clamored in her mind's ear, angry and foreboding. And Emile—she assured herself that she'd known perfectly well that he liked men instead of women, but . . . Going to his apartment was not going to be a problem. And now that it was a safe daydream she lingered on it and savored the aftertaste of danger with regret.

She saw her position in a new light. She had thought herself valued and secure, but she had deceived herself: in fact, she could see, she was entirely dispensable. She had scrounged the odds and ends of other people's jobs. There was nothing she did that other people in the kitchen could not do better and faster. If she were to vanish, they would all work just as they had the day before she appeared.

Her days were numbered at Le Coq d'Or. Even if her nest were to remain undiscovered, things would not be the same. Nicky would have had his day off to think things over. He might sack her on Tuesday. Or just stop creating work for her. Or just stop giving her money.

Nicky had his own problems. She would not blame him if he kicked her out.

But what else was there?

Give up?

Go home?

She prowled, pondering, until she noticed where she was. The kitchen was suddenly a colder and more complicated place than it had been. So cozy before, when it had been her refuge, but now it was one more field of contention. The compressor motor on the freezer had been almost like a great, reassuring pulse, day and night, but now it seemed to her merely a noise.

She had to get out, to walk around, lurking cops or no lurking cops.

Out on the street she pulled up the collar of her peacoat, dug her head into her shoulders, and walked fast. She liked it, striding into the cold wind and not feeling delicate. She kept her eyes peeled, ready to duck or run, but she saw no enemies.

At the used bookstore she paid seventy-five cents for a worn paperback anthology of Romantic poetry. Ms. Dieter's class was reading that period. The purchase made her feel connected and responsible.

She bought a purple lipstick. Why, she thought? But then she thought, Why not? Just to try. To please herself. And perhaps prove something to Nicky. She certainly had not handled Nathan well. The thought of Nathan was enough to make her stamp with anger and chagrin. And *should* she have known about Emile and Arthur? She saw that she had mistaken, misjudged, miscalculated—made a fool of herself in every direction simultaneously. A total capacity for self-deception. No judgment, no sense. Stupid, blind, and helpless. She broke into a run and pelted despairingly along the street until she was winded.

What with one thing and another, she discovered, she was a little hungry.

She bought a hamburger and sat at a counter facing the teeming shopping street. While she ate she watched the shoppers and nomads, beggars and hustlers, venders and cops as they hurried along, drifted, lingered, hovered, hunkered. A derelict stood between two newspaper racks with a vague expression on his face and a spreading puddle of urine at his feet. Essie propped up her book of Romantic poetry and ate french fries while she read "Lines Composed a Few Miles above Tintern Abbey, on Revisiting the Banks of the Wye during a Tour" by Wordsworth, which Elliott had mentioned. Her mind skipped off it like a stone.

But the world was brighter when she had something in her stomach.

So Nicky had his own priorities. Nicky wasn't trying out for Mother Teresa, he was trying to run a business. He was entitled to some latitude. She would not wait around on Tuesday to see what he would do; she'd go to him and flat-out apologize for not handling Nathan very well. He should give her another chance—he wouldn't be sorry. She was *not* useless. She'd pull her weight.

I'd go for that, if I were Nicky, she thought.

And anyway, she thought, it's not as if things were life and death. Nothing is forever. Emile—prime example. Now, Elliott—Elliott has virtues, even if he doesn't have a cute accent. Elliott is dependable. Emile was always a little scary, but it wasn't like that with Elliott.

Drifting along the street she thought, Wow, I wish I knew whether he really likes me more than he likes Shelly. I wish I could call. God, I *really* wish I could call.

Her life seemed very far away. She peered hopefully as she came up to each newspaper vending machine, wanting to see BOY FOUND. Only she did not see it. She scanned fearfully for her own picture: GIRL SOUGHT. But she did not see that, either.

Browsing in a variety store window she suddenly felt that she would be bolder if she had a fake tortoise shell compact with seven different shades of eye shadow and an applicator. And inside the store her eye fell on a display of skimpy black brassieres.

Essie had never owned any undergarments other than substantial and white. Once only she had ventured to express an interest in something more glamorous. Her mother said, "It doesn't make any difference what you wear unless someone is going to see it." Then she did that mock-quizzical look of hers and said, *"Is* someone going to see it?" which ended the discussion.

But even if no one was going to see it . . . Nicky had called her a kid.

She thought, Girl, if you want to be bold, be bold. Her mother, in any event, would not see it. She plucked down the most daring number she could imagine wearing, added it to the makeup, and strode bravely to the front. The cashier was a cocky-looking young man. For a moment she imagined him eyeballing her chest and saying contemptuously, You're too young to wear this. Instead, he accepted her money and bagged her purchases with the weary air of one who sells naughty underwear to runaways all day long. Essie regained the street with an exhilarating sense of assertion.

On the other hand, it had been an expense she had not needed. Bra and makeup were not expensive, but what with one thing and another, her cash was considerably depleted. All told, her whole reserve amounted to twelve dollars and change when she turned into the head of the alley and saw Charlotte sliding a portfolio into the backseat of a rented car. Another portfolio and several small paintings were leaning against the wall by the open stairway door.

"I'm off for a few days," said Charlotte when she saw Essie. "I've made a contact with a dealer in L.A. A *real* dealer. I'm going down to talk to him and show him some of my stuff. And if he doesn't work out, I'm going to spend some time looking around. It's time to get off the dime."

"How long'll you be gone?" said Essie.

"Maybe three or four days," said Charlotte. "Maybe ten. I'll stay till I score, unless it's hopeless."

"God, I'll miss you," Essie said, sounding lost, which was not what she intended.

Charlotte had just picked up a painting. She put it down again and said, "Listen, Jo. We've had kind of a deal about not prying and not giving each other advice. But now I'm going to give you some. You're trying to make a mother out of me."

"Oh, no," Essie said.

"Yes, you are," Charlotte said. "And if you're that desperate, maybe you ought to think about going home. 'Cause you sure don't act like you have the perfect life, as things are. And I can't take on responsibility for you. I like you, I'm glad to have you for a friend—this has been a rough time in my life, and you've made a difference to me—but I've got other things to think about. I've got my way to make, and I'm starting old."

"You're not old," said Essie. "You . . ."

"Shut up and listen," said Charlotte. "Shut up and think about this. I'm not a mom. Not yours, not anyone's. If you need one that bad, maybe the one you need is your own."

"I dunno," said Essie, meaning, Tell me how I could make it happen.

"Think about it," said Charlotte. She picked up the painting again and turned back to the car.

Paul and the boy stood by the river in gray overcast. For once it was Paul who was pensive and withdrawn and the boy who was energetic. Paul had sat on the bank struggling to assess the ebb and flow of his luck while the boy gathered a substantial pile of target wood. When he judged it sufficient, he plucked on Paul's sleeve.

"Ready," he said.

*The Perfect Parent* urged the importance of being responsive in such moments. Paul dragged himself up and began to throw the sticks. He cheered and groaned as was customary, but without enthusiasm, and before long—before the pile of targets was exhausted—he said, "One more, and then I have to go to work." He threw, and Jeremy threw. He began to turn away.

"Just these," said the boy, pointing to the pile. There were six or eight pieces left.

"No," said Paul. "I have to go to work."

"Just three, okay?" said the boy, running downstream a few yards to gather another handful of the small, smooth rocks he favored.

"No," said Paul.

*"Yes please!"* said the boy. He stamped. *"Yes! Just three please!"*

"No," said Paul, and turned away. A stone whizzed past him, very close to his head. He spun back in amazement. The boy had already cocked his arm back to throw another. For a moment he hesitated, meeting Paul's eyes, then he dropped his arm and released the rock. He took a step backward; his lip began to tremble. But Paul made no move at all. He stared reproachfully at the boy and slowly shook his head.

"I taught you how to do that," he said at last. "I taught you to throw. Do you remember that? You couldn't get your weenie out of your pants before you came here. So don't you give me a hard time. Now *c'mon,* goddamn it. I have to go to work." He held out his hand and gave it an impatient shake.

The boy trotted forward, eyes on the ground.

He did not want to take Paul's hand.

Paul continued to hold it out, and for a moment they stood there among the trees, the boy biting his lip and looking at the ground, Paul waiting, arm extended.

"What d'you think this means, eh?" he said quite soon. He shook his hand again, and when the boy did not immediately take it, he said, "I guess you've forgotten about the closet. Eh? Is that it? You don't remember spending all night in the closet? But all night isn't as long as boys stay in the closet sometimes. It can be all night and all day, and all night again, and even longer."

Slowly, still not looking, the boy put his hand in Paul's. Paul smiled grimly and nodded. Then he squeezed down hard, grinding the bones together and raising a yelp that rang in the woods.

"Don't you *ever* do that again," he said. Sharply he squeezed again, harder, and got a scream. Each time he was rewarded by the extremity of the boy's agony—the expression on his face.

# 36

"Another afternoon and evening of cramp and boredom," said Walt as he and Toby headed for their cars. And then, to head off any remonstrance, added, "Love it, of course."

"Good," said Toby.

"Yeah," said Walt. He filled his lungs with air and snorted exuberantly. "Got any hot premonitions? Is tonight the night?"

"I don't think I get premonitions," said Toby. "Do you?"

"Nope. At least, not ones you can count on. Get these strong feelings sometimes, that something's going to happen, except usually it doesn't."

"And tonight?"

"Nothing. Nothing one way or the other."

Charlotte gave Essie a genuine hug before she drove off, but it was perfectly obvious that her head was already in Los Angeles. Essie's ears burned with shame. Each day seemed to bring as a revelation something that had been under her nose all the time: yesterday that Emile was not for her; today that Charlotte was not, had never been, and would never be, her mother. She stood in the silent alley and stared in the direction of the bus terminal. She had run away from trouble and just found more. She could just gather up her stuff, walk on over, and be home in an hour.

Putting it that way made it seem very immediate, very tempting. Following that train of thought, she pictured herself arriving at the bus stop where she had started out, the half block to her house, the front door. There she stuck. Inside would be her parents. Would the police come? And then what? Would anything have changed? For better or worse? She could form innumerable conjectures, but none carried conviction.

Better, perhaps, to try to stay on as she was. She felt isolated and unsure: Charlotte had her own fish to fry; Nicky remained to be conciliated; her love life, or more properly, its illusion, had turned to smoke; she was cut off from her friends. But Essie told herself firmly that the bold girl would not be dismayed in her situation. It was in this spirit that in the early evening she cast aside her loneliness, plucked up her courage, and with her new makeup and brassiere in hand, strode resolutely into the ladies' room.

The purple eye shadow was fine, but the purple lipstick was something else. The black bra was distinctly visible through Essie's white blouse and so thin that it showed her nipples plainly. This was an effect she had noticed on stylish women, and she thought it imparted an air of confidence and unconcern. She was not at all sure that she could carry it off in front of witnesses—in fact, she was certain that she could not—but at the moment there were no witnesses.

Her blouse was buttoned almost to the throat, as usual; she undid the top button and then the next. That did not actually reveal much, but it was thrilling in its novelty. She stood as far back from the mirror as she could and tried to take in the whole effect. What would Nicky think? What if Elliott could see her? Her ears reddened. But then, Elliott could *not* see her. She arched her back and preened a little and boldly struck a voguish pose or two for Elliott. And if Jeremy saw her? She swallowed and pushed down the thought, while it was still half-formed, and focused on the mirror. Even the lipstick . . .

She was entirely absorbed in this when Nathan appeared in the doorway.

She jumped and froze, mouth half open.

He was stopped in the passageway just outside the door, three feet from her, taking in the makeup, the lipstick, the black bra trumpeting through the blouse. He did not speak; he stared frankly, as if she were a picture in a skin magazine. She reached feebly for the door to close it. But he said "No," and her hand dropped back to her side.

It was a tiny room; he nearly filled the doorway; there was no place she could go. She stood. His gaze pressed over her like oily hands on her lips, her bare neck and throat, her breasts, then down her belly, lingering at her crotch and thighs, settling again on her breasts. She could feel her bust rise slightly each time she breathed, feel the blouse tighten slightly; she knew it made the bra show blacker, her nipples more prominent. She was afraid to breathe. She was afraid to hold her breath. She was afraid to move. She wanted to fold her arms over her chest to cover herself—wanted to in the worst way. But she was afraid to acknowledge where he was looking, and she held her hands still at her sides.

It was unnatural to stand locked in that pose, and after a minute, she moved slightly. She half expected that he would move as well, that the sudden encounter would be ended and some sort of normal exchange would begin. But he only dropped his gaze to her hips as she shifted her weight, and she froze again.

Then abruptly he stepped back and said, "After you," nodding toward the kitchen.

Her alternative was to try to slam the puny bathroom door and hope that it would hold him off. It was no alternative at all. Slowly, with a thousand hesitations, she came out into the passage, as close to the wall as she could move, brushing past him. He did not touch her, but he was very tense. The kitchen was the only place to go. She went as far as the big table, and then turned to face him.

He dangled a key and said, "When you fire someone, always change the locks." He laughed. He arched his eyebrows, inviting her to join in his amusement; when she did not, but only stood watching him, he shrugged.

From the stocks in the refrigerator he produced a bottle of Le Coq d'Or's best champagne. Smoothly, adroitly, the veteran waiter, his eyes still fixed on her, undid foil and wire and eased the cork. There were glasses by the sink. He poured two, and with a friendly, almost deferential inclination of the head, pushed one along the table to her. He said, "The fag didn't give me very much severance. I've come back for a supplement. I wasn't expecting to find anyone here, as a matter of fact. I was going to have a sort of Easter egg hunt, and see what the fag's left hidden around for me." He lifted his glass and said, "But since you're here, you can help me celebrate. Here's to my supplement."

He waited for her to lift hers. She shook her head.

"Please," he said. "Join me in toasting my supplement. I won't tell you what this champagne costs Nicky, but it costs the customers a hundred and twenty-five dollars for each and every bottle."

"I don't drink," she said, lying smoothly.

Nathan placed his own glass carefully down on the table, took up the bottle, and suddenly, viciously, hurled it against the wall behind her where it burst in a shower of foam and green glass. His eyes never left her face.

Essie goggled at him, horror-struck, knowing she showed it, past pretense. They were both past pretense. There was no one else there. He was standing next to the telephone. He was planted between her and the front door. To get the alley door open she would have to back the beam out of its socket, lift it out of the brackets, and heave it out of the way; she was only three feet closer to it than he was. The butcher's block with Harry's knives in it was closer to him than to her.

"Go ahead," he said, nodding to her glass and again taking up his own.

Her voice felt tiny inside her. Her lips moved very slightly. Almost inaudibly she said, "No."

"What's the matter, little girl?" said Nathan. "Afraid you might get carried away?" He said this as if he considered that her getting carried away was highly probable. "Afraid you might do something *dirty?*"

There was no answer to make. She saw that his eyes were fastened on the bareness of her throat and neck. She had actually undone the top two buttons herself—for *Nathan.* She could not believe it.

He stirred a little, as if he were about to push away from the wall.

"I can make you," he said.

She shook her head very slightly, meaning, No, don't.

"Yes, I *can,*" he said, suddenly louder, his voice rising in pitch. "I *can.*"

There was nothing to say. They stood six feet apart, his eyes fixed on the third button of her blouse, her eyes on the wall next to his shoulder. Her hands held the table behind her as if she would draw it forward around herself and bring it between them.

Why can't you just fly out of places if you want to badly enough? Even at that moment she registered the monstrous injustice of her being unable, despite her fervent, desperate wish, to disappear, or be as strong as Nathan was, or produce a weapon, or conjure up a protector.

"I'm waiting," he cried, almost shouting now, slapping down his glass so that the champagne foamed over the sides, standing free, swaying with anger and excitement right in front of her, his breathing deep, his chest rising and falling.

"No," she said. To hell with it. She fumbled at the second button, trying to fasten it.

*"NO!"* He grabbed her wrists, irresistible. She thought, This is it: Mom will kill me. Then suddenly he stopped and said, "How did you get in here?"

She said instantly, "Nicky and Charles let me in."

It was the first thing that came into her head, and she recognized at once that it was improbable. But the best lies have the merit of being unexpected, and trusting to instinct she plunged on. "I'm getting your job. They dropped me off and told me to get made up while they went to pick up some stuff. Then they're coming back to start training me."

"I don't believe you," said Nathan, but she could see from his face that he did not know what to believe; he had never understood Nicky and Charles. At first he had pulled her toward him, but now he was beginning to hold her away. Out of the corner of her eye she could see the clock above the phone; it showed 9:22.

"They said they'd be back by nine-thirty."

Nathan glanced at the clock, then at her face. She tried to pull herself up a little more confidently, squared her shoulders, tried to make her chin jut like a woman who does what she pleases and doesn't take shit from anyone. The movement made her bust more prominent, but she did not care.

Nathan had not moved, but suddenly he seemed to be getting smaller.

Wow, she thought. She edged her chin higher still, amazed at herself.

"I can make you," he said less certainly, his chest still rising and falling. But his hands were relaxing on her wrists. He was stepping back. And then his pride, if not his courage, returning, he thrust out an accusing finger. "I *will* make you."

But instead, he turned and disappeared quickly down the passage. A moment later she heard the street door open and close.

She found it difficult to stand.

She did not know for sure that he had gone out—she had only heard the door. If he had gone out, she wanted to lock it between them.

But he might still be in the dining room.

She drew a short boning knife from the chopping block, the sort of knife which, she was astonished to find herself calculating, would be easy to swing and hard to see coming. She crept to the passage. She could see nothing, hear nothing. But except for the light from the streetlamp under the trees immediately opposite, the dining room was dark; she could not see the corner nearest the door, and she could not see behind the cashier's desk. He could be in any of a number of places at that end, or he could have opened and closed the door and then come back to the kitchen end of the dining room. He could be right around the corner at the other end of the passage, ten feet away, waiting for her to come past him or to relax so that he could dart in after her. If he were there, the knife would not save her. If he were not there, there was no need to go through the dining room to lock the door.

She wanted a line of retreat. She backed through the storeroom, removed the bar, and opened the back door.

Now what?

She quickly became aware that it was cold.

You can't stand here in the alley.

Charlotte is gone.

You're not safe in Le Coq d'Or.

You can't live on the street.

Go home.

There is only so much that can happen to you at home, and the same is not true of the present situation.

She thought, I'm an underage girl. I'm going home.

She peeked in at the door. Wherever he might be, Nathan was not visible; she slipped in through the storeroom and scrambled up the ladder. Pausing every few seconds to listen again, she bundled on her reindeer sweater, her sweatshirt, and her peacoat.

She'd have to find something else to do for Jeremy.

She would call Heather. Together they would figure something out.

She divided her twelve dollars between the right and left pockets of her jeans. She swept what she could into her duffel and slung it over her shoulder. Still holding the knife, she surveyed the storeroom as well as she could from the top of the ladder and then descended, braced to swing out from one hand and strike with the other. At the alley door she hesitated. When you leave places you lock up, you turn out lights. Surely, she owed it to Nicky. But Nicky would not expect her to creep back through the kitchen and passage to the office, rummage for a key with her unprotected back to the dark pantry, and then traverse the dining room to the front door—not when Nathan might still be there. Nicky would say, *Go,* girl.

A moment later she was out the alley door, the knife unobtrusively down by her leg, sprinting up toward the street.

No Nathan at the mouth of the alley or up or down the street. Into the pocket of her jacket went the knife, and she strode off in the direction of the bus terminal. She knew the neighborhood pretty well by now, knew the shortcuts, knew the quickest way.

# 37

They watched, they waited.

Zip.

Toward the end of the shift Toby raised Walt on the radio, and he came over.

"Been kinda keyed up tonight, for some reason," said Walt. "Keep seeing little Essie-size people wandering in and out. More than usual, anyway."

"I know what you mean," said Toby. "I'm getting balmy. I keep wondering if she could disguise herself. I want to chase everyone I see and get a look at them."

"There," said Walt abruptly, plucking up his binoculars.

A young woman in a peacoat had emerged briskly from the head of the alley half a block away and now strode purposefully across the street. He watched for a moment. "I can't see her face."

"Nah," said Toby. "The size is about right, but Essie doesn't move like that. That one's too assured, too old. Essie's a little mouse."

"No, there's something about that one," said Walt. "Take a swing past and get a closer look."

"We'll be out of position," said Toby, but he started up and pulled out sharply. They rocketed down to the corner where the light was red and the cross traffic bothersome. Looking up the street to the right, they could see the girl. She was covering ground. It was a short half block from the alley to the next street, and she was already crossing it. By the time they got around the corner and up the block she was several doors up the long block to the east. It was a one-way street heading west.

"Damn," said Toby. There was no unobtrusive way to follow her up a one-way street in the wrong direction. "We'll have to make the block."

The light was red, and there was enough traffic that they had to wait for it. Then they shot up to the next street, turned east, drove the long block, turned south, and finally west on the block where they had seen her before.

"Don't see her," said Walt.

"No," said Toby. "I think there's another alley midblock."

There was. They stopped at the end of it and looked up, but the girl was not visible.

"I'm going to let her go," Toby said, "and work around to our spot again. I don't think that was her. We could shake this block all night and not find her. She could have gone into any of these buildings. And in the meantime we're away from the most likely places."

"I'm with you," said Walt. "Too many variables in this business. Drop me at my car and I'll get back to my spot. We're wasting eyes, all clumped up like this."

"Paul is gettin' *worse*," said someone. "He was in here a few minutes ago, and it's doom and gloom every time he opens his mouth. Tragedy this and tragedy that. That man don't look on the bright side at *all*."

"Paul has been under a lot of stress," said Sergeant Wren. He lowered his voice. "For your information, I had a little chat with him about his relations with his coworkers. I gather there have been personal disappointments. He doesn't like to talk about his personal life, and he doesn't really spell things out, but I think that's what it is."

"That'll do it," said someone else. "That's all it takes, right there."

"It's a hard time for him," said Sergeant Wren. "We have to make allowances."

Essie paused at the door of the terminal. She had not been there since the day she met Kit. Reflexively, she reconnoitered the waiting room, but Kit was not visible. She entered, consulted the schedule, and found that the next Green Line bus left in less than ten minutes. She found a phone and, with a deep breath, dialed Heather's number. She got the answering machine.

She pressed down the hook and breathed again. Heather might well be baby-sitting, and that would probably be at the Parkmans'. In the past she had often called Heather at that number, and she dialed it now.

"Hello?" It was the one voice in all Essie's world that she wanted to hear at that moment, who would tell her what she ought to do.

"Hey," she said.

"Essie? *Oh wow, Essie, is that you?*"

"Oh, *Heather,*" she said. She glanced around the room, scanning for Kit. She could still almost smell Nathan.

*"Essie, are you all right?"*

"Oh, wow, Heather," said Essie. "I want a hug so bad."

"It's kind of hard over the phone, dummer," said Heather. "Where *are* you?"

"I'm not far," said Essie. "I'm coming home."

They did not have much time to chat. Heather could not meet the bus because she could not leave Adam and Joss. Essie did not want to go back to her family without support from some neutral adult party; for preference, she wanted to surrender—so she envisioned the process—to Walt.

"Walt and Toby Parkman are in the city looking for

you even as we speak," said Heather. "Fun*ny*. But they have to go by the station on their way back, so if you call Sergeant Gadek's office and leave a message on the machine, Walt'll get it when he goes in. He's supposed to be in at eleven." She gave Essie the number. "And if he isn't there to meet you, then just wait. I'll come as soon as one of the Parkmans gets in. Okay?"

"Yeah," said Essie. "I've got to make that call and run or I'll miss my bus."

"Oh, wow, Ess. *Wow,* I'm glad you're coming home."

It was shortly before 10:30, toward the end of his shift, when Paul finished a cataloguing chore in the basement and returned to Service Division. Sergeant Wren was not in a tranquil, end-of-the-day mood, however, because there were computer glitches that happened to impede and irritate the watch commander, and Sergeant Wren was always fretful when something within his span of responsibility was not in order; he was stalking back and forth behind the on-duty computer guru's chair, muttering exhortations.

"Oh, Greber," he said. "Just step down the hall to Gadek's office and see if I left my tickler file on his desk, would you? If it isn't there I can't imagine where it is." He was still exclaiming against his failing memory and the onset of old age when Paul left the room.

The tickler file lay in plain sight. The phone rang as Paul reached out his hand, and immediately the answering machine kicked in.

"Officer Kramer, this is Essie Beal."

Paul staggered.

For a moment he heard her hem and haw as people do when they hope that the person they are calling is really there and might pick up the phone; but then she spoke more quickly and to the point. She would be arriving at the end of the Green Line in half an hour.

Would Officer Kramer please pick her up, and help her to start dealing with her family. She couldn't call anybody else. She didn't know what else to do. Please would he help her. Then there was a click on the line, the tape whirred briefly, and the red message light began to *blink,* pause, *blink,* pause, *blink.*

Paul stood in the quiet office for a long moment, eyes fixed on the tiny light, his breath fast and shallow.

Here it was: It had been hanging, and now it was about to fall.

Tomorrow morning the long-missing Essie Beal would be sitting right here, talking about the man in the light sedan who was parked in front of the Broome house at the time of the kidnapping.

She would identify him. She wouldn't hesitate—why should she?

And then he thought, Unless she went right on being missing.

Why not?

She sounded meek. He liked all the "pleases." Submissive. How old was she? Fourteen? She sounded younger. She was small, he remembered. There was a pile of circulars on the desk, and he picked one up: five three, ninety pounds. He could handle that.

Maybe this was his break—maybe luck was running his way for once. Maybe things could work out after all. He would meet the bus.

It seemed like a good plan. It would clear away the one big threat that loomed over him, and then he could start again with a clean slate. Getting too close before the grab was the only mistake he'd made. He could correct that in the future. Live and learn.

Thoughtfully he reached past the desktop clutter and, with ever so slight a hesitation, pushed the Rewind button. The tape whirred again, and when the machine had reset itself the red message light shone steadily, unblinking.

Paul spent the last part of his shift in remote locations of the building, gathering his strength.

"Well," he said at the usual time, passing Sergeant Wren's desk, "I'm off home. I'll be glad to get there. I feel a little poorly. I wonder if I'm coming down with something."

Sergeant Wren was absorbed in the foibles of electronic devices. "Take care of yourself," he said absently.

"I will," said Paul.

Essie had been hoping to speak to Walt, and the answering machine was a disappointment, but Heather had said that he would get the message. Saying that she was coming back, acknowledging that she would be returning to her family, asking for help—saying all this out loud was so different from thinking it, juxtaposing her future so immediately with her present—that she felt a little stunned as she replaced the receiver and ran for her bus. The door was closing, but she called, "Wait, wait, wait!" and the driver opened again. As she dropped into a seat it occurred to her that a month ago she would have let the bus go and waited humbly for the next one. *Yeah,* she thought, I would have.

But everything was different, now. She had gotten through things. Yeah. Half an hour before, there was Nathan. That was luck, getting out of that, but still— she hadn't done what he wanted. *Yeah.* She'd been scared so badly she could hardly stand, but *she hadn't done what he wanted.* People can do things to you, but you don't have to help.

She still had the boning knife in her pocket. That was Harry's knife—a chef owns his own knives. She'd have to send it back to him. Or not—maybe she'd send him some money, instead. Maybe she'd keep the knife.

She didn't think of the knife as a kitchen implement, now; she thought of it as a weapon. She thought, I'll keep it.

It was a sort of promise to herself.

Maybe she hadn't done so badly. Yeah. Maybe she hadn't done so badly, these weeks.

There is no terminal building where the Green Line ends in downtown Bancroft. There are bus stops on both sides of the street where riders can transfer to locals, and there is a rank of taxis. Everyone gets off there, and on this occasion everyone but Essie got onto a local, or into a taxi, or into cars that were waiting, or else walked away through the downtown.

Walt was not there.

There was a clock visible in the store on the corner: 11:15. Either Heather or Walt should be there any minute.

She wondered if she would have a chance to change her bra before she had to face her mother.

It was about a quarter past eleven when Toby and Walt reached Gadek's office to deposit their customary memorandum of failure and frustration.

The phone rang as they opened the door, and Toby picked it up. It was Heather.

"Is everything okay?" she said happily.

"Okay?" he said. "Sure. What . . ."

"C'mon, *tell,*" she said. "How's Essie?"

He looked at Walt. "Essie?" he said.

* * *

A plain, light-colored sedan pulled up to the curb next to her. A man reached across to the passenger side and rolled the window partway down.

"Essie?" said Paul.

A little carefully, she said, "Yes."

He showed her a badge and said, "I'm Officer Fielding. Officer Kramer is tied up. He asked me to come get you. Hope you don't mind the car—undercover isn't very glamorous. Hop in."

They pulled away from the bus stop, and the hardest part was done. He had her, and nobody else would know. End of problem. He grinned to himself—he almost laughed. All these weeks he'd worried so much, and now the long-missing Essie Beal had dropped right into his lap.

"Better put on your seat belt," Paul said kindly. The release button on the passenger seat belt was broken—you had to stick a screwdriver into the buckle to undo it—and when Essie had fastened it, he knew that she wasn't getting out of the car in a hurry.

"That's better," he said.

The Hall of Justice is not far from the bus stop. They passed it a block to the south and continued west. Essie noticed this. And she knew this man from somewhere—where?

Paul glanced over and smiled. She's small, he thought. She can't be all that strong. He noticed the purple lipstick. Made up like a whore, too.

He thought, I could use her.

He thought, Why not? I don't have to wind things up tonight. A couple of days—why not? She's too old, but hell. I've lost enough sleep over her, God knows—she can make it up to me.

Better and better.

"Where are we going?" said Essie. She was trying to place him, and she wanted to hear his voice again.

The question was polite, but she didn't sound as meek in person as she had on the phone. There was a physical assurance, too. It put him off his stride so

274

that there was a little hesitation before his answer, and she noticed it.

"Kramer's working in the West End tonight," he said, smiling a little too late, oleaginous. "You know these detectives, they're all over. He wanted me to bring you there."

Heather said that Walt had been in the city with Toby Parkman, looking for her, and then would come back to the station—why would he now be working in the West End? It wasn't right. Kit had smiled like that. She didn't say anything, but she was tight as a drum. She never would have distrusted a cop before, but there had been the spruce cop, and now she saw what she saw. She would not have believed that Kit was someone who could affect her life, but he had. She would scarcely have believed Nathan, but she was still pumped from that encounter.

"Where is he working?" she asked. There was an alertness in her voice, and it was his turn to notice.

"Where I'm taking you," he said. He was rattled. Things were getting off on the wrong foot. He had always worked very gradually and with younger kids. This one had an attitude, he could see that.

"Let me out," she said suddenly. "I'll find Walt myself." There was no supplication about it.

"Now, don't get het up," he said. "We're almost there."

This street led to the interstate and to little else.

"Let me out." Her hand was on the door.

She was sounding tough, and Paul did not like it. But there was no going back. Even if she could not connect him to the boy, there was no credible explanation for what he was doing now—going to pick her up, or for this detour. She would not hesitate to betray him—he was committed.

And besides, she was small, still a little boyish. He would enjoy the next couple of days. Her attitude wouldn't matter, the way she'd be. But it was time to establish control.

They were not far from the freeway entrance. He turned into an industrial side street, deserted at this hour, and again into a deep parking lot enclosed on its three inner sides by a high chain-link fence. At the far, dark end he stopped.

"Now, young lady," he said, "you're a runaway, and you're under arrest. The department rule is that everybody under arrest has to wear these." He produced a pair of handcuffs from his belt and reached for her arm.

"It's for your safety," he added, still attempting a soothing smile.

Essie jabbed at the button on the seat belt with one hand and reached for the door with the other. The button wobbled fruitlessly, the buckle held firm, and Paul slapped the cuff onto her nearer wrist with a rippling metallic *clatch*.

"Now, c'mon," he said, drawing her toward him, straining against her seat belt to reach her other arm. The car was not large—he was half on top of her. She fended off his hand but he was gaining, pulling her in to him by the handcuff, which he held by the chain in his right hand, while with his left he seized her upper arm and began working his way down to her free wrist. She struck upward with her hand and caught him under the chin, more a slap than a blow, but he bit his tongue and tasted blood. He swung heavily at her with his left fist, ineffectively in the tight space, but he caught her on the side of the head and half stunned her.

She dropped her hand into the pocket of her coat and closed on the knife, blade upward as if she were about to bone a lamb. His left was cocked back to swing again, so she struck hard at his right where it clutched the cuffs, jabbing forward so that the slender point engaged the underside of his arm just above the wrist and slipped deep, scraping along between the two long bones; in that moment Essie saw the pale blade lying silvery along the red muscle and the bright, clean bone before he recoiled violently against the driver's side door, pouring blood and pressing himself away with his feet, yelping. He clamped the wound with his other hand and goggled in astonishment as she hacked savagely at the fabric of the seat belt. She was almost through it—freedom—disaster. He struck at her again and then again, more or less at random at her head and body while she struggled with the last strands of the belt. Disoriented, she realized that the knife had slipped out of the nearly completed cut and she was starting in a new place. She flailed at the air with the knife like a great soiled claw, trying to counter his blows, losing track of the belt. She threw open the door and lunged sideways, outward, thinking to break free, but still the belt held; she was fallen partly out, lying now so that she was doubled over the cut and unable to pull herself back up to get at it. Paul heaved open his own door and panted around the car to where she hung halfway out and almost upside down, sawing weakly at the belt in a new place that she could reach. He had every advantage now. He kicked the knife loose from her hand and then leaned down and used his weight, punching and slapping almost at random.

He hung over her for a minute, one hand on the roof and the other on the open door, gasping for breath. She still hung from the seat belt, helpless now, eyes open but punch-drunk and only semiconscious.

Paul's heart seemed to beat in slow, heavy spasms. He felt a giddiness that was not merely the adrenaline and the sudden exercise. In the struggle he had forgotten his wound after the initial sting, but now he could see that he had a serious problem. He was losing a lot of blood; it ran freely from his right arm and soaked into his pants.

Paul had often handled wounds suffered by others. Without thinking, he clamped his right forearm in his left hand, which reduced the flow considerably. What he could not stop oozed down his left arm and spotted his belly and pants. There was an old shirt in the backseat. He bound up his arm as firmly as he dared. The wound was long and deep—some major vessel must have been cut. The bleeding slowed with pressure but did not stop. Well, it was all he could do. Perhaps it would stop of its own.

His breath was almost recovered.

Now for his problem.

He could not dump the baby-sitter where she was. He wanted her to stay disappeared, not present the investigators with a new beginning and new possibilities. It was going to be hard enough to explain this wound, assuming that he could not conceal it, and he did not want so remarkable a circumstance to be noticed in conjunction with her death.

He had a hole all ready—the boy's hole in the shed. He would take her there.

Paul kept a screwdriver in the glove compartment for the purpose of jimmying the seat belt buckle if that should be necessary; he reached over Essie and fumbled around until he found it. When the belt parted she rolled out onto the ground. Shakily, putting out a hand for support, Paul moved to the back and opened the trunk. When he returned for her, he found he could barely lift her, small as she was; her feet dragged, and it was all he could do to get her upper half across the sill, and then lift her legs and tumble her in. She lay on her side with her left arm stuck out behind. Paul drew her right arm back with the handcuff still dangling from the wrist and snapped it over her left wrist so that her arms were cuffed behind her. Just in case she wakes up, he thought, slamming down the lid, just in case she doesn't die on the way.

He heaved himself back behind the wheel and maneuvered his way out of the lot. At the street he paused and looked up and down; on the right side he was looking through a window smeared across with blood. He could not drive around in a car in that condition. Reluctantly, he heaved himself out, and with the tail of the shirt binding his arm he wiped the window and door at least mostly clean. He felt heavy when he sat down again, quite remarkably heavy. He turned into the street and headed for the nearest entrance to the interstate, driving carefully so as not to attract attention. His arm was workable; it bled slowly, dripping onto his leg, but the loss was not serious as yet, and the pain was not much. In an hour or two, he knew, it would be more.

And he had to give some serious consideration to the question of keeping the baby-sitter for any length of time. That had been his first reaction—try her out, at any rate, and if there was any amusement in it, hang on to her. But if he kept her, she would need much more serious restraint than sufficed for the boy. And hurt the way he was, he obviously wasn't going to feel like using anyone for a day or two. He felt terrible, woozy and ill—that was loss of blood. When the serious pain began, he wondered if he would have the strength to handle her or be clear-headed enough to improvise restraints. Of course, she was not exactly in fighting trim herself when she went into the trunk. He shook his head in amazement. Did she seriously think she could just have a few free cuts on him, that he would just sit there and take it?

Perhaps the best thing would be to leave her in the trunk overnight. He would be rested in the morning. He could worry about it then. And if she still had so much spit that controlling her was going to be a problem, he could just close the lid again and leave the car in the sun for a few hours until she was a little wilted. That would take care of it. But in any case, he wouldn't have to worry about it until the morning.

"Leo, it's Toby. Did I wake you up? Listen, we've got something going, but it's unclear exactly what."

Walt paced slowly up and down between the three

desks in Gadek's office while Toby talked. He inspected the labels on Gadek's case binders and the titles of his training manuals. He looked at Wanted posters and Missing posters, and heaps of Offense Reports in trays, and little cups filled with paper clips, dry pens, cartridges of a caliber no longer issued. The answering machine—an *answering machine?*—fercrissakes, Heather has her own voice mail, and the Detective Division is still using an answering machine. The dingy off-brand computer. The dingy fax machine. The dingy phone. Walt had seen all of this before. Fortunately, the call was not a long one.

"He's on his way in," said Toby, hanging up and beginning to sift through the heap of manila file folders on Gadek's desk. "Somewhere here there's a list of the kids she's been calling, and we're going to start checking to see if she's turned up to stay with any of them. She may have gotten to the bus stop and then chickened out about coming to us. And while I'm looking, call over to Patrol, would you, and ask them to start a sweep downtown, working north toward her house. She may be walking. Or she may just be sitting someplace, trying to get her head together."

# 39

Essie was not entirely unconscious when Paul put her in the trunk, and she regained her senses steadily from there. Her first sensations were of pain—she hurt everywhere—without remembering why. She had a splitting headache. She tasted blood in her mouth. One nostril was partially occluded with a soft clot, and when she was conscious enough to explore her upper lip with her tongue, she encountered salty crust.

She felt carpeting against her face and thought that she was in her nest; then she felt the handcuffs, hard, cold, and sharp, and her arms pulled behind her. After that she remembered quite quickly what had happened: the creep had beaten her.

She tried to stretch out a little and found that she could not. Her left ear seemed very dull, but she could hear well enough with the other; from the space and the sounds and the motion, she knew where she was.

There was no doubt in her mind what was going to happen to her.

Her immediate reaction was anxiety that Heather would be offended that she did not appear as promised. Her next was to find the means of escape.

Essie wondered how, exactly, the bold girl would handle this problem.

The motion of the car was changing, she noticed. It was moving more slowly along a winding road.

Now that she thought about it, Essie seemed to remember virtually dozens of stories on the news and in the papers about people who get carried around in the trunks of cars for days or weeks. Apparently they are not able to get out. Sometimes they can attract attention by pounding and shouting. But unless the car stopped, and she could hear that there was someone around to hear any noise that she might be able to make, there did not seem to be much point.

What else?

Trunk lids have locks—can they be opened from the inside? Would the bold girl know how to do it? Does *anyone* know? Is there, in fact, any way to do it? Does it depend on the car? What about *this* car?

It was awkward to explore with her hands cuffed behind her, but in fact she was already lying jammed against the rear of the trunk. She began to run her hands over the parts she could reach. From the floor upward was all some sort of smooth paneling. If there was any mechanism there, it was inaccessible. She could feel the top of the sill and the rubber weather-strip, but no higher. She rolled a little more onto her stomach so that she could get her hands on the lid itself. She seemed to put weight onto bruises, whatever she did, but the pain did not stop her for a moment; she noticed this and was pleased, even then.

Now she could reach the part of the lock on the lid. There was some sort of open-sided metal cover, with a cable running into it from one side—the driver's trunk release. She ran her fingers around the cover and felt several metal parts; one had a flat surface and yielded when she pressed on it—the release.

The car was moving more slowly now, swaying more, and the surface was clearly bad. Wherever they were going, they must be almost there, and then it would be too late.

The creep would have to notice if the trunk lid opened. She would have to just do it, jump, pick herself up as fast as she could, and run—wherever. She did not know where she was or how long they had been traveling. But if it was still night, and they were out in the boondocks somewhere, she would have a pretty good chance—she was pretty sure she could outrun the creep—hide, find help—something.

Unless she broke something jumping. But Essie preferred the risk of breaking things to whatever it was that the creep had in mind. She took a breath and pressed the release. The lid popped up six inches or so and floated between its spring and the flow of air. She had a glimpse of a few yards of irregular and much-patched asphalt lit red by the taillights. The car was moving little faster than a fast run. She hunched herself up to her knees, lost her balance when the car swayed, and fell back, but with her shoulder braced against the side and her head pressing the lid up; she swung one leg around and over the sill.

Paul heard the trunk open but did not immediately place the sound. He was sunk low in his seat, faint and sick. His wounded arm lay in his lap, already hurting badly. His mind was on the road, on steering with his good hand, on getting home. The sound was behind him. After a moment he looked up at the rearview mirror and saw faintly red-lit trees, which was what he always saw on that road at night. Then he saw the trees disappear from the bottom up, which puzzled him. Then he understood—the trunk was open.

He knew what it meant. He had no idea how long it had been open. If she was gone—one of those stop-sign intersections miles back—the game was over. In panic, desperate to know, he slammed on the brakes and the slowly moving car jerked to a stop.

She was going to put both legs out, heave herself clear, try to roll when she landed, and run like mad for those trees. Ten seconds' head start into the night and he would never find her again. She tried to get the second leg out, but the sill was too high to manage it while she still sat on the floor, and too narrow to get her balance on it; she could not reach anything helpful with her hands. She would have to throw herself out in a lump. She had pulled herself up onto one knee, crossing the sill sideways, almost free, when the car suddenly jammed to a stop and she was catapulted forward into the deepest recesses of the trunk, striking her head sharply against the lid as she fell.

Badly frightened, Paul staggered around to the back and looked in. Without the slipstream to hold it down, the lid bobbed up gently at the sky, and the trunk lamp came on. Essie struggled in the bottom, blinking at the light; she did not know what had happened. She still had one ankle over the sill, and she was trying to hold with that and pull herself out again.

*"Whore!"* shouted Paul. His voice rang in the woods. Her ankle was the nearest thing to him: He grabbed, raised it, smashed it down again against the sill, and got a scream out of her. He reached in with his left arm and grabbed her coat, trying to pull her toward him, but he was too feeble, and he had only one arm to use; ineffectually he pummeled her, leaning in. He got hold of her hair and yanked it to and fro, trying to beat her head against the floor. She screamed once or twice more, wildly frightened but not much hurt, flailing at him with her legs. He was behind her where she could not see him or get a fair aim at him, but one of her kicks grazed his wounded arm and cost him such a jolt of agony that he howled and fell back several steps from the car. He grasped at his wrist with his other hand and swayed, dizzy, gasping, listening to her gasp and struggle, hearing the engine idle. He looked around the small circle of woods lit by the car's lights.

They were alone.

He was almost back to the cabin. Another five minutes.

Her ankle was dragging at the sill again—she was still trying to pull herself out. He lunged forward and tried to slam the trunk lid down on it, but she was turned around enough to see it coming. She yanked her leg in, and the lid slammed shut and locked.

He was almost home—just keep it together another five minutes.

A sudden paroxysm of anger overwhelmed him, and he landed a flurry of blows on the trunk with the flat of his fist and shouted, *"You'll pay for that!"* There was no answer.

The kick had set Paul's arm to pulsing in the most painful way. He was desperate to lie down. He worked his way around to the driver's door again, holding the roof as he went. He could barely hold himself up. He pulled the door closed and started again, watching the trunk carefully in the mirror and every short way throwing on the brakes.

The little whore is running up quite a tab, he thought when he was not thinking about the pain in his arm. She'll be sorry she started this fighting business. She's going to have a lot of paying back to do.

Of course, when he thought about it, sick as he was, Paul was relieved that the baby-sitter's escape attempt had happened when it did. Earlier, on a more traveled road, someone might well have seen it; and ten minutes later he would have been in the cabin, and she could just have traipsed off into the night. But now he was forewarned, and he was angry enough— at the escape, and especially for kicking him—that humanitarian considerations were not going to prevent him from making sure of her.

He drove through the gate, stopped, and locked it carefully after them. He checked the trunk. Then he drove on to the house and stopped among the trees, close to the porch. No one would see him get her out. She could make all the noise she wanted—no one was close enough to hear.

During the brief last stage of the drive she had reoriented herself in the trunk, and as he began to open it she lunged up, jumped, and almost succeeded in barging past him—he caught one leg as she landed. Handcuffed, she could not regain her balance, and she went down hard, face first into the dirt. He dragged her up by the arm with his one good hand, let go, and swung a haymaker that caught her on the head. Inept as it was, it had enough momentum to knock her down again. When he pulled her up again, she was completely disoriented but still trying to run. He took advantage of that to get her indoors pretty much under her own steam, clenching her collar and thrusting her in brutal little jerks in the direction he wanted. He propelled her straight to the closet, jammed her down onto the floor, slammed the door, and shot the bolts closed top and bottom. At first he sagged with relief. Then, moved by another paroxysm of rage, he drummed viciously on the door with the flat of his hand and shouted so that the veins in his neck stood out, *"Goddamn whore!"* There was no answer. He drummed again and bellowed, *"Are you listening? Are you fuckin' listening? You hurt me. You are gonna suffer! You are gonna fuckin' wish you had never been born!"* There was no response from the closet, and Paul began to beat on the door again, then kick it as if it were the baby-sitter behind it, frantically punishing the wood until a spasm of pain in his arm froze him in midstroke, bringing the sweat to his forehead and a long, deep hiss from his pale mouth. He stood perfectly still and silent for several minutes until the pain had receded to a level he could bear, and for that time there was not a sound in the house, not from the closet, not from the bathroom, where the boy, Paul knew perfectly well, was awake and listening. The boy took in everything.

Paul drew back the bolts on the bathroom door and opened it. Jeremy was standing right up against the wall beside the toilet, as far back from the door as he could be, eyes huge, perfectly still.

"It's okay," said Paul as reassuringly as he could, a little proudly now that he had an audience. "It's all under control. You can come out now." Jeremy crept past into the main room, glancing surreptitiously at the closet door as he passed, and dropped down in his place. The hand Paul had crushed hurt him badly, and he carried it against his chest with the other. It was only that morning that he had thrown a stone at Paul. As bad as Paul's retribution had been, Jeremy had been sure all day that there would be more when he came home, but now it seemed to be forgotten.

"Don't go near the closet," Paul said, his mouth working with pain. He looked awful, and the wound on his arm, the blood-soaked clothes, were frightening. Jeremy shook his head. He was not about to go anywhere near the closet.

"Well, let's see," said Gadek. "It's almost two-thirty. Why don't you two go on home. I can deal with the bus driver when he calls and spring a body or two from Patrol if I need help with calling or whatever. Why don't you report here at eight tomorrow morning. We ought to have our next step figured out by then."

"We can perfectly well do an all-nighter, if you'd rather," said Toby.

"No," said Gadek. "No point to it. I'd rather have you fresh tomorrow."

"Four hours of sleep is better than none," said Walt cheerfully, and they departed. "I notice Gadek isn't turning in," he added as they walked out to the parking lot.

"I don't think he can sleep at times like this," said Toby. "He gets too keyed up. He worries that he's going to miss something."

"And you?" said Walt.

"Oh, I worry, too," said Toby. "I won't get any sleep."

"Nor will I," said Walt, who had just put his key in the car door and now pulled it out again. "So if we're not going to go home and sleep and be fresh, why don't we stay and do whatever there is to do?"

"Beats me," said Toby. "Let's go back."

In the office they found Gadek slouched as far back as possible in his old oak swivel chair, feet on the desk, hands behind his head, eyes closed, breathing slowly and regularly; but perhaps the sound of the door opening penetrated because he opened one eye, registered their faces, and suddenly was wide awake.

"Christ," he said, pulling his feet off the desk and sitting up. "Did I oversleep? I was just going to grab a little nap till Patrol checked in." He looked out the window and saw that it was still dark. He consulted his watch. He said, "I thought you two were going home."

"We wanted to stay and play," said Toby.

It was late, very late, when at last Paul sank carefully onto his bed. He felt weaker and sicker by the minute, and his arm hurt him so badly now that sleep was unlikely. It had almost stopped bleeding in the car, where he had laid it along the seat back and not moved it, but as soon as he moved it, the bleeding started again. He had done plenty of moving, dealing with the baby-sitter. The rag it was wrapped in was soaking through. He dripped.

He had been right about the pain. It prevented him from sleeping in any healing way, but for three or four hours he passed continually in and out of consciousness, sometimes thinking, sometimes dreaming, in a welter of confusion and anxious, resentful thoughts.

*That little bitch*—who would have thought she would have a knife? He had been good to so many children. He had never done these things to be thanked—he tried to find the satisfaction in himself.

It was still dark when the throbbing in his arm awakened him. The bleeding had started again— perhaps he had been moving it around in his sleep. The bedding around his middle was spotted.

He had not been sleeping long, if sleeping was what he had been doing—not nearly long enough. He was still groggy, but he remembered everything.

It was very quiet in the cabin and very quiet outside. By the wall the boy slept fitfully.

The windows showed dim gray. Dawn was coming. What to do with her?

It was a serious problem. If he kept her, she would have to be restrained somehow—he could not stand over her every minute. He was going to need medical attention soon, that was clear. He ought to be thinking of some story he could tell the doctor so that the cops would not be called, not thinking about how to lock up baby-sitters.

Then, animated by a new thought, he rose, almost unconscious of the pain in his arm, and stepped forward to the fireplace, to the pictures on the mantel. So many of them. He could remember them all, what they were like, the things they liked to do.

He struck a big kitchen match against the stones of the fireplace and lit candles. It took several matches before he had them all lit.

The pictures glowed and shifted in the wavering golden light. So many memories. He studied the faces and bodies.

After a while his fatigue drew him back to the mattress. He could not see the pictures so well from there, but he knew them from memory.

He stared, mesmerized. Sometimes he dozed.

Captain Claypool had scarcely filled his enormous crested mug with the villainous Detective Division coffee and seated himself at his desk before Sergeant Gadek, chipper despite his sleepless night, was at his door. Now he listened with magisterial attention to the most recent mysteries connected with the comings and goings of Essie Beal.

"The call from Kramer's stepdaughter was the first Kramer and Parkman knew about Essie Beal coming back," Gadek said. "They tried the answering machine and her message was right there. The tape had been rewound, but no subsequent calls had come in to cover hers. Kramer and Parkman are sure that the message light was not blinking when they came in at about eleven-fifteen. They're sure they didn't rewind the tape themselves."

"Why were they in the office at that hour?" said Captain Claypool.

"They were there to leave their surveillance report for me," said Gadek.

"Very well," said Captain Claypool. He reached elaborately forward to his pen-and-pencil set, withdrew the pencil, made a note on the leather-bound pad that lay squarely in front of him, and then, with equal elaboration, replaced the pencil.

"They went immediately to the bus stop, and didn't find her. They presumed that the bus in question had come and gone some time before. They notified Patrol—lots of units available—they cruised the downtown and all along the route between downtown and the Beals' house, in case she decided to walk, without result. They called me at home. We called the transit company; the driver of the bus she was supposed to be on was still on duty. He remembered that she was on the bus, and he was sure that she got off at the end of the Green Line downtown. After that, we don't have anything. No one saw her leave or meet anyone. We called all her known friends in case she'd changed her mind and gone to one of them instead of coming to us or going home. Zip. So for the moment, at any rate, she's still missing, or missing again, depending."

"Ah," said Captain Claypool to show that he appreciated the distinction.

"So that leaves us with questions," said Gadek. "And the most worrisome one is, can it be coincidental that someone erased Essie's message and that she then disappeared from the bus stop?"

"Mmm," said Captain Claypool.

"We checked the machine," continued Gadek, "and it's functioning normally. We've called everyone who works around that office, and nobody admits to hearing or erasing the message or to being in the office after nine-twenty, when Footer went home.

"Except, of course, for Kramer and Parkman," said Captain Claypool.

"Yes," said Gadek. "The machine can be activated and rewound by phone if you know the code, and it could have been done by someone we haven't talked to—the code's no big secret—that's still unresolved."

"You dusted the button?" said Captain Claypool.

"A smudge," said Gadek with a discernible note of reproach. "Unusable." Captain Claypool nodded judiciously.

"So we have two apparent possibilities," said Gadek. "The first is that the tape and Essie's whereabouts are unrelated. Somebody erased the tape by accident, and more or less simultaneously Essie changed her mind and went out of sight again. That seems unlikely. The obvious alternative is that the tape was erased intentionally. Somebody heard the message and then erased the tape—either by remote or in the station—and went to meet her, and did not bring her back here.

"Now, what it looks like to me is that the person who rewound the tape is also the person who picked her up, that he is an insider, and that the intention was not good."

Captain Claypool leaned majestically forward and raised a large, firm hand.

"Leo, Leo, Leo," he said, in the tones of a veteran scoutmaster calmly calling his rambunctious charges to order. "I think we're letting our imagination run away with us. Let's keep a sense of proportion here. Possibilities must be treated according to probability. You are taking it almost for granted that a member of this department has abducted a young woman. This is within the range of possibility, of course, but it's highly improbable. Highly improbable."

Gadek shifted uncomfortably. He had known Captain Claypool for a long time. In his younger days he had been known as Sergeant Mudpuddle, from his ability to obscure the clearest issues.

"What happened, if you ask me," continued Captain Claypool, "is that the tape was rewound accidentally. Somebody laid something down on top of the machine and activated the rewind function inadvertently or forgot, in a moment of abstraction, that the message hadn't been transcribed yet. Parkman and Kramer, for example." He smiled forgivingly at the careless errors of young red hots. "It was late, and they were undoubtedly tired. Well, there are a thousand explanations that are more probable than that a member of this department is a kidnapper. I think we can very reasonably pare away the wild possibilities in favor of the simple explanation. The fact that something is *possible*—well, anything is possible. I think the 'insider possibility' will clear itself up quickly enough."

"Well," said Gadek. "That's what it looks like to me on the basis of what I've got now." He stopped, settled back a little more comfortably in his chair, and waited with an expectant expression on his face. He knew that Captain Claypool would not have the nerve to call off such an investigation with leads hanging, however unlikely or unpalatable the apparent end, and Gadek had found that it was better to let him come to these realizations himself. The next thing he said would have to be either Go or Stop.

An uncomfortable pause. Then Captain Claypool said, "How do you propose to proceed?"

"There is the next round of people," said Gadek. "People who don't work in DD but have occasional business here. There were a lot of people in the building last night, and most of them have perfectly good reasons for going into my office from time to time. We tried to narrow it down; most of the action at that time of night is in Patrol's end of the building. We called Wren, who was working then and who spends a lot of time right in the middle, and asked him who he noticed heading toward DD after ten-thirty."

"Of course, there are other routes," said Captain Claypool.

"Of course," said Gadek. "Wren gave us four names—Turin, Johnson, Greber, and Miyasaki. We can't get ahold of Greber because he doesn't have a telephone at home, but the others check out. Johnson and Miyasaki were in the field working cases until after midnight, so they couldn't have been involved, and Turin was researching a case in Juvenile, which we can verify."

"Imagine not having a phone," said Captain Claypool, chuckling. "Quite an eccentric choice in this day and age. The chief wants all the staff to carry cellular phones in our cars now—there's no escaping."

"Yes," said Gadek.

"Well, I don't doubt that Greber will check out, like the others," said Captain Claypool. "What else have you got?"

"Zip," said Gadek. "I've got zip else. We can go back downtown tonight, do an area check, and see if we can find anyone who was there last night who might have seen something. We can meet the late buses, interview the passengers, and see who remembers her from last night, and what they might have noticed. We can do all that. In the meantime, I want to check out Greber. Wren says Greber was working all around the building, and he knows he went to my office during the last part of the shift."

"I concur," said Captain Claypool. "There are a thousand possibilities, and Greber might be able to cast some light on them—might have observed something. Who knows? And who were you thinking of sending?"

"Me," said Gadek.

"No," said Captain Claypool. "That's simply over-reaction. For you to go personally is making him the public focus of suspicion. We have to clear this up, of course, but this whole thing is highly speculative—very thin. I won't have our people feeling accused and alienated for no good purpose. A fine message that would send, if a kidnapping occurs and our first reaction was to devour our own. Send one of your troops to see Greber. Tell him to keep it low-key. The focus is on that answering machine."

"Okay," said Gadek, "that's what we'll do."

"And I want you to work on developing other lines of inquiry," said Captain Claypool. "I don't believe this insider possibility is going to pan out. I don't believe it for a moment. Putting all our big guns on Greber is simply distracting ourselves and giving the real responsible a longer and longer head start. The fact closest to your nose is not always the most important fact, Leo. Try to remember that."

"I want you two to go see Greber," Gadek told Toby and Walt. "Plain clothes, obviously."

"Right," said Toby.

"Yeah," said Walt, and then added, "I thought you said the captain said to send one."

"I'm making a little tactical adjustment," said Gadek. "Chances are, the captain's right. At any rate, you'd like to think so. But we have to check out what Greber knows, and as long as you're doing that, it only makes sense to keep your eyes open. Keep it cool, but don't relax. Got it?"

"Right."

"Right. And by the way, Greber shoots, even though he doesn't carry a gun on duty. I've seen him at the range. He's at least so-so. Don't blindside yourselves."

"You think he's our guy, Leo?" said Toby.

"I'm certainly not saying yes," said Gadek. "I'm not saying no. I'm saying stay awake. Let's see—it's almost nine now—you ought to be on his doorstep by ten-thirty."

# 41

The sun was well up, such as it was behind the December overcast, and still Paul loitered on his bed and stared at his pictures. Jeremy had been awake for hours, huddled as invisibly as he knew how, perturbed. He knew that something had changed. He could see that Paul was hurt. The candles had never been lit at that time of day. It had always been just Paul and him at the cabin, and now there was someone in the closet.

Paul's mind was in many places. He was aware that night had become day, but he did not entirely comprehend it. He was aware that his thoughts were scattered, but this morning, of all mornings, he felt no urgency to collect himself. He was aware that today was to be a day of action, of decision, but he did not move. His dreams held him stupefied. I'm getting to be like my dad, he thought.

He did not forget the baby-sitter, but the closet door was around the corner, out of sight; he felt no immediate need to deal with her. He had decided during the night that he was not going to keep her. He was going to enlarge the hole in the shed that he and the boy had dug—or rather, he was going to encourage *her* to enlarge it—and then he was going to help her into it herself. It was just too complicated to keep her.

And—now that he was thinking of her, of that part of the cabin—what was that noise? A scratching.

His eye fell on the boy—he was not making it. A bird on the roof?

He lost the thought of it for a time, but it recurred, and at length he could not ignore it: something felt, more than heard, through the fabric of the cabin. A slow, faint scratching, repeated again and again.

"I really don't know Greber at all," said Toby as they turned off the freeway onto the county road. "The guy's around all the time, but I have no sense of him."

"*My* sense of him is that he's not my favorite," said Walt. "I don't know him well, either, but he's one of those people I've never had any interest in knowing well."

Paul stirred on the bed. The noise was coming from the closet, he was practically sure of it. The baby-sitter was making that noise. She was trying to get out of the closet. Paul swung his legs hastily over onto the floor and heaved himself to his feet.

The movement was too quick. His head swam, his legs folded, and he crumpled back onto the bed, almost fainting, only by a miracle saving himself from falling onto his bad arm. For a brief time he lay only semiconscious, aware of little more than his heart heaving in his chest.

He had not realized he had lost so much blood—he was seriously affected. His strength came back to him, such as it was, but it was alarming. He could not afford to be passing out. Not today.

And there was that scratching still. It was not his imagination or some trick of hearing; he could see that the boy was listening to it, too.

More slowly this time, more carefully, Paul rose to his feet, anxious and angry. Slowly he moved around the bed, steadying himself with a hand on the mantel; slowly he approached the kitchen doorway.

There was no doubt about it: she was doing something in the closet.

More quickly now, Paul stepped forward and began to slide back the bolts. It was hard to do with his left hand, and when the bolt came free from the socket and slammed back the last inch, the impact, slight as it was, ran a twinge down his bad arm that made him gasp. The bottom bolt, a foot above the floor, was even harder.

Drawing the bolts was by no means silent. There was no taking her by surprise. Paul knew that sometimes a prisoner will wait until a jail door is unlocked and then hurl himself against it to knock his keeper back and take him off-balance. Paul had had one or two try this, and now when he began to open the door, he kept his foot against it to block it if she tried to fling it wide. He had to keep control of it; he thought that he could not stand the pain of a sudden movement.

The door opened with an unaccustomed resistance, dragging along its outer edge. Through the widening opening he could see the baby-sitter on one knee, scrambling to her feet. She had gotten her cuffed hands in front of her—Paul had had prisoners do that before, pulling the cuffs around their butt and feet. Good for her, but he knew how to handle it. He yanked the door wide to get at her before she was up. There was a weak splintering sound, and the door fell straight away from the frame, so that he had to jump back to avoid it as it crashed flat on the floor. Essie was stumbling out over it, glancing at Paul but breaking for the back door beyond the table. Her second step threw her weight on an ankle obviously swollen, and it failed her so that she fell almost at his feet, but she half rolled and was up again, snatching at the door. It was bolted top and bottom, and it held against her. Paul was on her in three steps and struck into her stomach, weakly, but hard enough to take the wind out of her. He reached down and grasped the chain that connected the cuffs so that she could not use them like weights to strike at him, and pulled her around.

She could not immediately straighten at the waist. Shrilling, she dragged for breath. The cut on her right cheek was black, the right eye was swollen half shut, most of that side of her face was purple, and what was not discolored by bruises and crusted with blood was unnaturally pale. There were still visible traces of purple eye shadow and lipstick, which gave her whole coloration the effect of some bizarre and grossly ill-judged party joke.

A can opener lay on the closet floor, found by touch in some forgotten corner during the night. With this she had clawed the wood of the door down to the hinge screws, completely on the top, and almost on the bottom. Paul saw that a good heave would have thrown it down hours before. Perhaps she had not realized. Perhaps she had been trying for silence.

Essie knew that she had almost gotten away, and her fury and frustration seemed to pulse out of her as if all her pain and fear and outrage had condensed themselves into a blinding acid light. Face and body, she blazoned such an unbridled and wolfish malignance that Paul flinched, despite himself. He had been pulling her up by the chain; now he pressed his arm out straight to hold her off. Still with her hands reaching past the cuffs, she pulled in on his arm as if she meant to claw her way up until she reached his face. She could not; Paul knew how to twist back on the cuffs, cutting into her wrists to press her halfway to her knees and hold her where he wanted her, but her wildness shook him. Weakened as he was—even weakened as *she* was, and small, in any case—she was a live, instant threat every moment. He was going to have to use great care. Simply let her do her digging, help her into the hole, and get this over with.

Jeremy was in the kitchen doorway. He said, "Essie."

She realized for the first time, at that moment, that he was there.

He was staring at her face. He said, "I love you."

"Love *her?*" cried Paul. "You love *her?*" He heaved Essie away from him so that she stumbled over the fallen door and collapsed against the wall. He rounded on Jeremy. "You love *her?*" There was a glass on the kitchen counter beside him, and he snatched it in his good hand and hurled it violently at the boy. It hit him on the shoulder and shattered against the wall. There was a cast-iron skillet. In his fury he tried to grab it with his bad hand, gasped at the pain, and dropped it on the floor. Essie was scrambling to her feet. Paul took a step forward and swooped down for the skillet, swooping up again and cocking back his arm. The movement was too sudden. He swayed, his face suddenly ashen. He fainted and fell.

Essie tottered past him to the door. She had to get a chair to open the top bolt, but it yielded. The bottom one came more easily. She held out her cuffed hands to Jeremy, who took them without hesitation, and in a moment they were wobbling down the steps into the little space between cabin and shed, she leaning on him like a crutch. From there she could see past the front of the house to the track—it disappeared among the trees, and they would be out of sight before they had traveled a hundred yards. Past the shed, in the other direction, the trees began at once, alternating with grassy meadow sloping down to where substantial groves mingled with tall bushes and dense underbrush along the river. She could not see any other house where they might get help. Speed was everything—the creep would not be unconscious forever, probably not for long—and when he came to, he would be after them. If they followed the track, they would be out of sight quickly, but they could not outrun his car. Down the hill would get them out of sight almost as soon, and once they were in the trees they could go anywhere.

"C'mon, kiddo," she said, and they started down the hillside, Essie limping and hopping, clinging to Jeremy.

"I love you, Essie," he said, looking up as he staggered along beside her.

"Oh, God," she said. She could scarcely believe it: After all these weeks, in the middle of madness, here he was. But she was not letting her mind run on that theme, she was trying to stay focused on the immediate problem. Her ankle seemed to be on fire, she hurt in every part, her head was splitting, and even the gray daylight hurt her eyes. "I love you, too," she said, without slowing for a moment. "I love you, too, but hush. I love you, too, but you have to be quiet now."

She glanced back. She could not see Paul, but she could see that they were leaving a plain, broad swath through the tall grass. When he came, he would follow it right to them. What would the bold girl do about *that*, she wondered. Maybe the bold girl had been a Girl Scout. Maybe the bold girl could fly. Still, if they tried, she found, they could step between the clumps rather than going directly over them, which softened their trail a good deal. And once they were farther along among the trees the grass grew sparser and their way clearer; only now the ground was softer, and they began to leave noticeable footprints.

A gas station attendant had given Toby and Walt careful instructions on locating the turn onto Paul's track, which was a very good thing, they found, because even with this advantage they almost missed it. They moved slowly around the blind curves, partly to avoid running into somebody coming the other way, but also to see where they were going, if possible, before they actually got there. There were mailboxes stuck on posts by the road, and some of these had numbers.

"That was twenty-eight," said Walt as they passed one. "We want eighty-six."

Toby said, "I wonder what it's like to work one of these little vineyards."

"You'd have to have a straw hat," said Walt.

"That's okay," said Toby. "I wouldn't mind having a straw hat. Sara looks great in straw hats. It seems like a wonderful thing to do."

There was no number on the mailbox when they reached Paul's gate.

"Still, this must be it," said Walt.

Essie and Jeremy were still in the yard outside the kitchen door when Paul came to himself with the sick realization that he had been unconscious for some unknown period. He knew from the silence of the house that the baby-sitter and the boy were gone. He pulled himself slowly to his knees and then to his feet. He had trouble focusing his eyes at first—the world seemed vague and gray. He was giddy, exhausted, and in pain, but if he did not bring them back he was a dead man.

Paul was not going to go to prison. That had been a given with him for many years. He knew what happens in prison to men like him.

The first thing was to get his revolver from its hiding place under the bed. It was all he could do to find the doorway and stagger through it to the bed. The revolver was there. He could not hold it in his right hand, which was a problem; Paul had never been good for much with his left hand. Officers, he knew, had to learn to shoot with either hand, but aides do not carry weapons, and he had never had that training. He stuck the revolver in his waistband and tried to draw it again, but he gripped it badly so that the muzzle pointed lower than it should and the trigger was awkward to pull. Well, he would not have time to practice. It would have to do, the way the baby-sitter had left him.

With the pistol in his hand he lurched to the front door. He pictured them running along the track toward the main road. He could catch them in his car. The bolts were hard for him, but he cleared them. It was not until the door was open, and he was staring drunkenly down the track, that he knew that they could not have gone out that door and then refastened the bolts behind them; he turned, and realized for the first time that the kitchen door stood open.

He stepped out the back door and into the yard. They could have gone in any direction from there. His first sense, again, was that they must have gone out along the track, and that he should get in his car to give chase before they could reach one of the side roads or start pounding on the doors of his neighbors. But in fact they might not realize that there was help in that direction. They could also have gone down among the trees toward the river. He hurried along past the cabin and looked down the slope to the west and northwest, but he could see nothing. There were many irregularities in the ground that might conceal them briefly, and if they were moving among the trees, they might be hidden much of the time. He watched for half a minute, and then, growing uneasy—they could be disappearing just now on the opposite slope—*were,* in fact, just then disappearing on the opposite slope—he hurried along the crest until he could see to the southwest. Again he waited and watched until he could bear it no longer, turned back, threaded his way between cabin and shed, and came out on the south. There he saw the broad and plain new trail leading through the grass down toward the trees.

Then he knew they were to be his. The river was invisible but not far. The water was too deep and swift with the autumn rains to wade across, and he did not believe that the baby-sitter could swim the way he had left her, especially with the boy in tow. The riverbank looked merely verdant from above, but when you got down to it, he knew, there were large, impenetrable tangles of brambles and every sort of sharp and unyielding shrub. If they were down there, they could not just dodge around: the river was a dead end. Paul settled the pistol in his belt, and with an exultant heart, he started down the slope. Anyone could follow this trail. At the range he planned to be when he did his shooting, his left hand would be plenty good enough. First the baby-sitter. Then the boy.

## 42

The gate was securely padlocked, they discovered.

"Well," said Toby. "It can't be too far from here. Let's hoof it."

The gate was no obstacle except to a vehicle. They stepped around it and started down the track beyond. The wind blew fitfully under the gray sky and stirred the rank yellow grasses this way and that. Trees and bushes obscured the cabin, and until Toby and Walt were quite close, they could see very little of the building itself. A nondescript sedan stood in front near the porch.

"That's his car," said Walt. "I guess he's home."

And then, glancing in as they passed, he murmured, "Waitaminute waitaminute waitaminute. Look at *that,* willya."

They peered in. The driver's seat and the back of the passenger's were thickly spattered and stained with blood. The passenger's seat belt was hacked almost through, close to the buckle, and deeply notched in several other places. A blue gym duffel lay on the floor on the passenger side.

"Bingo," said Toby. "Essie was carrying a duffel like that when she ran away."

"Looks like a crime scene to me," said Walt. "Trouble. Big trouble."

"Y'know, does this change our position?" said Toby. "What if we back off, call Gadek, regroup, and come back?"

"Well, we can't leave this car, 'cause it's full of evidence, or my name isn't Detective Kramer," said Walt.

"We can't just stand here in the open," said Toby. "We're sitting ducks from anywhere. And I suppose we can't leave one of us to watch the car in any case, because if he's armed, it'd be one on one with the best cover on his side."

They had to go through this slowly because neither of them had been in quite this position before. If they were faced with these questions in Patrol, in their own jurisdiction, they would just get on the radio and buck the decision up to a sergeant.

"Well," said Toby, "retreat is out and staying here is out. Dividing up is out."

"Then let's roll," said Walt. "If Essie was in that car, we want to get our hands on her tootsweetly."

More cautiously, but moving fast, they headed for the cabin.

"I hope it wasn't Essie who was doing all that bleeding," Toby said.

"Shh," Walt whispered. "The wind will carry our voices."

They stepped gingerly onto the porch, trying not to make the old planks creak.

It was not until they came to the water that Essie comprehended the magnitude of their problem. The ground was soft behind them, and from the path through the grass they had left a clutter of footprints that the most inept city boy could follow. The undergrowth in both directions was impossible. Even if they could force their way through it, which she doubted, they would leave a trail even plainer than they had done so far, and which the creep could follow far faster than they could lead. The river was fast and looked deep. What else was there? There were holes in the undergrowth that would probably conceal them if it were dark, but she doubted that it was as late as noon. Whatever happened was going to happen long before dark.

She looked again at the water. She knew that riverbeds have a shape, and although the water was high enough now to cover the stream from bank to bank, it was not a uniform channel. In the summer—happy bather that she was, and timorous possessor of a bathing suit cut up to here and down to there that she always had to be plucking at to preserve any decency at all—Essie had picnicked on—which?—the inner bank of a curve or the outer bank? Where was the beach? The inner bank. Just in front of where she and Jeremy stood now. If she was correct, there would be a gravel bar with shallow water extending out well beyond the overhanging brush. They could wade along this bar and come back in to the bank at some private and unexpected place, leaving no traces of their passage.

"C'mon, kiddo," she said, and together they slipped off the mud and into the stream.

It was over knee-high for Essie—pushing waist-high for Jeremy—and very fast. The footing was almost liquid as their feet stirred the gravel into the current. It was very hard to balance without the use of her arms independently. She knew she could not carry Jeremy, and she wondered if she could hold onto him.

"Back," she called, almost shouting to be heard over the tumultuous water, and they struggled back to the bank, barely out of arm's reach but still a trial to gain. When they were secure, no more than ankle-deep, Essie pulled off her belt and ran it around Jeremy's chest just below his arms. The long loose end she knotted over the handcuff chain.

"Okay," she said, and again they set out into the current. Essie turned upstream, as offering the best concealment from the cabin and the shortest route to woods that could conceal them. She wondered what her mother would say, seeing her baby girl lead this innocent out into a winter flood. She wondered what Gabriella would say.

"Too bad they're not here to make suggestions," she cried aloud, and surprised herself.

"Hush," cried Jeremy. "Gotta be quiet now."

Paul had never been so tired as when he started down the slope, but he persevered. Clean up this problem and all would be well. There were satisfactions, despite his fatigue; the trail through the grass could scarcely have been clearer. He would catch them up, probably gibbering in fright at the water's edge.

Then he thought of the car. *The car.* Hell, I've got to clean the car. It's got blood all over—all over that textured vinyl—never get it out of all those little holes and creases. And even if I could get it clean, the seat belt's cut. How do you explain that?

Then he thought, I can torch it. Yeah. Blood'll burn. The upholstery, the seat belt, it'll all melt and burn. End of problem.

But a fire'll be visible for a long way. The fire

department'll come, and maybe cops. I don't want them to find this problem here. First I have to get rid of this problem here.

So much to do. Paul picked up his pace, almost loping down the slope along the plain trail through the grass. He did not miss the transition when they began to step between the clumps, and as the grass thinned, he saw the footprints plainly in the mud. Stupid kids, he thought. Stupid, stupid, stupid.

At the water's edge he stopped. There they were. They were fifty yards upstream, five yards out from the bank, laboring along, moving slowly. Very slowly.

A man-size target at fifty yards is reckoned by cops to be a long but entirely practicable pistol shot; they are trained to do it, preferably with a rest—a building or a tree. And they are taught to do it right- or left-handed. Paul had observed this being done at the range—he knew about rests, but he had never tried to use one. Now he picked a convenient tree, drew his revolver, placed his right hand on the trunk with the thumb extended for a rest—and realized that he could not shoot that way; his arm was too painful. He let his right arm hang and simply steadied his left hand against the trunk. He cocked the hammer so that the trigger pull should be lighter, and squinted along the sights.

It was more than a hard shot. Waving branches intermittently obscured the view. The light was not good. The viper was half the bulk of the "man-size" targets that cops practice on, her dark coat disappeared into the dark trees on the farther bank, and Paul was, in any case, tired, dizzy, weak, and under great strain. He had never before attempted to kill, and felt a certain awe. Still, he aimed as best he could under the circumstances, and pulled the trigger.

Essie saw the splash of the bullet, well beyond them. She guessed immediately what it was, and having guessed, sorted back through the last moments of sound from the rushing river and realized that she had heard the shot as well. The thought she found time for at that moment was that being shot at, inconceivable on the previous day, now seemed a perfectly consistent expression of her world.

She was not surprised, but she was frightened; and what frightened her most was not the thought that she would be killed but that Jeremy would and she would not; that she would be brought back somehow to her old life to be reproached for having lost him a second time.

*"C'mon, kiddo,"* she said, pushing him in front of her. *"We gotta go."* But they were already going as fast as they could. The only choices she could see were to go forward, to clamber back up on the bank and run for it, or to swim.

Running was out.

Swimming was out.

Forward, then. But the bar they were traveling would peter out very soon as the curve of the river reversed itself, and the sloping inner bank became the vertical outer one. The bar would snake upriver in an ever-narrower band until it fell off into the deepest, fastest part of the channel. Essie had assumed that if they could shake off the trail at the point where they went into the river, they would be able to make their next move unobserved. But when they got to the end, the choices would still be to climb the bank and run, or swim; and now, it was clear to her, they would not be able to make this choice without the creep's seeing what they did.

Paul cocked and fired again. Essie was looking back this time: she saw the flash among the dark trees, saw the thin puff of smoke, saw the splash less then ten feet behind them and only slightly to the side, and an instant later heard the report.

Essie had never fired a pistol or any firearm. She did not attribute the wider and the closer shots to the operation of luck within the limits of the creep's skill. She had heard the expression "getting the range," not realizing that it applied to howitzers and battleships; she thought that the creep was correcting his aim through some inexorable scientific method. At that rate of improvement, the next shot would hit them. It scarcely mattered which of them he hit because they were tied together, and whichever of them was not killed by a bullet would inevitably be dragged down to drown. This was the end. She could not believe the injustice of it. She pressed Jeremy upstream of herself, and half turned, stopped in the stream with the turbulent water bursting right over them and screamed, "ASSSSSSSSS HOOOOOOOOOOOLE!"

Paul saw them stop in the stream, saw the baby-sitter push the boy out of sight behind her. He saw her face contorting, saw her cock her body back and then lash forward almost to the surface, hurling the unheard words as if she could spit poison flat across that distance. Almost at the same moment the boy appeared beside her and launched a stone that only raised a piddling spout halfway, but for line was fair and true.

Paul cocked, laid on the wavering, spume-shrouded figures, and fired a third time.

Essie saw the flash and puff and the quick, ragged splash, short by twenty feet, and way off to the side. By far the worst shot of the three.

*Not* the end. She had thought they were dead, but they were *not* dead. She thought, "I'm scared to death," and then she thought, *"Move, girl, move, move, move."*

*"C'mon, kiddo,"* she called. With painful care they turned, rebalancing themselves on the shifting stones below their feet, and labored off upstream again.

*"Shoot, you scungy son of a bitch!"* she shouted to herself, not looking back, thoroughly scared now that she thought they might even yet get away. She had

picked up the rhythm of his firing with three repetitions. As the moment for the fourth shot came, she felt her whole back swelling, enormous, glowing, beckoning the smoking hot slug, enticing it. "SHOOT!" she screamed into the water in front of her. "SHOOT, SHOOT, SHOOT!"

*"Hush!"* shouted Jeremy, struggling along beside her, frightened, wild, ecstatic. *"Huuuussssh!"*

"Be QUIET!" Essie screamed over the river, beginning to laugh. "Beeee QUIET!"

"Be QUIET!" yelled Jeremy, hurling himself against the current. "Be QUIET, be QUIET, beeeee QUIET!"

A small, low porch with a single old metal spring chair by the door. Two front windows opaque with dirt and covered with heavy shades inside. Paint peeled and trim curled. Dead grass and all manner of windblown detritus banked up around the chair and along the wall except where the opening of the screen door had swept it clear.

"Lonely," said Toby softly.

"Goddamn depressing," said Walt.

At every moment they expected Greber to come sauntering out the front door with a silly grin on his face saying, Why, what a surprise. They expected him to be friendly and have some line of gab.

"What do you make of that?" Walt whispered. He was pointing to spotting on the porch floor.

"It looks like blood to me," said Toby.

"Sure does," said Walt.

The front door hung ajar. They stood more cautiously to the side than they would have done before looking at the car. There was no sign of anyone. With some care they peered in. Toby called, "Greber?"

Dim light through the thick old shades was augmented by the numerous candles still burning on the mantelpiece. There was plenty of light to see the furnishings, such as they were, the crudely wire-meshed windows, the mass of pictures covering the chimney. Most were small, but some he could see from the door, and he could certainly get the idea of the whole.

"Wow," whispered Toby. "Trouble."

Walt looked past him and whispered, "Real trouble."

They could see more blood spots in front of the fireplace, smeared where they had been walked on. Someone had spent a good deal of time there, bleeding on the floor. Someone had lain on the mattress and bled there, too.

"We better find whoever's doing all that bleeding," murmured Walt, " 'cause he must be getting pretty woozy. I hope it isn't Essie." He ran his eyes over the mantelpiece. "Trouble," he said softly. "Real trouble."

"Screw search warrants," said Toby, louder. "I'm looking through."

"Y'know, I even think we're clean on this one," Walt said. "But in any case, I'm with you." They went in as quietly as they could.

There was the one room, the kitchen, the bathroom, and the closet with its broken door lying on the floor. They found more blood stains, an odd assortment of toys, odd clothes, Greber's uniforms. The mess was considerable, but from the clothes and toys, it appeared that a man and a child were in residence.

They did not find any direct sign that Essie had been there, but the broken closet door, together with the rest of it, was ominous.

The shed was visible from the kitchen door, perhaps ten yards away.

"Let's have a look at that," Toby said, and they moved cautiously down the steps into the muddy little yard.

"Listen," said Walt, and they both cocked their ears, straining to hear over the wind.

"Someone's shooting," said Toby.

Paul saw the failure of his third shot with keen disappointment. It was only going to get worse: The range was lengthening—slowly, but lengthening, and the light was worsening, if anything; in their attempts to go faster, the baby-sitter and the boy were pumping and plunging in completely unpredictable ways; Paul's hand shook, and it was his left hand anyway. He had only the six cartridges in the revolver; he had not thought to bring reloads. He had been anticipating executions at the shortest possible range. By the time he labored back up to the cabin to replenish and labored back down again, they would be much too far to hit if they were still in sight at all. With that much time they could be anywhere.

So as a practical matter he had three shots left. The odds were against him in these circumstances, and rising.

Unless he could get closer.

In his condition, going into the water was out. He knew what the footing was like. He could not move any faster than they could, and he might slip or drop the pistol.

Struggling through the undergrowth along the bank was too slow, so that was out.

But he could cut back up the slope to open ground, circle around the heavy undergrowth, and come down to the water again—where? *There*—at the end of the bar, where the channel sweeps right under the bank, where they must choose between landing or swimming. He would have them ten feet away. If the baby-sitter resisted, he would threaten to shoot the boy; that would bring them in. Then he could do what he liked, which was what they deserved, he thought, as he turned hastily back into the trees and retraced his steps toward the open slope.

Essie did not want to look back, did not want to see the flash of the fourth shot, did not want to know when it was coming, did not want to be so scared again. Still, when it did not come at the anticipated moment, she could not help herself; she threw a glance over her shoulder and saw the creep stumbling away through the trees and out of sight. She could guess perfectly well where he was going and could see that they would be lost if he got there.

So now she had to think again.

There had to be something other than to walk up to the end of the bar and into his arms. She looked hungrily across the channel to the opposite bank, perhaps twenty feet away. No way, girl, she thought. It was as much as they could do to wade in the shallows against the force of the stream. Already once or twice it had lifted Jeremy right off his feet and nearly pulled her along.

*"Can you swim at all?"* she shouted. Jeremy shot a panicked look about him. He had in fact learned to paddle along, with Gabriella wading close beside calling congratulations and encouragement, but in his mind that cheerful, noisy accomplishment applied to dulcet summer days and the shallow ends of swimming pools with grass and big fuzzy towels and no running. His mind barely connected the basic skill in question with this wild place and the fast dark water. Vehemently he shook his head, which was no more than she had expected.

So they could not swim across it. They could just let

go, she thought, try to float downstream and hope to come up on the opposite bank, or someplace far away; but she knew that a river in spate is full of rocks to run against, odd currents that can take you under, and snags to hold you there. She could see some of these, and the boiling surface was evidence of more. She doubted that she could stay up for more than a few moments in her already waterlogged peacoat, in handcuffs, with Jeremy belted tight to her wrists. She would not cast him loose.

If worse came to worst, she supposed that swimming was a better speculation for her than going back to the creep's closet. But surrender would be the best chance for Jeremy when the creep reached the end of the bar, and whatever they did, they were going to do it together.

What else?

The thick, coarse growth overhung the bank close by them. If they could push into it far enough, they would be invisible from above and invisible from the river, too. He would guess where they had gone easily enough, but he would not be able to get at them quickly. Delay was not safety, but it was not surrender, either.

It was all she could think of.

*"C'mon, kiddo,"* she shouted, and turned for the bank. They might have two or three minutes before the creep reappeared on the bank ahead.

The water was not deep, nor the bank high, when they struggled into it. The undergrowth was fierce, but they wiggled through, pushing branch and bramble aside and then pulling them back again behind, until Essie was sure that they could not be seen from any direction. They did not have to lie down—they were already crawling flat along the ground—they had only to stop moving forward. The river still roared a few yards behind, and the wind agitated the foliage overhead. Essie felt herself spinning into the ground, cold as she was, out of breath, shivering violently. She huddled on her side and put her wrists over Jeremy's head to pull him against her, so that his head lay on one arm and her other lay across his chest, pressing him close. The cuffs galled her, but they locked him in, and that was what she wanted.

"Hush," she whispered. "I love you. But we can't talk at all. Understand?"

They were still close to the creep and still boxed in between the open slopes and the river. But he could not see them, he could not shoot at them. He would not have more than a general idea of where they might be. If he tried to come in after them, searching through the hundreds of square yards of undergrowth, it would take him a long time. Finding them would be sheer luck, and she could see that he would have the additional problem of not daring to get so involved in one part of the thicket that they could just boogie on out and disappear before he could disentangle himself. And when night came on it would be a whole new ball game. After dark she would think again.

She had been living minute by minute for many hours, and now that the next minute required no action or decision, reality began dropping away from her. Sleep mastered her in rushes, interrupted by sudden starts of consciousness as she tumbled between memory, apprehension, and the precipitous onset of dreams. Once or twice she jerked suddenly, falling, and almost immediately slipped off again. Her first, immediate dream was that the belt was parting and Jeremy was being swept away by the river. She clung to him, and he pressed back against her, both of them shaking violently with cold.

Paul was already out of breath when he cleared the densest part of the trees and turned along the more open slope paralleling the riverbank. He could see the place where he wanted to come back down to the water. They would be *right* there—looking back at the bank where he had been, thinking they had lost him, until they looked up and saw him almost close enough to touch.

Toby and Walt were not far from the cabin before they saw Paul through the trees, right below them on the slope, perhaps seventy yards away, laboring drunkenly along with his eyes on the river. His face was very pale, his eyes sunken; his right arm, which he held gingerly in front of him, was coarsely bandaged; they could not see his left hand in the tall grass. He had not seen them. Walt angled abruptly off to the left, working ahead of him, and Toby to the right, so that they could cut off escape either way. They picked up their pace. When they had halved the distance Toby called, "Hey, Greber!"

He stumbled to a halt and squinted up the slope at them, utterly surprised.

Incautiously, not having seen the pistol, they moved out beyond the last of the trees that lay between them and him, stepping quickly down through the meadow. Toby called, "Greber—it's Parkman!"

Paul could see Toby perfectly well. He could see Walt. He knew who they were. He had no idea how they came to be there at that moment, but he saw that somehow he had been discovered.

He had often considered this moment in his mind. If he killed them, he was still a free man. If they killed him, he would not suffer prison. He had nothing to lose. Without hesitation he turned, leveled his pistol at Toby, and fired. He was holding too low on the grip, and the trigger was awkward for him, but the range was close; he missed only by inches.

"Greber!" called Toby, who found this all very sudden. He drew.

"Police!" yelled Walt, drawing, dropping into a crouch and swinging his pistol forward.

Paul corrected and fired a second time at Toby, who saw the flash almost directly over his own gunsights.

The bullet plowed up a flurry of dirt on the slope, well beyond. Paul corrected again, and this time all three fired together, their orange muzzle flashes faintly visible in the dull light, crisscrossing the golden falling ground. Toby and Walt were comfortably within their practiced range, with a clear sight at a good-size target; they each hit Paul in the upper body, knocking him right over into the long, spindly grass.

The whole encounter could not have lasted five seconds.

Walt hustled quickly down the slope, pistol forward, muttering, "Shitshitshitshitshit."

Toby hurried in, too, approaching so that they were spread at right angles to each other. Paul still struggled on the ground, trying to roll over, straining for traction with his feet. His revolver lay close beside him, but he was not touching it, and Toby did not think he knew where it was. His labors fell off as they came close, his gasping breath slowed sharply, and by the time they were up to him he was still. Toby snatched up the revolver and jammed it into his pocket. Holding his own pistol wide so that Paul could not by any chance grab it, he reached down and felt for the pulse in his neck.

"Nothing," he said.

Essie stirred at the half-heard tumult of voices and shots just up the slope, beyond the undergrowth. They were puny noises in the open space, partly drowned by the river and muddled by the wind, but they shaped her dream. She dreamed that several Pauls had surrounded the hiding place where she lay with Jeremy and were working their way into it, firing and shouting. She stirred again, whispering almost inaudibly, *"Hush, hush,"* in her sleep.

Jeremy heard, also. He peered in the direction of the sounds, wide awake, drawing Essie's arm more tightly across his chest.

Toby thought, I'm alive. He's dead but I'm alive.

Walt had backed off a couple of steps and stood looking alternately at Toby and at Paul. Ten minutes before, this dead man had been simply an odd, sad somebody you know at work.

"He did shoot," said Toby. He had no doubt about it, but he wanted to hear Walt say it.

"Oh yeah," said Walt, hopped up. "Yeah, he did."

"Three." Toby realized that he sounded as hopped up as Walt did, now that he was noticing.

"Three," said Walt. And then, "No choice."

"No," said Toby. "No choice at all."

Paul lay very awkwardly, with one leg bent under him. His eyes were open. His mouth gaped.

"Well," said Walt, pointing to Paul's arm. "That's where that blood came from." And then, "Y'know, we oughta call the cops."

Even simple things seemed very hard to get organized.

"Let's look around first," said Toby. "He was really going after somebody. If he's the one who picked up Essie, and she got loose, she must be right around here."

Walt said, "Y'know, Tobe, just between you and me, I wonder how much anybody's really going to regret what's happened."

"No," said Toby, thinking of the pictures in the cabin. "Maybe not much." But he thought he heard a new note in Walt's voice, as if Walt regretted it already. Toby regretted it. Once the shooting began, there had been no options, but did the shooting have to happen at all? He wished he could sit right down and work it through, to settle his mind about it. Could they have done it any other way? What if something was overlooked? What if it *didn't* have to happen?

Abruptly, physically, they shied away from that thought, turning in opposite directions along the slope, working down to the bank when they could, peering into the undergrowth, calling her name.

Essie thought she was awake. She could not be sure whether she had slept or not. She tried to remember what she had heard. Had there been shots? And voices? Whose? She was stupefied with fatigue. She remembered that night was important, but she could not remember why. Had she decided to lie low until dark, or escape while there was still light? She could not remember which she had decided on, nor why.

Her name again. Someone *was* calling. It did not sound like the creepy man's voice. If it was anybody else, it must be help. Or must it? She distrusted herself. She struggled to make sense of it. She tried to calculate their chances of getting away by themselves. The more she considered the matter, the more chancy it seemed. If there were other people there, it might be their best chance. It might be worth taking some risk to find out.

"C'mon," she whispered to Jeremy. "We have to be very quiet. We're going to try to find a place where we can see what's going on."

Already there was a turkey vulture circling overhead. Remarkable how quickly they pick up on an opportunity, Toby thought, but it presented another problem. They did not want the body eaten. The local police would investigate the shooting. They could not just say, Well, we're cops and we wasted this scumbag for our own good reasons. Questions would be asked. It would all be looked into, measured, documented, photographed—treated as a potential crime scene. It was important that nothing be disturbed until all this had taken place. Toby watched the vulture and wondered, What else eats carrion? Crows, certainly. Dogs, very likely—there might well be dogs running around. Raccoons? Possums? Aren't they nocturnal? Toby was a city boy and did not know the answers, but clearly he would have to stick close.

Walt ranged farther upstream along the hillside, calling.

Toby was fascinated by the body. It lay just as it had when he felt for its pulse. It was so like and unlike life, contorted, strained, with that leg turned sharply under. Toby had always found it odd that bodies do not move at all, not even to ease themselves when they are facing eternity in uncomfortable positions.

Questions would be asked, Toby knew. Questions will always be asked, and the right answers are not the same in all times and places. Society permits life to be taken for expediency's sake, to avoid worse things, but society reserves the right to say afterward, Hey, wait a minute, let's take another look at this. When we said you ought to do this sort of thing, maybe this isn't what we were thinking about.

Why couldn't the damn fool just surrender? he thought. Would have saved me a lot of pain, no doubt about it.

He wondered what Sara would think. In theory, he was sure, he could waste kidnappers and pedophiles all day long without hearing a peep from Sara. But this was not theory, this was a particular case. He wondered how she would react in practice.

He could make out tiny flying shapes around Greber's face. At the police academy there had been a lecture about how to tell how long someone has been dead by examining the insect life that has taken up residence on the corpse. That was disgusting, but the more he thought about it, the less it bothered him. In any case, he thought, he wasn't going to stand there fanning the son of a bitch to keep the flies off him. He was not feeling tender toward him. Screw it, he thought. Let nature take its course.

Then Essie emerged from the trees thirty yards downstream. She was limping, and he could see even at that distance that she had been battered. She was cuffed, holding in both her hands the hand of a little boy. Toby knew Jeremy Broome only from photographs, but he recognized him at once.

"I thought I heard you, but I wasn't sure," she called when they were still some distance off. She was hurrying along toward him now, with Jeremy, looking wary, pressing tight beside her. "I wasn't sure what I heard. I didn't know . . ."

She had come quite close before she saw Greber's body lying in the grass, and the two of them pulled up abruptly, staring.

Flies buzzed around the slack mouth, flying in and out.

"You don't need to see that," Toby said, coming down toward them, but Essie was stepping forward. Jeremy jibed and pulled his hand loose from hers, backing, but she was up to the body before Toby could stop her and, leaning low, spat inexpertly, but with astonishing conviction, square in the middle of the vacant putty face.

# 45

Ten days after the shooting, Gadek told Toby, "I went by the Broomes yesterday to see if Jeremy had mentioned anything interesting to her that he hadn't told us. It happens a lot—kids can know something perfectly well, but you don't get it if you don't ask 'em right, and then they'll drop it to someone they trust. So I was just checking.

"At one point she said, 'Trevor still blames me.'

"I said, 'That's wrong. It wasn't your fault.'

"She said, 'No, I've thought about it a lot. I don't think so either. Trevor is a blaming son of a bitch. I'm divorcing him, unless . . . No, I'm divorcing him. Anyway, it was bad luck. That's what everybody says. Bad luck.'

"Then I said, 'Do you think you could say that to Essie?'

"She dropped her head and shook it and said, 'I'm not ready to talk to Essie yet.'

"I said, 'Y'know, she probably saved his life.'

"She stared out the window for a little while, and then she said, 'It didn't have to happen at all, you know. The door was open. It all stems from that. I don't think it ever would have happened at all, except for that.'"

On the second Friday afternoon after Essie's return she received a phone call. A few minutes later she appeared in the living room, excited and a little anxious. She was wearing her peacoat and purple lipstick.

"I'm going to meet Elliott downtown," she said to her parents as they peered up from their books, blinking like twin owls. "We're going to get wired on cappuccinos and then have pizza and maybe do a movie. Expect me when you see me, okay?" Her hand was on the doorknob.

"So long as we see you by midnight," said Esther, succeeding on the whole in making the traditional answer sound like a friendly confirmation rather than the traditional fiat.

"Yeah," said Essie, and darted out.

Norman and Esther exchanged uneasy looks. They stepped together to the window and saw their only child loping toward the bus stop, one arm extended, while a bus, which had pulled halfway out into the traffic lane, halted abruptly and waited for her.

"I don't know," Esther murmured to herself. "I don't know." One minute her daughter was silly and fourteen, and the next she was making buses stop for her. She had lived by her wits for several weeks, stabbed a man, and been lucky to escape with her life. On her first morning home she had brought out the stuffed animals consigned to her closet years ago and strewn them over her bed, as they had been when she was a child. She giggled more than she used to and cried easily. But at other times she seemed years older, contained and watchful to a degree that startled Esther. She walked straight down the middle of halls now, and straight into rooms, and looked people in the eye. But the prospect of pizza with Elliott clearly flustered her, and when she announced her plan to her parents, she still put a question mark at the end.

Esther hastened to her daughter's room and opened the second bureau drawer. The black bra nestled there among its chaste white kin, halfway to the bottom.

This garment had come to symbolize for Esther the

parts of Essie's recent history that remained unknown to her, and which time in its fullness might or might not reveal. She had been wearing it when they arrived at the hospital to pick her up, and they saw in it the concrete expression of some—not all—of their reasonable and natural fears about the life their child might have led in her exile. That was not the time or place to inquire into the matter, and in the succeeding days there seemed to be no better occasion.

The bra had been in Essie's laundry a few days later when Esther sat on the bed in Essie's room, chatting and watching her sort and put away. In a manner not overtly defiant but conscious, Essie neither concealed it nor called attention to it; Esther neither commented on it nor pretended not to see it. They both knew that she *had* seen it. Each kept her eyes more to herself than usual, and they discussed anything else.

In the past Esther would simply have insisted on an explanation, but no longer. She might make other mistakes, but she was not going to push her daughter out again.

Naturally, Esther associated the bra with Le Coq d'Or. The Beals were not much accustomed to stylish places. When she had called to make reservations for Saturday night, the person who answered the phone had sounded highly sophisticated—a word to which, in that context of worldliness, Esther did not attach necessarily positive connotations. And when she told him who they were, and why they were coming, and he assured them that their dinner would be *"my* treat—*entirely* my treat"—she feared that flamboyant lingerie might be the least of their challenges.

Still, that challenge was for tomorrow. Now she returned to the living room, where her husband had gone back to his reading, and said, "I think all is well." He heard her and looked up, pleased.

# 46

Erin and Essie were waiting at Erin's door when Lizby's father dropped her off. She was carrying a gift-wrapped book, and Essie groaned when she saw it.

"You didn't get my present in," she said before Lizby was halfway up the steps.

"Nope," said Lizby. "Gabriella saw right at the door that I'd brought too many. I never thought anybody would ask about presents at a Christmas party. Maybe I looked guilty. Anyway, she guessed. She asked me to please leave it on the porch."

"I really wanted to come," Essie said, "but she didn't invite me."

"I know, Ess," said Lizby. They had been talking about little else for days.

"I really wanted to be there." There were tears in her eyes.

"I know, Ess," said Lizby. "It's okay."

"C'mon up to my room," said Erin. "You can't just stand there blubbering."

"God, Gabriella looked totally out of it," said Lizby, starting up the stairs. "Like she'd taken a pill or something."

"She's drinking a lot, too," said Erin.

"That's totally hearsay," said Lizby sharply.

"Which I believe," said Erin.

"You shouldn't believe everything you hear," said Lizby.

"I heard it from you," said Erin, and Lizby flushed.

"So tell," said Essie impatiently, bouncing onto Erin's bed.

"Tell," said Erin. She flopped down on the bed, too, so that Lizby was left to choose between the straight-backed desk chair and the floor. She chose the floor, kicking off her shoes and settling back against the wall.

"Gabriella keeps all three kids really close," she said. "It's like she never lets them out of her sight. I've been over there three times now to sit, and each time she decides at the last minute that she can't leave. She fixes dinner, and I entertain the kids, but she wants us to stay in the kitchen."

"God," whispered Essie to herself, remembering the kitchen so clearly.

"Jeremy asked if you were coming, and I said I didn't know. I didn't want to get into the middle of that. He kept looking around for you.

"He seems okay, pretty much, except he spent most of the party being right next to me—I mean touching. And he does *exactly* what he's told—it's creepy. Except that last week he picked up a plate and broke it for no reason at all, and his therapist says that was a good sign. But he still won't talk much. And he still gets night frights where he'll be just petrified for hours."

"He had night frights before," said Essie.

"They totally know we're lying when we say that everything is okay," said Erin.

"There are scary things," said Essie.

Erin and Lizby hung for a moment. They were waiting for her to say something profound on the subject of scary things, but she did not.

They all gazed at the floor.

"What is there about things?" said Essie. "Why don't things end? Why do things have to be so complicated? Did I screw up so badly or not? Y'know, I still don't know. The night it happened, Toby said it was bad luck and it wasn't my fault. But he sounded as if that was what he had decided he ought to say. It's been like that ever since. Everyone says this and that, but they always sound as if they mean something else. And if I say, Please, *please* tell me what you *really* think, they say, Oh, no, that's what I really think. But that isn't all they're thinking. All I want is someone to say, Look, this is what you did right, and this is what you did wrong—just exactly that mix."

"You don't ask for much, do you?" said Erin.

"Why not?" said Essie. "You think honesty is so important. Why not tell me what *you* think?"

"I've told you," said Erin. "Lizby's told you. We're saying it wasn't your fault, but we're thinking we don't really know whether it was or not. The fact that you want to know doesn't mean we're able to tell you. There. That's honest. Bet you're sorry you asked."

They all stared at the floor. Then Erin said, "Shelly found out that Elliott's going to ask you to the dance. The girl is deeply hostile to the entire concept."

"Well, excuse *me*," said Essie in a feistier tone. "It's not as if she *owned* him or something."

"You can be the one to tell her that," said Erin.

"Maybe he likes me more than he likes her," said Essie.

"You can tell her that, too."

*"Has* he asked you yet?" said Lizby.

"Not yet," said Essie, sighing. "I'd just go ahead and ask *him*, but Robert says I'd be humiliating him. It's a manhood thing, Robert says."

"Maybe Robert should set him a manly example by asking *me*," said Erin.

Essie said, "Heather says that Toby keeps seeing the kidnapper's face the way he looked when they shot him. Sees it in reflections, clouds—all over. It really freaked him at first."

*"God,"* said Erin. "I can't believe I actually know someone who knows someone who's actually shot someone with a gun, like TV. I mean, is this ridiculous or something?"

"I dream about it, too," said Essie. "Last week I dreamed I was boning a leg of lamb, and then I noticed it was his arm. But by the time I'd noticed, Harry had already cooked it, and the waiters were serving it. I ran out into the dining room and said, No, no, please don't eat it. But I didn't dare raise my voice in the dining room, so nobody heard me. Everyone was eating it and saying how good it was."

"I guess I think that's funny," said Lizby.

"I definitely think it's funny," said Erin.

"I guess I think it's funny, looking back on it," said Essie doubtfully. "But I wasn't looking back on it at the time. I know I didn't think it was funny at the time."